"Kelly Irvin's *Matters of the Heart* is wonderfully written and paints a complete picture of the joys, trials, and tribulations of the average Amish community. It is filled with beautifully flawed characters you will laugh with, cry for, and then rejoice in their happiness when they finally find love."

—AMY LILLARD, BESTSELLING AUTHOR

"I do love a quick-paced, entertaining novel, and *The Heart's Bidding* is just that. I was immediately drawn into Toby's and Rachelle's stories and found myself rooting for them page after page. Kelly Irvin's latest belongs on the everyone's keeper shelf."

—*NEW YORK TIMES* AND *USA TODAY* BESTSELLING AUTHOR SHELLEY SHEPARD GRAY

"Strangers at first, Maisy Glick and Joshua Lapp find solace in their unhappy circumstances in Kelly Irvin's *Every Good Gift*. Joshua, full of sorrow and doubt. Maisy, full of regret. Together, they forge a path forward in ways that will surprise readers. Irvin's knowledge of the Plain people shines in this endearing tale of love and redemption."

—SUZANNE WOODS FISHER, BESTSELLING AUTHOR OF *A SEASON ON THE WIND*

"A beautifully crafted story of mistakes, redemption, healing, and grace. Kelly Irvin's *Every Good Gift* will captivate readers and tug on the heartstrings as characters brimming with real human frailty try to work through the consequences of their lives and choices with love and faith."

—KRISTEN MCKANAGH, AUTHOR OF *THE GIFT OF HOPE*

"Just like the title, *Warmth of Sunshine* is a lovely and cozy story that will keep you reading until the very last page."

—KATHLEEN FULLER, *USA TODAY* BESTSELLING AUTHOR OF THE MAIL-ORDER AMISH BRIDES SERIES

"This is a sweet story of romance and family that will tug at heartstrings. It is another great story and great characters from Irvin."

—*THE PARKERSBURG NEWS AND SENTINEL* ON *LOVE'S DWELLING*

"*Peace in the Valley* is a beautiful and heart-wrenching exploration of faith, loyalty, and the ties that bind a family and a community together. Kelly Irvin's masterful storytelling pulled me breathlessly into Nora's world, her deep desire to do good, and her struggle to be true to herself and to the man she loves. Full of both sweet and stark details of Amish life, *Peace in the Valley* is realistic and poignant, profound and heartfelt. I highly recommend it!"

—JENNIFER BECKSTRAND, AUTHOR OF *ANDREW*

"With a lovely setting, this is a story of hope in the face of trouble and has an endearing heroine, and other relatable characters that readers will empathize with."

—*PARKERSBURG NEWS AND SENTINEL* ON *MOUNTAINS OF GRACE*

"Kelly Irvin's *Mountains of Grace* offers a beautiful and emotional journey into the Amish community. Readers will be captivated by a heartwarming tale of forgiveness and finding a renewed faith in God. The story will capture the hearts of those who love the Plain culture and an endearing romance. Once you open this book, you'll be hooked until the last page."

—AMY CLIPSTON, BESTSELLING AUTHOR OF *A WELCOME AT OUR DOOR*

"Irvin's fun story is simple (like Mary Katherine, who finds 'every day is a blessing and an adventure') but very satisfying."

—*PUBLISHERS WEEKLY* ON *THROUGH THE AUTUMN AIR*

"This second entry (after *Upon a Spring Breeze*) in Irvin's seasonal series diverges from the typical Amish coming-of-age tale with its focus on more mature protagonists who acutely feel their sense of loss. Fans of the genre seeking a broader variety of stories may find this new offering from a Carol Award winner more relatable than the usual fare."

—*LIBRARY JOURNAL* ON *BENEATH THE SUMMER SUN*

"The second entry in Irvin's Amish Blessings series (after *Love's Dwelling*) delivers an elegant portrait of a young Amish woman caught between two worlds . . . Irvin skillfully conveys Abigail's internal conflict ('How could Abigail put into words the longing that thrummed in her chest? The sense of loss, of missing out, of missing it all,' she reminisces about Amish life). Fans of Amish romance will want to check this out."

—*PUBLISHERS WEEKLY* ON *BENEATH THE SUMMER SUN*

"A moving and compelling tale about the power of grace and forgiveness that reminds us how we become strongest in our most broken moments."

—*LIBRARY JOURNAL* ON *UPON A SPRING BREEZE*

"Once I started reading *The Bishop's Son*, it was difficult for me to put it down! This story of struggle, faith, and hope will draw you in to the final page.... I have read countless stories of Amish men or women doubting their faith. I have never read a storyline quite like this one though. It was narrated with such heart. I was fully invested in Jesse's struggle. No doubt, what Jesse felt is often what modern-day Amish men and women must feel when they are at a crossroads in their faith. The story was brilliantly told and the struggle felt very real."

—*DESTINATION AMISH*

"Something new and delightful in the Amish fiction genre, this story is set in the barren, dusty landscape of Bee County, Texas . . . Irvin writes with great insight into the range and depth of human emotion. Her characters are believable and well developed, and her storytelling skills are superb. Recommend to readers who are looking for something a little different in Amish fiction."

—*CBA RETAILERS + RESOURCES* ON *THE BEEKEEPER'S SON*

"*The Beekeeper's Son* is a perfect depiction of how God makes all things beautiful in His way. Rich with vivid descriptions and characters you can immediately relate to, Kelly Irvin's book is a must read for Amish fans."

—RUTH REID, BESTSELLING AUTHOR OF *A MIRACLE OF HOPE*

MATTERS OF
the Heart

Other Books by Kelly Irvin

AMISH CALLING NOVELS
The Heart's Bidding
Matters of the Heart

AMISH BLESSINGS NOVELS
Love's Dwelling
The Warmth of Sunshine
Every Good Gift

AMISH OF BIG SKY COUNTRY NOVELS
Mountains of Grace
A Long Bridge Home
Peace in the Valley

EVERY AMISH SEASON NOVELS
Upon a Spring Breeze
Beneath the Summer Sun
Through the Autumn Air
With Winter's First Frost

THE AMISH OF BEE COUNTY NOVELS
The Beekeeper's Son
The Bishop's Son
The Saddlemaker's Son

NOVELLAS
To Raise a Home included in
An Amish Barn Raising
A Holiday of Hope included in
An Amish Christmas Wedding
Cakes and Kisses included in
An Amish Christmas Bakery
Mended Hearts included
in *An Amish Reunion*

A Christmas Visitor included
in *An Amish Christmas Gift*
Sweeter Than Honey included
in *An Amish Market*
One Sweet Kiss included
in *An Amish Summer*
Snow Angels included in *An
Amish Christmas Love*
A Midwife's Dream included
in *An Amish Heirloom*

CONTEMPORARY FICTION
The Year of Goodbyes and Hellos

ROMANTIC SUSPENSE
Tell Her No Lies
Over the Line
Closer Than She Knows
Her Every Move
Trust Me

MATTERS OF
the Heart

KELLY IRVIN

ZONDERVAN

Matters of the Heart

Copyright © 2024 by Kelly Irvin

This title is also available as a Zondervan e-book.

Requests for information should be addressed to:

Zondervan, *3950 Sparks Dr. SE, Grand Rapids, Michigan 49546*

Library of Congress Cataloging-in-Publication
Names: Irvin, Kelly, author.
Title: Matters of the heart / Kelly Irvin.
Description: Grand Rapids, Michigan: Zondervan, 2024. | Series: Amish calling; 2 | Summary:
   "He's the community's jokester auctioneer. She's the serious caregiver for her siblings who
   also works at the local plant nursery. What future could they have together?"—Provided by
   publisher.
Identifiers: LCCN 2023058505 (print) | LCCN 2023058506 (ebook) | ISBN 9780840709417
   (paperback) | ISBN 9780840709424 (e-pub) | ISBN 9780840709431
Subjects: LCSH: Amish--Fiction. | LCGFT: Christian fiction. | Romance fiction. | Novels.
Classification: LCC PS3609.R82 M38 2024 (print) | LCC PS3609.R82 (ebook) | DDC
   813/.6--dc23/eng/20240105
LC record available at https://lccn.loc.gov/2023058505
LC ebook record available at https://lccn.loc.gov/2023058506

Any internet addresses (websites, blogs, etc.) and telephone numbers in this book are offered as a
resource. They are not intended in any way to be or imply an endorsement by Zondervan, nor does
Zondervan vouch for the content of these sites and numbers for the life of this book.

Zondervan titles may be purchased in bulk for educational, business, fundraising, or sales
promotional use. For information, please email SpecialMarkets@Zondervan.com.

Printed in the United States of America

24 25 26 27 28 LBC 5 4 3 2 1

*To Tim—thanks for making it possible
for me to go on. Love always.*

So to keep me from becoming conceited because of the surpassing greatness of the revelations, a thorn was given me in the flesh, a messenger of Satan to harass me, to keep me from becoming conceited. Three times I pleaded with the Lord about this, that it should leave me. But he said to me, "My grace is sufficient for you, for my power is made perfect in weakness." Therefore I will boast all the more gladly of my weaknesses, so that the power of Christ may rest upon me. For the sake of Christ, then, I am content with weaknesses, insults, hardships, persecutions, and calamities. For when I am weak, then I am strong.

2 Corinthians 12:7–10

Featured Families

Lee's Gulch, Virginia

Aaron and Katherine King

Bethel   Enos   Claire   Robbie   Judah   Liam   Melinda

Silas and Joanna Miller (grandparents)
Charlie and Elizabeth Miller (parents)

Toby   Jason   Elijah   Declan   Layla   Emmett   Josie   Sherri   Sadie

Jason (brother) and Caitlin Miller

Zachary   Zander   Mary   Retta

Karl and Cara Lapp (grandparents)
Adam and Leah Lapp (parents)

Rachelle   John   Dillon   Mark   Steven   Kimmie   Emma   Mandy   DeeDee

Jonah   Sean   Sam   Michael   Darcy

Atlee and Hilda Schrock (nursery owners)

Ben   Harriet   Hannah   Nan   Amos   Kendell   Lulu

Luke and Deana Beachy

Andrew   Christine   Ryan   Corrine

Bartholomew "Bart" (bishop) and Miriam Plank

David   Henry   Nyla   Hannah Matthew Timothy Esther

Martin (deacon) and Cindy Hershberger (grocery store owners)

Bella   Sophia   Justin   Harry   Finn

Jedediah "Jed" (minister) and Martha Knepp

Sarah   Carol   Isaac   Will   Thomas

Noah and Mary Eash (parents' committee member)

James Melanie Catherine Robert

Micah and Layla (Miller sister) Troyer

Glossary of Pennsylvania Deutsch*

aamen: amen
ach: oh
aenti: aunt
bewillkumm: welcome
bopli, boplin: baby, babies
bruder, brieder: brother, brothers
bu, buwe: boy, boys
bussi: cat
daadi: grandpa
daed: father
danki: thank you
"Das Loblied": Amish hymn of praise sung at all church services
dat: dad
dochder: daughter
dumkopf: blockhead
eck: corner table where newly married couple sits during wedding reception
eldre: parents
Englischer: English or non-Amish
eppies: cookies
es dutt mer: I am sorry
faeriwell: good-bye

Glossary

fraa: wife
Froh gebortsdaag: Happy birthday
fuhl: fool
gaul: horse
Gelassenheit: a German word, yielding fully to God's will and
    forsaking all selfishness
gern gschehme: you're welcome
Gmay: church district
Gott: God
gut nacht: good night
gut: good
hallo: hello
hanswascht: clown, silly fellow
hochmut: pride
hund: dog
jah: yes
kaffi: coffee
kapp: prayer cap or head covering worn by Amish women
kind, kinner: child, children
kinnskind, kinnskinner: grandchild, grandchildren
kossin, kossins: cousin(s)
kuss, koss: (noun) kiss, kisses
maedel, maed: girl, girls
mamm: mom
mammi: grandma
mann: husband
mudder: mother
narrisch: foolish, silly
nee: no
niess: niece
onkel: uncle

Ordnung: written and unwritten rules in an Amish district

rumspringa: period of "running around" for Amish youth before they decide whether they want to be baptized into the Amish faith and seek a mate

schweschder, schweschdre: sister, sisters

sei so gut: please (be so kind)

suh: son

tietschern: teacher

wunderbarr: wonderful

*The German dialect commonly referred to as Pennsylvania Dutch is not a written language and varies depending on the location and origin of the Amish settlement. These spellings are approximations. Most Amish children learn English after they start school. They also learn high German, which is used in their Sunday services.

A Note from the Author

Matters of the Heart continues the exploration of both developmental and intellectual disabilities through the lens of its Amish characters and their corresponding worldview begun in *The Heart's Bidding*. As I mentioned in the author's note for that first book in the Amish Calling series, I want to note that I'm keenly aware of the tender issues that may be raised by the disability community when encountering the Amish term "special" children and their view that these children are "gifts from God."

As a writer, I know better than most the power of words to hurt, demean, make feel less than, and perpetuate stereotypes. First know that I'm a Christian writer living with a disability. I came by my disability later in life. My struggle to accept this disability is ongoing. I don't see it as a gift from God. However, I respect and value the Amish perspective as Christlike and beautifully loving. Readers will see that Amish believe all children are gifts from God. They employ the term "special" for these babies as a term of affection and love. Therefore I use it in the context of my Amish characters' points of view. These are their views, not mine, as I walk a narrow path between portraying what the "English" world finds acceptable and representing an authentic Amish voice.

I say all this to respectfully ask readers to honor the Amish view as loving, kind, and so much more Christlike than the worldly view of some would-be "English" parents who hold the belief that bringing a child into the world with disabilities is a choice that can be rejected. I have no doubt that Amish parents agonize, worry, and even shed tears over their "special children." But they choose an attitude of gratitude. I hope you will read and enjoy *Matters of the Heart* in the spirit in which the Amish Calling series is offered—to edify, provoke thought, and shed Christ's light in the world. God bless.

Chapter 1

ot even a blustery March wind propelling a heavy mist across the Knowles County, Virginia, fairgrounds to the auction platform could stop Declan Miller. Not when he had a microphone in one hand and a beautiful surrey-style buggy parked in front of an enormous crowd hanging on his every word.

"Here we go, folks, only a few items left, so get those bid cards ready for another workout." Declan pointed at the buggy. "Take a good gander, folks. This will make a fine surrey for a family. It's practically new." He switched to Pennsylvania Dutch. "Let's give the Hershbergers a great send-off to Pinecraft. You know what a buggy like this should go for."

And then back to English. "This excellent piece of workmanship has headlights, taillights, warning lights, and running lights. In addition to the bench seat in front, it has two smaller flat seats in the back and plenty of storage. Nice green carpet in the interior, a dashboard made of inlaid pine with a roomy glove compartment, and two cupholders. I'd be tempted to bid on it myself, if I had a wife and kids. Maybe this buggy would be just the thing to get a woman to finally say yes to me."

"You have to ask her out first, *hanswascht*!"

Silly fellow. Grandpa's deep bass, once his best auctioneering tool, carried from his spot in a lawn chair on the front row. Since his retirement a year ago as the founder of Miller Family Auctioneering, Grandpa liked to attend the local auctions to watch his grandsons in action so he could critique them afterward.

Silly fellow indeed. That was Declan. The clown, the class cutup. With three older brothers and one younger one all working in the family auctioneering business, clowning around was his way of standing out. "Someday I'll catch up to the right one, *Daadi*, I will. Even if all that running after her wears me out."

A big grin split Grandpa's face. Laughter ran through the crowd. The folks around Lee's Gulch's three Plain districts had known Declan since he was a kid. At twenty-four he was a little on the old side to still be a bachelor, but no one was stewing about it yet—except his mother. Mom wanted all of her older children happily married as soon as possible—if not sooner.

"Declan."

Despite the noisy crowd, the sound of his father's voice—that same deep bass as Grandpa's—filtered through to Declan from where the older man stood checking off auction items as they were moved to the front of the line. He waggled his index finger toward the sky. The clouds had turned black. They were poised to lower the boom. *Stop messing around. Get a move on.* Dad could say so much in two syllables.

Right.

"We could get some rain any minute, so we'd better get busy. Here we go. I'll start the bidding at $2,500. Who'll give me $2,500?" The buggy was worth far more and the Plain men and women knew it. Bidding would be fast and furious. Declan let his gaze rove the crowd. His brother Elijah pointed out a Plain man from Nathalie. Declan nodded. "Fine, 2,500. Who'll give me 3,000? 3,000, 3,000 . . . got it. Who'll give me 3,500?"

The bids soared rapidly to $5,000, becoming a three-way fight among the Plain stranger from Nathalie, newlywed Mark Schrock, and an Englisher named Kyle Jenkins. Kyle had a business hauling around English tourists who had a hankering to see Plain farms outside Lee's Gulch and visit their stores.

"$5,500. Who'll give me 5,500? Bid 6,000. Now 6,000—"

"$6,000." A man wearing a purple windbreaker and a Norfolk Tides cap stuck his bid card in the air for the first time. "I'll give you $6,000."

"Whoa! We've got some serious competition going on here. That's what I like to see." Chuckling, Declan swung around and pointed at the Nathalie bidder. "What do you say? Are you still in the game?"

Nathalie shook his head. Same with Mark. Kyle's grin was grim, but he nodded. Declan cleared his throat again. His voice was getting scratchier. "All righty then. Who'll give me 6,500? Bid 6,500. 6,500. Now 6,500."

Kyle lifted his bid card. "$6,200."

"I can work with that. 6,200. Bid 6,200. Now 6,200. Bid 6,200 . . ."

The newcomer's bid card popped up. "6,500."

"6,500. Bid 6,500. Come on, folks, you know this buggy is worth more. Now 6,500. Bid 6,500 . . ."

"Too rich for me." Kyle tucked his card under his arm and shot darts with his eyes at the newcomer.

A few more scans of the crowd. His bid spotters, Elijah and Emmett, both shook their heads. Declan lifted his flat-brimmed straw hat toward the newcomer. "Going once, going twice, sold to the gentleman in the purple jacket. What's your number, sir?"

Leaving Elijah to get the man's particulars, Declan grabbed his water bottle and emptied it in a few swallows.

"Hey, *Bruder*, why don't I finish up?"

Declan turned. His oldest brother, Toby, strode across the platform. It was like catching himself in a mirror—not that he ever did that. Toby had the Miller look—tall, broad shoulders, blond hair, slate-blue eyes, dimples. Declan was slightly shorter, but otherwise a carbon copy. "Did you finish your auction already?"

"*Jah*, all the livestock is done." He picked up the mic Declan had laid on the podium. "*Dat* says you sound terrible. All hoarse and scratchy. Are you catching a cold?"

Declan's throat had been sore when he hopped out of bed this morning. Nothing a cup of hot tea and some of Mom's homemade horehound syrup wouldn't fix. "*Nee*. It's likely allergies. All the trees are budding like crazy." He nodded at the crowd. "They're getting antsy. There's only a few items left. I can handle it."

"Dat wants you to give it a rest."

Dad and Toby shared supervision of Miller Family Auctioneering since Grandpa's retirement. Declan glanced over Toby's shoulder at their dad. He was in front of the platform. He jerked his head toward the two trailers that sat to the right of the auction site. His intention was clear. *Get off the stage.*

No way. Nothing was more enjoyable than auctioneering. As a boy Declan had lived for the day when he could take over the platform. He'd worked his way up from checking inventory, unpacking and packing equipment, and bid spotting to auctioneer school and then the best job in the world—one he'd been doing for three years now. Dad and his brothers would have to pry the microphone out of his cold, dead fingers. Declan shook his head and mouthed, *I've got this.*

Dad scowled. *Nee. You don't.*

"It's about to pour." Declan tugged the mic from Toby. "We don't have time for this. I'll wrap it up quick."

"I don't know who's more stubborn, you or Dat." Pulling his black rain slicker's hood over his straw hat, Toby glanced at the sky. "I'll let you two thrash it out."

There would be no thrashing. "Tell Emmett to get that pony cart moved up front."

"Will do."

Declan took the microphone and swung around to face the crowd. "Come on, folks, let's finish up quick so you can get home, dry off, and eat a hot supper."

Many of the English attendees had already scattered for the makeshift parking lot on the Hershbergers' east pasture. Rains earlier in the month had softened the ground covered with only sparse weeds. It would quickly turn to mud, as would the dirt road that led to the highway. Visions of their pickup trucks stuck in the mud surely danced in their heads.

"I reckon you've already taken a peek at this sturdy pony cart, great for *kinner* to drive to school or church. I'm starting the bidding at $500. Who'll give me 500, 500, bid 500—"

A jagged bolt of lightning crackled across the sky. Thunder bellowed. The mist turned into a deluge of rain driven by a suddenly fierce, icy north wind.

"Sorry, folks, we're done here." Declan pulled his windbreaker's hood up over his straw hat before the wind could send it sailing. "Get to your buggies. Be safe. Drive safe."

Everyone swarmed at once.

Declan didn't take time to tug on his raincoat. The speakers were already covered. He stuck the mic in its hard-shell plastic case and went to work moving equipment. In seconds rain soaked his jacket and his thin cotton shirt. His black denim pants hung heavy on his legs. Shivering, he pushed a dolly loaded with speakers toward the trailers parked a few hundred yards from the platform.

As expected, the ground had already turned to the consistency of corn mush. The dolly's wheels clung to it, resisting forward movement. Declan's steel-toed leather boots sank into the mud. He mustered all his strength to pull them out. The mud made a sucking sound with each determined step. Rain sloshed from the exposed brim of his hat, making it hard to see.

"Watch where you're going, *sei so gut*."

The entreaty delivered in a soft, concerned tone brought Declan to a halt. He released the dolly handle long enough to shove his hat back and wipe at his face with the back of his hand. Bethel King stood in his path, both hands on her brother Robbie's wheelchair handles. Her younger sister Claire pushed brother Judah's chair. The younger kids' clothes were bedraggled and their faces unhappy.

Bethel's clothes and bonnet were soaked. Her lilac cotton dress clung to her pleasing form. Yes, the dress's hem was black with mud, but her cheeks were red with exertion and her eyes, the color of hot cocoa, were dark and serious. She was still as pretty as she had been during their days in school together. Declan put both hands in the air. "Sorry, I didn't see you there. After you."

Nerves zinged from the tip of his nose to his toes. As usual. Whenever he saw Bethel he turned into a blathering buffoon.

"It's okay. I just didn't want you to run into my *brieder*." Bethel strove to move Robbie's chair forward. The wheels sank deeper into the mud. She lifted the handles and heaved. The chair lurched forward. "We'll get out of your way."

Despite doing her best to deliver on that promise, she wasn't able to move the wheelchair more than a few inches. She had plenty of practice pushing her brothers' wheelchairs. Robbie, eleven, and Judah, ten, lived with a rare form of muscular dystrophy seen mostly in Plain families. They'd been stricken almost simultaneously as four- and five-year-olds.

"I can't, *Schweschder*." Claire, a skinnier, shorter version of Bethel, struggled valiantly, but Judah's chair remained mired. She glanced at Declan. "*Es dutt mer.* Could you give me a push?"

"Don't be sorry. I'm happy to help—"

"I'll do it." Bethel let go of her charge's chair and hustled back to Claire's. "Declan has expensive equipment that shouldn't get wet."

Everyone in the district knew the Millers' sound system had been stolen the previous year. They'd only recently raised enough money through fundraisers and generous donations from their Plain community to replace them.

"The speakers are covered. They're in no danger." Here was his chance to do something nice for a girl—now a woman—who was known for her kindness but never seemed to warm up to Declan. Ignoring the *shmuck-shmuck* sucking of his boots, Declan waded over to Judah's chair. He bent low, so as not to tower over the boy. "I reckon I needed a bath. How about you?"

"Just in time for church tomorrow. I wish I'd brought soap." Judah pushed back his slicker's hood and grinned. "*Mamm* says it doesn't count unless I use soap."

"Es dutt mer, I can't help you there." Declan straightened and reached for the handles. His hand collided with Bethel's smaller one. She startled as if a bogeyman had popped out from behind the closest tree. Why was she so jumpy around him? He summoned a reassuring smile. "I don't bite, and I don't have cooties—contrary to what my *schweschdre* say."

"I don't want to put you out. We're fine."

"You can't push both of them. You push Robbie. I'll get Judah. We'll be a team."

Could she read between the lines? Did she even consider in the farthest corner of her mind what it would be like to be a two-person team with Declan?

It was so unlikely. Bethel had been the smartest girl in the class—in the school—but she never let her head swell. When the other kids played baseball at recess, she sat on the sidelines reading a book, pausing to cheer them on at exactly the right time.

He became a base-hitting machine just to earn her cheers. And she had been generous with them. Sometimes she even jumped up and clapped as he ran the bases. Hearing her yell, "Way to go, Declan!" had spurred him on to more than one headfirst slide into home plate.

She worried her lower lip with her teeth for a few seconds. "What about your equipment?"

"It's in its covering and then double-wrapped with heavy plastic. Plus, folks around here are far more likely to push it to the trailer than take it."

Her forehead wrinkled. She nodded as if coming to an important decision. "*Danki*. We really appreciate your help."

A chance to be helpful. Bethel always seemed so competent, so self-contained. She didn't need anyone's help, let alone Declan's. Head bent against the wind and pelting rain, he followed her lead toward the line of buggies, his hands tight on the chair handles. "Knock, knock."

Judah yelled over the wind, "Who's there?"

"Oink, oink."

"Oink, oink who?"

"Make up your mind. Are you a pig or an owl?"

Judah and Robbie chortled. Bethel, her shoulders hunched over the wheelchair, didn't seem to hear.

Declan kept up a steady stream of jokes as they slogged through the field, across the muddy road, and into the pasture where the buggies were parked in the sprigs of grass foolish enough to sprout so early in the spring season. Wasn't entertaining the boys another way of helping? Plus laughter was excellent free medicine.

Fortunately, the King buggy was close to the road. Her voice high and breathless, rain dripping from her bonnet and nose, Bethel waved at Declan. "I'm sure Claire can get it from here. Danki."

"I've come this far—"

"Really, we're fine."

"Was it the jokes?"

"Nee, of course not. They were . . . funny," she sputtered. "The boys love silly jokes."

Declan swiveled. Claire lagged behind by several yards. She had a strange waddle-like walk. "What do you think, Claire?"

"I can get it from here." She didn't sound convinced, but she marched forward. "Danki."

A gust of wind knocked Declan back a step. A fit of coughing overcame him. He hunched over. Between the wind and the cough, he couldn't breathe.

"Go, go, you need to get out of this wind." Bethel took the wheelchair handles. "Go home and have a cup of hot tea with plenty of honey and lemon. Sit by the fire."

"I'll be fine." Bethel had enough on her plate without worrying about Declan. He sought a more serious tone—she seemed to prefer serious. "I promise. You get yourself and these *buwe* home and do the same."

"Go!"

"Going." Declan turned. Having his back to the wind would help. He needed to skedaddle before Dad found the abandoned speakers. He picked up speed. His boots encountered a wet, slick clump of grass. They slid out from under him.

Whomp. He landed flat on his back, cold rain running into his nostrils and open mouth. Not great. Not great at all. Gasping for air like a stunned fish, he stared up at the clouds. Two of them looked like old men with long gray beards grinning down at him.

"*Ach*, are you okay? Are you hurt?"

Bethel's concerned face appeared over him, along with Claire's. The rain dripping from their bonnets joined the deluge threatening to drown Declan.

His back and behind hurt.

But not as much as his pride. Or was it his dignity? So much for impressing Bethel with his strength and dexterity or whatever else it took to get her brothers squared away.

"Knock, knock."

Frowning, Bethel swiped rain from her face. "I'm serious. Are you hurt?"

Too late to backtrack now. "Knock, knock."

She shook her head. Rain sluiced down her face. Claire had no such compunction. She jumped in. "Who's there?"

"Pecan."

"Pecan who?"

"Pecan someone your own size."

Chapter 2

*I*t wasn't funny. Okay, maybe a little. The joke. Not the fall. Laughing would be unkind. What if Declan had been hurt? Bethel allowed herself a small smile as she peered down at him. A fallen giant. Not really a giant, but he *was* tall compared to her five-foot-four-inch frame. Here he was doing them the huge favor of helping with the wheelchairs in the middle of a deluge and he'd fallen. And still he'd managed to keep his sense of humor. That should count for a lot—it took strength of character, really. She held out her hand. "Let me help you up."

Instead, Declan rolled over on his knees, pushed off the ground, and hopped up. He whirled around and bowed with an elaborate flourish. "I meant to do that."

"You did not." Maybe he had. He was such a cutup. That's what she remembered from their school days. Quick with a joke, a harmless prank, and a smile. He had a nice smile. A really nice smile. Then and now. He also didn't have a serious bone in his body then. Or now. "Are you sure you aren't hurt? You didn't hit your head, did you?"

"I know how to fall. There's an art to it." Mud coated his shirt and pants. Smudges decorated his clean-shaven cheeks and forehead. He'd lost his hat. The rain flattened his thick blond hair. He was a mess, and yet he seemed pleased with himself. His grin widened. His dimples deepened. "Go ahead, laugh. It was funnier than the joke."

They were standing in the middle of an open field in the pouring rain. A flash of sizzling lightning lit up the sky. Thunder boomed only seconds later. "Danki, but nee. There's a time and place for fun, but this isn't it. It's lightning out. The kinner are soaked and chilled to the bone."

"Jah. Of course. You're right. Going." Declan scooped up his hat. He slapped it on his head. Raindrops rolled down his face. "Be careful getting home. The roads will be full of water."

"You too. Very careful."

Coughing, he took off across the field.

He really was kind. Over the years his signs of interest had been obvious. Yet he'd never actually asked her to take a buggy ride. Why remained a mystery. He always spoke to her at the singings. He never failed to say hello at frolics and at church. A few times he appeared on the verge of saying something serious, but a joke sallied forth instead. He was nice, funny, and kind. And pleasing to the eye. But somehow Bethel couldn't imagine Declan stepping into the trials her family faced. A woman in her situation needed a serious man to stand with her. No matter how his sunny smile and sweet attitude tugged at her heart, Declan didn't seem like that man.

She went to work getting Robbie into the buggy. He didn't weigh much. The wheelchair folded up neatly. "Claire, can you get Judah in?"

A wail met Bethel's inquiry. She turned. Claire had her arms under Judah's armpits. She struggled to lift her brother from his chair. Frustration shone on her freckled face. "I don't know what's wrong with me today. I can't get him out."

A shiver that had nothing to do with the icy wind ran through Bethel. She clomped through the mud to Judah's chair. "Did you eat your oatmeal for breakfast?"

"Nee, I didn't have time. I dropped my bowl, and I had to clean up the mess."

"That must be it, then." Bethel patted her shoulder. "You're just low on fuel, that's all."

Sei so gut, Gott, sei so gut.

Together they lifted Judah into the buggy. Bethel stowed his chair in the back. She wiped her hands on her muddy apron, for all the good it did. "Let's get home. We could all use a hot cup of tea and one of Mamm's cinnamon rolls."

Ninety minutes later the boys, dressed in dry clothes, were ensconced in thick quilts in front of the fireplace holding mugs of chamomile tea spiked with lemon and honey. Little sister Melinda had talked them into playing Connect 4 with her. Mom had lit a fire in the wood-burning stove in the laundry room and heated water so Claire could take a bath after her cup of hot tea and a handful of gingersnaps.

"This weather. The sun was shining when we left the house this morning. It's supposed to be spring, but winter just doesn't want to let go." Following the tantalizing aromas of onion, chili powder, and sweet cornbread baking, Bethel went to the huge cast-iron pot of chili bubbling on the propane stove. She picked up the ladle and stirred. The heat warmed her cold hands and feet. "I wouldn't have taken the boys if I'd known it was going to storm."

"You should've brought them home as soon as it started to sprinkle." Mom pulled a huge pan of jalapeño cornbread from the oven. The billowing heat turned her cheeks red. Her tone held no condemnation, only concern. "You know how easily they catch colds."

"Colds are caused by viruses, not rain." Bethel softened her tone. Mom meant well. She and Dad had spent more than their share of time at the Center for Special Children in Lancaster County, where Robbie was first diagnosed with limb-girdle muscular dystrophy, and then Judah. The realization that intermarrying among the Plain people resulted in this rare genetic disease had been hard on both her parents. They never complained, but occasionally the weight of the yoke of guilt showed itself in their slumped shoulders. "But the cold wind probably carries a lot of germs with so many people gathered in one place. And then all the pollen in the air might cause them to be congested. We'll keep a close eye on them."

"When did you get your medical degree?" Mom didn't have a mean cell in her body. She set the cornbread on a trivet and closed the oven. The oven mitts landed next to the pan. She sighed. "I know the boys can't stay home all the time. They deserve some fun. I keep reminding myself of that."

"The doctor said fresh air is good medicine."

"Fresh air, not gale-force winds, and sunshine, not a cold rain." Mom came over to the stove. She took the ladle from Bethel. "Did you try the chili? Is it spicy enough for your dat?"

Bethel accepted the bite her mother offered. The tangy concoction woke up her taste buds. Garlic, chili powder, canned tomatoes from their garden, chopped onion, green and red bell pepper, and tender chunks of beef stew meat. Mom's chili was legendary at church picnics and school fundraisers. "That's yummy, Mamm, as usual."

She handed the ladle back. Mom took a bite herself. "It just needs to simmer. Your dat, Enos, and Liam won't be back from delivering the bed set to Farmville for at least another hour. That'll give the spices time to meld."

The lyrics of an old Plain hymn floated through the open door that led to the laundry room. Claire loved to sing. She had a high, clear voice that hit every note with a sweetness that made Bethel's heart squeeze. "Mamm, have you noticed anything odd about Claire lately?"

Mamm dropped the ladle. She scooped it up and laid it on the counter. She turned her back on Bethel and stepped over to the shelves where the dishes were kept. "Nee. What do you mean?"

Her words said one thing, her tone another.

"She couldn't push Robbie's chair through the field today. Fortunately, Declan Miller came by and helped us out or I would've had to push them both. She had trouble lifting Robbie from his chair." Bethel went to her mother. She took the stack of bowls from her. "She dropped her bowl of oatmeal this morning."

"Gott provides." Her expression was stoic, but Mom's voice quivered. "I'd hoped Claire was getting too old to be affected, but Gott's will be done."

Even with her fourteenth birthday coming up next week, Claire wasn't too old. This form of LGMD was as unpredictable as it was vicious. Bethel could cite all the symptoms. They all could. They'd watched them consume Judah and Robbie. They still watched and waited to see if Enos, Liam, and Melinda would be spared. The age of onset could be anywhere from three years old to early adulthood, but the average was thirteen and a half. Usually it involved the legs first, causing difficulty walking and climbing stairs and causing falls. In three to five years, the muscles wasted. The earlier the onset, the more rapid the progression. That might be the silver lining, if Claire was indeed affected.

People with the disease could still live to a ripe old age. Women could still have children, but being in a family way made the weakness worse, making it even harder to care for the baby. Plain women were expected to cook, bake, clean, garden, and care for as many children as God gave them. Almost impossible with

LGMD. And then there was the probability of passing the disease on to her children.

Bethel could only aspire to have a faith as stoic and as strong as her parents' faith. She set the plates on the table and went to her mother. She hugged her quick and hard. "Whatever happens, we'll deal with it. I'm always here for you."

"Nee. You must marry, have a *mann*, have kinner. That's your place in this world." Her mother drew back. Her expression lightened. A sly smile stole over her face. "Declan Miller, eh? He's a hard worker, that one. A bit of a clown, but a sense of humor is a good thing. It can help a family get through tough times. It's certainly better than being married to a sourpuss."

So true. "I've always thought he was nice, but to *never* be serious?"

Serious problems required serious people who knew how to solve them.

In the days when she never missed a singing, Bethel had taken a few buggy rides, but none of the men—still boys, really—interested her because she had too much responsibility at home to fritter away her time on courting. Declan had spent most of his time horsing around with his buddies, pulling pranks, and singing at the top of his lungs—often off-key—trying to impress the girls. Occasionally Bethel would catch him staring at her, a curiously somber look on his face, but then his glance would dart away, followed by more hilarity.

He'd taken Jana Yoder for buggy rides for at least a year, but next thing everyone knew Jana was married to a man from Bird-in-Hand and moved away.

The gossipers didn't know why, and Bethel didn't want to know. It wasn't her business.

"There's nothing wrong with making people laugh. If you ask me, and even if you don't, you're far too serious. Your laugh muscles could use a workout."

"I laugh plenty, but when it comes to spending the rest of my life with a man, I need to be sure he can be serious when the need arises."

"Some boys take longer to mature than others." *Mudder* had plenty of brothers and cousins to use as examples, plus Bethel's brother Enos, but he was one of the most serious people Bethel knew. "My experience has been they're worth the wait. Declan's not bad to look at either."

"Mamm!" The kitchen suddenly seemed too warm. Bethel waved a dish towel at her mom. Who could help noticing a man built like he came from a long line of laborers used to swinging an ax and pushing a plow? Add that to the perpetual smile, dimples, and blue eyes, and a woman might be a bit tongue-tied in his presence. "Was Dat the class clown?"

"More of a smooth talker, I guess." Mom smiled at the memory. "But I wasn't one to fall for smooth talk. I made him work for it—two long years."

And now they'd been married twenty-seven. What did that kind of love feel like? To weather the hard times as well as the good ones? Which brought Bethel right back to the topic at hand—babies born with a terrible disease inside them waiting to unveil a litany of dreadful symptoms like painful falls and wasting muscles.

"You are blessed." The words cut Bethel's tongue like a finely honed knife. Blessed by a curiously heavy yoke. Babies were gifts from God—all babies. "I just want to help with the buwe however I can."

"Your *daed* and I will care for the buwe until we can't. Then you and those who can will take care of those who can't."

It was the way of the Plain people. Bethel's throat ached. Her stomach roiled. Her dreams of having lots of babies had begun in childhood when she'd been blissfully ignorant about genes and hereditary diseases like limb-girdle muscular dystrophy. Chances were far too great that her children would inherit this disease as well. She had a deep well of strength, but she'd used so much of it caring for her brothers. One day her parents would no longer be able to do it. Then it would be up to her again. Enos and her. Maybe Claire. Maybe Liam. Or maybe not. And what about little Melinda, who just turned four?

Should a man be asked to marry into such a quagmire? What hidden genes as a Plain man from her community would her as-yet-unknown groom bring to the marriage? It was like opening Pandora's box as a wedding present.

"What's wrong? You both look like the sky is falling." Claire stood in the doorway. Her freshly scrubbed face glowed a healthy pink. "Don't be mad, Mamm. The buwe will be fine."

"I'm not mad, you silly goose." Mamm rushed to the stove. "Get the pitcher of water from the refrigerator and fill the glasses. Your dat and brieder will be here any minute."

Still humming the hymn, Claire did as she was told.

Bethel went to work setting the table.

Glass shattered. Claire shrieked. Bethel whirled. Her sister had dropped the pitcher. It shattered on the vinyl floor. Water puddled at her feet. She dropped to her knees. "Ach! Es dutt mer, Mamm. Es dutt mer."

"It's okay. It was an accident." Bethel strode to her side. She knelt and brushed Claire's hands away. "Let me. You'll cut yourself."

She glanced up at their mother. Her expression wooden, Mom shook her head. She twisted the dishrag in her hands. "Jah, just an accident."

Chapter 3

The patter of rain on the metal roof usually lulled Declan to sleep. Not tonight. He gritted his teeth, willing the tickle in his throat to disappear, taking with it an annoying cough. No such luck. He coughed into the crook of his arm. Not only did his throat hurt but his ears as well.

Elijah's steady breathing didn't change. His brother had worked hard for the last two days. He needed his sleep. Declan rolled over on his side. He rearranged his pillows so his head was higher. Another coughing fit burst out. This time Elijah moved restlessly. Toby's wedding likely couldn't come soon enough for him. Then Elijah would move into Toby's old bedroom. As the next oldest sons Elijah and Declan would both have their own rooms.

Or maybe Declan should have his own house. If he started his own auctioneering business, he would need his own property from which to launch it. Declan contemplated the thought that liked to tiptoe into his brain late at night when he couldn't sleep. The Miller Family Auctioneering Company covered five states. His grandpa and dad had expanded it steadily over the years. They had more business than they could handle.

A man who had his own business was a man to be taken seriously.

A spate of coughing consumed Declan. Along with a dash of guilt. What made him want to be the son who split from the family business? Amish families stuck together.

To be taken seriously by a woman like Bethel, whom he had known since they were both learning to walk, would take some doing. Especially when jokes were his fallback whenever he was nervous. Bethel made him nervous. Women made him nervous. He'd learned early on that people liked to laugh. Making them laugh was nice.

More coughing.

"Bruder, sei so gut," Elijah muttered, rolling over and sticking a pillow over his head.

"Es dutt mer." Declan sat up. He threw his legs over the side of his single bed pushed against the wall to make a walkway between the two beds. And immediately coughed. The muscles in his stomach ached. Poor Elijah. Listening to someone else cough was almost as annoying as listening to a guy snore. Declan slipped from the room and padded barefoot down the stairs. A light flickered in the kitchen. He wasn't the only one not sleeping.

Reading glasses perched on the end of his nose, his father sat at the kitchen table engrossed in a thick book. After six months of tutoring by Toby's special friend, Rachelle Lapp, Dad had made great strides in overcoming his reading disability. He was making up for lost time.

"You couldn't sleep either?" Dad picked up a mug with a tea-bag string hanging over the side and took a sip. "I heard you coughing before I came downstairs."

"Allergies, I reckon."

"Or a cold from being out in the rain and wind today."

"Colds are caused by viruses, not cold, wet air. Plus it wouldn't happen that fast." Declan wanted the words back as soon as he uttered them. His father meant well. He had no idea his words made Declan feel like a six-year-old. He softened his tone. "I'm fine. Nothing a cup of chamomile with honey and lemon won't fix. And some of Mamm's cough syrup."

"Since when did you get a medical degree?"

About the same time you did.

Thankful the words didn't pass through his lips, Declan clenched his jaw. He was twenty-four, a full-grown man, still living at home and working year-round with family. The Plain people counted that as a good thing. Most of the time it was.

But a little wiggle room would be nice. To be able to stretch out his arms and not bump into someone with the same last name. That was a most un-Plain sentiment, one Dad wouldn't understand.

What was wrong with him? Maybe he *was* coming down with something. Declan concentrated on pouring the already steaming water from the teapot on the stove into his mug. He cut up some lemon and helped himself to a large dollop of honey. He sat across from his father. "Did you ever think about doing something besides auctioneering?"

Dad laid the book on the table. Frowning, he removed his reading glasses. "I thought you loved auctioneering. You've been chomping at the bit to get on the platform since you were five years old."

"I do. It's the best." Declan dunked his tea bag a few times. "Did you ever think about going out on your own?"

Dad's lips turned down. He shook his head and shrugged. "Nee. Why would I? Your daadi needed my help. And I liked it."

"But your brieder didn't go into the business."

"Nee, my brieder chose other paths."

"We cover a lot of territory. Maybe too much."

"What's your point?"

"What would you think if I split off? Maybe started my own . . . branch, so to speak? What the Englischers call a satellite location."

"You want to compete with Miller Family Auctioneering?" Dat's incredulous tone matched his scowl. "Why would you do that?"

"I'm . . ." A spasm of coughing hit Declan. He sipped his tea. The hot liquid helped. "It's just a thought that keeps niggling at me. It wouldn't be competing; it'd be supplementing. There's so many of us. Elijah and Emmett coming up behind me. Toby and Jason already full-time auctioneers. We don't have a lot of auctions big enough to need three auctioneers, four with you."

"You're not getting enough time in the spotlight?"

Acerbic sarcasm soaked his words.

"Nee. It's not like that."

"What is it like?"

"People see me as the clown. I want them to know I can be serious. I am serious."

"Serious men don't leave a dolly filled with speakers all by their lonesome in the middle of a field during a thunderstorm." Dad's voice was almost as hoarse as Declan's. "It seems to me you earned the clown title. It always seemed like you wanted people to laugh at you. Never understood it myself."

Dad never missed a thing.

"They were wrapped up good and tight. They didn't get wet."

"*Gut* thing they didn't get stolen."

"Only Plain folks were around."

"You know that for sure? Where'd you run off to?"

Timing was everything. He'd given his dad a reason to discard his idea out of hand. Dad didn't see him as capable of running his own business. The realization cut like a sharp ax. Heat that had nothing to do with the steaming cup of tea coursed through Declan. His pulse beat in his ears. "I was helping Bethel King get her brieder into their buggy."

One hand stroking his gray beard that hung almost to his waist, Dad stirred more honey into his tea with the other. His frown faded, replaced with a small grin. "That was kind of you. Wasn't Bethel in your class at school?"

"I know what you're thinking." Declan rose and went to the window over the sink. The conversation about his business plan would go nowhere. Not tonight. Another day. He would show his dad he could handle a business on his own. "You're as bad as Mamm with her matchmaking. Jah, Bethel was in my class. She was—and still is—one of the smartest girls I know. I reckon she's too smart to put up with the likes of me."

The rain had stopped, but the wind still shook the branches of a Japanese maple near the back porch, causing a shower of drops. Nothing like the rain that poured on Bethel as she frowned down at him while he lay staring up at her. He'd been clumsy and played it off like a buffoon. Leaving her with the same impression as his dad's. The Miller brother clown.

"I would never matchmake." With a chuckle, Dad picked up his book and turned the page as if he were not the least interested in talking about such a ridiculous topic. "I leave that nonsense to your mamm. She did gut with your schweschdre and brieder."

His sister Layla and her husband, Micah, had beaten Toby and Rachelle to the altar by several months.

Dad's satisfied tone tickled Declan. He turned around to face his father. A sip of tea soothed his throat for a few seconds. "At least wait until after Toby and Rachelle's wedding to start on Elijah and me."

"I'm not starting on anybody." Dad displayed his best innocent look. "I'm just saying everyone knows Bethel King works hard taking care of her brieder. She is a gut and faithful believer. She even works at the nursery to earn extra money to help out her family. She'll make somebody a gut *fraa*."

"No doubt."

But would she take a man with a reputation for being a jokester seriously? Jana Yoder had tried and given up. Her point was well taken. He'd never opened up to her. The truth was he should've ended the relationship himself much earlier. He'd liked Jana. He was sure it would grow into more, but it never did. He'd started dating Jana because he didn't have the guts to ask Bethel and risk rejection.

"No doubt what?" Elijah wandered into the kitchen. He stretched and scratched his armpit. "What are you two doing up?"

"Just getting something for my throat. You?"

"I can't sleep without you tossing and turning and coughing in the other bed. It was too quiet." Elijah went to the counter where he removed the lid from a plastic container filled with Mom's butterscotch chip–pecan cookies. "Besides, I'm hungry."

Elijah was the one brother who didn't want to auctioneer. No point in rehashing Declan's business idea with him. "Dat's matchmaking."

"Am not."

"Are too." Declan rummaged through the cupboards where Mom kept her store of medicines out of the little ones' reach. "Dat's trying to marry me off, when it's your turn first."

"Elijah needs to come out of his shell before he'll have a special friend." Dad accepted the cookie container as his due. Elijah was the shy brother. He'd yet to call his first auction even though he was two years older than Declan. "Get me a glass of milk, will you?"

"I don't have a shell." Elijah stacked another cookie on his napkin. "I'm fine just the way I am."

Like Declan. Another brother in denial.

Declan set the bottle of cough syrup on the counter and took care of his father's request. Cookies and milk sounded good, but the cookie would make his throat hurt and the milk would only add to his congestion.

"What's going on here? A family meeting?"

Toby had joined the crowd.

"What are you doing up?" Elijah picked up the cookie container and held it out. "You're just in time. Dat almost grabbed the last ones."

Toby waved away the container. "I'm hungry, but I want eggs. With toast."

He pulled the cast-iron skillet to the front burner on the stove. "Anybody else?"

"It's four hours until breakfast." Dad brushed crumbs from his beard. "Your mudder will be irritated if she makes breakfast and we don't eat it."

"That'll never happen. We're growing buwe." Toby grabbed the eggs from the refrigerator and set them on the counter. "She'll be more upset if we leave a mess in her kitchen."

"Or she'll be upset when she realizes you can actually cook for yourself." Declan coughed into the crook of his arm. He squeezed past his big brother to retrieve the syrup. "Personally I don't want to be around when she finds out you used her gut skillet without her supervision."

Unperturbed, Toby dumped a chunk of congealed bacon fat into the skillet. He adjusted the flame under it. "I heard you coughing earlier. Is your throat sore?"

"It's fine." Declan dumped a few ounces of syrup in a cup. He pinched his nostrils closed and gulped it down. Despite a bitter taste that was a cross between licorice and root beer, the syrup went down easy. Likely because of all the honey Mamm's recipe included. "This syrup will fix me up."

"You're only supposed to take a teaspoon," Elijah objected. "That's gross."

"This bug—if it is a bug—calls for a double dose."

Maybe triple.

"That's what happens when you don't rest your vocal cords the night before an auction." Toby had switched from his big brother voice to his boss voice. "You went to a singing at the Eashes' last night, didn't you?"

"Not even. I went to pick up the band saw Noah borrowed from us last week. James challenged me to a game of chess. Mary and the girls started singing while they were working on their sewing." Music soothed Declan. Singing was a joy, especially when Mary and her daughters had such fine voices. "It was an impromptu thing. They were having fun, and James, Noah, and I joined in."

"I can see that, but singing strains your voice. Did you drink plenty of water?"

Toby was such a big brother. They all knew how to take care of their voices. The "rules" had been impressed upon them in auctioneer school, and first Grandpa, and then Dad, had kept them fresh in their minds. "I did. I promise."

"Your voice is your most—"

"Your voice is your most important tool as an auctioneer!" Declan, Elijah, and Dad chorused. "We know."

"Just saying." Toby turned back to the stove. The scent of bacon wafted in the air, accompanied by the melted lard's crackle in the skillet. Toby cracked a dozen eggs into a bowl in quick succession. He picked up a fork and whisked them together. "After all, pretty soon I won't be around to remind you. I'm going to miss playing big bruder in the middle of the night. There's always someone in this kitchen, day or night."

"I reckon Rachelle will be happy to keep you company in the kitchen any time of the day or night." Declan returned the syrup to the cupboard, then leaned against the counter to watch Elijah make toast while Toby dumped the eggs into the skillet. The blossoming scent stirred memories of many mornings gathered around the breakfast table, talking, planning, and laughing with his brothers. "Are you getting cold feet?"

"Nee. Never."

Toby had always been popular with the Plain women in their community. He was good-natured and smart, worked hard, and was a striking figure on the auction platform. Heads turned when he walked by. The only reason he'd waited so long to marry was his concern over bringing a wife into his life as an auctioneer on the road for six months out of the year.

Growing up in Toby's shadow—not to mention the shadow of his brother Jason, who was already married—wasn't easy. It didn't seem to bother Elijah. He was happiest in the woodworking shop he'd built out back of the house. His children's furniture and wooden toys were beautiful. His needs were few.

Toby, Jason, and Elijah seemed to have found their places in the scheme of life. Why couldn't Declan? After a minute or two, the scent of toasted bread became less appealing. More acrid. Elijah didn't seem to notice. Declan tapped his arm. "Hey, you're burning the toast!"

Elijah jumped. He jerked the long-handled, multipronged fork back. One of the slices fell to the floor. "Whoops. Who likes their toast well done? Open a window, will you?"

Declan obliged. Elijah tossed out the remaining slices. "I like to share with the birds."

"*Dumkopf!*" Chuckling, Toby shook his head. "Always daydreaming—even at night."

"Hey, no name-calling." Declan scooped up the errant slice and threw it in the trash. "Everyone gets distracted."

"Enough with the bickering." Dad stood, stretched, and picked up his book. "I like spending time with my *seh*. But there can be a thing as too much togetherness. See you in the morning."

Exactly Declan's point. Although these middle-of-the-night gatherings were among some of his best memories. On the road, they sometimes sat in diners and talked until the wee hours of the morning. It had become a bit of a tradition. He would miss these moments as his brothers married and moved into their own homes.

Every business plan had pros and cons.

"Don't leave now, Dat. The eggs are ready." Toby scooped scrambled eggs that also appeared overly done onto plates as he spoke. "We don't have to have toast."

"I'll wait until your mudder makes breakfast in the morning." Dad shuffled toward the door. "Don't leave a mess and don't stay up too long. Daylight will be here before you know it. No one in this family has a pass to be late for church."

"I smell food." Sadie, her blonde hair loose, no glasses, zipped into the room. The ten-year-old's tendency to run when her clumsy gait—caused by her Down syndrome—kept her off-kilter often resulted in tumbles. "I am hungry."

"Nee, nee, now this really is out of control." Dad tucked his book under his arm. He reached for her, but Sadie danced away. "Come now, back to bed, *maedel*. Mamm will make you breakfast before church in the morning. You won't want to get up if you don't sleep now. And if you sleep in church, Bishop Bart will be upset with you."

Sadie wouldn't want to upset Bart. He kept Tootsie Pops in his pockets, and he liked to share with the kids.

"I'll bring her, Dat." Declan caught his sister from behind and swung her into the air. She smelled of homemade lavender soap and shampoo after her Saturday night bath. "Sadie, how long do chickens work?"

"I don't know."

"Around the cluck."

A chorus of groans greeted the joke, but Sadie giggled and clapped her hands. "More, more."

"Why shouldn't you play basketball with a pig?"

"Why, Bruder, why?"

"Because he'll hog the ball."

"Sei so gut, make him stop." Toby tilted his head back and raised his hands as if appealing to God Himself. "I can't take it."

"You love it." Declan kissed Sadie's mussed hair. "Schweschder, how did you see to get down here without your glasses?"

"My nose show me."

"Interesting. Big bruder will show your nose how to get back to bed."

"Eppies."

"Nee. No eppies, no toast, no eggs. Sleep." Declan tossed her over his shoulder. He took the stairs two at a time. His sister's sweet tooth was legendary. Sadie would eat cookies—or cake or pie or fry pies or whoopie pies—for breakfast if no one saw her helping herself. "You don't want to oversleep and miss church. Jonah will be there."

Jonah Lapp, who also attended classes for children with developmental and intellectual disabilities at the English school in Lee's Gulch, was Sadie's best friend. Giggling, Sadie patted Declan's tousled hair. "Mamm take eppies to church."

Not if her sons had eaten them all while she blissfully slept. Declan smiled and kept that thought to himself. No matter how many times belonging to this big, messy family made him feel hemmed in, there were just as many times when family felt good. Very good.

He halted in the doorway, torn between futures that appeared so different. Which one was best?

Sadie tweaked Declan's nose. "You fall asleep, Bruder?"

"Nee, nee," he whispered. He slid the girl down so she landed on her feet. "Shhh. Don't wake your schweschdre."

"*Gut nacht,* Bruder."

"Sweet dreams."

Declan withdrew. Sweet dreams. That's all they were. As the fourth brother behind his dad, Declan earned less than his three older brothers. Everyone received a salary, but while living at home, all of them contributed to the family's budget. Soon Toby would have his own home and family but still would be number two behind Dad. Then Jason and then Elijah. Declan was number five in the hierarchy.

The numbers for sound systems, trailers, drivers, insurance, property, and other expenses ran through his brain as Declan returned to his bedroom. The numbers, his cough, and the memory of Bethel peering down at him and laughing took turns keeping him awake long after Elijah returned and slipped back into slumberland.

Chapter 4

A delighted whoop followed the slap of the red bag on the wooden cornhole board. Grinning at her little brother's enthusiasm, Bethel high-fived Robbie. She stepped out of the way to allow Judah his turn in the bishop's backyard, which they'd commandeered for a game after church and lunch. Robbie's black bag not only hit the board; it slid into the hole. He beamed and pumped his fist. "Three points!"

"See, I knew you two had a knack for this game." Bethel stood between the two boys' chairs, her hands on their bony, bent shoulders, waiting for Sadie Miller and Jonah Lapp to take their turns from behind the other board. "You just have to aim and calculate the distance."

Moving the boards closer than the regulation twenty-seven feet had helped. Giving the kids do-overs as needed also helped. Rules were made to be broken when fun was the object of the game. The previous day's storm had brought a cold front with it. Despite the sunshine, the March breeze still held a chill. The rain had made it too muddy for the baseball or volleyball the kids usually played after church. Which was just fine. Bethel's brothers couldn't play those sports, and it was hard to see the longing on their faces when they watched other kids their age run the bases after a hit or jump high to spike the volleyball.

Robbie and Judah went to school with Sadie and Jonah in Lee's Gulch. They were best buddies on the weekends too—especially after church when the others sometimes forgot to include them in their games.

"Ha, it's not over until it's over." Rachelle Lapp nudged her little brother, who hopped up to a spot behind the foul line in front of the other board. "Fire away when ready, Bruder."

Jonah dumped his winter coat on the ground and shoved his church hat back on his head of dark brown hair. He settled his black-rimmed glasses on his nose. His tongue came out and curled across the corner of his mouth. He let the red bag fly. It landed on the board just shy of the hole.

"Yay!" Robbie stuck both of his skinny arms in the air, hands fisted. "Gut shot, Jonah."

Claire, who was stretched out in a lawn chair next to her best friend, Nyla Plank; Bethel's best friend, Hattie Schrock; and Layla Troyer, Declan's married sister, led them in applause and noisy congratulations. Every game needed enthusiastic spectators.

Why did Bethel now think of Layla, whom she had known since her diaper days, as Declan's sister? No reason. No reason at all. She brushed the thought away.

"How many points is that, Jonah?" Rachelle had been their teacher before the English school district invited Plain parents to send their children with developmental and intellectual delays to their school in town. All the occupational, speech, and physical therapy that came with that offer, plus the fact the families already paid school district taxes and previously received nothing in return, made it an offer they couldn't refuse. Now Rachelle never let a teaching moment pass. She simply couldn't. Jonah rolled his eyes. Rachelle shook her finger at him. "Come on, you know."

"One."

"See, that wasn't so hard."

Next up was Sadie, Judah's partner. The ten-year-old didn't bother to shed her heavy coat. She was a doll of a little girl with Declan's blonde hair and blue eyes—Miller family traits. Her eyes were made big by her thick brown-rimmed glasses. Her dimples popped up whenever she smiled—which was all the time. Another feature shared with Declan. Something about yesterday's encounter in the muddy field had left Bethel with Declan on her mind. She'd known him her whole life. Why now? *Stop it!*

Giggling, Sadie sashayed up to the line, tucked the bag under her arm, and proceeded to go through a series of exaggerated stretches of her throwing arm.

"You're such a ham." Bethel threw her hands in the air in mock despair. "Come on, maedel, my hair is turning gray standing here. Let it rip before we die of old age."

Sadie spun with her arm in the air like a windmill and did just that. The bag sailed through the air far beyond the boards, whooshing past the boys, just missing Bethel, who ducked, and finally landing at the feet of Jonah's dog, Runt. Runt dropped the hot dog he'd stolen from Sadie's plate. He snapped up the bag and raced it back to Jonah.

The kids roared with laughter, as did their cheering section. "Way to go, Runt," Claire yelled. "Five points!"

Hattie and Layla joined in a chorus of "Five points, five points for the *hund*!"

"Ten points." Sadie danced around the dog. "Ten points for Runt."

"Uh-uh. No points. Gut job, hund." Laughing so hard he tumbled to his knees, Jonah hugged the dog. "Take to Robbie. Go on. Go."

His tail whapping back and forth, Runt did as he was told. He gently deposited the bag in Robbie's lap and backed away, panting, his tongue hanging from his mouth.

Tears of laughter on his cheeks, Robbie patted his head. "Gut hund."

Still grinning, he peered at the cornhole board with deep concentration. "Here we go." Robbie let the bag fly. It plopped into the hole. "Three points. Three points!"

Doing the math in her head, Bethel knelt so she could hold up the pegboard. Elijah Miller had done a beautiful job building the cornhole boards with one compartment underneath to store the bags and another for the pegs. "The score's tied up at twenty-one all. I think we can call it a game. Everybody wins."

Jonah and Robbie grumbled, but neither one outright argued. Judah and Sadie cheered. "We won, we won."

"Everyone won." Rachelle nudged Sadie and Jonah toward the King boys. "Go tell Robbie and Judah gut game."

Sadie immediately dashed over to Judah. "Gut game. I win. You win. We all win."

Judah smiled for real then. "Gut game, Sadie."

"You like eppie? I bring you eppie. And lemonade. Come on, Jonah."

She dashed away. Grinning, Jonah shrugged and turned to follow.

"Jonah, your coat," Rachelle called after him. "Mamm will get you if you lose your coat."

Scowling, he stomped back to the coat. He threw it over his shoulder.

"Wear it, Bruder."

More scowls, but he tugged on the coat, then took off at a dead run.

"They have so much energy. I love that about kinner. Keeping up with them makes me feel like a *kind* again." Most days Hattie had no problem acting like a child. Her parents probably wished she acted a bit more grown-up. "I don't mind mopping floors or doing laundry as long as I can turn it into a game. Being a grown-up should be fun too."

"Chores are fun, but by the time I get done, I'm too tired to play." Claire had a dusting of freckles across her turned-up nose and cheeks, products of the bright sunshine. "I could sleep all day and all night."

"Not today." Nyla hopped up. She grabbed Claire's arm and tugged. "Let's go find the other girls. I'm tired of sitting around. We can walk to my house. We have a new batch of kittens that are the cutest ever. Maybe we can take a ride on the horses."

Claire tugged back. She remained firmly seated in the chair. "You go ahead. I think I'm coming down with something."

Nyla, a round girl with wheat-colored hair and green eyes half hidden behind thick glasses, stuck her hands on her hips. "Are you sure? You didn't come hiking with us last weekend. You don't want to do anything anymore."

"Next time, I promise."

"I'm holding you to that."

Nyla turned and nearly collided with Enos and Liam, who took turns sidestepping her.

"Whew! Where's the fire?" Enos's booming laugh, though rarely heard, echoed the one their father had. He and Liam were the spitting image of Dad—hair the color of dark toast, cocoa-brown eyes, and built like bulldogs—solid, all chest, and not much height. "No need to knock us down."

"Sorry, sorry." Nyla's face turned tomato red. She ducked her head and rushed away, still muttering, "Sorry."

Apparently unaware of the effect he had on the girl, Enos cocked his head toward Bethel. "We just came to steal the boys from you, Beth. Mamm wants us to take them home. Are you ready, guys?"

"Mamm is worried we caught cold in the rain yesterday." Judah's disgruntled tone matched his scowl. "Tell her we kept our coats on, like she said. We're fine. Aren't we, Beth?"

"You're fine, but you have school tomorrow, so it's not a bad idea to call it a day." Bethel tucked a scarf Mom had insisted Judah wear more snugly around his neck. "I can come along."

"Nee. No need." Enos cocked his head toward Claire. "Mamm says you should come too, Schweschder."

Frowning, Claire struggled to rise from her chair. It wobbled. So did Claire.

Hattie popped up and steadied her from behind. "Do you need a push?"

"I'm fine. Just tired."

Enos took Claire's hand and pulled her upright. "You need to eat your spinach, maedel."

"Like I said, I must be coming down with something." Claire's cheeks, dusted pink from the sun, turned a deep red. "Or maybe it's just because yesterday was a long day."

No teenage girl should be tired after a good night's sleep. Bethel swallowed those words. They left a bitter taste in her throat. "I'll bring your chair. See you back at the house."

"Danki." Her shoulders hunched, Claire waved good-bye to the other women. "See you soon."

Bethel heaved a sigh and relaxed in her chair. It was nice to be relieved of duty. God knew what He was doing when He made Sunday a day of rest.

"Does Claire have it?" Her dark brown eyes full of concern, Rachelle spoke in a soft voice. "Muscular dystrophy?"

Rachelle was so observant and so empathetic. Bethel forced a nod. "We think so, but Mamm's calling tomorrow to make an appointment at the Clinic for Special Children. They'll do the tests to confirm."

Another five-and-a-half-hour trip through Virginia, Washington, D.C., and Maryland to Strasburg in Lancaster County, Pennsylvania. More medical bills. The clinic thrived on fundraisers and donations that allowed them to keep their fees down, but the costs still added up.

If Claire had the disease, surgery, braces, canes, ankle and foot orthotics, walkers, mobility scooters, and eventually a wheelchair would likely be needed. Both Judah and Robbie had surgery to lengthen their tendons in an effort to prolong their ability to walk. Eventually, their leg muscles became too weak even then. Robbie's had progressed more quickly than Judah's. There was no way of knowing how quickly Claire's would affect her.

"I'm so sorry." Layla laid her hand on Bethel's. "It's a hard row to hoe."

"I know we have to believe Gott's will is being done in all this, but it's hard to see." Another sibling who would need care. How many would there be? Robbie and Judah were sweet, loving boys. It broke Bethel's heart to see them struggle. "Mamm keeps saying Gott has a plan for the buwe. He has a plan for Claire too. I know it's true. I don't begrudge a single second of taking care of them. I just can't understand why He allows them to suffer like this."

"What is that saying?" Hattie rubbed her crinkled forehead as if thinking hurt. "Sometimes the test comes first, then the lesson . . . That's it."

"Is it wrong to say I don't like this test?"

Kelly Irvin

"Nobody does." Rachelle pulled her lawn chair closer. "Everyone in our family has had to think about Gott's hand in Jonah's life. Every family ponders these issues when a special *kind* joins it. All we know for sure is that every bopli is a gift from Gott."

"Kinner come in all shapes and sizes. Look at me. The silly goose." Hattie, short for Harriet Rose Schrock, the daughter of nursery owner Atlee Schrock, had a penchant for saying odd things. One of her many traits that had turned her into Bethel's best friend in first grade. She held out her paper plate. She'd filled it with monster cookies, snickerdoodles, gingersnaps, kiss cookies, and brownies. Hattie had a sweet tooth and loved to share. "Just looking at me makes people laugh."

It wasn't the wiry orange-red hair or immense sea of freckles across her nose that made Hattie stand out among her friends. It tended to be the lopsided prayer cover, wrinkled dress, and inevitably stained apron along with a propensity for talking nonstop.

"Gott made you in His image, and you're only a silly goose when you want to be." The steel binding around Bethel's heart loosened a tad. Serious Hattie appeared at the least expected moments. Bethel took a kiss cookie and passed the plate to Rachelle. Kiss cookies were the best because they were a two for one: a cookie and a chocolate candy. "You always make me smile. I just need to stop whining."

"You're no whiner. I wish I had your patience." Rachelle pulled her crocheted shawl more tightly around her shoulders against a frisky north wind that had loosened a lock of dark brown hair from her prayer covering. Her fair cheeks were rosy. "I've been where you are. Wondering what Gott's plan was for me in all this. I struggled with giving up teaching our special children because I wasn't sure of my future. I wished He'd use the clouds to spell it out across the sky or in the fields like those crop circles people talk about. Something plain as day."

"Mamm needs me. The buwe need me. Not only will Claire be less help, but she will need more help as time goes on."

"Remember, though, it's not all on your shoulders. It's *hochmut* to think you're the only one who can take care of their needs." Rachelle tempered the words with a smile. "I was sure I was what was best for my special kinner. Come to find out, they're doing just fine at the English school without me. I only made it harder for them by hanging on so tightly."

The sound of a child counting at the top of his lungs mingled with laughter and shouts as kids raced through the yard, intent on a game of hide-and-seek. So carefree. Their bodies so strong and able. Such joy for them. Such blessing. For that, Bethel would always be grateful. She simply had to work harder to find the blessings in the trials borne by the people she loved. "When did you figure it out? Was it because of Toby?" Bethel put her hand to her mouth for a second, then let it drop. "I'm sorry. That's awfully personal, isn't it?"

"Maedel, Rachelle loves to talk about Toby." With a snort, Hattie flipped her hand in the air as if she were tossing out Bethel's comment. "Go on, tell Bethel how he wore you down until you knew you couldn't live without him."

"Eww, this is my bruder we're talking about." Layla pretended to cover her ears. "Toby is a gut guy, but I don't want to think of him like that."

Bethel joined in their laughter. When it died away, she broached the subject that was most worrisome. "You don't have a history of muscular dystrophy in your family, do you?"

"Ach, is that what you're worried about? More special children?" Rachelle's eyebrows arched, but her ochre eyes filled with empathy. "We Lapps have our own special child, as do Toby and Layla's family. I consider it an honor to care for Jonah and will happily do the same for Sadie someday. If Toby and I have more, then Gott's will be done."

"Absolutely. I hope and plan to do the same." Bethel felt her way gingerly along the narrow, pitfall-filled path this conversation followed. To compare diseases or disabilities was unthinkable. Each had its own challenges, each its own means of coping and overcoming. "It's just that LGMD is so hard on the kinner. It doesn't show up right away. After a while you forget to keep your guard up, and that's when it pounces. Watching the kinner struggle to understand and to accept is hard. I would never say anything to them. They're so resilient, so determined to live life the best they can.

"I'm the one who falls short, Gott forgive me. To watch them struggle breaks my heart. First it's no more running, no more baseball or volleyball and other sports. Then it's walking. No hiking. No hunting. It's harder and harder to finish simple tasks. They start to realize they won't be able to farm or do most jobs. Even with physical and occupational therapy twice a week, the simple tasks like taking a bath or combing their hair get hard. After a while, even brushing their teeth is hard. They're so brave. I'm the one who questions. If they do, they never do it in front of me. I try to trust in Gott. I try to have faith. I try."

Bethel halted. The quiver in her voice was shameful. It was the most she'd ever shared. Why today? Why now? Because the disease seemed to have skipped her and gone for Claire instead. Why her little sister and not Bethel? "If I could somehow spare Claire this trial, I would. I'd gladly carry it for her."

"I believe you would. I know you would." Rachelle tipped her chair to one side. She gave Bethel a one-armed hug. "But it's not up to you to question Gott's plan—for her or for you. We don't have to know why Claire will bear this cross and not you. We only have to accept it as Gott's will and do everything we can to support her. You also have to think about your mamm. She needs you to help with the younger kinner."

"I know. How can I marry and leave her to take care of three kinner—or more—with the disease? The therapy sessions, the stretching, all the care they need." Bethel kneaded her apron's soft cotton with both hands. "Setting that aside, I wonder if it's fair to ask a man to marry me, knowing what the future may bring."

"Getting married won't keep you from helping your mudder. Others will step in to help too. That is the way of our community and our faith. The key word is *may* bring." Her tone gentle, Layla patted Bethel's shoulder. "If we worried about these diseases, none of us would get married or have *boplin*. I can't wait for my first bopli to come along."

Come what may.

"That's for sure and for certain." Hattie passed the dessert plate again. Bethel passed it right back. The last thing she needed was more sugar. Hattie's expression said *Yay, more for me.* She selected a snickerdoodle and held it up as if inspecting it. "I want to have as many kinner as possible. If James ever gets around to asking me the big question."

Of course she did. All Plain women did.

"I heard you and Declan had a run-in yesterday." Rachelle's observation came with a slight smile. "Maybe that's why the subject of kinner is on your mind."

Declan helped them in a deluge of rain despite a terrible cough. He'd gone out of his way to be helpful, and all she'd done was judge him. "Nee, nee, that's not it. It was nothing like that. He just helped us out."

"Then why is your face turning red?"

The more the women laughed, the more heat toasted Bethel's face. "Stop!" She couldn't help herself. Their laughter was contagious.

Declan knew how to make people laugh. Maybe that was the gift God had bestowed on him. "Stop it. It's not that funny."

Yet she giggled with them.

"What's so funny?"

Bethel swiveled in her chair. So did her companions. Declan strode across the gravel driveway toward them. Her friends' peals of laughter grew. Bethel bit back her own. Declan frowned, then glanced down. "What? Did I spill something on my clothes?"

"Nee. It's not you." Her fit of giggles fled as quickly as it had come. "It's nothing."

That set Hattie off again. Which sent Rachelle and Layla into another gale of laughter.

"Really. It's nothing."

Suddenly it *was* all about him. Or maybe it was simply the power of suggestion. Bethel allowed herself a glance at Declan's half-bewildered, half-willing-to-smile expression. He wanted to make the world a happier place.

Who could argue with that?

Chapter 5

These women had a serious case of the giggles. Declan forced a smile and forged ahead. Something about the knowing glances they exchanged suggested he might be the butt of the joke. Jokes were good—when he told them. Had Bethel told them about her encounter with him the previous day? A good report or a bad one? He'd paid for his efforts. His voice was so hoarse it barely registered above a whisper. After coughing all night—not to mention the impromptu family reunion in the kitchen—he'd had trouble staying awake in church. Which only irritated his father, who offered a couple of tooth-picks "to prop up his eyelids." One peek at Bethel sitting with his sister Layla and future sister-in-law Rachelle and chatting in the bishop's backyard had him wide awake now.

"As you know, I like a gut joke." He didn't mind being the punch line as long as he was in on the joke. He picked up his pace and strode in front of their lineup of chairs. "What is it?"

"Just girl talk." Layla smothered another laugh with both hands. "Nothing that would interest you."

The muffled words sounded more like "nuffin tat wood inrest you." "Okay. No more *kaffi* for you, little schweschder." Declan used his thumb to gesture toward the road. "I think Micah is looking for you. He said something about leaving you to walk home. You'd better hightail it to the buggy."

Micah had said no such thing. The man was daft for his wife. Layla was opinionated, good with math, a smart-mouth, quick with a joke, surly in the mornings, and a snapping turtle when tired. But Micah seemed to love her anyway. He barely let her out of his sight.

"Your voice sounds terrible, Bruder." Layla's laughter faded, replaced with a concerned tone. "You need to stop talking and rest it or you won't be able to call an auction come Friday and Saturday."

"I'm doctoring it." The cold March wind wasn't helping. Declan shifted his gaze to Rachelle. "They offered you a ride, too, if you need one. Your *eldre* took off a few minutes ago."

"Nee, I think I have a ride, but danki."

Rachelle didn't need to elaborate. With the announcement of their banns at church, everyone now knew about Toby and her.

Declan had at least two weddings to attend in the coming weeks. Everyone was getting hitched—except Elijah and Declan. Fortunately for Declan, Mom was more focused on Elijah, since he was two years older. Regardless of Dad's comments the previous night, he too was prone to nudging their shy son along. Elijah refused to go to the singings. He spent most of his time in his workshop when he wasn't on the auction circuit. What he lacked in social skills, he made up for in determination to go his own way.

Good for him.

The geese took off, leaving one poor goose to fend for herself. Bethel closed up her canvas chair, then did the same with a stray lawn chair. "I reckon I'd better get moving as well. My mamm is probably ready to go too."

"She was chatting with your *aentis* the last time I saw her. They didn't seem like they were in any rush." Declan reached for the chairs. "Let me carry those for you."

Bethel frowned. She clung to the chairs. "They don't weigh much."

No, but they would make a good reason for Declan to walk with her to the Kings' buggy. He wavered, hand still hanging out there all lonesome. Bethel's frown disappeared, replaced by an odd expression that was hard to decipher. She thrust the chairs toward him. "But since you offered so kindly."

He didn't have to be told twice. Declan accepted her offering. She led the way. He adjusted his stride to hers. Now what? Now make conversation like a normal human being. "How are the buwe? No ill effects from getting caught in the thunderstorm yesterday?"

"They're fine. Like I told Mamm, rain doesn't cause colds—"

"Viruses do." Declan finished the sentence. "I said the same thing to my dat last night."

Bethel laughed. Such a nice sound. One it would be good to hear more often. "You do sound like you're coming down with something. And your face is flushed like you might have a fever."

Or be embarrassed because he didn't know how to talk to a woman without being a goof. At least that had been Jana's complaint. He was all fluff under the fluff. "It's chapped from the cold wind yesterday." He turned up his jacket collar to provide puny protection against it. "It's probably allergies."

"My mamm says locally harvested honey is best."

"Mine too, mixed with horehound to make a syrup."

"Time tested and true."

The subject exhausted, they walked in silence for a few yards. She wouldn't be interested in the auctions. She spent her days caring for her brieder. "How do the buwe like the English school now that they've had time to adjust?"

"They like it okay. They miss their friends and Corrine, but the speech therapy, PT, and occupational therapy have been gut for them."

"Sadie likes it, but she has Jonah with her. Those two are two kernels of popcorn in the same pot. Always jumping up and down, but usually in the same direction."

More steps. More silence. Had it been this hard with Jana? "Layla says you're working part time in the Schrocks' nursery. How's that going?"

"I like it. I was helping Mamm with the bookkeeping and sales at our furniture warehouse, but the nursery lets me bring in money to help with the medical bills." Her tone sounded almost grudging. "If I have to be away from home, I'd rather be repotting plants, watering, and weeding than stuck in a stuffy store behind a counter."

Something else for Declan to stow away in his mental file of Bethel facts. She was a homebody who'd rather be outside than inside. "I've never had to work inside. I wouldn't like it either."

Bethel stepped closer, leaning in as if straining to hear him. "I like gardening and mowing and even hanging laundry on the line while the kinner are at school." Her expression was almost guilty. "The furniture shop is fine, but sometimes it's gut to talk to people besides family."

Exactly Declan's thought some days when it was Miller brothers twenty-four-seven on the auction circuit. Another thing they had in common.

The community had pitched in when the King boys had their surgeries and helped to pay for their wheelchairs. Barbecue plate sales had attracted all of Lee's Gulch's residents, not just Plain families. "We're fortunate the district helps to pay medical bills, but I know they can still be overwhelming for families like yours. I ate three plates at the last fundraiser. I almost popped a seam in my shirt."

"We appreciate the support." She smiled up at him. Declan almost forgot how to put one foot in front of the other. Her tone warmed, which didn't help with the walking thing. "Judah loves the joke book for kinner you gave him when he was in the hospital. It was gut practice for his English too."

"Gut. I'm glad it helped."

"It was kind of you. They've done the puzzles you gave them twice—they took them apart and redid them."

Rehabbing from the surgery had taken time. Boys who were used to being active had to find new ways to occupy themselves. "I broke my leg when I was in second grade. I had surgery." He held up three fingers. "Cast. Rehab. Stuck at home."

"I remember that. Vaguely. Didn't you jump off a roof?"

"Flying. I was flying. Even Elijah thought I was part eagle. Dumkopf, that was me."

"Not dumkopf. Foolhardy, maybe. But definitely imaginative. And adventuresome."

"Kind of you. Anyway, I know sitting still isn't easy. And I only had to do it for a while." Not a lifetime. "Never hear Judah or Robbie complain."

"They don't. I'm amazed at how accepting they are. We can all take lessons from them."

"We could."

They'd arrived at the Kings' buggy far too soon. Declan waited while Bethel opened up the back so he could stow the chairs in the storage area. She scooted back. He leaned in close enough to smell her scent of sweet and chocolate. Somebody had been eating a kiss cookie. "There you go." He took a step back. "Any other chores you need done . . . ?" A cough snuck up on him. He hid his face in the crook of his arm until it passed. "I work for tips."

He sounded like an old man who'd worked in the coal mines for a hundred years.

Her smile faintly puzzled, Bethel touched the bag slung over her shoulder. "I don't have—"

"I'm kidding."

"Of course, jah. Always the kidder." Her smile faded, replaced with a frown. "Mamm and Dat are headed this way."

Was it because of his joke or the fact that her parents would see her with Declan? "Do you work tomorrow?"

"Nee. Not until Tuesday. Why? Are you in need of plants?"

"Maybe. My mamm can never get enough flowers for her garden. You know how crazy she is about the native flowers she planted last year. I imagine she'll want to make it bigger this year." He studied his church boots. They were muddy and in need of a good polish. Really, it was just a poor attempt to prolong this conversation. She must see right through him. "I was wondering if you'd be there when she comes in."

"Don't wander too far. You'll get lost."

That sounded vaguely like she was poking fun at him. Declan peeked at her face. Her smile had resurfaced. *Nice.* "If I did get lost, would you join the search party?"

She took a turn studying her black penny loafers, also muddy, also scuffed. Finally she raised her head and met his gaze. "Nee, but I would make kaffi and cinnamon rolls and serve them hot to the men."

"Gut enough."

This time the pause wasn't awkward. Declan couldn't tear his gaze from hers, and she seemed to make no effort to look away either. Warmth that had nothing to do with the afternoon sun peeking through the clouds flooded Declan. Even his throat felt better in that moment.

"Humph."

The sound of a throat clearing forced Declan's gaze from Bethel's pretty face. Her father had stepped up his pace. Her mother lagged behind, but both of them would be at the buggy in seconds.

He tipped his black hat and spoke quickly. "Will you take a buggy ride with me?"

Would she want to take a ride with a man she could barely understand?

Her smile faded. Her forehead wrinkled, even as she studied him with a cast of conflicting emotions he couldn't begin to identify. "Can I think about it?"

"I—"

"There you are, Dochder," Aaron King called out. "We were waiting for you."

"I was helping the buwe play cornhole until Enos and Liam took them home." Sounding flustered, she ducked her head. "Claire went home with them too."

"I'd better go too." Declan made a wide berth around Aaron and Katherine. They both nodded in dismissal when he strode by. If they were curious why he stood talking to their eldest daughter by their buggy, they didn't ask. *"Faeriwell."*

"Declan."

He glanced back. Bethel's smile enveloped him. "Danki for carrying the chairs. Tend to that cold. Get well."

Declan touched the brim of his hat. *"Gern gschehme.* I will."

The conversation hadn't been a rousing success. On the one hand, Bethel hadn't said yes to a buggy ride. On the other, she hadn't said no. And that last smile was reason to hope. Wasn't it?

Chapter 6

The *chug-a-chug-a-chug* of the wringer-wash machine cheered Bethel. Such a happy sound. The astringent smell of bleach and fresh scent of soap brightened the laundry room as much as the sunshine streaming through the windows. She grinned to herself. Arms full of the boys' pants and shirts, she let her nose lead the way as she trudged through the kitchen back into the laundry room. Others might associate all this with work. No, it meant dirty clothes were getting clean, and therefore, all was right in the world. Mondays were laundry days. Nothing should impede this time-honored tradition.

A strangled sob stopped Bethel in her tracks. Contentment fled. "Claire?"

Her little sister, who'd pleaded a stomachache and stayed home from school, whirled so her back was to Bethel. Both hands to her face, she ducked her head. "I didn't know you were there."

The words were muffled but the angst in them unmistakable.

"What's the matter, Schweschder?" Bethel added her load to the piles of dresses, shirts, and pants on the floor next to the wash machine. She approached her sister's hunched form with care. "Aren't you supposed to be lying down? Is your tummy still bothering you?"

"I'm fine." With a swipe of her face, Claire turned to face Bethel. "I figured since I'm home I might as well help with the chores."

"If you don't feel gut, you shouldn't be up."

"My stomach is better."

"Uh-huh." Bethel swung the machine's wringer over the huge sink she'd filled with cold water. Time to run the clothes through the wringer into the rinse. "What's really going on?"

"Nothing."

"Then why are your eyes red and your nose running? Is it a cold, or were you crying?"

"I don't want to talk about it."

Bethel fed towels through the wringer, one after the other, careful not to feed her fingers with them. She waited.

A hiccupping sob and a huge sigh filled the silence. "Mamm says I have to go to the clinic," Claire whispered. "I don't want to go. There's nothing wrong with me. I'm just clumsy, that's all. I trip over my own feet. I get in a hurry and drop things."

The words were jerky and filled with shades of denial, uncertainty, and belligerence.

Bethel peeked over her shoulder. Her expression stricken, Claire knelt next to the pile of clothes, sorting whites from colors. Her freckles stood out against her pale skin. She chewed her lower lip. Why her and not Bethel? Why Robbie and Judah?

Bethel ran another towel through the wringer. Her heart went with it. Crushed by the weight of her grief. *It's not fair, Gott. Not fair. Don't give me that line about life not being fair. This is my little schweschder.*

What would Dad say about such a prideful, ugly prayer? God might smite her. Surely He understood. Surely she wasn't the first. Nor would she be the last. She drew a long breath and counted silently to ten. The bitterness receded on a tide of love for her sister. Such angry emotions would do Claire no good. "I'm wondering if it wouldn't be better to know for sure. Then we could start helping you make adjustments. You can go to physical and occupational therapy with the buwe. We have experience. We know what to do to help you stay on your feet."

No need to speak the rest of the sentence. Claire could finish it for herself. *For as long as possible.*

"Nee. Jah. I don't know." A bitter laugh accompanied the words. "I didn't think it would happen to me. I don't know why. It's weird. It feels like it's happening to someone else. It's like a surprise, only a bad one. Know what I mean?"

"Jah, I do. Only I worried it would happen to me. And then it hasn't." The cold water chilled Bethel's fingers. It was hard to hang on to the heavy, wet towels. Even harder to hang on to a faith that demanded she accept this trial for Claire, for their parents, for Bethel—indeed, for the whole family. "I still wonder if it will."

"You're too old." No bitterness marred Claire's statement. "You're okay."

"Maybe. I thought maybe you were too old. I'd hoped you were." Bethel dropped the towel into the sink and knelt next to Claire. "I'm so sorry." She rubbed the girl's back. "We'll get through it. Mamm and Dat and me and your brieder—we're all here for you."

Claire leaned her head against Bethel's chest as if it was too heavy to hold up. "I know. I'm being weak." She sniffed and wiped her nose on her sleeve. "I like playing volleyball. I like riding horses. I like jumping off the bluff into the pond when we go swimming. I like jumping on the trampoline with my friends. And riding my bike. I want to go to singings and run around during my *rumspringa.*"

Her voice dropped to a whisper. "I want to get married and have boplin. What Plain man will have a fraa who can't take care of boplin, cook, clean, and do laundry?"

All fair points. All fair questions. Unlike English women—with disabilities or not—Plain women aspired to one future: marriage and children. It would take a special man to make a woman with LGMD his wife. A certain kind of all-encompassing love that could surpass the aspiration of having children. Did he exist? No words of wisdom came to Bethel. Nor could she offer false hope. "Scripture says Gott can use all things for our gut."

Those words, repeated in sermon after sermon by bishops, deacons, and ministers who received divine appointment through the lot, did nothing to erase the misery from Claire's face.

She was barely a teenager. Enough of a child to still like to play, but enough of a blossoming woman to dream of romance and marriage. Better to focus on the former and pray for the latter in the difficult days to come. "Think about all the fun stuff Robbie and Judah still do. They play basketball and volleyball and cornhole in their wheelchairs. There's nothing that says you'll be using a chair anytime soon. You might use a cane or a walker." Bethel hugged her hard. "The buwe drive the pony carts. They still do chores. Don't think you'll get out of doing yours."

She tickled Claire, who half sobbed, half giggled. "I was hoping I wouldn't have to clean the chicken coop anymore."

"No way you're getting out of it."

Claire straightened. She managed a watery smile. "Do you think I'll still go to the singings when I'm old enough?" A pink blush spread across her pale skin. She buried her head in Bethel's chest again. "It's stupid."

"It's not stupid." *Sei so gut, Gott, let there be such a man out there for Claire. Sei so gut.* "We'll pray for Gott's will and ask Him to give you your heart's desire. A man who will love you as you are, a gut, loving, hardworking, kind, devout woman—when you're old enough to be that woman."

"Do you think that there is such a man? In our community?"

"I know so."

Was that a lie? Lying was a sin. So was doubting God. And worrying. *Forgive me, Gott. I only want to give Claire hope. Is that a sin? Chalk up another for me, then.*

No answer. God probably didn't answer snarky prayers like that one.

Dad's voice echoed in Bethel's head. God answered all prayers, but not necessarily the way a person wanted.

"More laundry. Melinda wet the bed last night and forgot to mention it." A basket of bedding in her arms, Mamm bustled into the laundry room. Melinda trailed behind her, the picture of innocence. She held a doll in one arm and a roly-poly puppy that might be part red cocker spaniel, part mutt in the other. "No more water before bed for you, kind."

Mom halted so suddenly Melinda walked right into her. The little girl squawked. Puppy and doll slipped to the floor. "Mamm!" Melinda scrambled to gather her precious cargo, but the puppy waddled beyond her reach. "Ginger, come back."

"Es dutt mer, kind. What's going on here?" Mom settled the basket next to the machine. "I don't see a lot of laundry getting done."

"We were just talking." Bethel hopped to her feet. "I'll finish rinsing the towels so we can get them hung up while the sun's shining."

"Uh-huh." Mom's knowing gaze bounced from Bethel to Claire. "If you're sick, you should be lying down, Claire. If you're not, you should've gone to school. What's the problem?"

"My stomach's better." Claire scooped up Ginger. She rubbed her face against the puppy's silky fur. "It didn't feel right lying around while you did laundry."

"Worrying does no gut."

"I know."

"It's a sin."

"I know."

"We know, Mamm." Bethel pulled a towel from the sink and ran it through the wringer into an empty basket below. Time to rescue Claire. "It's just hard, that's all. Don't you worry at all, even just a little bit?"

"I try not to. It doesn't do the least bit of gut." All the same, some of the oomph had leaked from her determined tone. "It just steals joy from today. Why would you want to do that?"

"I don't—"

"Then let's not. Let's pray for Gott's will and wait to see what the doctor says." Mom held out her hand to Claire. "I called the clinic. I thought we would have to wait until the buwe' appointments in April, but they had a cancellation on Thursday. How's that for Gott's provision?"

"This Thursday?" Claire's wail startled the puppy. He wiggled free and ran as fast as his fat legs would carry him to Melinda, who pulled him into her lap with a delighted giggle. "So soon? Before my birthday?"

"You know your aenti Emma will want to celebrate your birthday. And we'll celebrate with the kinner when we get back. You'll get two parties." Mom managed to make it sound like Claire was getting a special present. "Isn't it better to know sooner rather than later?"

Despite the matching droop of her shoulders and mouth, Claire nodded. "That sounds gut, I guess."

"You'll get to take a road trip all the way to Lancaster County, just you, Mamm, and Dat." Bethel cast about for silver linings. "You'll get to see Aenti and *Onkel* and our kossins. I bet Aenti will make her buffalo wings and pizza and dump cake with ice cream for your birthday."

Dad's sister-in-law Aenti Emma always cooked something special when the boys came for their appointments. Family in the area converged on Uncle Ray and Aunt Emma's house for a mini reunion. It took some of the sting from the reason for the visit.

"Won't that be nice?" Mom's smile was thin but firmly fixed. "Now grab that basket of towels. Get them hung up. You know they take longer to dry. We're wasting daylight."

Claire did as she was told. "I'll hang up all the clothes, Bethel. I figure I should do it while I can."

"There you go, buying trouble again." Mom's scowl matched her tone. "Take Melinda with you. That hund needs to go back to his mudder in the barn."

"Nee, nee, my hund." Melinda hugged the puppy close. He yipped and wiggled free. She hopped up and chased him out the back door. "Ginger, come back, Ginger."

Chuckling, Mom scooped up the pile of dresses and sank them one at a time into the soapy water. "Keep an eye on her, Claire. She'll be down to the shop badgering your dat to make her more wooden animals. The last time it was a baby horse. The kind doesn't know when to stop."

"She probably runs faster than I do now." A dramatic sigh accompanied Claire's observation. There was a kernel of truth in her words. Still, she hefted the heavy basket of wet towels into her arms and headed after her sister.

She'd barely cleared the door when Mom sagged against the machine's caldron of water. The lines around her mouth and eyes deepened into grooves of worry. "We have to be strong for her, Bethel."

"I'll do my best."

"I know you will. You have been a great help with the buwe."

"We'll get through it."

Mudder heaved a sigh not much different from Claire's. "You'll be in charge of the kinner while we're gone. We'll have to leave on Wednesday. The appointment is at nine o'clock on Thursday morning. Depending on the tests they'll want to schedule, we may be gone until Saturday, maybe even longer."

"We'll be fine. Enos will help."

"He'll need to be in the shop keeping up with orders." Those worried grooves deepened. "After we come back, you may need to ask for more hours at the nursery—just for a while. Our furniture orders are down a bit. With the cost of food and gas so high, people don't have the money for custom-made furniture."

Medical bills would pile up. The elders would step in to help. They might decide to do more barbecue plate fundraisers in town. The need to organize, to plan, assailed Bethel. First things first. "I'll talk to Atlee at the nursery tomorrow. Spring is the busiest time of year. The next few months, they'll need more help. He's offered more hours in the past, but I turned him down."

Because she preferred to help at home, whether it was cooking, cleaning, or keeping the books for Dad's business. Whatever her parents needed. It took some of the burden off her mother. Dad wasn't much for book learning, especially in the math department. Mom had been a schoolteacher before she married him.

"I know you'd rather be at home." Mamm sorted through the piles of clothes with expert hands. "But Gott blessed you with a gut job, working at a Plain business. He provides and He expects us to use His provision to the best of our ability."

"I will. I promise. I just hate leaving you to carry such a big load here."

"My shoulders are broad, Dochder. Don't you worry." No hint of self-pity marred her expression or her tone. She hefted a load of pants into the wash machine and shoved them into the water. "We each have our jobs to do. I thank Gott for our blessings."

How could Bethel complain—or worry—in the face of her mom's stalwart faith? *"Aamen."*

Chapter 7

"*T*oot-toot, toot-toot, coming through."

Bethel glanced up just in time to see the flatbed cart full of cauliflower, brussel sprouts, broccoli, rhubarb, and onion plants swerve crazily between the nursery's rows of blooming annuals, headed straight toward her.

Clutching a flat of purple, yellow, and pink pansies, she lurched to the left in time to save herself and the tender flowers. "Hattie, slow down!"

Her nursery coworker halted within a quarter inch of a display of petunias, marigolds, and zinnias. Grinning, she wiped at her face with the back of her grimy sleeve. "Sorry about that. It almost got away from me."

"I noticed. What's the big hurry?"

Hattie gave an exaggerated shrug. "No hurry. I just felt the need for speed. Don't you ever feel like dropping the trowel, rubbing mud on your face, and running through town singing '*Das Loblied*' at the top of your lungs? Don't you think Gott would love that—I mean, really love it?"

In light of Hattie's muddy apron, smudged forehead, and usual lopsided prayer covering that didn't cover much of her hair, it seemed she'd already prepared for the run. Bethel buried a chuckle. She'd learned the hard way that one should not encourage Hattie. "I reckon Gott would find it funny. While the bishop might like the idea of singing a hymn of praise to Gott, I suspect he wouldn't like us calling attention to ourselves."

"Stick-in-the-mud," Hattie muttered. "No one ever said you can't have fun while praising Gott—or working, for that matter."

"That's true." Work frolics were some of the best fun Bethel had ever experienced. Friends, family, chatter, food, and elbow grease provided a recipe for an enjoyable day for Plain people. Bethel went back to removing dead leaves and blooms from the flowers that spread in a sea of gorgeous spring colors before her. Working at the nursery was fun, too, which meant more time spent there wouldn't be a hardship. The worried look on her mom's face in the laundry room the previous day spurred Bethel on. "Speaking of work, do you know when your dat is coming in?"

"He went to the bank. He'll be back lickety-split. He doesn't like leaving me in charge. Mamm is home with a touch of the flu, so Dat had no choice." Hattie sounded philosophical. Her long-suffering father's aversion to leaving his daughter to mind the nursery wasn't a secret. Since his oldest son, Hattie's brother Ben, married and moved with his wife to be near her family in Lancaster County, Atlee had found it necessary to give in a little to his daughter's loudly stated desire to share in managing the family business. "The flu has been going around. Better not get too close to me. I could have the germs and not even know it."

Bethel clipped dead leaves and bided her time. When Hattie paused for breath, she jumped in. "He hasn't hired any more help, has he?"

"Nee, but he's planning to. I heard him and Mamm talking. Why? You got someone in mind?"

"Me."

Hattie wrinkled her freckled nose. Her pale blue eyes held mirth. She cackled. "You already work here, silly goose."

"I need more hours." Bethel stifled a laugh. Hattie's giggles were catching. Having a serious conversation with her could be a challenge. "As many as I can get."

"I thought you wanted to spend more time helping your mamm with the bookkeeping at the shop. And with the buwe." Hattie stopped hopping around like a potty-training toddler. She squeezed past the cart and came around to where Bethel stood. "What's up?"

Bethel waited for two English shoppers to select a flat of black-eyed Susans and another of daisies. While they passed by, she studied her clippers. "Mamm and Dat are taking Claire to the Clinic for Special Children." She kept her voice low. The number of shoppers browsing the plants had grown steadily since the nursery opened at 8:00 a.m. sharp. March's brisk north winds hadn't dampened everyone's urge to get a jump on their spring gardens. The excellent chances of more freezing temperatures all the way into April didn't deter most people. "That means more medical bills."

"Don't you worry. Dat will give you more hours with a snap of his fingers." Hattie demonstrated with her own dirty fingers. "You're already trained, you work hard, and you put up with me."

"All true." Bethel patted Hattie's arm. Her friend's blithe acknowledgment of her own idiosyncrasies made her all the more appealing. "Especially the last one."

"It's so nice to hear laughter on this fine spring day! It goes well with the scent of lavender and mulch—two of my favorite smells."

Bethel peeked over Hattie's shoulder. The sentiment belonged to Elizabeth Miller. Also known as Declan's mother. She held a pot of lavender in her arms. Layla Troyer, Declan's sister, pushed a cart laden with vegetable plants that could be expected to survive cold soil. She waved and went back to sipping from a Styrofoam cup of steaming liquid, likely coffee.

"I see you're ready to start your spring garden. Mamm's itching to get ours going too." Bethel surveyed their cart. Peas, broccoli, cauliflower, rhubarb, onions, radishes, lettuce, spinach, and peas. "You have your work cut out for you."

"Plus I need to restock my medicinal herbs." Elizabeth held up half a dozen seed packets. "Declan's been going through my horehound syrup and tea. He's depleting my supply. I need to grow more horehound. Rosemary, thyme, and peppermint too."

The herbs could be planted in pots indoors, keeping medicine cabinets stocked year-round.

Something about Elizabeth's small smile was suspect. Or maybe that was Bethel's imagination. "His throat is still bothering him?"

"Jah. He says it's just allergies, but Mamm thinks he might have a cold. So he told you about it?" Layla pounced on Bethel's question before the sound of her words had a chance to fade from the air. "That must've been when he helped you get your brieder to your buggy after the auction got rained out."

"Or was it when he carried the chairs to your buggy after church?" Elizabeth chimed in. "My mann and I saw you talking. You were deep in conversation."

Declan's mom didn't seem the least bit concerned that this conversation occurred so publicly. She had a reputation for match-making. She probably thought she'd single-handedly brought Layla and Micah together as well as Toby and Rachelle. Better not give her more fodder. "The buwe like Declan. He makes them laugh. They like to practice their jokes with him."

"The buwe?" Elizabeth's eyebrows rose and her forehead wrinkled. "Jah, Declan is gut with kinner. He's kind and funny.

He's a gut bruder to Sadie and his other schweschdre. He'll make a gut daed one day."

"Maybe he gets along with the buwe because he still acts like one." Hattie scooped up a pot of chamomile. "You should add this to your herb pots. It makes gut tea, and it has pretty flowers."

Leave it to Hattie to say what everyone else was thinking. Scowling, Elizabeth took the pot. "Declan's—"

"Hattie! There you are." Atlee Schrock's voice boomed from the doorway that separated the covered outdoor greenhouse from the storefront. "You have customers waiting at the cash register."

Saved by the boss. Bethel let Hattie squeeze by her, then scooped up her pruning tools. "I'd better see if that customer needs any help. Her cart is about to overflow. It was gut to talk to you."

"Bethel, wait."

Not fast enough. Maybe she just had a question about the plants on sale. Bethel turned back.

Elizabeth added a flat of peonies to her cart. "We're planning another pie booth to raise funds for the school at the livestock auction in a few weeks. I thought maybe you and your mudder would like to work a few shifts. We're asking all the women to pitch in with at least four pies. You know how fast they go."

How could Bethel say no? She couldn't and Elizabeth was fully aware of that. Five or six hours in a ten-by-ten booth with Elizabeth would give Declan's mother plenty of time for her sales pitch.

Bethel didn't need the pitch. The ledger was weighted heavily toward Declan's good qualities. He worked hard. He was one of the best auctioneers around—and that was saying a lot in his family. He was kind, generous, good with children, and, as her mom had pointed out, not bad-looking. Many would put his penchant for joking squarely in the good-quality category.

Besides, Bethel was by no means perfect. Having children with LGMD could drive the smile from any man's face, even a funny guy like Declan. Would he still be able to joke while lifting his sons and daughters from wheelchairs to the buggy or making those long treks to the clinic or paying those medical bills?

Buggy rides didn't necessarily lead to wedding vows. She was getting way ahead of herself. "I'll tell Mamm. I'm sure she'll want to help."

"Bring the buwe and Melinda. Sadie loves to play with them, and I reckon Rachelle will be there with Jonah. She goes to every auction when Toby is in town. She's going to make a *wunderbarr* fraa."

Hint, hint. "And Toby will be a gut mann. They are blessed." Better to move this conversation away from the danger zone. "I reckon Mamm will want to make fruit pies. We have plenty of canned peaches and apple pie filling."

"Elizabeth, is Bethel getting you everything you need?" Atlee squeezed past an English woman's double stroller and halted next to Bethel. "Do you need any potting soil or fertilizer?"

Always upsell. That was Atlee's motto.

"Almost everything." Elizabeth's tone was wry. "I'm awfully particular, but Bethel's a gut maedel and a gut salesperson."

"That's why I'm about to increase her hours." Atlee beamed. "Hattie says you want to work full time."

"I do need more hours, at least until school is out, but I can't work full time until next week."

"What's going on?" Elizabeth leaned closer, her eyes bright with curiosity. "You can always depend on us to help out—whatever you need."

"Nee, we're fine, we're fine."

"Hattie said Claire has the LGMD." Atlee's thick carpet of gray eyebrows wiggled. "Did my scatterbrained daughter misunderstand?"

"Nee, jah, it's what we think, but Mamm and Dat are taking her to Strasburg on Thursday so the doctors can run the tests and confirm it."

"Tell your mudder not to worry about the pies." Her tone brisk, Elizabeth stretched across the plants until she could reach Bethel's hand. She patted it. "You either. I imagine you've got your hands full. If there's anything we can do, let us know. I'll send my girls over to help with laundry or cooking or cleaning, you name it."

She really was a kind woman. Elizabeth had nine children of her own, but she never failed to show up for frolics, volunteer for fundraisers, or offer to babysit little ones. Bethel shook her head. "I can still make pies. Melinda and Liam love to help. Robbie and Judah entertain each other, especially if I make an extra pie for them."

"Gut. You're such a gut schweschder and dochder." Elizabeth's smile returned. "There's no doubt in my mind you'll make a gut fraa someday soon."

Maybe. Being a good sister and daughter would have to come first.

Chapter 8

*M*om's news only made the phone shanty colder. Despite icy fingers, Bethel finished buttoning her woolen coat with one hand. She used her elbow to push shut the door against a gusty morning breeze. Mom sounded determinedly cheerful. "Claire had the tests and the lab work yesterday. We go back this morning for the consult."

Claire and their parents had left for Strasburg on Wednesday, done the tests on Thursday, and today they would likely have Claire's diagnosis. "But the doctor thinks it's the early stages of LGMD?"

"He says it's likely, based on the physical exam, the EMG, and her CK levels. He says they don't need to do genetic testing right now since they have our family history. He also said because she's older, her LGMD symptoms wouldn't likely progress as fast as Robbie's and Judah's. So that's gut news."

Most people would think Mom spoke a foreign language, but it was one all families who went to the Clinic for Special Children learned. Bethel shuddered. The EMG, an electromyography, sounded awful. It involved sticking needles in various muscles to measure their reaction to stimulus. CK stood for creatine kinase, an enzyme that leaked out when muscles were damaged.

What a way to celebrate a birthday. Bethel held the receiver away from her ear for a moment, just long enough to corral a sob that threatened. "How's Claire taking all this?"

"She's a brave maedel. She didn't cry during the EMG." A quiver in her voice betrayed Mamm. A sigh filled the line. "But she hardly touched the pizza and wings your aenti made for supper. I heard her crying when I passed the room where she bunked with her kossins last night, but when I stuck my head in, she pretended to be asleep. Emma wants to throw a big birthday celebration tomorrow, in case we leave on Sunday. I'm hoping it will cheer her up, but I'm afraid it may make her feel worse. It's hard to know what to do."

So hard. "I think it would be worse to ignore her birthday, but either way, we'll celebrate when you get back. Will Dat add another bedroom downstairs for her?"

"Jah, if necessary. We'll know more after we talk with the doctor today. Which means we won't be home until tomorrow at the earliest. How are the kinner?"

Not great. How much should she tell her mother? All four of the younger children woke up coughing and with stuffy noses. Robbie and Judah had fevers. With the other kids, a person wouldn't worry too much, but her brothers had weakened lungs. A simple cold could become so much worse for them.

Mom couldn't do a thing from where she was, and she didn't need any more to worry about. "They went out to the shop with Liam and Enos yesterday. Enos has so much patience with them."

A quick trip into town to their doctor's clinic was in order. If it turned out to be something, then Bethel would tell Mom and Dad.

"What about Melinda?"

"Enos and Liam are keeping an eye on her. You know how she is. Where Liam goes, she goes."

67

Liam was only eight but used to having his little sister tag along. Melinda had no other siblings close in age, so she'd latched onto Liam as her best buddy.

Enos was getting the buggy hitched so they could head to town as soon as Bethel finished the phone call. Liam insisted on helping, which meant Melinda did too. All the more reason to think they weren't too terribly sick—not yet, anyway.

"That's gut. I'd better go. We have to be at the clinic by ten o'clock. I'll call you tonight if we have to stay until Monday for some reason. If you don't hear from me, we'll be home tomorrow night."

"Gut. Tell Claire I'll make caramel popcorn and Chex mix for game night Sunday."

Two of Claire's favorites. Game nights, which featured Dutch Blitz, Scum, Life on the Farm, Scrabble, and checkers, among other games, used to be for winter nights. Now the King family made them a year-round tradition that suited all their children's abilities, along with huge puzzles, story reading, and tall tales. The last one was Dad's favorite. No one could beat him at telling the tallest tales.

"I'll pass along the message. You tell the kinner we'll be home as soon as we can."

Her way of saying she loved them. Mom and Dad rarely said those words aloud, but it wasn't necessary. Everything they did shouted the words.

"Gott willing, we'll see you tomorrow night." Bethel put the receiver on the base. She took a deep breath and blew it out. *Gott, forgive me for not telling her about the kinner. And let it be nothing bad. Heal their bodies, Gott, sei so gut.*

She stepped out of the shanty. The wind nearly tore the door from her grasp. It stole her breath. She quickened her step to a near run. They'd have to wrap the boys up in blankets over their coats.

Why had winter decided to muscle its way back into the Virginia countryside, blocking spring's arrival?

Enos had parked the buggy next to a wheelchair ramp he and Dad built leading up to the front porch. He was nowhere in sight. Probably getting Robbie and Judah ready to go.

"Hey, Beth, can I drive the buggy?" Liam leaned out from the front seat. He had the reins in one hand as if ready to take off. "I know how. I practiced with the pony cart—"

"Nee, me. Me. Me!" Melinda popped up next to him. She swiped at the reins. "I know how."

The new black standardbred Dad had bought at auction just weeks ago raised his head, snorted, and whinnied. He jolted forward. The buggy took off, gravel spurting from under its wooden wheels.

It took a second for the situation to sink in. "Nee, wait. Stop him, Liam, stop him."

The buggy picked up speed, leaving Bethel behind. Liam's face, mouth and eyes wide open, flashed in Bethel's vision. Melinda's too, but she was laughing.

Fingers wound around her skirt, lifting it up, Bethel shot after the runaway buggy. "Pull back on the reins! Pull, Liam, pull!"

The buggy didn't slow. The startled horse refused to stop, and Liam didn't have enough strength to force him to halt.

Gasping for breath, Bethel pumped her legs hard. She was out of shape. Still, she gained on the buggy. The back end was within reach. The buggy's rocking motion flung the door back and forth.

Come on, come on, come on. She stretched her arms out, grabbed the wooden frame.

Got it, got it. Gut.

She stumbled and lost her grip. *Gott, please.*

The buggy rocked. It swerved left, then right, into an empty field yet to be planted with alfalfa. It rocked harder.

Screams.

Melinda? Liam?

Bethel raced across the field. Her shoes sank into the soft dirt. She struggled to get traction. "Melinda! Liam!"

There. Two small figures lying in the dirt. *Gott, no. Sei so gut, Gott, seis so gut.*

Her heart slamming against her chest, she stumbled, fell, and pulled herself up. "Liam! Melinda!"

Liam popped up. He'd lost his hat. He cradled his left arm against his chest. "We're okay. We're okay."

Not okay. Nothing was okay about this.

Bethel charged across the field. Adrenaline faded, replaced with anger so hot that it turned her vision purple. She was too out of breath to yell.

"That was fun!" Melinda crowed, still lying flat on her back. "Can we jump out again?"

"Nee, nee, nee." Bethel heaved a deep breath. *Get a grip.* She breathed in and out, in and out. The red wave of anger receded. "Not fun, not fun at all. Jet and the buggy are who knows where. You could've been killed. Jet could be hurt. The buggy could be damaged or destroyed. Not fun!"

Melinda jumped to her feet. Her face crumpled. "I sorry. I didn't mean to scare Jet."

She didn't seem hurt physically, but now her feelings were hurt. She would get over it. Bethel focused on Liam. "Are you hurt, Liam? Did you really jump out of the buggy? Why would you do that?"

"We didn't jump. Melinda started to fall out. I grabbed her and we both went over the side." Liam clutched at his left arm. He winced. Splotches of dirt decorated his face. "I think I broke my wrist. But I'm okay. I'm gut."

If he broke his wrist, he wasn't okay. "Let's get you back to the house. Enos can search for Jet and the buggy." *Sei so gut, Gott, let them be in one piece.* The poor horse had barely been introduced to his new family and home. The buggy was their newest one. Dad would be furious if anything happened to either. The cost of replacing either or both would be tremendous on top of the new medical bills.

And it had happened on Bethel's watch.

She gritted her teeth against useless tears. Crying would accomplish nothing. She put her arm around Liam's shoulders and took Melinda's hand. They trudged across the field. Melinda was short. It would take forever to get back to the house. They still had to get to the doctor's clinic, only now they would have additional bills after the doctor treated Liam's wrist.

Bethel counted silently to ten while the muscles in her shoulders and neck gradually unknotted. Liam and Melinda were young, but not that young. Mom and Dad had so much on their plates right now. They didn't need a damaged buggy, injured horse, or, worse yet, hurt children. "You both are old enough to know better, but especially you, Liam. What were you supposed to be doing?"

"Putting clean blankets on the shelf under the seat." His nose was running and his cheeks were scarlet—from the wind or a fever? "Mamm washed them. Enos said to put them back since it was so cold this morning."

"Uh-huh. And you, Melinda, what did Enos tell you to do?"

Melinda's forehead puckered. Her nose was running. Her lower lip protruded. "Take snack bag to buggy. He said wait for you."

"Where do you suppose the snack bag is now?"

Melinda pointed toward the field. "Jet has it."

"Did you wait for me?"

"Nee, I no wait."

71

"What about you, Liam?"

He coughed into his elbow, an ugly, hoarse cough. "I didn't mean for it to happen. It was an accident."

That was the nature of accidents. No one meant for them to happen. But often they could've been avoided. "What do you think Dat will say about it?"

Tears trickled down Liam's face. "Do we have to tell him?"

"Bruder, don't you think he'll notice a cast on your arm? Or that the buggy is gone or broken? Or that Jet is gone or hurt?"

"Dat will be awful mad." Melinda's voice quivered. She sniffed and wiped her nose on her sleeve. "I sorry."

The tears nearly melted Bethel's heart. What would Mom and Dad do? "Rightfully so, don't you think? But let's do our best to make the situation right before they come home. Hopefully Enos will find Jet and the buggy—and neither will be the worse for wear."

"I'll search too." Liam swiped at his face with his sleeve, smearing snot and dirt across his cheek. "I ride better than I drive."

No doubt about that. "You can't ride with a hurt wrist, Bruder. I'll take the other horse and go."

After what happened with the buggy, was it a good idea to leave Liam in charge? Probably not. "We'll figure it out."

Melinda halted, forcing Bethel and Liam to do the same. "We pray?" She tugged her hand free from Bethel's grip, then clasped it together with her other grimy one. "Gott will help us. Bart says so."

Unless He wanted to teach them an important lesson. Bethel bit her lip to keep from sighing. "Jah, we can pray. Just know Gott does what's best for us. That's not always what we want Him to do."

"But He knows it's not Jet's fault. Jet shouldn't have to pay for our sins."

Liam was a wise little man. Bethel patted his skinny shoulder. "You're right. Let's pray."

So they silently prayed in the middle of the field, horseless and buggy-less.

The fact was it took only a minute—a second, really—for something bad to happen. It wasn't any more the children's fault than it was Bethel's. She was supposed to watch them. She was responsible for them. *Forgive me, Gott. I let them down. I let Mamm and Dat down. I let You down.*

"Bethel." Liam's plaintive voice forced her to open her eyes. "Es dutt mer."

"I know."

"Do you forgive me?"

"Of course you're forgiven."

"Do you think Dat will forgive me?"

"Of course he will. Scripture says we're to forgive seventy times seven."

Truth be told, Dad and Mom would be relieved and thankful their two youngest children hadn't been badly hurt or worse. Runaway buggies were common occurrences in Plain communities. Sometimes it didn't end well.

They were almost to the road when the sound of horse hooves pounding on the packed dirt road reached them. Liam broke away and ran ahead. Melinda tried to follow, but her short legs refused to cooperate.

"It's Martin and Harry!" Liam shouted. "They have Jet and the buggy."

Bethel saw as much. Deacon Martin Hershberger drove his buggy, and his son Harry drove the Kings' buggy. Both buggy and Jet appeared none the worse for wear.

"I believe we have something of yours." Martin halted. Harry did the same with the buggy. "I hope no one was hurt when your *gaul* decided to make a run for it."

Despite the cool weather, Jet was lathered with sweat. He dipped his head and whinnied, obviously in a snit about being returned. Bethel hurried the remainder of the way to the road. "Liam hurt his wrist. Otherwise they seem to be okay. It was quite the ride, though."

The deacon's gaze fell on Liam and Melinda. "They took off without permission, I reckon."

"Jah. Danki for bringing the gaul and buggy back." Bethel approached Jet cautiously. She held out her hand. Jet tossed his head and neighed. "It's okay. You're okay. It's not your fault."

She grasped his halter so she could smooth his tangled mane. "Easy, easy, you're fine."

A horse wasn't just a means of transportation. He was also a living, breathing creature that should be treated with care. Bethel ran her hands over his withers while she examined him head to hoof. No visible injuries. "Gut gaul, gut gaul." She glanced up at Martin. "Danki for bringing him back. Where did you find him?"

"No need for thanks. He stopped at the creek that cuts across the field behind my house. I guess he was thirsty after all that running."

"I'm so thankful he wasn't hurt." Bethel turned her attention to the buggy. She strode around it, examining it from top to bottom the way Dad would after an incident of this magnitude. "Or the buggy damaged."

"Gott's provision." Martin studied Liam and Melinda some more. "Are your eldre in Strasburg still?"

"Jah, with Claire. They hope to return tomorrow night."

He wrinkled his long nose. After a few seconds, he nodded. "All the same, if you need anything, we're right down the road. We can help out with the kinner."

"Danki, but we're fine. Enos is here. Between the two of us, we've got it covered."

Even if it didn't seem that way.

"Hop in. I'll drive you the rest of the way." Harry seemed perfectly happy to remain in charge of the Kings' buggy. "Jet likes me."

"Danki, I can take it from here."

Before Harry could argue with her, Enos appeared on horseback, coming full tilt toward them.

"What's going on?" Bethel's brother yelled as he reined in the chestnut standardbred. "Where did you get to?"

Bethel whipped through a quick explanation. Enos's scarlet face turned a deeper shade of red. "What were you thinking?"

"We've already covered all that." Bethel guided Melinda toward the buggy as she spoke. "Let's just get back to the house. The buwe will be worried."

"Right." Enos's countenance said he wasn't through expressing his thoughts, but he thanked Martin and turned his horse around. Bethel helped Melinda and Liam into the buggy and followed.

The boys were waiting on the porch when they drove up. Bethel explained what had happened while Enos made his own thorough inspection of the buggy and Jet. She went inside and grabbed a washrag and towel. Melinda wasn't happy with the wipe-down, while Liam took it stoically. "It'll be okay, Bruder." Bethel dabbed at a smudge of dirt on his cheek. Tears welled in his eyes. A bruise was already forming along his jaw. "Does your arm hurt?"

"Not much." He sniffed and hung his head. "I hope I don't need a cast. Dat needs my help."

Bethel hugged him. He was only eight. "We'll figure it out."

Once Enos was satisfied no damage had been done, he helped Bethel get Robbie and Judah into the buggy. Bethel settled onto the bench and let him worry about the driving. Her oldest brother had dark circles under his eyes and the tip of his nose was red. He coughed almost as often as Robbie.

"Are you feeling poorly too?"

He nodded but added nothing. Enos wasn't much of a talker. A peek over her shoulder revealed that Melinda had crawled into Liam's lap and fallen asleep. Liam's eyelids were drooping too. Robbie alternately coughed and sneezed.

"I'm dreading telling Mamm and Dat."

"They have to know. Liam is old enough to know better. He has to be punished."

"Maybe the tumble, his injuries, and the fright are enough punishment."

"You can't be softhearted about these things." Enos was the spitting image of Dad with his big cocoa-brown eyes, thin lips, and flyaway sandy-brown hair. "He has to learn now, better than later. Dat will decide his punishment."

"It's just that Mamm and Dat have enough on their shoulders." In a soft voice, aware of her siblings behind her, Bethel shared the conversation she'd had with their mother earlier.

Enos's stern expression opened a crack, revealing pain for a second or two, then closed shut tightly again. "Claire is a gut maedel. She's strong. Whatever it is, she'll do fine."

True. True. Wiggling on the bench, Bethel bit her tongue. *Let it go. Be as strong as everyone says Claire is.* Claire didn't have a choice.

"She's had more years without the disease than the buwe." A hard truth. As usual, Enos took a page from Dad's book. "She'll have many more years. It's not our place to question Gott."

Don't you think I know that? It's just so unfair. Bethel breathed a prayer of thanksgiving that she hadn't said those words aloud. "Don't you ever wonder why you haven't gotten it? Why Robbie and Judah and not you?"

It was Enos's turn to squirm. He snapped the reins. "Get along, Jet. At this rate it'll take us all day to get into town."

Jet tossed his head and snorted, as if to say, *Don't take it out on me.*

So Enos didn't want to talk about it. Fine. Bethel shifted to her right so she had a better view of the countryside and Enos had a better view of her shoulders. The dogwoods were starting to bud. "I hope we don't have another freeze. It got close last night. Thirty-eight according to the thermometer on the porch."

The weather made a good topic any day of the week.

"I do think about it."

Bethel shifted to her left so she could see her brother's face. He immediately glanced away. It was hard for men to admit fear or uncertainty. Bethel didn't like it much either. "Me too. Why Claire and not me?"

"Bart would say it has to do with Gott's plan for you and for me. I reckon he's right. What else can it be?"

It was the bishop's job to speak God's truth. "I don't know. Could it be Satan trying to make us so mad at Gott we lose faith and are lost?"

"I'm no theologian. I can't make heads or tails out of the Articles of Faith. I'll probably be the first Plain man to flunk baptism class."

Those were the most words Enos had ever said to Bethel. When he was worried and hurting, who did he talk to? He had men friends. He went to the singings. Did he have a special friend? She'd been so busy taking care of her younger siblings, she'd never given much thought to her oldest brother's life. He always seemed so self-contained, so able to care for himself. He probably felt as if he had to do that, given Robbie and Judah's disease. "I don't think you can flunk baptism."

"It don't matter. This isn't about me. I'm glad I can help Dat. I'm not as gut at building furniture as he is, but I do okay. It's just me and Liam right now."

He didn't finish the sentence, but his meaning was apparent. Unless Liam was destined to get muscular dystrophy too.

Bethel was in the same boat. She would become their mother's only helper now, and Claire would need the same additional care as the boys. All the more reason she should put marriage and children out of her head.

Immediately a picture popped up, filling that space where her duty to family should be. Declan, his face smudged with mud, grinned up at her from his resting place in a rain-soaked field at the fairgrounds. *"Don't pecan me."*

Mom was right about one thing. A man with a good sense of humor was far more appealing than one who wouldn't smile if a person paid him to do it.

It didn't matter. Bethel had no time for either. She had too much work to do. Even Enos needed her. She'd neglected him. Shame enveloped her. "I can help you study the Articles of Faith."

"'Preciate it."

"I'm sorry I didn't offer sooner."

"That's so like you."

"What do you mean? I'm serious. I should've—"

"To apologize when it's my fault for not asking for help. Not everything is your responsibility or your fault." Enos snorted. Jet followed suit as if agreeing. "You're not a mind reader. You're not required to take care of everyone and anyone. You're allowed to have a life."

No, not really. "I like helping people—especially family."

"You probably think it's your fault Liam and Melinda spooked Jet and ended up in a runaway buggy this morning."

"I should've been watching them—"

"I was supposed to be keeping an eye on them."

"You were taking care of Judah and—"

"You can't take care of the whole world. It's hochmut to think you can."

Maybe so, or maybe God saw her as a helper. He gave her that nature, didn't He?

Enos turned the buggy onto Pine Street and then into the parking lot behind the medical clinic. The lot was almost full, mostly of cars but a few buggies too. One held a solitary man who seemed to be deep in thought. Bethel peered closer.

Declan.

Chapter 9

*H*llergies. Just allergies. Or a cold. Could be a cold. Right? Maybe it was a bad case of strep. Declan shooed away the thoughts that kept circling his brain like dogs chasing squirrels they'd never catch.

He'd parked his buggy in the lot behind the medical clinic a full ten minutes earlier. Most of the slots were full. Which wasn't a good sign. The waiting room would be full as well. He turned up the collar on his jacket in hopes of keeping the cold wind away from his sore throat. Six days and the pain was no better. It was worse, in fact. This morning he'd awakened to find he couldn't speak above a whisper. Not even horehound syrup or gingerroot tea helped. If only he didn't have to swallow or cough, he'd be fine.

Dad insisted he come into the clinic. Toby backed him up. They were right. Anything that kept Declan from stepping onto the platform, microphone in hand, had to be dealt with right away. He would not miss his turn calling an auction. He'd waited all winter for the weather to warm and the auction dates to start filling the calendar. The time had arrived, and now his throat decided to act up.

Not only that, but Toby's wedding was coming up. Toby had chosen Declan as a witness. He was also in charge of the table and chair setup with Elijah and Emmett—in the barn, in the house, outdoors if the weather cooperated. They expected a crowd with the Millers and the Lapps coming from enormous extended families and having big broods of their own.

Commitments. Declan had commitments. Which made going to the doctor unavoidable.

Straightening his shoulders, he raised his face to the sun. Maybe its warmth would help. Not likely. Not if Mom's sage-echinacea spray and her apple cider vinegar with honey concoction didn't give him any lasting relief. His gaze fell on the buggy that had just pulled into one of the few open slots.

Bethel.

Maybe this day wasn't so bad after all. Suddenly his arms and legs decided to work. Declan hopped from the buggy and trudged toward the Kings. Bethel climbed down from their buggy in a graceful move. She headed for the back as if she hadn't seen him. Had she not seen him?

"Bethel?" His feeble attempt to call out to her fell flat on the asphalt.

His eyes unblinking, Enos stared at Declan from the other side of a gorgeous black standardbred. "Hey, Declan."

"Hey. That's a fine gaul. Is he new?" His words didn't amount to even a whisper.

Enos's eyebrows rose. He might look like his dad, but he had his mom's long face and sturdy build. "You got the laryngitis?"

Declan nodded.

Bethel spun around. "Ach, nee. Your throat isn't better after almost a week?"

"Nee." His lips moved but no sound came out. He coughed, which only made his throat hurt more. "Not much."

"Hopefully Dr. Matthews can give you something to cure it."

In time for the next day's auction. Declan nodded again.

"You shouldn't be standing out here in the wind." Bethel gestured toward the clinic's double back doors. "You'd better get inside."

Shaking his head, Declan strode around the buggy. He grabbed a wheelchair and hoisted it to the asphalt.

"Nee, we've got this." Bethel tugged at the chair. "You're sick."

Declan mouthed, *Never sick.*

Almost never. Until now.

"She's right." Enos cocked his head toward the glass double doors. "I'll handle the chairs."

They *were* right. Yet Declan lingered. Bethel's cheeks were red. Her lips were chapped. Her crooked prayer covering didn't hide her chestnut hair. That wasn't like her. *Who's sick?* he mouthed.

"The kinner. All four of them." Her shoulders hunched. "Coughs, sneezing, running noses, congestion, tummy aches. They don't want to eat."

"Colds." Although the flu, croup, and strep throat had been running rampant through the district. "Tea and cough syrup?"

Declan was so full of licorice tea, ginger tea, and the apple cider concoction that he couldn't drink another drop.

And his throat still throbbed.

"It's almost impossible to get the little ones to drink the teas, but they like the syrup." Bethel's concerned expression matched her worried tone. She moved aside so Enos could pull out the second wheelchair. "Robbie and Judah have fevers. We can't be too careful with them."

That made sense. Plus if the boys had the flu, the others would have it soon enough. Sickness spread like spilled marbles in Plain families. Children almost always shared not only bedrooms but beds. "Doc's got this—and Gott does too."

Pretty soon he'd be reduced to hand signals or chicken scratches on a notepad.

The worry in her face didn't fade. "Plus Liam and Melinda decided to have an adventure with the buggy this morning. Liam hurt his wrist."

Declan eyed the boy, who sat with Melinda draped across his lap, sound asleep. He did look the worse for wear. "I'll help you out."

"Nee, I've got her." Liam attempted to rise, but his little sister was deadweight in his arms. "Wake up, Melinda, we're here."

She mumbled in her sleep but didn't move.

"I've got her." Declan gently tugged her into his arms and laid her head on his shoulder. "Come on, Liam. I'll give you a hand down."

Between Enos and Bethel, they managed to get the wheelchairs moving in a wobbly parade to the clinic. They took turns holding the doors open. Inside almost every chair was full, mostly moms with children. They'd probably been waiting on the doorstep for the clinic to open this Friday morning. Coughs, sneezes, whines, and the occasional sob filled the overly warm, heated air. Along with a tsunami of germs, no doubt. They parked the wheelchairs next to a bank of chairs in the back. Enos took Melinda from Declan so he and Bethel could get in line behind several others waiting to check in with the receptionist.

"You first." Declan nodded toward the receptionist. "Kinner first."

"Nee, we have four kinner who need to be seen. You're just one person." Bethel didn't move. "You've lost your voice. You go first."

Not just his voice. He couldn't work if it didn't come back. *Be smart, go first.* "Kinner first."

"That's on ships." She clucked and shook her head. "Don't be stubborn. You have to get better or you can't auctioneer."

Her tone was soft, kind. The one she'd used with the kids as she helped get them situated. It soothed his anxious soul, if not his hoarse throat. A fit of coughing overcame him. He leaned over, one hand on his thigh, the other to his mouth. His whole body shook.

Okay, he'd go first. "Danki," he whispered.

The heat in the clinic turned her cheeks even redder than the cold wind outside. Despite being tired and bedraggled, Bethel was still pretty. She stared at him. Her expression turned puzzled, then uncertain. "Are you going first, then? It's our turn."

He'd been standing there like an idiot, mooning over her. "Jah, jah."

Mentally popping himself on the head, Declan whipped around and strode to the counter. After a few seconds of trying to communicate with Declan, the receptionist pushed a pen and a notepad toward him on the counter. "I can see you're in pain. It sounds like you have a throat ailment. Write your name and date of birth down for me. I assume you don't have an appointment, no insurance, and you're willing to wait while I try to work you into the schedule."

Relief coursed through him. The clinic staff members were so caring and helpful. "Yes. Please."

The woman handed him a clipboard with the usual forms. He stood aside and waited while Bethel went through the same routine. When she was done she turned and nearly ran into him.

"Entertain the buwe?" His voice was reduced to a squeak of its former bass. *Just a cold, it's just a cold.* "Tell a story?"

She shook her head. "They're fine. Rest your voice."

He stopped at the water dispenser with little paper cups. Maybe a drink would help. He hit the red button for hot water. The few swallows felt good, but the pain immediately returned. *Just a cold.*

A seat was open next to Robbie and Judah. Declan grabbed it. Enos sat to his little brothers' right, still cradling a sleeping Melinda in his arms. Liam sat stiffly in the chair next to his brother. Bethel took the one to Declan's left. His eyebrows lifted, Enos shifted in his seat. He frowned but said nothing. A single Plain woman sitting next to a single Plain man in public might cause talk.

If Bethel noticed his reaction, she didn't let it bother her enough to move.

"Are you worried?" Leaning closer, she voiced the question softly. Enos's frown grew. She didn't seem to notice. "Or just tired?"

Declan rubbed his sweaty palms on his pants. The waiting room was too warm. "Not gut to worry."

"It's your voice."

He closed his eyes, savoring the sweetness of *her* voice for a second, then opened them. "Cold. Allergies."

"Probably."

Except he had no stuffy nose, congestion, fever, or achiness. "I'm fine."

"Rest. If you fall asleep, I'll elbow you when they call your name."

Declan closed his eyes again, but he couldn't nap. Not with Bethel sitting next to him. Her nearness, her fresh scent of soap, her barely contained energy—every aspect of her combined to keep his body too tightly wound. The time ticked by, each second jittery with nerves, longer than a trip to the moon and back.

He nudged Judah. "What did one flea say to the other?"

Judah sat up straighter. He grinned. "I dunno. What did he say?"

"Shall we walk or take a dog?"

Judah giggled. Enos groaned. Robbie hooted. "Another one, another one."

"What did the cowboy say when his dog ran away?"

The boys shook their heads.

"Well, doggone."

"That's awful." Despite Bethel's words, she chuckled. "Surely you can do better."

"Okay, how about this one?" he whispered. "Why are elephants so wrinkled?"

"I'm afraid to ask."

"Have you ever tried to iron one?"

The boys laughed. Enos snorted.

Bethel did neither. "Danki."

"For what?"

"For being you."

Warmth flooded Declan's body. Even his throbbing throat felt a tad better. "I think that's the nicest thing anyone has ever said to me."

She smiled. "You should get out more often, then."

Melinda yawned and stretched like a sleepy kitten. "What's so funny?"

"Not Declan." Enos squirmed in his chair. "Go sit with Bethel, little one, while I visit the restroom."

Melinda did as she was told. She snuggled up against Bethel's chest. "Songs, Beth, songs."

"Okay, but you have to sing with me." Bethel tugged a tissue from her bag. She wiped Melinda's nose. The little girl ducked and squirmed, but Bethel got the job done. "How about 'The Itsy Bitsy Spider'?"

Melinda's forlorn expression gave way to delight. She wiggled around in her sister's lap to face Declan. "You too, Declan, you too." Her chubby fingers began the climb up the waterspout. "*The itsy bitsy spider went up* . . . Sing, Declan, sing."

"He can't sing, Schweschder. He has a sore throat." Bethel stretched her arms in front of her sister so she could do the motions with her. "Let's show him how it's done."

Declan couldn't sing, but he could send the spider up the spout and back down in a whoosh of rain with the best of them. Melinda giggled and sent her spider rushing after his. Bethel sang softly, but Melinda preferred to belt out the tune at the top of her lungs. A little boy in blue jeans and a Mickey Mouse T-shirt stopped crying long enough to join in. His mom telegraphed a weary smile of thanks.

Bethel returned the smile and waved at the boy. He hid his face. "What a cutie." Her expression pensive, Bethel stroked Melinda's back. "Isn't he sweet, Melinda?"

"Sing, Beth, sing."

So Bethel sang. She had a nice voice, high, soft, soothing.

Declan's muscles relaxed. The tension in his shoulders eased. His mind stopped searching for jokes and hilarity. He didn't have to be on. He could just be. Like Melinda, in the moment. Sitting next to a beautiful, kind woman who would one day be a good mother. She already had the patience and the endurance. Kindness and generosity of spirit.

Everything a man would want in a wife. Everything a child would need in a mother.

"Declan Miller."

Declan jumped.

"Sorry. I didn't mean to startle you." The nurse gestured toward the hallway behind her. "You're up next, Mr. Miller."

"I'm praying for healing," Bethel called after him. "That the doctor fixes you up."

Declan hadn't thought to pray about it. God must be disappointed in him. *What she said, Gott. And while You're at it, could You see about getting Bethel to think of me as someone besides the class clown? To think about me as someone worthy of courting . . . or even more than that?*

He hadn't even taken her for a buggy ride, but no ride was necessary. Bethel was the one. She'd always been the one.

Chapter 10

S o if it's not strep, it's just a cold, right?" Declan stuck his cold, sweaty palms under his armpits. A sudden chill ran through him. The exam room was cold—compared to the waiting room. He'd waited at least fifteen minutes for Dr. Matthews after the medical assistant weighed him and took his blood pressure and temperature. He shivered. "I told my dad there was no reason for me to bother you with a sore throat." He stood. "I'll just get out of your hair now. You have a waiting room full of sick kids out there."

"Whoa, Declan, hang on." Dr. Matthews motioned for Declan to return to the exam table. "When a cough, earache, and sore throat linger as long as this one has, it's better to come see me. It's certainly no bother. That's what I'm here for."

"You said the strep test was negative. I don't have a fever. My lungs are clear. I don't have an ear infection. What else could it be?"

Dr. Matthews tucked his stethoscope around his neck. His forehead wrinkled, he pushed his dark-rimmed glasses up his nose with one finger. He frowned. "I'm sending you to an ENT—"

"A what? The kind who takes care of you in an ambulance? I don't need an ambulance—"

"That's an EMT," Dr. Matthews broke in gently. "An ear, nose, and throat specialist. The fancy name is a laryngologist, but ENT is a lot easier to say and remember." He extracted a small cloth from his white jacket pocket, removed his glasses, and proceeded to polish them. "I'm a little concerned about the swelling in your throat, but I'm just a country GP, not a specialist in throat ailments. Given what you do for a living, I'd rather you see a specialist."

A specialist. That didn't sound good. "Why?"

"A visual exam, coupled with your symptoms, suggests you may have developed polyps, nodules, or cysts on your vocal cords. This isn't uncommon in people who use their voices in their professions—singers, teachers, public speakers, salespeople—"

"Auctioneers."

"Exactly."

"So what's the treatment for those thingies you're talking about?"

"It depends on what exactly you have. An ENT specialist can perform an endoscopy, which involves putting a little tube down your throat with a camera on the end of it that sends images to a video screen that the specialist watches for signs of abnormalities. Or he could do a laryngoscopy to examine your vocal cords specifically."

Declan's gag reflux kicked in. He swallowed against it. Swallowing hurt. It was a vicious cycle. "Sounds expensive."

And painful.

"It's not cheap, but this isn't something you want to mess around with." Dr. Matthews stuck his glasses back on his nose. His magnified pale blue eyes were full of empathy. "There's another possibility. I'm not trying to scare you, but it's my job to share the facts with you so you're fully informed about your health and can make good choices."

"Appreciate that." The concern in the doctor's voice sent up big red flags. "What's the other possibility?"

"Throat cancer."

The room went from cold to frigid. The fluorescent light was too bright. "Throat cancer?"

"I didn't say it was that. I simply want to impress upon you the importance of following up with the ENT. He's in Richmond. I'll send a referral to him and give a copy to you. Since you don't have a phone where his staff can reach you, you'll need to make the call to set up the appointment."

Declan was still back at the word *cancer*. Cancer was never good, but of all places, his throat. His livelihood. His family's livelihood. The Miller men's family tradition. He was an auctioneer. He'd never thought of being anything else. His stomach rocked. The coffee he'd had for breakfast burned his throat. Dark spots danced in his periphery. "Whoa. Whoa. You think it could be cancer?"

The word seemed to stick in his swollen throat. Two syllables with so much reach and tenacity and strength, they could simply wrap themselves around his throat and squeeze until he blacked out. Or worse.

"I'm not saying it's anything at this point." Dr. Matthews's tone softened. "I'm just covering all the possibilities, however farfetched they may be. If the ENT sees abnormalities when he does the procedure, he can pass surgical instruments through the scope and collect a tissue sample."

A choking sensation threatened to overcome Declan. His hand went to his throat. He swallowed. It burned. "How big are those instruments?"

"It's a microsurgery. Don't worry." Dr. Matthews smiled wryly. "They're tiny. And you'll be under general anesthesia while the procedure is performed."

Gee, that made it so much better. "It sounds expensive. We don't have insurance."

"I know, but we can't afford to mess around with something like this when your voice is a tool of your trade. I send Amish folks to this ENT regularly. He's used to making arrangements for payment. No worries."

No worries. "But it could just be these polyps or cysts or whatever."

"It could be."

"I wouldn't lose my voice."

"In any case, the ENT and the surgeon will do everything possible to preserve your voice, whether it's polyps, nodules, cysts, or cancer." Dr. Matthews leaned forward, elbows on his knees. He clasped his hands as if in prayer. "Much of it depends on where the abnormality is and how widespread it is. For example, with cancer, if it hasn't spread, they might be able to treat it with radiation."

More expensive treatment. More time away from home and the auction circuit. Declan had come in with a simple cold and would leave with a wheelbarrow full of medical bills, worries, and potentially funeral costs. "And if it has spread?"

"It might require surgery, radiation, and even chemotherapy. But let's not borrow trouble. You can cross that bridge when you and your specialist get there."

A wave of anxiety slammed into the bridge, washing it away. "It's probably just nodules from overworking my voice. I don't need a specialist. I just need to rest my voice."

"Hiding your head under the blankets won't heal your voice." Dr. Matthews switched to a stern teacher tone. "Do not put off this appointment, Declan. I'm serious. The sooner you know what's causing your symptoms, the sooner you can get treatment and get back to normal. Postponing will only give it a chance to worsen. You do understand that, right?"

Declan clenched his jaw. Finally, he nodded.

"Good. You're right about resting your voice. No auctioneering. No public speaking at all. No singing. Drink plenty of fluids, lots of tea and honey. Speak as little as possible. I'm going to prescribe a cough medicine and something for the throat pain."

No working. The days ahead loomed in front of him, suddenly empty. "I could use a vacation," he whispered. "Virginia Beach is nice this time of year."

Not really. It was still too cold.

"Very funny. No talking except when absolutely necessary." Dr. Matthews stood. He was a short man who barely reached Declan's shoulder. He was starting to stoop with age. "Try not to worry. I know that's easy for me to say, but it could simply be nodules or cysts. The best thing to do is let them get in there, see what it is, and take care of it."

It *was* easy for the doctor to say. "Okay. Thanks."

Dr. Matthews put his index finger to his lips, then let his hand drop. "Shush. Have your mother or sister or someone call to make your appointment for you today. This afternoon."

In one breath he said not to worry. In the next he made it sound urgent. Declan gave him a thumbs-up.

Not talking was a good thing. It gave him an excuse not to share this news with his family. No sense in worrying his mom and dad.

He strode down the hallway, through the door, and into the waiting room. Every chair was full. A man leaned against a wall, a baby in his arms. Kids sat cross-legged on the carpet, playing tic-tac-toe.

A voice called to him. People were shadowy figures blurred by the pall cast by the word *cancer*.

He kept walking. Not stopping. Not thinking.

"Declan. Declan!"

Bethel.

He should've stopped to make payment arrangements. But he didn't. Better to not have to explain his predicament to Bethel. She didn't need to know about the nodules or the cysts, but especially about the cancer.

She had enough on her plate with the boys and now Claire's diagnosis. The last thing she needed was another complication, another burden. She was already a caregiver. She didn't need to court someone with medical issues.

Gott, forget my prayer earlier. Turn her gaze elsewhere. If I'm in treatment for the long haul, if I can't do my job as an auctioneer anymore, I'm in no position to court any woman, least of all one like Bethel. Sorry for the confusion.

God would think he was nuts. Of course, God already knew that and He knew the plan. Too bad He wouldn't let Declan in on it.

Chapter 11

So he just walked on by like he didn't see you? How rude."

The disbelief in Hattie's tone matched Bethel's feelings about her encounter with Declan in the doctor's office that morning. They'd had a good conversation before he went in. She'd prayed for healing—which of course came with no strings attached—but still it seemed strange that he would act like he didn't know her thirty minutes later.

"Not rude necessarily, just odd. Like he went into the exam room with a sore throat and came out blind." Bethel flapped the fresh sheet in the air so it came to rest covering most of the boys' double bed. Hattie grabbed the other side and tucked it under the mattress while Bethel did the same on her side. Hattie was a good helper, but Bethel appreciated even more having her ear to bend about the day's events. "We sat next to each other before he went in first. I keep wondering if I said something that offended him—"

"You? Never. You're the kindest, sweetest, most caring person in the world." Hattie tucked a pillow under her chin, grabbed a clean pillowcase, and tugged it over the pillow. Once done, she let it drop onto the bed. "I bet you did everything you could to make him feel better. You probably told him to sleep until they called his name."

So Bethel had, but that was just common courtesy. *Hattie* was the kindest, sweetest, most caring friend in the world. She'd shown up at the door minutes after they'd returned from town. She brought with her a large pot of chicken noodle soup, banana bread still warm from the oven, homemade sugar doughnuts, and a bag of oranges for making fresh-squeezed orange juice for the sick children and their caregivers. "That would be you. I don't know what I'd do without you. Not having to cook supper is a huge help. The doctor said the kinner need lots of fluids. Soup is perfect. The OJ will give them vitamin C. And the doughnuts will improve their moods."

All four kids had the flu. Dr. Matthews had prescribed an antiviral drug that was supposed to cut down on how long the flu would last and how severe the symptoms would be. Liam's wrist was a sprain, not a fracture. The doctor had wrapped it and advised giving him ibuprofen for the pain.

"I can't take credit. My aenti saw your aenti in town. She mentioned that the buwe were sick and maybe Melinda too." Hattie's tone was airy. "Mamm suggested the soup. I was all about the doughnuts. I'd planned to come anyway to make sure you're going to the singing tomorrow night. Now I'm even more sure you need a boot in the behind to get moving. You need to march right up to Declan and demand to know why he ignored you after you'd been so nice to him."

"Very funny. I'll do no such thing." Bethel motioned for Hattie to pick up the other end of a quilt so they could spread it over the bed. Bethel hadn't gone to a singing in ages. It didn't seem likely that Declan went either—given how much he traveled. Plus he had to be at least twenty-three or twenty-four. "Besides, the kinner have the flu. I certainly won't be going to a singing with them sick."

"Aren't your eldre supposed to be back tomorrow night?"

Bethel hadn't tried to get in touch with her parents to share the bad news. Not yet. "Jah, but they'll be exhausted after the clinic visits and the drive. I'm not leaving them to take care of four sick kinner."

"Your mamm will be the first to tell you she can handle sick kids. She's been doing it since you were a bopli."

"And now she has me to help her."

"Beth, Beth, Beth . . ." Melinda's cranky whine floated in from the living room. "I need you."

"Go. I'll finish with Liam's bed." Hattie flapped her hands toward the door. "Enos can help me get them situated. Go see what the maedel needs."

What she needed was a clean nightgown. Melinda had vomited on the couch. "I pooed in my undies." Her eyes huge, she announced this development with grave concern. "I never do that anymore."

Indeed she didn't. Bethel helped her stand. "You're sick, sweet pea. Let's get you cleaned up."

"Don't tell Mamm." Tears rolled down the girl's bright red cheeks. Her nose needed wiping. "She'll be mad."

"Nee, she won't. I promise. Things like this happen when you're sick."

Unfortunately for all of them. The next several hours were spent cleaning up after bouts of diarrhea and vomiting. The boys were better about doing their business in the bathroom. Bethel placed plastic buckets in strategic locations so they didn't have to worry about making it there in time if nausea hit.

Liam and Robbie managed to eat some soup and toast. Melinda sipped flat ginger ale. Judah tried but couldn't keep any of it down.

By eight o'clock they were blessedly all asleep. Bethel flopped into a chair at the kitchen table and laid her head on her arms.

"I'm dog-tired." Hattie slid into the chair across from her. "You look like a horse rode hard and put up wet."

Bethel raised her head and peered at her friend with one open eye. "You're not exactly ready for church either."

"Danki." Hattie blew a lanky piece of hair from her eyes. It had escaped from her prayer covering hours earlier. "If only your friend Declan could see you now. I think you have dried vomit on your apron."

"He's not my friend." Not in the way Hattie meant it, but he did have good qualities. He was good with kids. He'd sung—or at least gone through the motions—with Melinda. He'd proven himself with the boys long before this morning's encounter. He didn't seem to be interested in her anymore. None of that mattered. Bethel sat up straight. "At least I don't have poo on my apron."

Hattie jerked back, chin tucked against her neck, staring down at her apron. "Eww. You're right. That's just gross."

"Take it off." Bethel stood with one hand on her chair. "I'll make tea."

"Tea and doughnuts. And banana bread." Hattie stripped off the apron. She held it gingerly with her fingertips while folding it into a small square. Then she tucked it into her canvas bag. "I heard some ladies dressed in yoga pants talking in the nursery the other day. They called it *carbo-boosting*. We need to carbo-boost."

"I have no idea what that means." Bethel stuck the teakettle on the burner and turned the knob on the propane gas stove. "Do you ever think about the kinner you'll have?"

"For sure. I think about how nice it'll be to have someone to hang up the laundry for me. I hate doing laundry."

"Hattie! I'm serious."

"That's called putting the gaul before the cart. In this case the gaul before the buggy." Hattie cut four thick slices of banana bread and laid them on a plate next to four puffy cinnamon-sugar dough-nuts. Apparently she thought they were having guests who would arrive shortly. "James is taking his sweet time with this courting stuff. He hasn't even kissed me yet. He's barely holding my hand."

"Hattie." Bethel's friend didn't have a discreet bone in her ample body. She and James Eash had been courting for about six months. Not so long. "I know you're my best friend, but you probably shouldn't tell me that. It would embarrass James to know you talked about it to me. Maybe he's just shy. Or wanting to take it slow."

Look at you, talking about courting like you know something about it. That snarky voice again. Bethel fought the urge to stick her fingers in her ears. She had courted. Early in her rumspringa, but neither brief foray into buggy rides led to more. Something hadn't felt right. No welling up of love from deep in her heart when she saw either man. No sudden rush of longing when either wasn't around. No tingling anticipation for either's touch.

Nice. Very nice. Nice didn't rise to the level of love. As much as Mom insisted the feelings would grow, she knew they wouldn't.

"Sorry. I just can't wait to experience that first *kuss*." A look of bliss on her freckled face, Hattie gave an exaggerated shiver. "Can you? Seriously? It must be so wunderbarr."

There had been a time when Bethel daydreamed about first kisses. Now reality invaded her daydreams, filling them with babies and doctors and wheelchairs. Hattie's family didn't have any children with physical or developmental delays. Neither did James's family. It was easy to espouse the Plain belief that children with disabilities were gifts from God—something Bethel believed with all her heart—but living it was a pothole-filled road that wound through the lowest valleys and highest mountains. First kisses led to marriage and to babies. "Kissing someone I love, who loves me, will be wunderbarr, jah."

"Why does it sound like there's a big *but* in there somewhere?"

Bethel marshaled her thoughts while pouring hot water over tea bags in two oversize mugs. She carried them to the table where Hattie had arranged the plate of goodies beside butter, honey, and a pile of napkins. "It's not a *but*. It's more of a warning."

"What could possibly be wrong with kissing someone when you're in love?" Hattie slathered butter on her banana bread. Her generous mouth turned down in a pout, and she pointed the knife at Bethel. "Don't take the fun out of my daydream, sei so gut. All I have to sustain me until James catches up with me is the thought of what it'll be like when he finally gives me a big smooch-a-roony."

Where did she get these words . . . these thoughts? Despite herself, Bethel chuckled. Hattie's face broke into a big grin. She toasted Bethel with her bread, then took a huge bite. She chewed with great enthusiasm. Oh, to be so happy-go-lucky. So sure life would deliver on her dreams. One of the many traits that made Hattie a great friend.

"I promise not to rain on your parade—however imaginary." Bethel took a doughnut and laid it on her napkin. She stirred honey into her tea.

"Come on. Stop procrastinating. Spill it. What's making you look so constipated?"

"Hattie!"

"That's my name. Don't wear it out."

Bethel heaved a sigh. "I worry about having boplin with LGMD. It runs in my family. And not just LGMD. There's nothing that says I won't have kinner with Down syndrome or one of the other genetic disorders that occur more often in Plain families."

To know for sure that Hattie didn't have family members with these rare diseases would take research into her family's genealogy and genetic testing. "The King family traces its ancestry back to the founding families in Lancaster County. For generations, we've only married other Plain members of our community. That means genetic variety has been lost over time. Recessive genes are taking over."

Hattie's face screwed up as if she was the constipated one. "Huh?"

"Because of that, we get all sorts of diseases you almost never see in the rest of the world. Some of them I can't even pronounce, but there's a certain kind of dwarfism, a particular type of deafness, and something called maple syrup urine disease. Then there's the regular diseases you find in the world that happen much more often in Plain communities. Like cystic fibrosis, Down syndrome, muscular dystrophy—"

"Whoa, whoa!" Hattie put up both hands, palms out. "Stop before my head explodes. You sound like a doctor or a mad scientist. How did you get to know all this stuff?"

"I went to the library in town. I did research." Bethel glanced around the kitchen as if her mother might be hiding behind the stove or the half-open door. Her conscience wasn't guilty—not much. "I got on the internet and read everything I could find. It's like a disease buffet. Something called microcephaly that kills babies. There's even one called Troyer syndrome that is only in a certain Plain community."

"All because we marry other folks in our districts?"

"Jah, because outside people with fresh blood, so to speak, almost never join our faith. And we have big families with lots of kinner so there's more chances of those pesky recessive genes getting together and making boplin with these rare diseases."

"I only understand about a third of what you're saying." Hattie's frown attested to the truth of her words. "I also don't understand why you'd do it. Why do all that research? Why do you want to know?"

"I wanted to understand why this was happening to Judah and Robbie. The doctors said it could happen to any of Mamm and Dat's kinner. Including me. The statistic I saw online said that kinner who have the disorder have to inherit two mutations, one from the daed and one from the mudder. So my eldre both have the gene. That means one in four of their kinner will get the disease. Two in four will be carriers. One in four will have neither bum gene. I'm past the age for getting LGMD, but there's a gut chance I'm a carrier. Wouldn't you wonder and worry?"

"The bishop says it's Gott's will. I figured the man knows what he's talking about. Besides, knowing doesn't change anything. If anything, it just makes you worry more. Talk about buying trouble." Hattie washed down a bite of banana bread with a sip of tea. All the usual teasing silliness disappeared as grown-up, wise Hattie materialized. "If we worried about such stuff, none of us would ever have a bopli. Only Gott knows. If He gives me a special bopli, I'll know He has a reason. I'll know He thinks I can handle a special kind. Me and my mann together. It'll be a gift from Him to us. If anyone knows that, you and your eldre do."

"You're right. You're so right." Bethel held her mug with both hands so it hid a sadness she couldn't shake.

Hattie talked a good talk, but she had no idea what it was like to watch a boy race across the yard chasing a kite or a ball or an older brother. Then a run became a walk. Then a stumble. Then a fall. A cane and braces gave way to a wheelchair. Hands that once had caught a high fly ball or handled a bat or hit a ball down the first base line for a home run could no longer brush teeth or comb hair.

Laughter turned to tears shed onto a pillow after the lamp was extinguished at night. Dressing himself was a thing of the past. Dreams of working alongside his dad building furniture or farming or being a farrier one day turned to ashes. Dreams of marrying and having children, wisps of smoke blown away by a cold wind.

And what about her sister? A teenager still two years from her rumspringa. Claire had dreams of a first kiss too. Dreams of being a wife and mother. Wasn't it cruel to wait until she was a teenager to put a damper on those dreams? God wasn't cruel. He was merciful and gracious. His ways were simply unfathomable. That's what the bishop would say.

What would the children say? Was it a gift for them? Did they feel special?

Why, Gott? Her people weren't supposed to question God's will. *I know. I know. Thy will be done.*

Mom and Dad had made it seem easy. Bending to God's will. Neither ever complained. At least not in front of their children. Did Mom smother her tears in her pillow at night? Did Dad take his pain out on the wood when he chopped kindling for the fireplace, heaving that ax with the fury of a father hurting for his children?

Bethel didn't dare ask. Then they would know how little her faith sustained her.

"I'm a doofus." Hattie popped the last bite of banana bread into her mouth. She reached for a doughnut. "You have experience with these things. I have none. Easy for me to say. You're tired. I'll clean up the kitchen and head home—as soon as I finish my doughnut."

"Nee. It's already dark out, and you're just as tired. Spend the night." Bethel savored a bite of her doughnut. No one made them better than Hattie. Because she made them with such anticipation of how good they would taste. "You can sleep in Claire's bed. I don't want you driving home in the dark."

"Fine. Dat wouldn't want it either. He's almost as big a worry-wart as you are."

"I'm not—"

"Don't deny it. Aren't you the one worrying about boplin when you haven't even taken that first buggy ride with Declan? You think he wouldn't want to take a chance on having special kinner? He has Sadie. He loves his schweschder."

"Who said anything about taking a buggy ride with Declan?"

"I saw your face when you were telling me about him rushing out of the clinic. Your feelings were hurt. Which means you like him. Which means you've been thinking about taking a buggy ride with him."

"Only because last Sunday he asked me if I would."

"Whoa, and you're just now telling me? Shame on you. What did you say?"

"I asked if I could think about it."

Hattie spewed bits of doughnut. "Ach! What? You two have been pussyfooting around each other since I don't know when. Everyone knows you like each other."

"They do not. Who says that?"

"Everyone, just not to your face." Hattie reeled off the names of several of their friends: "Corrine, Rachelle, and Layla, and all the girls in our class at school. We haven't forgotten how you used to yell his name at the baseball games. You cheered way more for him."

"Did not. Besides, that was a hundred years ago. I was just a kind. So was he."

"You're always staring at each other at frolics and in church. You think we don't see you? You look and he ducks his head. Then he looks and you duck your head."

"Do not."

"Do too. Why wouldn't you want to go out with a guy who is so straw-hat-over-work-boots for you?"

It really wasn't all that obvious. Was it? "Because."

"'Cause why?"

"Because he tends to be so . . . not serious, and it will take a solid, grown-up man to face the problems my mann and I will likely have. Because I bring my own heavy burden to courting that he might not want to shoulder."

"In the first place, it's just a buggy ride and not a life commitment. In the second place, there's nothing wrong with having a sense of humor, Bethel King." Hattie grabbed a napkin, wiped her face, and cleaned up around her plate. "A sense of humor can get people through hard times. It can get a mann and a fraa through many trials. Declan uses humor to make your brieder smile, doesn't he? He makes people smile all the time. There's a lot to be said for that, Miss I'm-Always-Serious."

What did Hattie know about trials? Her parents were wonderful, her sisters and brothers healthy, and she'd never been married. But she was right about Declan. "I agree, but he hasn't had to cope with this kind of disease. It's a hard life. Don't let anyone tell you differently."

They finished eating and cleaned up their mess in silence. Hattie folded the dish towel and laid it on the counter. She came to Bethel, arms open and wide. "I know it's not much help, but a hug's all I have."

"Hugs help a lot."

Hattie had the best hugs. "Give it to Gott," she whispered. "Let Him guide you and keep you. I don't know much, but I do know He has a plan for you and for your brieder and for Claire." Her face creased in a sly smile. "And for Declan."

The lump in Bethel's throat eased. Her heartbeat slowed. Wise, grown-up Hattie's appearance had perfect timing. "Danki."

"What are friends for?" Hattie pulled away. "Tomorrow you'll find Declan after church—"

Silly Hattie was back. Bethel eased away. "Number one, we don't have church tomorrow. It's our Sunday off. Number two, why would I do that?"

"Because you want to know if he's all right. You want to let him know you were worried about him. You can track him down at the singing or a frolic."

"Neither one of us go to singings. And he probably won't ask me again since I didn't say jah the first time."

"We'll see."

"Jah indeed, we will, missy."

Hattie just smiled that smile. The one that said she was always right.

Chapter 12

A surprise birthday party might not be the best idea. Bethel racked her brain for a way to break this news gently to Nyla and Claire's other friends who'd shown up on the front porch a few minutes earlier. They were so excited. They'd brought the food, cake, ice cream, presents, a homemade banner, and an assortment of equally creative posters. They were so sure Claire would be thrilled they'd planned a celebration on the day of her fourteenth birthday. They couldn't know how difficult this day would be for their friend, who'd just received hard news. She would surely need time to adjust to this difficult reality. Too bad Hattie had left for home right after breakfast. She was better at saying what needed to be said.

"They're supposed to be back this afternoon, right?" Nyla held out a huge card made from poster board. The front read Froh gebortsdaag, Claire. "Since we didn't have church today, we had plenty of time to prepare. We thought we could welcome her back and wish her a happy birthday. If the news wasn't gut, she'll need cheering up. Two birds with one stone, you might say."

Nyla, Charlotte, and Deanna, Claire's best friends since first grade, didn't know Claire's diagnosis, but they knew what bad news would mean. Claire often enlisted them to play games with Robbie and Judah. All three girls always joined in with obvious goodwill and enjoyment.

"The news isn't gut." Bethel took the card. How could she argue with such good intentions? "And you're right. She'll likely need cheering up. It's just that the kinner are sick. They have the flu."

Melinda's fever had broken. So had Liam's. The other unpleasant symptoms had slowed down by morning. Both had eaten some soup for lunch and were now napping. Judah and Robbie were less fortunate. They still had fevers and all the accompanying issues. "I don't want you *maed* to get sick. Your mudders would be really upset with me."

"Ach. Claire will need our hugs more than ever." Nyla's smile disappeared. Her lower lip quivered. She turned to Charlotte and Deanna. "All the more reason for us to give her a party to take her mind off her troubles. We're willing to take a chance on getting sick, aren't we, maed?"

They nodded and linked arms. "For Claire, for sure and for certain."

"Maybe we could have the surprise party in the front yard. The sun is shining. The wind has stopped blowing. We can hang the banner on the porch." Nyla's face brightened. "Then we won't get sick and we won't bother the sick kinner."

"I don't know . . ." Bethel stopped. The van lumbering up the road toward the house made her objections moot. Claire had returned. "Just don't be surprised—"

"They're here, they're here!" Charlotte snatched one end of the banner. She tossed the other end to Deanna. "Let's go. Hurry!"

The girls trotted down the steps and stretched the banner out. Nyla grabbed a poster and followed. "You can hold up a poster too, Bethel. Claire will love it."

If she could see past her disappointment and worry to how much her friends cared and wanted to support her, yes, she would. Claire had a good heart. She loved her friends. But it seemed wrong to ask her to feign excitement and appreciation to make them feel better.

It would be a lesson in growing up. A person learned to put the feelings of others before her own. Bethel sucked in a breath, squared her shoulders, and picked up a poster. A smile firmly in place, she joined the girls on the grass next to Nyla's buggy.

The van pulled up and stopped a few feet away. Mom alighted first. She smiled and clapped. "A welcoming committee. You maed are so sweet." She turned and leaned into the van. "Claire, the maed are here."

No response.

Dad hauled himself from the van's front seat and closed his door. "Perfect timing, I reckon. I hope there's cake and ice cream with that banner."

"There are." In her excitement, Deanna dropped her end of the banner. It sagged to the ground. She scrambled to right it. "We brought chocolate-covered pretzels, PayDay candy bars, Sour Patch Kids, taquitos, sub sandwiches with pastrami and swiss cheese and pickles and mustard, Doritos, fruit salad with whipped cream . . ."

She ran out of breath. Still no Claire.

"Claire, come out here. Your friends are waiting."

A few seconds later, Claire climbed out of the van. She wasn't smiling.

"Froh gebortsdaag!" Nyla laid aside her poster and scooted across the grass. She threw her arms around Claire. "We brought all your favorite snacks, and wait until you see your presents. You'll be so surprised."

"Danki." Claire burst into tears.

Nyla hugged her harder. Claire pushed her away. "I have to go in." She brushed past Bethel, tottered up the steps, and disappeared into the house.

"It's okay. I'll get her." Mom started after her.

Bethel stepped into her path. "Let me."

Her mother threw out one arm in a "be my guest" gesture.

Bethel hustled to Claire's room, where she found her sister huddled on the floor, her back against the bed, knees pulled up, arms around them, head down.

Bethel dropped to her knees. "It's okay to be sad. The maed know. They want to cheer you up."

Claire raised her head. "They're only doing it because they feel sorry for me."

"It feels that way, but Nyla and Charlotte and Deanna are gut friends. They wanted to make you feel better, so they made a plan and they did something. I think that's better than people who avoid you or give you that sad, pitying look I sometimes see people giving the buwe."

"I reckon that's true." Claire wiped her reddened eyes. Her nose was running and her lips were chapped. "Nothing will be the same now. They'll graduate in April and get jobs. Pretty soon they'll be old enough to go to singings. I'll be hanging around here, being a burden."

"Do you think of Judah and Robbie as burdens?"

"Nee. They're my brieder."

"Jah, they are." Bethel waited.

Arms tight around her knees, Claire rocked gently. After a few seconds, she flung herself into Bethel's arms. "I'm just feeling sorry for myself."

"You're allowed . . . Just not forever."

Claire straightened. She left wet tearstains on Bethel's apron. "Where are the buwe? Why weren't they out front with the maed?"

109

"They have the flu. So do Melinda and Liam, but they're already getting better."

"Ach, poor boplin." Claire struggled to stand. "I can help with them. I can still help."

"Jah, you can, but first you have a birthday party to enjoy."

Bethel helped Claire to her feet. Together they returned to the front porch. Dad had set up two card tables in the grass, along with folding chairs. Mom was busy tacking up the posters on the porch railing. Everyone was all smiles. They immediately broke into a ragged, off-key, but enthusiastic rendition of "Froh Gebortsdaag."

Nyla escorted a beaming Claire to her seat. "I made carrot cake cupcakes with cream cheese frosting, so leave room."

Claire hugged her friend. "Wunderbarr. Danki for being so nice. I'm sorry I ran—"

"Forget it. Food first or presents?"

"Presents."

Deanna and Charlotte carted the gifts wrapped in brown paper and adorned with yarn bows to the table.

A half dozen Janette Oke novels from Nyla. Mom muttered under her breath, something about whether Claire was really old enough for sweet romances. Then a five-hundred-piece puzzle of wild mustangs galloping across a valley, Wyoming mountains behind them, from Deanna, and an assortment of games, including Uno, Password, Brain Quest, and Trivial Pursuit, from Charlotte. She proudly announced she'd bought them at a yard sale, but they were in perfect condition.

They hadn't known Claire's diagnosis, but they'd prayed for the best and prepared for the worst. They weren't so very young after all.

Bethel plopped onto the porch steps and heaved a breath. Crisis averted.

"So what happened while we were gone?" Mom eased into the space next to Bethel. She had a funny expression. Like a cat about to pounce on a mouse. "Enos walked up here from the workshop. He stayed long enough to mention something to your dat about a runaway buggy and a doctor visit."

"A lot has happened—"

"Mamm, Mamm, you're here." The screen door slammed. Bethel swiveled. Melinda trotted barefoot across the porch. "Jet ran away so me and Liam jumped off the buggy. I pooed my panties and threw up in a bucket. I'm all better now. Not Robbie, though. Or Judah."

Mom sighed so big that the neighbors down the road likely heard her. She pulled Melinda into her lap, settled back, and peered at Bethel with raised eyebrows. "You were saying?"

Chapter 13

*N*osy families were the worst. They made it hard to do anything in private. Even a simple phone call. Declan glanced left. Then right. None of his eight siblings or Mom or Dad was in sight on the dirt road that meandered past the shack. No one on foot. No one in a buggy. No one on horseback. *Seize the moment.* He opened the phone shack's door. It squeaked. He paused. Looked left. Looked right. *Now.* He slipped inside.

This was ridiculous. A grown man sneaking around like a teenager on his rumspringa intent on leaving the house for a kegger in some farmer's pasture.

Not that Declan had ever done that. Well, once or twice.

Meow. Meow.

Declan jumped. He hit his forehead on the low doorframe. "Ouch." He whirled and stuck his head out. Sadie's cat Matilda, an orange tabby full of attitude, slipped past him into the shack. "What are you doing here?"

Wherever Matilda went, Sadie was sure to follow.

The cat didn't answer. She hopped onto the chair, plopped down, and began to lick her paws. "Hey. Nobody invited you in here. I don't need your company." His words were less a whisper, more a croak. "Or anyone else's. Go find Sadie."

Only Sadie was at school this gusty, chilly Monday morning. March might be almost over, but it still felt like winter. Her tail flicking side to side, Matilda the Cat—Sadie insisted she be called by her full name—yawned widely, yowled once, and went back to cleaning herself.

"Ach. Fine." Declan was reduced to mouthing the words. "You can stay, but you need to move. That's my seat."

Matilda the Cat yawned again. Apparently cats didn't read lips or they simply didn't take orders from men who whispered.

Declan picked her up and deposited her on the scarred student's desk that held the phone and old-fashioned tape recorder. The new accommodations seemed to agree with her. The bath continued. After settling onto the old desk chair on wheels, he tugged the piece of paper the nurse had given him from his pants pocket and unfolded it. Dr. Shane McMann, otolaryngologist, specializing in laryngology. Who could even pronounce those words?

Declan laid the paper on the desk. He smoothed out the creases. He worked to steady his breathing. He couldn't put it off any longer. Better to know than not know. Better to get it over with. Better to have a plan.

Maybe it was nothing at all. Just overworked vocal cords.

If that was the case, why weren't they getting better? Dad and Toby were good with Declan taking a week off the auction circuit. Dad hadn't said a word when Declan stayed home from a Sunday visit to family in Nathalie. A deep wrinkle in her forehead, Mom went to work making more horehound syrup and teas after she returned late in the afternoon.

He would have to tell them the truth soon. Not that he'd lied. He simply hadn't told them everything Dr. Matthews had said.

Stop messing around. Declan picked up the receiver.

"What's up, Declan? Who are you calling?"

Layla peeked through the open doorway.

Purring loudly, Matilda stopped grooming herself, hopped from the desk, and went to greet their visitor.

Traitor. "No one," Declan whispered.

Layla squeezed into the shack. It was only big enough for one person—comfortably. Certainly not a full-grown man, an oversize tabby cat, and a tall woman who'd become slightly rounder since marrying a few months earlier. "Really? Just sitting in the phone shack with the receiver in your hand, Sadie's cat keeping you company for no reason?"

"Making a call."

"I figured as much."

Her expression expectant, she waited. Declan stared back at her. Dark circles ringed her slate-blue eyes. Her prayer cover lay crooked, revealing some of her blonde hair. Her normally fair skin was slightly green. Her hand went to her mouth. She hiccupped.

She looked worse than he felt. "What's going on with you?" Declan asked.

Her eyebrows lifted, Layla shrugged. "Is it a secret?"

Sort of.

"I've seen that expression before. When the buwe got caught eating a pie Mamm had cooling on the windowsill an hour before supper." Her hand went to her stomach. She winced. "You can tell me. I'm gut at keeping secrets."

Layla was terrible at keeping secrets.

"A doctor," he croaked. "I'm calling a doctor, and you look like you could use one too."

Layla's smile disappeared, replaced with full-on concern. Maybe even a bit of fear. The exact reason Declan hadn't told their parents. He didn't want to see that concern on their faces. Why worry them until he knew more?

"Dr. Matthews? Why are you calling him? Mamm told me at church yesterday that you said he gave you some prescription medicines and told you to rest your voice. No auctioneering. No talking, period. Lots of fluids and such. Yet here you are making a call. You have to talk on the phone to do that."

It would be nice to tell someone, to share the scary possibilities weighing on him like a truckload of boulders. Only then his sister, virtually a newlywed still finding her way as a wife, would have to carry that truckload too. "Everything is fine," he whispered. "He just wanted me to see a doctor in Richmond. For more tests."

Layla leaned against the shack's wall. Her hand went to her mouth again. She winced.

"What's wrong with you?" Declan stood. "Why are you here, anyway?"

"Caitlin is bringing the new baby over so we can all ooh and aah over her. Something I ate disagreed with me. I feel better standing. Don't change the subject." Layla drilled Declan with a fierce frown reminiscent of the one their mother employed when they bickered at the supper table in their younger days. Layla had perfected it. "What kind of tests?"

Jason and Caitlin's fourth baby had come a few weeks early and spent several days in the hospital. Everyone was excited that she was doing better now. Especially her grandmother. "That will be nice. Go on in then. There's nothing to worry about here."

"Declan, if you don't fess up right now, I'm going straight to the house to tell Mamm you're out here calling a doctor, which obviously you haven't told her about or you wouldn't be sneaking around like this."

"Fine." Declan pointed at the chair. "You sit and I'll talk."

Layla sank onto the chair. He ran through Dr. Matthews's scenarios with a minimum of words in a hoarse voice, barely recognizable as his own. "Now you know why I'm not saying anything. Not until I know more."

"You shouldn't keep such a big secret like that. It'll give you ulcers."

"Will not."

"Will too." Layla burped. She frowned. "Sorry about that."

"Are you sure you don't have the flu? Go to the house. Mamm will fix you up."

"I'm not leaving this shack until you call." Layla crossed her arms and glared. Matilda the Cat raised her head and meowed. Once. But sharply. "See, even Matilda the *bussi* agrees. Just do it."

So Declan called. It took less than five minutes to make an appointment for the following Monday. The earliest opening available. Another week of living with this uncertainty. Or more if they decided to do a bunch of expensive tests. Declan eased the receiver into its cradle. He heaved a breath. "Satisfied?"

"I'm sorry this is happening to you." The scowl was gone, replaced by a gentle smile full of concern. "I reckon it's scary. Your voice is your vocation."

She understood. Declan's pique disappeared. Layla was a good sister. "I never wanted to do anything but be an auctioneer like Dat."

"Toby, Jason, and you were like triplets. Dat and Daadi's shadows."

Declan nodded. From the time they were old enough to trail after the men at the fairgrounds or farms where auctions were scheduled, they had been given little jobs. Carrying boxes. Arranging items so they were ready to go up on the platform. Helping spot bidders. He'd sat in the corner on the platform, watching Dad's every move. Memorizing the cadence. Practicing in the bedroom late at night. By the time he was ten, he knew the auctioneer's spiel inside and out. By the time he was fifteen, he could do any of the jobs, but the only one he truly wanted was that of auctioneer.

He and his brothers had breezed through auctioneer's school, but Declan had been the one described by his teachers as a natural. Calling an auction was like breathing.

So what would not doing it be like? "As far as I'm concerned, it's the best."

"I thought you would pass out when Daadi handed you the microphone that first time."

"So did I. Want it again."

"You'll be fine, but you have to tell Mamm and Dat." Her voice quivered. She made a sound like humming. After a few seconds, the sound stopped. "You can't go to Richmond alone. Plus they'll have to talk to the bishop about the medical bills. You know that, right?"

"After the appointment." But she was right about the money. The scheduler hadn't seemed perturbed by his lack of insurance, but she had mentioned a down payment and payment plans. "You should go up to the house. Mamm will make you some soup and crackers. You'll feel better."

Layla's skin turned a deeper green. She groaned. "You had to mention food." She bent over and heaved on the phone shack floor. It spattered on the desk, chair, and Declan's pants.

Declan tried to dance back a step, but the tiny shack's walls hemmed him in. His stomach rocked. *Don't vomit, don't vomit.* He pinched his nose and gritted his teeth. *Get a grip.* Breathing through his mouth, he ignored the stench and took his sister's arm. "I'd better drive you home so you can get cleaned up."

"Nee. To the house. Mamm will know what to do."

"But you're sick. You don't want to give your germs to Jason's bopli."

"I'm not sick." Layla wiped her mouth with her sleeve. She leaned against Declan. "I'm in a family way. I've been throwing up for three weeks."

Ah. Not much Declan could say to that. Plain couples didn't make a big to-do about having babies. "I'll drive you up to the house."

Layla allowed him to help her into the buggy. In the time it took him to run around the buggy, she stuck her head over the side and vomited again. Declan climbed in and grabbed the reins while she heaved some more.

"By the way, I stopped by the Kings' yesterday." She wiped her face again and cleared her throat. "I took them a pot of vegetable beef stew. Bethel asked about you."

"You feel awful and you want to talk about Bethel?"

"It takes my mind off it. I can't wait to tell Mamm. She'll be so excited. She'll have you married off in no time."

"Does she know about the bopli?"

"Nee, but she will now. Don't you want to know what Bethel said?"

"Nee . . . Jah."

"She said you ran out of the clinic like your hair was on fire."

Her perception wasn't far off. "She didn't say that."

"She said you rushed out without saying good-bye. She wondered if everything was all right."

Bethel didn't need another person in her life with a medical condition. Declan couldn't do that to her. "She doesn't need to know my business. And don't tell Mamm."

"Why? Bethel likes you. I know you like her."

"She does not like me. She just can't help herself. When someone is sick, she automatically wants to take care of them. It's her nature. That's the only reason she asked about me."

"It was definitely more than that. I'm a woman. I can tell."

"You just take care of yourself, and I'll take care of my business." Declan pulled in next to Jason's buggy in front of the house. "I think you have plenty on your plate."

Layla hopped down on her own. She turned and looked up at Declan. "Being married makes me happy, Bruder. Even with all this sickness, the idea of being a mudder makes me smile. I want that for everyone."

With that, she grabbed the steps' railing, plastered a smile on her wan face, and trotted into the house.

Not everyone gets what they want. Declan kept that thought to himself.

Chapter 14

A wail grew into an angry squawk. Declan couldn't see the baby—what with his mother and sisters gathered around the latest addition to the Miller clan. Caitlin had gladly handed off her daughter so she could fix a cup of chamomile tea and a plate of soda crackers for Layla. Much discussion followed of morning-sickness remedies, and then Mom insisted her daughter take a nap—after getting cleaned up and donning one of Mom's dresses.

The women were in their element. Declan edged toward the door.

"Hey, Declan, how's the throat?"

Declan turned to find Jason, followed by their dad, striding into the kitchen.

"Okay."

Dad snorted. "Doesn't sound okay."

"Dat is right." Jason squeezed past Declan, then stopped. "Whoa, you stink, Bruder. What is that smell?"

Declan explained.

"Been there. Done that." Jason chuckled. He went to the counter and poured himself a tall glass of cold water. "You have to learn to dodge the splash zone, right, Dat?"

Glass in hand, he turned around and leaned against the counter. Dad chose a chair at the table. "Jah."

His frown said he didn't want to talk about this stuff. Declan didn't blame him. "Anyway, I hear the new bopli is doing better."

"She's fine. She's got a powerful set of lungs and she doesn't mind using them. Mostly in the middle of the night." Jason grinned. He straightened and ambled over to where Caitlin sat. The women parted. "Fraa, Onkel Declan wants to hold the bopli."

"That's okay—"

"Jah, jah." Mom's face lit up. "It'll be gut practice. Layla told me Bethel—"

"I'll hold the bopli." Declan took a seat.

Jason delivered the tiny bundle into Declan's arms. His brother handled her like the pro he was after three babies in six years, leading up to this one.

After searching a bit, Declan located a red, blotchy face under a spike of damp brown hair. Her eyelids fluttered, then closed. Meeting so many relatives had tuckered her out.

"Ach, poor thing is your spitting image." Surprise made Declan forget to whisper.

"Hardy-har-har." Jason grinned. His face was in danger of splitting in two. "I'll take that as a compliment. Meet Loretta Mae Miller. Retta for short, like her."

"It's a happy day."

"Indeed it is. Another grandchild for me." Looking as if he might break into song, Dad chortled. He shoved back his chair. "Let me introduce myself to Retta. I'll be one of the most important men in her life—behind Jason, naturally."

Declan moved to hand her over. Carefully, every moment awkward.

"Here, give the little thing to me." Dad took over the handoff. He expertly tucked her into the crook of his right arm. "She won't break. I promise."

"Nee, she'll just caterwaul at all times night and day, poop, pee, eat, and sleep." Jason rolled his eyes. "Then it's on to teething."

Dad didn't take his gaze from little Retta, whose lips puckered as if she might cry in her sleep. "It's best not to scare poor Declan to death before it's his turn."

His turn. Declan wanted his own babies. The thought sucker punched him in the gut. He swallowed against the fierce pain that traveled from his throat to his heart and beyond.

Cancer.

Shut up. Not today. Not now.

The words of a multitude of sermons preached by Bart Plank, Martin Hershberger, and Jed Knepp crowded Declan. *"Arm yourself with the Word of God in difficult times. It will sustain you. Don't spoil today's joy with what tomorrow might bring."* Some of Bart's favorite topics. It was a sin to be fearful. It was a sin to worry. God's will and God's plan were perfect. A believer didn't question. He certainly didn't worry. He had no reason to be afraid. The twin monsters of fear and worry destroyed today's joyful moments that were filled with God's goodness and grace.

"Yea, though I walk through the valley of the shadow of death, I will fear no evil: for thou art with me; thy rod and thy staff they comfort me."

A strong believer would have no trouble remembering Psalm 23:4. God would be disappointed in Declan. God would point to Psalm 112:6–8 and shake his head.

"Surely he shall not be moved forever: the righteous shall be in ever-lasting remembrance. He shall not be afraid of evil tidings: his heart is fixed, trusting in the Lord. His heart is established, he shall not be afraid, until he sees his desire upon his enemies."

"He shall not be afraid of evil tidings." In other words, "Suck it up, buttercup," as Hattie liked to say. Bethel's best friend had a slew of slang she picked up from her English friends during her rumspringa. She liked to trot them out now and again. That one was Declan's favorite.

He touched his hat in a silent tribute to Hattie's sweet idiosyncrasies. *Sucking it up now, Gott.*

Help me, Gott.

What a measly, half-hearted prayer. *It's the best I can do.*

Dad stood and handed Retta back to Declan. "I have to go check on the mechanic. He's working on the van again. Declan, wait until your new *niess* is a little older to tell her your first joke."

"No promises." Declan nestled Retta in his arms. She weighed nothing, less than a plastic bag full of air. He tucked the blanket more snugly around the baby. She peered up at him, her face wrinkled in what surely must be a question. *Who are you?*

"I'm your Onkel Declan," he whispered. "I don't usually sound like this, but I have a sore throat."

More than a sore throat, but Retta didn't need to know that.

She needed to know Uncle Declan planned to stay around as long as possible so he could get to know Retta and she could get to know him.

Her tiny pink lips turned up in a smile. She liked him. She wanted to know him.

Take that, cancer. "Hey, she just smiled at me."

"Boplin don't smile until they're older." Superiority tinged Jason's tone. Everyone knew this face—everyone but Declan. "It's gas."

"Ha! I can make her smile." Declan touched Retta's cheek. Her arms, fingers fisted, fluttered in the air. He leaned closer. "What do you do for a sick bird? Don't know? Let me tell you. You give him tweetment."

Groans erupted from the entire crowd. His family wasn't his best audience. Declan chuckled. He took the little girl's hand. Her fingers uncurled. They grabbed his index finger and hung on. "Do you worry about being around for your kinner?"

Jason swallowed a slug of water. He frowned. "What do you mean?"

"What if your days are short?"

Jason rubbed his thumb over a scar in the pine table's wood. He shrugged. "Gott will provide. Others will step in and be what my kinner need."

"That wouldn't bother you?"

"You're worried about dying, aren't you?"

"Nee, why would I—?"

"Layla told your mudder who told Caitlin who told me all about finding you in the phone shanty and the call you made."

So much for allowing Declan to deliver that news. "Ach."

"Women can't keep secrets. You know that."

Maybe some small part of him was glad Layla had saved him from having to do it. No, it was his place to do it. His duty. Declan snuggled Retta closer. "Bopli, never tell your mamm a secret. It'll no longer be a secret. I promise. These are your first words of wisdom from Onkel Declan."

"And here are some from your bruder to you, Declan. Live in this moment. You don't know what will happen in the next one, which one will be the last one. For any of us, not just you."

"I know—"

Retta chose that moment to wail. Hungry? Wet? Tummy ache? Wondering where Mama was? Declan laid her against his chest and patted her back. "It's okay, bopli, Mamm's right here."

Retta's wail rose to a crescendo that verged on earsplitting.

Caitlin broke away from the gaggle of women making lunch and trading snippets from the grapevine. "She's hungry."

"She looks like you." Declan didn't dare attempt to match Retta's volume. "I'm glad she's healthy."

"For such a little bitty thing, she's got a healthy set of lungs." Smiling, Caitlin tucked her daughter against her chest and swayed in an easy to-and-fro rock. "You'll see when you have your own. Gott willing, that won't be too far off."

Still smiling, she slipped from the room.

The gradual return to the soft murmur of the women chattering with the baby's ruckus receding should've been a relief. Instead, Retta's absence left an odd, lingering pain, like the spot where a splinter had been removed. God had offered him a sneak peek into what it must be like to be responsible for a new life. A life Declan's brother and sister-in-law created through God's provision. A life they would foster, nurture, and cherish all the days of their lives. They had no way of knowing how long that would be. For them or for this new life. *The Lord giveth and the Lord taketh away.*

Thy will be done.

Easy to say. Hard to stomach.

O ye of little faith.

The urge to hurl hit Declan. He'd been assessed and found wanting.

Chapter 15

This had to be how an injured pitcher in the dugout felt watching a teammate wind up and throw a strike during the World Series. Declan shifted between a hickory table with six matching chairs and an oak curio cabinet, the next two items up for sale at the Matthias Giron retirement auction in Nathalie.

Declan sipped chamomile tea from his travel mug. Its flavor with honey and lemon, once so pleasant, now tasted sour. He pulled his gaze from Toby, who had the crowd laughing as he urged them in Pennsylvania Dutch not to offend the women who crafted a beautiful king-size Starry Night quilt by lowballing their bids. Toby was a master at working the crowd. Declan had learned a lot from his brother. But it was Declan's turn to call the household goods and furniture auction. He would've settled for the livestock and farm equipment, but Jason had that spot.

"Stop stomping around like someone spit in your oatmeal." His deep bass just loud enough for Declan to hear, Dad tugged the reading glasses from their spot hanging from his shirt and anchored them on his long nose. He thumbed through a thick stack of papers listing all the items that remained to be sold. "You're scaring away the bidders."

"Am not." Declan managed a reluctant smile. Did his voice sound a little better, a little stronger after four days of almost complete silence? Nope. "Tea tastes bad."

"You'll go to this specialist in Richmond on Monday, he'll figure out the problem, and we'll deal with it."

The week had passed slowly and quickly at the same time. "Jah."

"Gott can bring gut from all situations. Scripture tells us so. Gott's will be done."

Mom and Dad had been more upset that Declan hadn't been forthcoming with them about Dr. Matthews's concerns than about the possible diagnosis that might follow. They were faithful believers. They trusted in God.

Gott, I know You find my faith lacking. Es dutt mer.

"No talking." His father grinned. He'd been in a good mood since baby Retta's visit earlier in the week. With his waist-length gray beard, thick gray eyebrows, and craggy face, Dad was every Plain child's idea of a genial grandpa. One who liked to let a few rules slide now that he wasn't the dad. "It's almost killing you to not talk, isn't it?"

Stop talking to me, and I'll stop responding. It took supreme effort for Declan to button up his lips. He'd always been a big talker, a good trait in an auctioneer. After weeks of barely a whisper, his head threatened second by second to explode. "Grrrr."

"Don't growl at me like a starving bear." Dad cocked his head toward the barn. "Watching Toby call an auction is surely like pouring rubbing alcohol in an open wound. Go check to make sure the inventory is in the correct order and ready to be brought out."

Busywork. Declan hunched his shoulders and did as Dad instructed. He trudged into the barn where it was cool and semi-dark after the sunny spring day outside.

"Gut. I need to run to the porta-john." Elijah, who was in charge of inventory today, held out a list like the one Dad had. "And get my water bottle from the trailer. I'll be back."

"No rush."

"You look like someone who just found out his dog died."

"Nee."

"No talking."

They were taking turns reminding Declan, half serious, half joking. Declan mustered a smile and nodded.

Elijah had done his work. The boxes of dishes, pots and pans, flats of canning jars, a wringer-wash machine, rocking chairs, and a seemingly endless array of household goods were neatly positioned, ready to be moved to the auction area as needed. Nothing to do here.

Still, Declan picked up the list and went to work. Sitting around like a lump on a log wouldn't make him feel any better. Or pass the time. He needed to be useful. Any man worth the air he breathed needed to be useful.

Seriously, Gott. Is that too much to ask? I worked hard to be gut at this job. The job I wanted since I was a little bu. I do it well. Is this about me having a swollen head? Me liking the spotlight? Hochmut? Is this punishment? How do I fix it?

No answer. Frustration welled in Declan, like hot lava spewing from a volcano that hadn't erupted in a hundred years. He grabbed a hammer and hurled it against a far wall. It smashed into the wood, then fell to a soft landing in hay strewn on the barn floor.

For a flash, it felt good. The frustration ebbed back into the volcano for the briefest moment. Then shame elbowed its way past the satisfaction. A Plain man didn't resort to violence. Ever.

"Hallo?"

"Ach." Heated shame flooded Declan. "Preview time has ended." He stuck his pencil behind his ear and turned. "This area is closed . . ."

Her face filled with concern mingled with surprise, Bethel stood inside the barn door. She wore a deep teal dress and a black jacket. She was too pretty for words. "I know. Are you all right?"

"I'm gut. Just resting my voice box. It has a habit of jabbering from sunrise to sunset. I put it in time-out like the English kinner."

Bethel didn't laugh. She didn't even crack a smile.

Declan plastered his comedian grin across his face. "I thought I'd practice hammer throwing. It's a thing now, only the English throw axes, I've heard."

"I saw you come in here."

"Do you want to throw a hammer? It's gut for what ails a person."

"Nee, I came to see you."

"Here I am. Fit as a farmer after a long summer in the fields."

Bethel's expression said she wasn't buying his act. She should leave. A single Plain man and a single Plain woman alone in the barn. People would talk.

"I wondered why you rushed past me at the doctor's office last week without even a good-bye." She studied her canvas bag as if it held important information. "I wondered if I said something that made you mad. Or did something."

"Nee, nee." He hadn't wanted her to see his panic, his worry. Instead, he'd hurt her feelings. "It wasn't you. I just wanted out of there. It was too hot. Too crowded. All those germs." Declan trudged through the winding, narrow aisles between household goods and equipment until he stood within arm's reach of Bethel. "I hope the kinner are okay. I didn't see you at church."

"I've been home with them. They have the flu. Mamm took over today so I rode here with Enos. He wants to check out a horse that's for sale."

"I hope the kinner feel better."

"They do." Despite this good news, faint exasperation colored her words. "Otherwise I wouldn't be here, of course."

If Declan told her about the doctor's concerns and about the appointment with the specialist, what would she think? Would she feel obligated to hang around? Feel sorry for him? Think she needed to take care of him? "That's gut. I'm glad."

This time her gusty sigh lifted a single strand of brown hair that had escaped her prayer covering and lay on her forehead. "Seriously, what's bothering you so much that it drove you to smash a hammer into someone else's barn wall?"

"It's nothing. Just blowing off steam."

Plain people didn't blow off steam. They accepted life's trials as a way of building faith.

Her brown eyes were so somber. Concern made them even darker, warmer. She exuded the kind of caring so enormous it was like a huge tent that could hold and protect all the people she loved. "What did the doctor say that has you so riled up?"

She already had too many people under her tent. "It's not your problem." Ignoring his heart's fierce protestations, Declan met her gaze head-on. "It's not your business."

Anger sparked in those huge eyes like a flash of lightning at dusk, there and then gone so quickly that Declan couldn't be sure he'd seen it at all. Then her expression turned neutral. Her chin lifted. "Of course. I'll leave. You seem to want to be alone."

Everything was slipping away. The future echoed like an empty house after a family moved out, leaving nothing but a dirty floor and a child's handprints on the living room wall.

Rocking a baby with newborn lungs as healthy as Retta's. Telling him jokes, watching him smile—no matter what Jason said, Retta had smiled. A man couldn't tell jokes to a nonexistent crowd. A man couldn't tell tall tales to his children if there were none. A man couldn't sing silly songs to a baby if that baby was never born.

"I don't . . ."

Bethel turned back. "You don't what?"

"Want to burden you."

The quiet concern was back. "It's not a burden when two people are friends. We're supposed to help each other out. That's what gut Christians do."

Friends wouldn't work. "Friends are other women. Friends are other men."

"I don't believe that. We're all human beings. Gott didn't say be kind only to other women or other men. 'Do unto others as you would have them do unto you' didn't specify men only or women only. 'Love thy neighbor' means all your neighbors."

She was simply doing her Christian duty. Declan was a charitable case to her. On the other hand, it was better than nothing. A seed planted might grow into a bigger feeling. She might see beyond his silly facade.

If you let her.

I don't want her caring. I want her love.

There it was. Plain and simple. How could he ask her to know him more if he might not even be around in a year or two? If he even had a year or two. "It can't be."

Her cheeks stained red. Her eyes darkened. "Because you don't want to burden me? Why don't you let me be the judge of that?"

A friend didn't make Declan's heart speed up like a guy in a buggy stuck on a railroad crossing with a train bearing down on him. A friend didn't keep a man awake in the middle of the night wondering what it would be like to kiss her. "Don't leave."

"Make up your mind. You can't have it both ways."

This is crazy. She'll regret it.

Let her be the judge.

Declan turned his back on her. He strode over to a stack of hay bales pushed to one side for the sale. He pointed. "Sit."

"If that will get you to talk, fine." She joined him, taking the bale across from his makeshift seat. "Now tell me what had you so riled up you practically ran out of the doctor's office."

Declan explained. Just the bare facts. In as few words as possible, softly, even though that meant Bethel had to lean forward to hear him. He stopped short of his worst fears. Cancer. That he might lose his voice permanently. That he might never call another auction. That his plan to start his own business might have died a sudden death before he'd even taken a single step toward it.

He could still work for his father, but he would never be on the platform again. Every job was important, but none as fulfilling as wielding that microphone and singing out those bids, joshing with the crowd, and making money for the owners.

That would be plenty awful. Even worse, though, was a possibility he barely let himself think about, let alone express to others. Cancer. He could die with cancer. God's will be done. That's what Mom said. And Dad. And the bishop. But no one would deny it was a hard word. One he shouldn't dump on Bethel.

"You're worried you'll never call an auction again." Bethel didn't simply have a good heart; she also had a head on her shoulders. "You've jumped way ahead of yourself, haven't you?"

"Wouldn't you?" Unable to bear the thought, Declan rose and retrieved his travel mug. He gulped down half of the tea. It helped him swallow the lump, but it also hurt. He sucked in a breath and strode back to their corner. "I have to accept Gott's will, but it's taking me a minute to get there."

"There's more to it, isn't there?"

Declan couldn't tear himself away from her keen gaze. He crossed his arms, then uncrossed them.

"What is it? Tell me, Declan, sei so gut."

Something about the deep caring in her voice was impossible to resist. "It could be cysts, nodules, or . . . cancer."

Her expression never changed.

"You'll cross that bridge when you get to it." She slipped across the few feet that separated them and sat next to him. Close. So close Declan could smell her scent of soap and something flowery. She took his hand in hers. Her fingers were cool, her touch delicate. "And there will be a bunch of people right there with you."

Goose bumps raced up his arm. His heart thrummed. His brain didn't want to form words. If only they could simply sit there, just like that, her hand over his, forever. "Like you?"

"Like me," she whispered, as if to match his soft voice. "Of course."

Declan turned his hand palm up so he could intertwine his fingers with hers. Her shoulder brushed against his. She smelled so good. Everything about her was good. It was impossible to pull away. Impossible. "Even if I can't joke."

"Even if you never tell a joke again." She favored him with a smile that obliterated the barn's dusky gloom. "I like serious Declan. I may even prefer him with just a sprinkling of the jokester."

"You . . . like me?"

"Of course I do."

Declan leaned closer, mesmerized by her dark eyes, her fair skin, and her red lips.

"Hey, Declan, where's that . . . ?"

Elijah's voice broke the spell. Declan thrust Bethel's hand into her lap. They jumped up simultaneously and shot apart.

Elijah tramped straight toward them. He halted. "Hallo!" His fair skin turned ruddy. He ducked his head and stared at his boots. "Uh, I, uh, need the box that has the set of cast-iron skillets in it. Somehow it got out of line."

"Right there." Pointing in the opposite direction of Bethel, Declan charged toward the area where he'd last seen the box in question. "You double-checked the list?"

"I did." Elijah's clean-shaven face turned a deeper red. He hunched his shoulders. "Sorry, I didn't know you were here, Bethel."

"It's okay." She scooted past Elijah without a glance in Declan's direction. "I need to get back home. Mamm will want help with getting lunch on the table."

Elijah had to be the shyest man in Lee's Gulch. He went out of his way to avoid talking to women—much to Mom's dismay. Declan picked up the box of skillets and held it out. "Run it out to Dat. He'll be waiting."

Obvious relief flooded Elijah's face. "You all just . . . you know . . . whatever you were . . . I mean . . ."

"Just go, Bruder."

He went—nearly running down Bethel in his haste. She stumbled back a few steps and put her hand against the barn door. "Bye, Elijah."

"Bye." Elijah's gaze swung toward Declan. "You're not supposed to be talking."

"Not talking," Declan whispered, but his brother was already gone. "Much." He went to Bethel. "Sorry about that. He's Elijah, if you know what I mean."

"I do. He's come into the nursery a few times, but he never lets me wait on him. If I try, he fidgets and runs away. I'm afraid if I get too close he'll melt into a puddle on the floor."

"It's gotten worse."

"There's nothing wrong with being shy." Bethel wrinkled her nose and squinted as if she smelled manure. "Not everyone wants or needs to be the center of attention."

Was that what she thought of Declan's love for auctioneering?

"I know." But his brother might never have a wife and children if he didn't find a way to break out of his shell. "But lonely?"

"It's sweet that you worry about your bruder. He will find a fraa one day." Her dark expression held an emotion Declan couldn't identify. Almost sadness, but not quite. "It'll just take the right girl at the right moment. That reminds me. I heard Caitlin and Jason had their bopli."

"Loretta Mae Miller." A small baby with a fringe of brown hair and a wrinkled face. "Ten fingers, ten toes."

"Another healthy bopli. Praise Gott. They must be so happy."

Bethel had that same pensive look on her face that she'd worn at Dr. Matthews's office when she'd been watching the little boy sing "The Itsy Bitsy Spider" with Declan and Melinda. Not just pensive—sad.

"They are." Declan fought the urge to touch Bethel's cheek. More than that, kiss her until that sadness disappeared. "Why sad?"

She shook her head. "Not sad."

"Huh, sharing only goes one way."

"I have to get home. You have work to do." She squeezed his hand, the movement so sudden and so quick, Declan didn't have time to hang on. It would've been nice to hang on for a few seconds.

She smiled, this time for real. "I expect to see you as soon as possible after you get back from your appointment."

How could she be so willing to take on his health problems on top of what she faced with her own family? "Let's see what I find out."

She stuck her hands on her hips and shot him a frown. "Nee. Friends are there, no matter what."

"You don't need to take care of another person." Especially when the man was supposed to take care of the woman. "Let's see how it goes."

"I should have a say in how this story goes."

If only they knew how the story ended. Most people didn't get the fairy tale. The happily ever after. Bethel deserved the happily ever after.

If he couldn't give it to her, he should back away and leave room for the man who could. "We'll see."

"Jah, we will. Who's going with you to Richmond?"

"Dat and Mamm."

"Gut." Still she lingered. "See you."

Maybe. Declan fought the urge to draw closer. Bethel moved into his space. She wasn't making this easy. She slipped her hand over his and squeezed. "Say it."

He stifled a groan.

"Say it."

"See you."

"That wasn't so hard." She let go. "In the meantime, don't throw any more hammers."

He might have to throw rocks instead, or baseballs—anything to relieve the pressure building behind his head at the idea of never getting closer to her than this. "I'll do my best."

"Promise?"

"Promise."

She touched his cheek, a touch so quick, so light, it might have been imagined. "Gut. Bye."

"Bye," he whispered.

Bethel strode away, her hands wrapped in her shawl, holding it close against a sudden gust of wind. She had learned his biggest, deepest worries. She said she wanted to stand next to him, whatever came next, but she carried some other burden, one that bowed her shoulders.

No matter how sweet her touch, Declan couldn't add to that burden. For her sake.

Chapter 16

The specialist's office was a far cry from a small-town doc's clinic. Dr. Shane McMann practiced with several other specialists in a two-story freestanding building in a busy section of downtown Richmond that held mostly medical care–related businesses. Declan had plenty of time to take in the pale blue walls, dark wood floors, landscape paintings, and forest-green upholstered chairs while waiting his turn to check in with one of four receptionists working behind the counter. The waiting room was three times the size of Dr. Matthews's.

Mom and Dad had taken seats in the plush chairs halfway between two flat-screen TVs hanging from walls at either end of the room. If they wanted to learn how to rehab a beach house, this was their opportunity. Fifteen minutes later, Declan had waded through a massive pile of paperwork. He stood in line a second time to return it. He'd barely retaken his seat when his name was called.

Dad stood. "Do you want us to go with you, or would you rather talk with him alone?"

"Better you come. I won't remember all the questions you and Mamm have or the answers to the ones I do remember to ask."

His mom had been the one telling jokes and stories on the long van ride to Richmond. Between jokes that made Dad wince in pain, she'd pointed out all the dogwood trees bursting with blooms this first day of April, the wildflowers budding along the roadside, and the fresh new foliage gleaming a vibrant green in the bright sunshine. She insisted they eat thick ham-and-cheese sandwiches, chips, and enormous snickerdoodles, all washed down by sweet tea in travel mugs. She wouldn't take no for an answer. It was easier to give in even though his breakfast of bacon, egg, hash browns, and toast— which she also insisted he eat—sat like a concrete block in his gut.

Now nausea made Declan's belly lurch. His throat burned. Swallowing hurt, but he had no choice. "Can my parents come with me?"

"We're just doing vitals and lab work for now." The woman, whose tag hanging from a lanyard read BEATRICE, MEDICAL ASSISTANT, spoke past Declan to his parents. "I'll send your son back to you in a jiffy. We don't have an open exam room yet."

For a fleeting moment he'd walked into a flashback. He was six and getting his tonsils and adenoids out in the Richmond hospital's pediatric wing. Mom had that same "I'm worried and trying to hide it" look on her face. Dad was his usual stoic self. The MA was so chipper, Declan—the little boy, of course, not the man—was tempted to pinch her arm.

No, he was all grown up now. Tonsils were easy, routine, a piece of cake. Cancer, not so much.

Mom opened her mouth to object. Dad took her arm. Her reluctance obvious, she sat. The medical assistant was right. Declan did return in a jiffy. His stomach settled. False alarm. No reason to get nervous yet. Five minutes later the willies in his stomach returned in triplicate. An exam room had opened up. It was bigger than Dr. Matthews's rooms but still a tight fit for three adults. And then five when Dr. McMann flew through the door, a transcriptionist pushing a rolling laptop cart right behind him.

"Hello, hello. Good to meet you." Dr. McMann raced through the preliminaries. He pumped their hands, then nodded toward the transcriptionist, whose name turned out to be something Declan couldn't pronounce. "Okey dokey, I've read through your doctor's report. I've received the report from scans you had done last week in Lee's Gulch. I'm glad Dr. Matthews sent you to me posthaste. You have some tiny growths on your glottis. What you would call your vocal cords."

Growths. A cold chill ran up Declan's arms. Goose bumps. He shivered. His dad shifted in his chair. Mom clutched her bag to her chest. "Could they be polyps or cysts?"

At least she still had enough wits about her to pose the question that ran around in Declan's head like a rooster whose head was about to be parted from its body.

"That's not what they look like to me or to the doctor who read your scans." He closed the folder, laid it across his knees, propped his elbows on it, and eyed Declan head-on. "But we won't know for sure what we're dealing with until we do a biopsy. First, let's get some preliminary questions out of the way and I'll do a physical exam."

The questions were the same ones Declan had answered when he had the CT scan done the previous week, and on the forms he'd just filled out, and the same questions Dr. Matthews had asked him. Did he smoke? Had he ever smoked? Did he drink alcohol? Had he ever drunk alcohol?

That last one was hard to answer in front of his parents. He was a grown man, but still. "A few times during my . . . when I was a teenager, but that was years and years ago." At keg parties in open fields on English kids' farms. Back during his rumspringa. After which he'd thrown up most of it. Declan didn't look at his mother. Her disapproval pierced the tender skin on the back of his neck. "Not a drop since."

A litany of other more innocuous questions followed. Why did they require forms to be filled out if the doctor wasn't going to read his answers? Declan pressed his lips together to keep from growling.

Finally, Dr. McMann slapped the folder closed and nodded at the transcriptionist. "Hop into my exam chair, Mr. Miller—"

"Declan."

"Declan, so I can examine you."

While Declan got situated, the doctor washed his hands and dried them. He proceeded to feel Declan's lymph nodes on his neck, under his ears, and along his collarbone. He peered into his ears and throat using doohickeys with lights and mirrors. He didn't say much, just an occasional "humph" or "uh-huh, uh-huh." Declan mostly tried not to cough. Or hurl.

After what seemed like hours, the doctor stepped back. "Okay, then. Next step is the panendoscopy."

"Panda-what?"

"It's a procedure that allows us to examine the inside of your nose, mouth, throat, esophagus, and trachea—that's your windpipe—with scopes. While the surgeon is in there, he'll snip a little piece of the growth on your glottis—your vocal cords—and we'll get it checked out."

Mom nudged Dad. He shifted in his seat. "Checked out for what?"

"To determine if those lesions are carcinoma. Cancer."

Mom let out a little squeak. Dr. McMann swiveled to face the two of them, Mom huddled in her seat, Dad ramrod straight, his face stoic. "I know this is easy for me to say, but try not to worry. Your son is in excellent hands. We have a solid team associated with our clinic and the hospital where I practice." He settled onto his stool and motioned for Declan to return to his seat. "The head and neck surgeon has twenty years of experience under his belt. We have a radiation oncologist, dentists, speech-language pathologists, a registered dietician, every specialty as well as me, your otolaryngologist, better known to you as the ENT that Declan might need, should this turn out to be cancer."

Cancer. That word. Mom straightened. Her scared frown faded, replaced by the same stoic expression on Dad's face. But the knuckles of her hand clutching her bag were white. She elbowed Dad again. He scowled at her but said, "When will you do this panda-thing?"

"ASAP. I know you're in from out of town. Let's go see my scheduler and figure out what we can do."

Declan and his dad traipsed after the doctor through a series of halls until they stood clustered around a smiling lady's desk while Dr. McMann explained in a rapid-fire delivery what he needed. By the time she was done making phone calls, Declan had an appointment the following day at a nearby hospital. This would be an outpatient procedure, Dr. McMann said, but it had to be done in an operating room. Declan would be under anesthesia while it was done.

"And then," Declan whispered, "how long?"

"The tissue sample will go to a pathology lab. Depending on how backed up they are, it could be a week, two weeks, three at the most."

"Three weeks." Mom snorted. Dad shook his head. She put her hand to her mouth.

"For now, let's concentrate on getting you ready for tomorrow's procedure. No food or anything to drink after midnight. You'll arrive at the hospital at 6:00 a.m. for paperwork and prep. That'll include lab work and some other tests."

Not eating wouldn't be a problem. The thought of the cost of the procedure was enough to kill any appetite Declan might have left.

Dad shook Dr. McMann's hand. "Appreciate it. Where do we go to settle up on your bill?"

Dad must've thought Declan was six again, a little boy getting his tonsils out. "Dad, let me talk to the billing folks. You and Mom can stretch your legs outside. The van should be back by now."

Their driver was probably napping in the van. The appointment had taken longer than expected. They always did. Mom started to protest, but Dad nodded and took her arm.

Dr. McMann waited until they were out of earshot to turn to Declan. "I understand you Amish folks don't have insurance. My billing staff is aware. I'll show you where they are."

"Thank you, but you have other patients waiting. I'll find my way. I just wanted to ask you something first."

Without his mom and dad there.

"Sure, shoot."

"Do you think it's cancer?"

"I do. I've been doing this a lot of years. But I've been wrong before."

"What happens then?"

"Surgery, for sure. Radiation, possibly. From what I see on the scans, it isn't widespread. I don't think chemotherapy will be necessary. The important thing for you to understand, Mr. Miller—"

"Declan."

"Declan, is that this is highly treatable. You're not going to die from it—not on my watch."

That was nice to know, comforting, really, but it didn't answer Declan's real question. "Will I lose my voice?"

"Completely? I can't guarantee anything right now, but my educated guess would be no. I don't expect we'll have to do a laryngectomy—that's when we remove the entire voice box. Even if we did—and I emphasize I don't think we will—we have work-arounds that allow people to speak in other ways. There's been tremendous progress in this arena. Let's just take this one step at a time."

He patted Declan on the shoulder. "I know that's easy for me to say, but try not to worry. I know your kind are praying people. Say your prayers and let the medical team do the rest."

He was right. So easy to say, so hard to do.

Chapter 17

eclan Miller hadn't kept his promise, and Bethel planned to call him on it.

She slipped past the cluster of men studying the blueprint for the new addition to her family's home lying on the desk in the living room. They jabbered among themselves about beams, load-bearing walls, measurements, insulation, drywall, and paint, sounding like women discussing a new recipe for bread. Measure this, add that, make sure you do this, that, and the other.

Declan stood shoulder to shoulder with his father, Toby, Jason, and Elijah. Declan, who'd failed to steer his buggy toward Bethel's porch after his doctor visit exactly one week earlier. Apparently, nothing she'd said that day in the barn had penetrated his thick skull.

Maybe Bethel was to blame. Maybe she'd been too forward. Caught up in the moment, she'd wanted him to know he wasn't alone. Few Amish people were ever alone. Declan had a boatload of siblings, his parents, and his grandparents. What did he need her for?

Maybe he didn't want to be friends. *Friends.* Was that weird or improper? Something in Bethel refused to allow her to keep her distance—as much as her brain insisted she should. Her heart kept tugging in the other direction.

That moment in the barn. His expression. He needed her. Moreover, he wanted her. Not just Bethel the caregiver. Bethel the woman. This was the Declan behind the clown. The one she'd been waiting to see.

Friends, just friends. Others might not see that as possible or even appropriate, but she did. People were people. Except in this case, Declan had his health problems. She had her family health history.

Not exactly a perfect match.

Bethel sped up. She whipped into the kitchen where the women were making lunch while talking a mile a minute about everything from baby Retta's colic to Grandma's sciatica to Corrine Beachy's wedding, now only a few days away.

"We're out of peach preserves and we need another jar of bread-and-butter pickles." Mom waved a peanut butter–smeared knife precariously close to Elizabeth Miller's face. Elizabeth gently guided her hand farther south. Mom chuckled. "Sorry, Liza. Can you send Claire down to the basement for them?"

"I'll get them." Bethel headed toward the basement door. "I know where everything is."

As if the basement was a huge warehouse stacked to the ceiling with all sorts of canned goods. A moment to regain her balance would be good. Seeing Declan again only made all those feelings well up again willy-nilly.

Maybe he felt the same way. Maybe he couldn't bear to share the results of his visit with her. He'd said he didn't want to make her share his burden. He'd meant it. Or maybe a wheel came off his buggy. Maybe his horse was sick. Maybe he held hands with girls all the time. Maybe, maybe. Bethel jerked open the basement door and stomped down the steep steps.

"I'll go with you."

Hattie's voice carried over Bethel's shoulder. The last thing Bethel needed was company—even from her best friend. "That's okay—"

Too late. Hattie's footsteps trod heavily behind her.

At the bottom, sneakers planted firmly on the cement floor, Bethel turned on the propane lamp. Then she faced her friend. "How's it going? I haven't talked to you since the kinner were sick."

"Don't change the subject."

"What subject?"

"I'll get the pickles. You get the preserves." Hattie marched past Bethel toward the wooden shelves lined with Mason jars filled with tomatoes, dill pickles, sweet pickles, relish, green beans, canned venison, peaches, pears, cherries, every kind of preserve, and a multitude of other canned goods. "So why do you look like you just stepped on an elephant-size cow pie? And why is your face red?"

Bethel did as she was directed. "I do not. I planted vegetables yesterday afternoon. It was my first time in the sun this spring. My face is red from the sun."

"Sure it is. You were fine until you went upstairs to change your apron. You came back looking like you whacked your funny bone."

"Nothing's wrong."

Hattie picked up a jar of pickles. She studied its contents like a judge at the county fair. "Declan's in the living room, isn't he?"

"Jah. So?"

"So his mudder told my mudder that he went to see a specialist in Richmond, and the news isn't gut."

"Did you tell your mudder that gossiping is a sin?"

"It's not gossip. We care about our neighbors, or brethren in Christ, our district members." Hattie added a second jar of pickles to her haul. The herbal sprigs floating in the juice pegged them as dill pickles, Hattie's favorite. "Mamm made a pot of chicken noodle soup and took it right over to his house."

The all-purpose medicine—better than any prescription. Also an excuse to get the latest news. Also an excuse to meddle in her brethren's business. Despite her earlier words, Bethel abandoned her search for peach preserves. "Did she talk to Elizabeth?"

"She did." Hattie's voice dropped a notch. As if there was someone around to hear her. "Elizabeth's beside herself and trying not to show it. They stayed two nights in a hotel in Richmond. Declan had some kind of deal where they examined his throat with a gizmo to see if he had any lumps or bumps or blisters. That's not what they call them, but like that. Then the next day they put him to sleep again and went in there with itty-bitty tools and cut out a piece of tissue so they could send it off to be studied."

Bethel's stomach lurched. Bitter bile scorched her throat. She went back to the shelves. Her vision blurred. She grasped a shelf to balance herself. The wood was rough and dry under her fingers. Cherry, grape, strawberry, apple, and finally peach preserves. Grandma Samantha's favorite. Grandma Sammy, as the grandkids called her, loved peach preserves on hot biscuits with plenty of butter. She'd had breast cancer a few years earlier. What Hattie had described was called a biopsy. Doctors did biopsies to see if a person had cancer.

Cancer. Declan was afraid of losing the ability to call auctions. And his life. Good Christian folk weren't supposed to worry. Scripture said so a few hundred times. Bethel's biggest concern was losing a loved one to a horrible disease—there were so many from which to choose. How could they not worry?

O ye of little faith.

"What's the matter? Ach, I see. Come." Hattie set the pickle jars back on the shelf. She put her arm around Bethel and led her to sit on the steps. She scooched in next to Bethel. "Don't you go borrowing trouble. I can tell by the look on your face you've already got him dead and buried from cancer."

"If Gott's plan is for Declan to die of cancer before he's had a chance to get married, have kinner, and grow old with gray hair, I'm going to have a problem with that." Bethel fingered a splotch of bacon grease on her apron that wouldn't come out. "I know how awful that sounds. Gott should smite me with a bolt of lightning. He knows exactly how many days Declan has in this world. Just like He has a plan for Claire, for Judah, for Robbie, and for you. I know that. Yet here I sit questioning Him. What is wrong with me, Hattie?"

"Nothing is wrong with you, maedel. It's who you are. You're so full of love, so full of caring, so full of nurturing, that you overflow with it. It's your nature to care so deeply it hurts." Serious Hattie made an appearance. "It doesn't feel gut to lose someone you care about, that's for sure and for certain. But you don't know that will happen. Not even Declan knows. He hasn't received the results yet."

"The waiting must be so hard. The things that must be running through his mind." The same scenarios running through hers—and she wasn't living it. "I feel for him and for Charlie and Elizabeth. For the whole family."

"Elizabeth says they are relying on Gott's plan. His will be done."

"Of course that's what they say. That's what we all say in these circumstances. We should all do that."

"You don't sound convinced."

"Are you?"

Hattie's arm came around Bethel again. She squeezed hard. "I believe. We can't expect to get the answers we want when we pray. It doesn't work that way. We have to pray and accept Gott's will—come what may."

"It's that 'come what may' that gives me hives."

The door above them flew open and banged against the kitchen wall. "Bethel, Bethel, where are you, Bethel?"

Sadie. Declan's little sister.

"I'm here, Sadie, with Hattie. What do you need?"

"Peaches. Mamm says I can have some on my sandwich."

Sadie's speech had improved so much since she and the other children with physical and developmental delays had started at the English elementary school in Lee's Gulch in September. "Coming." Bethel hopped up. "Get your biscuit ready. I'll be there in two shakes."

"Gut. I am hungry."

"We really don't know anything for sure." Hattie took her time getting up. "It's all leaves of the grapevine."

"All gossip, you mean." Bethel grabbed the preserves and hot-footed toward the stairs. "We're as bad as the older women, picking apart news that isn't even ours."

"So what will you do?"

Bethel brushed past her friend. Smiling up at Sadie, who was perched on the first step, Bethel took the stairs two at a time. "I'll find Declan and ask him myself. Getting the news straight from the horse's mouth is always the best policy."

"You're getting something from a horse's mouth?" Sadie giggled. "Brownie and Jasper and Red have big teeth. They chomp when they eat."

Her mouth wide, the little girl made loud chewing noises. "They might bite your fingers off. Not on purpose, though."

Such a talker. Like her brother Declan. "I'll be careful. I promise." Bethel handed Sadie the jars. "Can you give these to my mamm?"

"Jah. I do gut job."

"You always do a gut job."

Bethel wiped dust on her apron. With a quick peek to make sure her mother was otherwise occupied, Bethel slipped from the kitchen and went in search of Declan.

She found him outside next to the new cement foundation, where he'd created a makeshift table from sawhorses and wood planks. He wore a tool belt and had a pencil stuck behind one ear. The whine of a propane-driven saw filled the air. They already had one wall nailed together on the ground. Jason, Enos, Elijah, and a bunch of other men spaced themselves along the frame. Her dad yelled, "Up!"

In unison they heaved the frame upright. They set it in place and went to work attaching it.

Teamwork. Like one big, extended family.

The saw stopped. Declan whistled "Yankee Doodle." A cardinal chirped in a nearby oak. A bumblebee buzzed over the pink roses Bethel's mother had planted at the corner where the living room wall met the front porch.

How could she talk to Declan with half the district's men—more than half—buzzing like bees in a hive around the worksite? He was so absorbed in his work that he never even glanced up.

"Dochder, do you want to swing a hammer?" Dad noticed her first. He lifted his straw hat, wiped his forehead with his shirtsleeve, and returned the hat to its resting place. "Or did you come to take sandwich orders?"

They didn't do orders. They would serve the men around the picnic tables with "a little of everything" as Mom liked to put it. "Just seeing how things are coming."

Enos snorted.

"What was that, Suh?" Dad picked up a hammer and stuck it in his tool belt. "It sounds like you have a frog in your throat."

"That would be me."

Bethel hazarded a sideways glance at Declan. He offered a sunny smile as if absolutely nothing was bothering him. Fine. She could play that game. "You have a frog in your throat?"

"Something like that."

Excruciatingly aware of her father's presence and Enos's disapproving glance boring a hole between her eyes, Bethel clasped her hands behind her back. "I wanted to make sure the Igloo still has water. It's warm for an April day."

Bethel surveyed the men milling around in their side yard. The Igloo sat on a picnic table several yards from the worksite. "I'll just check the water supply."

"My throat is parched," Declan whispered. "On fire."

His footsteps followed her to the table. With her back to the men, Bethel pulled off the cooler's lid. Water still reached above the halfway mark. She glanced at Declan. "Still plenty of water."

"Gut."

"How did your doctor's appointment go?"

With an exaggerated grimace, Declan handed her his travel mug. "Doc said I talk too much. Wore out my voice box. Replacement on back order. Supply chain problems. Women got to them first."

"Very funny. What did he really say?"

"To send up smoke signals." Declan pointed at the sky. "Or Morse code, or get one of those computers that talk for you."

Bethel tugged the lid from his mug. "If you don't want to tell me what he really said, just say so and I'll get out of your way."

"You're not in my way." Declan's words were barely audible in the midst of the men's gruff voices. His Adam's apple bobbed. "I planned to find you as soon as I had a chance."

In his defense, finding her alone would be almost impossible at a frolic. Which was why he should've stopped by the house one evening earlier in the week. "Did your buggy lose a wheel somewhere along the road?"

"Nee." He took a long, elaborate drink of water. "It kept swerving toward my house. My horse decided he needed a vacation. Plus, the doctor said people need to do something called processing when something like this comes up. I reckon I process real slow, slower than a watched pot that refuses to boil."

"I see." Bethel didn't see at all. Should she be more understanding? The joking was typical Declan. He hid a world of hurt with humor. It wasn't about her. "I *reckon* I understand such a thing, being as my sister was just diagnosed with a horrible disease. If you ever need someone to help you *process*, come see me. Maybe I can help you speed up."

"I'm gut. Biopsy results will come back in another week or two."

"Not knowing is the hardest part." Knowing Claire had LGMD was hard, but now they could plan. They could build another first-floor bedroom. Raise money for her treatment and the equipment she would need. Care for her. "I'll pray for the peace that passes understanding."

"Danki."

"Gern gschehme."

With that she plopped the Igloo lid back in place and went back to the kitchen. Men didn't talk about their feelings, not like women. She'd have to be satisfied with that. Even though everything in her heart said a shared burden weighed less.

Maybe one day Declan would see that.

Chapter 18

*F*inally. After a three-hour service, Corrine Beachy and Henry Plank's actual wedding ceremony began. It would take all of five minutes. But what a five minutes. Trying to ignore her aching behind on the hard wooden bench, Bethel straightened. She fanned her warm face with her hands. Her fingers barely stirred the air. April had brought a tiny sliver of spring to the air, but the number of people packed into the barn for the wedding ensured stuffiness.

Corrine's cheeks were pink, her eyes wet with tears. Layla and Rachelle, her witnesses, couldn't quite hide their delighted smiles. Henry looked as if he wanted to hurl or faint or do both. Fortunately, Toby and Micah were there to help him if he did. How it must feel to stand in front of 150 or more folks and answer questions second in importance only to those asked on the day of their baptism.

"Do you promise that if she should be afflicted with bodily weakness, sickness, or some similar circumstances that you will care for her as is fitting for a Christian husband?" Bishop Bart Plank intoned the question without a quiver in his deep bass. How did it feel to preside at the marriage ceremony of his son? A bit of pride that he would quickly send packing. A touch of bittersweetness to see his son grown and assuming the role of husband and one day, God willing, the role of father.

Trying to ignore her mother's frown at her wiggling, Bethel leaned forward slightly. Declan sat ramrod straight, hands in his lap, across the aisle with his brothers, father, and grandfather. What was going through his mind? Did he wonder what it was like as well? Could he see himself standing before his family and community taking these vows? What if it wasn't his wife who was sick but his children?

Declan was a good man. A man baptized in the Plain faith. He wouldn't shy away from a trial. He was going through one right now. He should receive the results of his biopsy any day now. It must feel as if the weight of ten tractors sat on his shoulders. Peace in the waiting was so hard.

Henry's gruff but firm response resounded in the Beachys' cavernous barn. The smell of horses mingled with the scents of sweat and hay. A little boy whined for a cookie. His mom shushed him. Sun filtered through cracks in the barn walls, casting shadows on the occupants. Bits of dust swirled in the sunbeams. Such a breathless anticipation for the final words.

"Do you also solemnly promise with one another that you will love and bear and be patient with each other—"

A fit of coughing overcame Bart's words. Frowning, he flicked his gaze toward the men. Heads turned. Bethel wiggled in her seat. Still coughing, Declan stood, squeezed past his brothers, and strode from the barn.

Bart quickly finished the question. "—and shall not separate from each other until dear Gott shall part you from each other through death?"

Of course the answer was a resounding yes. Henry and Corrine returned to their seats on opposite sides of the aisle. Bart prayed for them, followed by the deacon and the minister. A Plain union was forever. Plain people took these vows seriously, as irrevocable. Newlyweds needed all the prayers they could get.

So did Declan, it seemed. *And Gott, heal Declan while You're at it, sei so gut.*

God heard prayers, but a person didn't always get the answer he wanted. *Sei so gut, Gott—*

A tug on her dress jerked Bethel from her pleading. She opened her eyes. Mom scowled up at her. Everyone was on bended knees for the last prayer. Heat scalded Bethel's face. She scooted from the bench to her knees and bowed her head. *Forgive me, Gott. You know what You're doing. I surely don't.*

Finally, they stood and everyone started moving toward the doors flung open by the older boys who'd been sitting in the back, waiting for the signal.

"Maedel, you try my patience worse than the kinner." Bethel's mom spoke softly, but her frown shouted. "What has gotten into you?"

"Nothing. Nothing at all. I'm just tired."

"More like besotted." Mom's frown faded as if the thought erased her ire. "Were you imagining your own wedding day, by any chance?"

"Today is about Corrine, not me."

"Uh-huh. That doesn't mean a maedel can't dream."

Her mother was right, but a woman shouldn't be so obvious about her thoughts. Especially when so many obstacles made it hard to imagine this dream coming true. A bittersweet thought. Again, this wasn't about Bethel. "I want to congratulate Corrine. See you in the kitchen in a bit."

Bethel squeezed past her mother and threaded her way toward the spot where a gaggle of women clustered around the newlywed.

Corrine's eyes were red and her cheeks tearstained.

"Why are you crying? It was a beautiful ceremony." Bethel slipped between Layla and Rachelle so she could offer Corrine a hug. Corrine's friends were teary-eyed as well. "I'm so happy for you."

"I guess this day was so long in coming, I'd begun to wonder if it ever would." Corrine hiccupped a sob. "I'm being *narrisch*. I'm just so happy."

So happy she was crying. Everyone was crying. The best kind of happy. "Gott has rewarded your patience."

"He'll reward yours too." Corrine tightened her arms around Bethel in a warm hug. "He knows how hard you try and how much you care for others. Your time will come."

"You're so sweet." Now it was Bethel's turn to swallow tears. "This is your day. Time to celebrate."

Corrine's family had no children with special needs, but her father had heart troubles that could signal a family history. Every family had a medical history. Heart disease. Diabetes. Epilepsy. Bart would say it went back to Adam and Eve and the fall of man. Somehow knowing that didn't help. Bethel thrust those pesky thoughts aside. Today was Corrine's happy day.

"You'd better stop gathering wool and hurry." Rachelle nudged Bethel with a sharp elbow. "There's a seat for you next to Henry and Corrine's *eck*."

No, no, the usual wedding reception shenanigans. Corrine and her friends had plotted to seat boys—they would call themselves men now—across from the girls they were courting or wanting to court. They would be seated next to the corner table where the bride and groom would preside over the meal. "Nee, I'm supposed to help in the kitchen."

"Nee, you've been excused." Rachelle threw her arm around Corrine in a half hug. "Isn't that right, Corrine? My mamm and Bethel's mamm agreed she should skip kitchen duty today."

Her smile radiant, Corrine nodded, but it was hard to say if she even heard the question. She was too new to the idea that she was now the wife of Henry Plank after all the waiting she'd done. Bethel took pity on her. "No worries, I'll check in with Mamm. If they don't need my help, I'll find my seat near your eck."

"You'll be in gut company." Rachelle and Layla linked arms. "Just so you know."

Good company. Declan. They couldn't know just how complicated that idea was.

Or scary.

One time. Plain couples made their marriage vows one time. Embarrassment coiled in his stomach. Declan had coughed in the middle of Henry and Corrine's. Finally the coughing had subsided. He left the spot where he'd taken refuge among the horses, who didn't seem to mind his gut-splitting coughing, and stomped across the yard toward the Beachys' house. The sunshine warmed his face, a reminder of God's infinite wisdom from the beginning of creation. The sun was so bright and hopeful on this first day of Henry and Corrine's wedded life. God expected Declan to be equally bright and hopeful on their behalf and on his own.

Being hopeful for Henry and Corrine was easy. They fit together like peanut butter and jelly sandwiches. Henry had waited until his chicken farm, decimated by avian flu, turned a profit again before asking Corrine to marry him. She'd waited patiently at his side for that moment. The district was losing a good teacher but gaining a new wife and mother who already knew how to love, care for, and discipline children. God would provide the right person to fill Corrine's post.

Still, God asked a lot of a faithful believer. When He peered down at Declan from His heavenly throne, He must be heartily disappointed. *O ye of little faith.*

Cancer.

Those two syllables were enough to make his heart as sore as his throat. The results were back from his biopsy and they weren't good. Not just cancer. Something called glottis cancer. That was easier to pronounce than the other word. Laryngeal. His voice box. The thing he needed to do his job. Finding God's hand in this new trial was hard. The doctor insisted he shouldn't worry. Surgery and radiation, then—boom—he'd be done.

Except for checkups once a month, then once every three months, then every six months, and so on. Up to five years. Or until a recurrence.

He never should have confided in Bethel. A moment of weakness had led him to burden her with his problem. Now he had cancer. He could die. She would never be able to rely on him.

His heart contracted so hard, he flinched. His hand went to his chest. He should feel nothing but joy for Henry and Corrine. *It's not about you.* Surely God's words spoken from on high. As if God deigned to talk to a lowly onetime auctioneer. Declan's calling days likely were over. He sucked in the crisp April air and immediately coughed.

"I could hear you coughing all the way up here. Do you want some water?" Obvious concern on her freckled round face, Hattie picked up a pitcher from one of the picnic tables already decorated with white tablecloths and Mason jars filled with daisies. "I happen to have a full pitcher right here."

"That would be great." Declan unclenched his teeth long enough to whisper his reply. "Danki."

"I have some cough drops in my bag."

He shook his head as he took the glass from Hattie. "Have some."

He was long past that point. Dr. McMann said the cancer appeared to be confined to his vocal cords, which the doctor called the larynx. "You're fortunate. It appears to be in the early stages. We should be able to save your voice. Surgery and radiation should knock it out—if the surgeon doesn't find any surprises when he gets in there."

Fortunate didn't belong in the same breath as *cancer*. The "shoulds" didn't add to Declan's confidence either. Nor did the phrase "any surprises."

"You look like someone stole your gaul." Hattie poured herself a glass of water. "And maybe your hund too."

"Nee. Just tired of coughing."

"When do you have your surgery?"

Declan froze.

"Sorry." Hattie picked up a bundle of silverware wrapped in a napkin. "Was I not supposed to know?"

If Hattie knew, Bethel would know in short order—if she didn't already. "How?"

"I heard your mudder talking to my mudder. They're friends."

His mother was friends with all the women in the district. "Does Bethel—?"

"I just found out, so no. Unless your mudder told her mudder."

Entirely possible. "I'd rather be the one to tell her."

"Why are you worried about her knowing? She has a heart bigger than the North American continent. It won't stop her from liking you."

Hattie said "liking you" as if it were a done deal. It was far from that. "Bethel has enough on her plate with her family. I don't need her thinking about me too. And I don't need her pity."

"You're an idiot."

Pure Hattie. She never felt the need to measure her words. "Excuse me?"

"Her caring is wasted on you if you really feel that way. Bethel likes you, idiot."

Declan peered around Hattie at the house. Where had this version of Hattie come from? Growing up, she was the female version of him. Funny, prone to pranks, the first with a zinger of a line. Despite her words, this Hattie stared at him with eyes full of kindness, empathy, and a certain unexpected measure of knowing. He broke away from her gaze. "It's not right to ask a woman—"

"It's not right for a man—if he cares about a woman at all—to make such a decision for himself."

"Does she really like me?"

"She sought you out in a public event, went into the barn to talk to you. She sought you out at the frolic in front of her dat and her bruder. Do you think she does that for just any man? She may be telling herself she's just concerned for you, but nee, she likes you. She's just not ready to admit it."

What did Hattie know about relationships? Did she have a special friend? If she did, they were doing a good job of keeping it private. Or more likely Declan was simply oblivious. Not that it was any of his business. Nor was his relationship with Bethel any of Hattie's business. Of course, as Bethel's best friend, she had certain buttinsky rights. "I'm still figuring out how I feel—"

"About having cancer, jah, but you already know how you feel about Bethel. That's been obvious forever."

"Maybe to you—"

"Ever since you used to try to hit a home run every time you came up to bat at recess back in our school days. You'd check to see if she was watching, to see if she was impressed."

"No way you noticed that."

"I notice everything when it comes to my friends."

"I'm still figuring out how to deal with this disease. There's surgery and radiation and who knows what else after that."

"I reckon I can understand that." Her tone softened. "The service is over. Bethel will be along shortly. You'd better go inside. There's a seat for you at the table next to the eck. Just remember, if you don't tell her, I will, and knowing Bethel, she'll be mighty irked."

"Danki for the heads-up."

"Gern gschehme." Hattie went back to filling glasses with water.

Hattie was right. He needed to tell Bethel. He'd told her he would and he should.

Declan strode inside. The mingled aromas of roasted chicken, baked ham, pastries, homemade rolls, and myriad other tasty dishes greeted him. Rows of tables had been set up, covered with tablecloths, and decorated with the same daisy motif. A back row offered an array of pies and cakes already cut and plated. His mouth watering, he approached the corner table. Tables connected to Henry and Corrine's would be reserved for their single friends, both men and women.

Knowing Corrine, Declan's chair would be across from Bethel's. Sure enough, a handwritten place card bearing his name sat on a white china plate two chairs down from Henry and Corrine's table. With a glance around, Declan slipped to the other side. Yep. Bethel's was on the plate across from his.

"I think you're on the girls' side."

Her sweet voice sent a wave of warmth through Declan. A smile came naturally at the sound. He doffed his Sunday black hat. "You're right. I got a little turned around."

"You were sneaking a look at the place cards." She had such fair skin, what his mom would call peaches and cream. Declan called it inviting. It invited him to touch her cheek. Her pale lilac dress complemented her dark eyes, currently filled with amusement. "Go on, admit it. Were you afraid you'd have to sit across from me?"

"Nee. The opposite." Declan forced himself to speak up over the din of family and friends pouring into the living room made bigger by removing a portable wall between it and the dining room. "People have been known to mess with the seating arrangement to make sure they sit across from the right person."

"Who knows which person is the right person?" Bethel grasped the chair's back with both hands. She cocked her head and gave a mock sigh. "Don't you find it hard to be sure you're on the right path?"

"Not at all, not when it's about the person." Suddenly the conversation no longer seemed light or flirty. Declan cleared his throat. It hurt. His hand went to his neck, as if of its own accord. He forced it to drop. "It's life that gets in the way."

Her gaze didn't falter. Her expression held a message, one hard to decipher. Or maybe he was just a dope, too shallow to interpret it. "I—"

"Hey, you two got this all wrong." Henry, with his hand clasped in Corrine's, approached. Their smiles stretched so wide, their cheeks surely hurt. "You're going to confuse everyone. Switch sides."

"Unless you want to sit side by side." Corrine shot Bethel a mischievous grin. "You can talk better that way."

That, of course, wasn't done. Corrine knew that. Bethel's cheeks turned cherry red. She squeezed through a gathering crowd of youngies all intent on finding their seats in this time-honored tradition of setting the springboard for more courting and, one day, more weddings. Declan did the same. In a matter of minutes that seemed like years, they were seated across from each other.

Now's not the time to tell her. Declan's mind sifted through topics suitable for this occasion. "How are your brieder and schweschdre doing? I saw Melinda and Claire in the barn, but not the buwe."

"Judah was running a fever this morning, so Enos stayed home with him and Robbie. Just in case."

"Ach. I'm sorry to hear that."

Bethel leaned over the table, obviously straining to hear.

"Sorry, I can't speak up."

"No worries. How are you doing—?"

"Here's your roast chicken with stuffing." Hattie leaned in between Declan and Dillon Lapp, who was busy talking to Hattie's younger sister Hannah. Hattie dumped a healthy portion of the main dish on Declan's plate. "Enjoy. Don't stuff yourself, though, because there's cake, dirt pudding, five kinds of pie, donuts—my favorite—and ice cream. Those are serve yourself on the tables along the wall."

With that sage advice and dessert pitch, she chuckled and winked at Declan or maybe the wink was meant for Bethel. "Somebody needs sweetened up."

Why wasn't Hattie seated at the table across from a would-be suitor? Then she wouldn't have time to matchmake for her best friend. Not a question a man could ask.

Fortunately she'd decided to move on. Right behind her came servers with his choice of lemonade or fresh-brewed tea, mashed potatoes, gravy, noodles, salad, coleslaw, and mixed vegetables. They piled plates high, barely giving folks on the receiving end time to reject an offering. As if they would. The food was delicious and hot, prepared in the wedding trailer with its load of propane stoves and ovens reserved by Corrine's parents months ago.

Any opportunity for serious conversation was gone, overcome by the sheer volume of silliness that occurred when young men and women gathered to celebrate the nuptials of good friends. And when young men attempted to impress their women.

Declan couldn't compete. Not with his throat on fire. Not that he wanted to. At twenty-four, he was the oldest man at the table. He focused on eating the mashed potatoes, gravy, soft noodles in brown butter, and rolls with apple butter. They went down the easiest. Later he would go in search of dirt pudding and ice cream. Soft and cold foods were his friends for now.

He pushed the coleslaw around on his plate. It was his mom's favorite spicy version often served at district weddings. A no-go. He glanced up. Bethel studied him with a faint frown.

Are you okay? She mouthed the words.

He shrugged and shook his head. That likely amounted to mixed messages. "I need to talk to you."

She nodded. She must read lips. "Maybe we can—"

"Declan." Hands squeezed his shoulders.

Declan swiveled and craned his head. Bart stood behind him. "Jah?"

Bart leaned down and spoke into Declan's ear. "Walk with me."

This couldn't be good. Declan tossed his napkin on his plate. He scooted back his chair. Tonight many of them would stay behind to help clean up and put the Beachys' house back together. *Tomorrow night.* He mouthed the words at Bethel.

She nodded. "Gut luck."

Plain folks didn't believe in luck, but her meaning hit home. "Danki."

He would need all the help he could get.

Chapter 19

A walk with the bishop could mean anything—but mostly nothing good. Declan contemplated possible explanations for Bart's desire to take a walk in the middle of the wedding festivities. The morning's sunshine had done a disappearing act behind clouds stacked high like white snow-covered mountains. A brisk breeze blew away the heat of a hundred-plus people crammed into the Beachys' house and spilling out onto the porch and yard. It felt good. He slowed and matched his stride to the shorter man's. The bishop had his hands clasped behind his back. He seemed intent on studying his black church boots, their shine hidden beneath a light coating of dust.

"I don't mean to interfere in your fun. It looked like you were done eating." Bart unclasped his hands. He used one to smooth his golden-blond beard streaked with gray and white. "I didn't want to wait too long to talk with you. So here we are."

"If I ate any more, I'd pop my buttons and explode." Declan produced a grin from a well he didn't know still existed. He patted his flat belly. "It's a gut thing you dragged me out of there. It'll leave some food for the other folks."

Bart didn't smile. "Your dat told me about the test results."

Dad and Bart had been friends since childhood. It wasn't surprising that his father sought counsel from a man who was a friend as well as his bishop. "It's not a big deal. The doctor says the surgeon will nip those ornery cancer cells out of my vocal cords like nothing."

Bart veered toward the long line of buggies parked adjacent to the gravel road that led to the Beachys' outbuildings. He picked up speed. "Your dat said you could lose your voice. He thought you might be anxious, but you didn't say much."

Declan surged past the bishop. He moved between two buggies to the corral where the horses were catching up on gossip with their neighbors. He put both hands on the corral fence railing and waited for Bart to catch up.

"Are you in a hurry?" Bart huffed a little. He still played a mean game of baseball, but he wasn't a spring chicken anymore. "A leisurely walk is better for the digestion."

"I have a lot of noodles to work off. Plus I need to make room for pie and pudding and ice cream."

Declan's horse tossed his head and whinnied. The animal made his way over to the railing as if to welcome Declan. Dad's horse joined him. "Hey there, guys. Relax. We're not going anywhere. Not yet."

"You always were one to make light, no matter the circumstances." Bart patted Caramel's forelock and smoothed his tawny mane. "You can drop the act. It must be awful hard to put up a front when you're hurting."

"I'm gut."

"You and your family will have the support of the *Gmay*, financial and otherwise."

"Dat will appreciate that."

"And you."

"I'm gut."

"You have a sore throat. I get that." Bart tapped on Declan's hand, a quick *tap, tap, tap*. "But it'll take two to have this talk."

"I'd think everybody would be glad I shut up for a while. I blab too much."

"Sometimes, maybe, but mostly your dat likes to hear your voice. He'd be sorry if it were to be silenced. I reckon you would be too."

Sudden emotion choked Declan. His hands clenched in fists. *Breathe. Just breathe.*

"Declan?"

"I call auctions. That's what I do."

"You're having a hard time understanding Gott's plan in this."

"Jah, I am." Anger sparked in Declan, surprising him. He had this under control. Dad and Mom didn't need him arguing with their bishop. "But His will be done."

That's what Bart would say. Might as well beat him to the punch.

"I haven't always been the bishop." Bart tugged two Tootsie Pops from his pocket. He held one out. Declan shook his head. Bart tucked one away again. "Even being a bishop doesn't make me stronger or more faithful than the next man."

"You were chosen by lot. Gott must've seen something in you."

"He saw a man He could use. Like so many of His servants, I'm weak and flawed, but He saw a vessel He could fill. He equipped me. He had a plan for me. He also has a plan for you."

"I wish He would share it."

"Gott doesn't have to share with us. Faith is believing even when you don't understand. Faith is believing during the hard times as well as the good times."

"I know. I *know*."

"Easier said than done, I *know*." Bart unwrapped his lollipop and stuck it in his mouth. "Chocolate's my favorite. Anyway, when I was a bu, my dat got sick. By the time I finished school, he was dead."

"What did he have?"

Bart propped his elbows on the railing, but he angled himself so Declan could see his face. Some sadness, but more a remembering of something good. "He had cancer in his kidneys."

If Bart intended to bolster Declan's spirits, he had a funny way of doing it. "Es dutt mer."

"It was a long time ago, but you can imagine how hard it was for a bu to understand losing his dat before he was even a grown man. I thought I needed Dat to show me how to be a mann and a daed. People said all the things we always say. Gott had a plan. Gott would take care of us. Gott had given Dat a certain number of days on earth, and his days were ended."

"Didn't help much, did it?"

"Truthfully, nee, but I was a bu. Now I'm a man."

A man like Declan, who'd taken his baptismal vows. He was a faithful believer. "It's easy to mouth platitudes until something happens and your faith is tested."

"Do you know what the meaning of *platitude* is? It's a statement or remark, usually containing a moral value, that has been repeated so many times, it's no longer thoughtful or interesting. But just because something is a platitude doesn't mean it isn't still true."

"So you think this is a test of my faith?"

"Scripture tells us in this world there will be trouble, but to take heart, because Gott has overcome the world."

That didn't answer his question. Declan adopted a similar pose, forearms on the railing, hands clasped. He shivered in the northerly wind. "So do you think Gott caused my cancer in order to strengthen my faith, or do you think He allowed it in order to strengthen my faith?"

"Does it matter which it is?"

Declan kicked at the pebbles in the dirt on the corral's edge. "It does to me. What would that bu have thought if he knew Gott had caused his dat to die of cancer? Wouldn't he have been mad?"

"He was mad. Regardless. Because he was a little bu. Even as a grown-up man, he still sometimes gets angry at what seems like an unfair burden . . ." Bart's voice trailed off. He ducked his head, then cleared his throat. "When my fraa and I had been married about a year, we lost our first bopli, a mite of a maedel born too soon."

"Es dutt mer."

"It's not the kind of thing you get over. We said all the right things. Gott's will be done. Even her days were numbered. Two days? That's no life. That's a few breaths." He shifted and straightened. "But we said those things because saying them helps to believe them. We kept saying them until we could believe them. It took time for our hearts to heal.

"It took a few years for us to have another bopli. But Gott is gut. When we finally had a bopli who lived, our hearts were so full we couldn't breathe, we couldn't talk. As Gott is our witness, we fell down on our knees in thanksgiving. Gott is gracious. He is merciful. He is omnipotent. Most of all, He is always gut. I will cling to that notion, come what may."

Declan swallowed the growing lump in his throat. He would not shame himself with tears. "I'm trying."

"Are you afraid of dying?"

A fair question that deserved a straight answer. If only one presented itself. "I don't know."

"You shouldn't be. Gott is merciful and just. You've been faithful."

"I'm not afraid. Not really." The memory of his mother standing next to the hole in the ground where his aunt Esther's casket had been lowered moments earlier rose to meet him. The anguish on his mother's face. The way she dashed away tears as if ashamed of them. "The way you felt when your bopli died . . . I don't want my family to feel that."

"They have the living hope that they'll see you again one day. That's cause for celebration."

"No more pain, no more tears, no more suffering."

"Does that go on your platitudes list?"

"Sorry."

"Don't apologize. I'd rather you be honest." Bart's smile had turned grim. "Nobody said it would be easy. Like the Scripture says, there will be trouble."

"Then I have another question."

"I'll try to have an answer."

"Why my voice? The one tool I need more than any to do my job."

"I don't know. I'd be lying if I said I did."

"Could it be that I was too full of hochmut? I like my job. I'm gut at it. I wanted people to see that I was gut at it." Declan glanced sideways at Bart, then away. Would he understand such a prideful attitude? Would he be shocked and dismayed? No stopping now. "I have all these brieder, and I wanted to stand out. I admit it. Maybe Gott decided I needed to be knocked down a peg or two or three."

"I'm not so full of hochmut as to think I can read Gott's mind. I know we are to be humble. But I also think Gott wants us to enjoy our work." Bart turned around and leaned his back against the railing. Declan swiveled to one side so he could see the other man's face. "It's gut to work hard and want to be gut at your job. It's far better than being lazy and doing a poor job. I suppose you could take it too far, but I never saw that in you. When I saw you on the platform, I saw a man determined to do his job and do it well. A man who enjoyed his job. That, too, is a gift from Gott. I like to think Gott sees the gut as well as the bad."

"I hope so."

"There's more to it than that, isn't there?"

Declan sucked in a long breath and exhaled. "I was thinking of starting my own auctioneering business. I wanted to carve out a piece of Miller Family Auctioneering Company's territory for my own. How's that for hubris?"

"I'd agree it's an odd thing for a Plain son to want. Especially one who likes his job so much. You and your brieder and your dat get along so well." Bart's forehead wrinkled. He crossed his arms. "What did your dat say about it?"

"I floated the idea in passing. It fell flat." Declan rubbed his throat. As if he could soothe away the cancer, along with the pain and the disappointment. "It likely doesn't matter now. It's possible I won't call another auction in my life, let alone start my own company."

"You don't know that. Why did you want your own company? Was it to be in charge? To boss others around? To keep all the money for yourself?"

"Nee, nee." Declan snorted. "Nee, I just wanted room to spread out. To be on my own."

"So someone would see you and not just bruder number four?"

"Isn't that a form of hubris? Wanting to stand out? We're not supposed to want that."

Instead, *Gelassenheit* was to be their goal. Dying to one's self. Surely God was teaching him a lesson.

"But you're human. If you learn nothing else, learn that. Only one perfect man has walked this earth. And we crucified Him."

Declan relaxed. His painfully rapid heartbeat slowed. Somehow Bart had given him permission to admit failure. He'd failed at faithfulness, but his sin wasn't mortal. He could pick himself up, dust himself off, and go on. To do what exactly? "I can't imagine myself doing anything besides calling auctions."

"You can help behind the scenes at the auction, like you're doing now."

"Standing on the sidelines, watching my brieder do what I love to do—it's too much to bear. Plus it doesn't allow me to earn a salary that helps pay my medical expenses."

"So what else do you like to do?"

Declan cast around for something he liked that would qualify as work, as gainful employment. His imagination flailed. "Hunt. Fish. Camp. Play baseball. I know, those aren't work. I never thought about it."

"We can't always have jobs we love. When we do, it's that icing on the cake we like to talk about." Bart bent and picked up a leaf. He twirled it around in his fingers, studying its motion. The lines on his face deepened. He sighed. "Sometimes jobs are simply work. They give us the satisfaction of earning a living and providing for our families. We take our joy from a job well done, regardless of whether we like the work. Surely something comes to mind."

Sunshine warmed Declan's face. He inhaled deeply. The citrusy scent of peonies floated around him. The knotted muscles in his shoulders relaxed. "I'm pretty gut at growing things. I like planting stuff."

"Growing things like your farming ancestors." His expression gleeful, Bart dropped the leaf. It spiraled in the soft breeze and floated to the ground. Bart rubbed his hands together. "Now we're talking."

"My only experience is our family gardens." They grew a variety of vegetables, fruits, and plants to sell at the family's combination store not far from the auction business's office. "I grub around and get my hands dirty. It feels . . . gut."

Not fun like auctioneering, but the smell of mulch and mud and the feel of dirt under his fingernails and the warmth of the sun on his back felt good. Bart was likely right. It was a deep connection to his family's not-so-distant past. Great-Grandpa Patrick had been the last Miller to farm full time.

"Gardening is farming on a smaller scale. Vegetable farming is a source of produce for restaurants and grocery stores. Produce can be a valuable source of income. It's a solid vocation from which a man can take satisfaction." Like a teacher expounding on his favorite subject, Bart ticked off these facts on his fingers. "Something for you to think about."

Something to think about? Could Declan support a family growing produce? Mom didn't need him to take over her garden. The women in the family took care of it. She didn't need him to run the store. Now that Layla was married, Josie did that. She wasn't as good at numbers, but she had an eye for arranging the displays and the customers enjoyed her good-natured chatter. They would like Declan's jokes, too, no doubt, but he was terrible at numbers.

He would have to resign himself to working in one of the stores in town.

Like the nursery where Bethel worked?

The thought caught Declan and held him.

"It's not just about the job itself, is it? You need to be able to support a family."

Bart's knowing gaze made it impossible for Declan to pretend otherwise. His heart sped up again. The muscles in his neck tightened. The next breath came hard. He couldn't talk to his bishop about a woman. Bart might be the bishop, but he was also a man and best friend to Declan's father.

"I promise not to spill the beans to your dat."

Either Bart was a mind reader or Declan needed to hide his feelings better.

"I don't see how I can support a family by gardening. One of the reasons I wanted to start my own business was to build up a nest egg so I could buy some property for my own house."

"Your dat will understand that."

Maybe. Toby and Jason hadn't seen the need to start their own businesses. Jason built a house a few miles from their home. It made it easier for him to work at the family business. Toby had bought property only ten miles away where he would start a family with his new bride.

"You want to build a house so you can start a family. That's only natural."

"How can I court a woman if I don't even know if I'll be around in a few months or a year?"

"You can't stop living. No one has a guarantee that he'll be around tomorrow or next week or next year." Bart straightened and stretched his arms over his head. He grunted and let them drop to his sides. "A runaway horse and buggy, a plow that overturns, a crash with a car on the highway, a drowning—we know all the ways death can come suddenly when we least expect it."

"But when there is a real possibility, a known possibility, is it right to ask a woman to take that risk?"

"To ask her to step out in faith? Isn't that what every couple does when they begin that complicated journey, first courting, then marrying, then having kinner? Take it from a man who has been married a gut many years. It's far better to take a chance on love. If I had been afraid to jump in feetfirst, I would've missed all the wunderbarr times with my fraa and my kinner. So many gut times. Sure, there has been some heartbreak, but the trials make the special times all the more special."

Declan rubbed his eyes. "You're right. I know you are."

"We will pray for Gott's guidance and His peace and direction." Bart clapped Declan on the back. "Then we'll step back and watch Him work. Take comfort knowing He's in charge. You don't have to be."

Declan shoved his hat down on his forehead to hide his eyes. Bart was too perceptive. Too wise. "Gut to know."

"Isn't it? Now go catch that girl and at least have a piece of pie with her before it's all eaten."

The festivities were just getting started. There would be singing and games and presents to open. And a lot more food. "I'll try."

"Go on then. Don't let an old man slow you down."

Bart wasn't old, but Declan took him up on the offer.

Chapter 20

*T*he *clip-clop* of a horse's hooves on the hard-packed road that led to the house brought Bethel up from the porch swing. Dusk had crept across the open fields and disappeared, taking with it the pine trees' shadows. The porch solar lights cast tepid rays on the front yard that stretched all the way to the corral and barn. She peered into the darkness. Declan's roan had a regal bearing. The buggy moved at a quick clip.

The waiting and wondering if Declan would show up were over. Bethel gathered her crocheted shawl around her shoulders and slipped down the steps to meet him. Her throat ached. Her heart joined in. Would this be the beginning of something special or the end before it had truly begun?

They required a meeting of two minds. Declan had failed to come find her after receiving his test results. He hadn't returned to the table the previous day after his talk with Bart. Or maybe she'd gone home before he'd come back.

She'd let her heart and her body do the talking for her in the barn that day. Declan's want and need had spoken to the nurturer in her. Tonight, her head had to hold sway. Declan faced an enormous challenge. His expression at the wedding reception had said as much. The fact that Bart wanted to talk to him spoke of an even greater one to come.

How could Declan handle the medical bills, equipment, and day-to-day needs of children with a disease like LGMD while dealing with his own disease? Cancer never truly went away. Once diagnosed, it was a permanent fixture in a person's life, even if and when the words *cancer free* were spoken.

Declan halted the buggy. He hopped down. No sunny smile. No big dimples. "Hallo."

"Hallo, Declan."

"Do you want to go for a ride?" He waved his hand toward the buggy. "It's chilly, but I brought a heavy sleigh blanket."

"Let's go inside." It would seem less like courting. Friends. They could be friends. "I'll make us some hot tea. Or would you rather have cocoa? I don't know about you, but kaffi keeps me up."

She was babbling. She didn't need coffee to keep her up lately. All the "should she, shouldn't she's" kept her awake.

Declan wrapped the reins around the hitching post. His face was hidden in the shadow of his straw hat. "Tea would hit the spot."

Bethel led the way through the dark living room down the hallway to the kitchen where she'd left the propane lamp burning. Everyone had been asleep for at least an hour, the little ones longer. "Have a seat. Help yourself to the peppermint–chocolate chip cookies."

"I looked for you after I got done talking to Bart yesterday. Hattie said you'd gone home. Something about the buwe."

"I took Enos and the boys plates of food. I'd promised them cake." After Hattie had spilled Declan's news. "Peppermint, apple cinnamon spice, or chamomile?"

"Not chamomile." Distaste resonated in his quick response.

Bethel shot him a sympathetic glance. "Tired of the taste?"

He nodded.

"I like Red Zinger myself."

The water was already hot. She made quick work of preparing the tea and carried it to the table. Declan was uncharacteristically silent. His sore throat or not knowing where to start? Bethel sat across from him. Time to let him off the hook. "I know about the results."

"I figured. Hattie 'Grapevine' Schrock?"

"She thought I should know, and she wasn't sure you would tell me."

"And I thought I was the one who never stopped talking." His chuckle sounded raw. "Hattie would give me a run for my money."

"She said you're concerned about being a burden to . . . who- ever . . . to the people in your life."

"Jah. I have a long road ahead of me. Surgery. Radiation. Retraining my voice." He shrugged. "Bart says not to worry, that Gott is in charge. Not me."

"I know he's right, but it sure is easier said than done." Did Declan find it as difficult as Bethel did? Was she the weak one— weak in her faith, weak in her worry? "You're blessed to have plenty of family and friends to support you."

"I have friends. I don't need more."

The words stung. His tone was defiant . . . belligerent. Like someone trying hard to be tough but not really feeling it inside. He wouldn't admit to being weak—not to her.

"Everyone needs more friends. The entire community will stand by you."

If anyone understood what he faced, Bethel and her family did. They all had to work to earn the money needed for medical care.

"I told Bart it wouldn't be fair to start something I may not be able to finish." He used one finger to draw circles on the tablecloth.

He hadn't touched his tea. "It's not fair to expect a woman to jump into courting with a man who can't do his job and might not be around for long."

"I reckon Bart told you not to assume the worst. You'll be back on the auction circuit in no time, Gott willing."

"Gott figures I've done enough talking for six people for a lifetime."

"You don't have to joke with me. I had an aenti who had cancer."

"Let me guess. She died."

"She did, but my point is—"

"You understand."

"I know I can't really understand. It's not the same as being the one with the disease." But as a caregiver, Bethel understood a lot more than most people. "I'm sorry for what you're going through."

"I'm sorry about Claire."

"That's what I wanted to talk to you about."

"It'll be all right, Bethel. Bart helped me work through it. Nobody has guarantees. Nobody has assurances. A mann could die in a farm accident or a hunting accident. A fraa could die in child-birth. My having cancer just helps us realize how fleeting life is and how important it is to live life to the fullest with the people you love."

"I don't expect you to court me, Declan. I'm not ready to court anyone right now." Maybe her brain agreed with this bold statement, but the ache in her heart ratcheted up another notch. It blossomed into outright pain. "We both have our own obstacles to overcome."

His smile died. His dimples disappeared. "You said cancer wouldn't be a stumbling block for you. You said we'd go through it together."

"We will. As friends." Bethel's hands wanted to reach for his face to smooth away the frown. He had a strong jaw, even teeth, full lips. What would that first kiss be like? The first of many . . . *Stop it.*

She tucked her hands in her lap. "It's not about your cancer. I promise you. I don't want to saddle a mann with more burdens than I have a right to expect him to carry. The problem is the founder effect and my family's genetic predisposition, plus I'm needed here to help care for the kinner and earn money to help pay their medical bills."

Frowning, Declan rubbed his temples. "Your predispo-what?"

"Predisposition. It runs in our family." Bethel swallowed hot tears. If only it weren't so. It would be so easy to draw closer to Declan, to kiss away the pain in his face as he grasped the meaning of her confession. But she couldn't. It was too much to ask. "So far I have three siblings with LGMD. We still don't know if Liam and Melinda will develop it. It's a costly disease. They'll need constant care as time goes on. I take that genetic mutation with me when I marry."

His expression darkening, he splayed his fingers along the edge of the table. "What does that have to do with us courting?"

Maybe his illness was affecting his hearing. Bethel bit the inside of her cheek. *Easy.* "Have you not heard of the founder effect?"

"Of course I have. We're all descended from families in Lancaster County. How could I not have?"

"But you don't have LGMD in your family. One child in nine with Down syndrome."

"And Sadie is no less loved than the other eight." Declan picked up the honey bear, then set it back down. "Children with disabilities are gifts from Gott, just as every bopli is."

"Of course they are. That's not what I'm saying."

"Then what are you saying?"

"I'm saying you need a woman who can stand with you through whatever health problems you face. Under normal circumstances we could focus on coping with that." Bethel worked to soften her tone. They weren't even courting yet, and they were having their first argument. It didn't bode well for either of them. "But I bring with me another challenge, a big one. It's too much for one man."

His right leg jiggled, his boot tapping. "Why don't you let me be the judge of that?"

"You're not thinking with your head right now."

"Are you sure it's not my cancer that's really the issue here?"

"I'm absolutely sure. Let's just be friends for now."

"I don't want to be friends with you." Declan grimaced. His hand went to his throat. "Are you saying you'll not court anyone, or is it just me?"

"I'm not in a position to court anyone right now." If Declan was the one for her, and her heart was determined to push aside her brain on this point, then she would simply remain a caregiver who lavished her love on her siblings. "My family needs me. That's where my focus has to be."

"You said you liked me the way I am."

"I do."

"You're a very serious person." His leg jiggled harder, his boot tapping faster. "Is it because I joke all the time?"

"I did have some reservations about that, but lately your humor has grown on me." Bethel picked her words with care. Hattie was right about the need for laughter in the midst of trials. "I know humor can be good medicine. But I also know there's a serious, hardworking man underneath the funny guy. I see glimpses of him."

"Making people laugh isn't a bad thing." Declan straightened. His shoulders went back, his chin jutting forward. "It can have a serious purpose. Like making your brieder laugh. Don't you like the sound of their laughter and the way their faces brighten when I tell a joke? Doesn't that laughter sound gut in your ears?"

"*Their* laughter *is* sweet."

"But you don't need to laugh? You're too grown-up? Too serious? Too smart?"

Again his words stung. "Nee—"

"You need to laugh as much as they do." Declan's voice grew raspier. "You carry such a heavy weight on your shoulders. It just becomes heavier when you don't give yourself a break."

"I do give myself a break. I work in the garden. I sew. I read books. But I also recognize my responsibility as the oldest daughter and sibling. A person can do both."

His expression softened. "I'm glad to know you can relax. I just wish I saw you doing it more often."

She relaxed when she could, just as her mother did and her grandmother before her. Plain women put families ahead of rest and relaxation. Bethel kept those thoughts to herself. She sipped her tea.

Declan did the same. Then he nibbled at a cookie. Silence reigned. The clock ticked. Ginger rolled over in her doggie bed by the back door. She woofed softly in her sleep.

"Did you ever dream of doing something different?"

His question hung in the air. Different than what? Family was Bethel's world. "What do you mean?"

"During my rumspringa I considered leaving the Plain faith."

How was that even possible? "Nee, really? You weren't sure you wanted—"

"Not because my faith was weak, but because I wondered what my life would be like if I wanted to make people laugh for a living. Instead of auctioneering, I would be a stand-up comedian. I watched them on TV with my English friends." A smile flitted across his face at the memory. "They were so funny. The people in the audience laughed so hard they cried. Making people laugh in a sad world is a gift, don't you think?"

"I do. I think people need faith more than they need humor, but jah, I can see your point."

"I'll grant you that—they need both." His leg had stopped moving. His dimples reappeared along with a smile. "I asked my English friend why they were called stand-up comedians. He said he didn't know. Some of them do their routines sitting on a bar-stool. Does that make them sit-down comedians? If they do both, are they up-and-down comedians?"

Declan and Hattie were a pair. Silly more often than serious. Maybe they should court. Bethel banished the thought. "You're doing it now, aren't you?"

"Doing what?"

"Trying to make me laugh."

"At least smile. Isn't it better to laugh than cry?" He pushed away the mug of tea, still full, and stood. "I might not get to sing 'Itsy Bitsy Spider' with Melinda again. I probably won't get to sit on a hay bale and hold your hand again. I might not get to see what's around the next bend. That makes me sad, but being able to laugh—that's a gift."

He pulled his hat down over his forehead and headed for the door. There was nothing to say to that. He was right. Bethel followed him out to his buggy. A cool breeze made her shiver. She pulled her shawl tighter. He climbed into the seat and sat still for a moment, staring down at her. His gaze enveloped her. It held her. This couldn't be it. It couldn't. It had to be. "When will you have the surgery, then?"

"I go to Richmond the day after Toby's wedding. The doctor didn't like putting it off, but what's a few days in the bigger scheme of things?"

The knot in her throat made it impossible to speak. She ducked her head and nodded.

He drove away. Bethel stood there on the front porch, watching, even when she could no longer see him. The night breeze ruffled the leaves in the oak trees, playing a sad, sad melody.

No one was laughing now.

Chapter 21

"A re you ready for this?" Declan brushed white fuzz from Toby's black coat. His older brother stood, arms stiff, a muscle working in his jaw, in the middle of his bedroom. A bright red flush splashed across his cheeks. Despite the cool April breeze wafting through the open windows, small beads of sweat dampened his forehead. Declan paused, staring. "You look—"

"He looks constipated." Chortling, Jason elbowed his way past Declan. "That happens when you wait until you're an old man to get hitched. You'd better have a sit-down in the bathroom before we go out to the barn. Three hours is a long time to hold it."

That was Jason. Everybody said Declan was the clown, but Jason was the brother who resorted to potty humor when he was nervous. Toby rolled his eyes. He elbowed Jason out of his way and went to the dresser where he picked up his black hat. He brushed invisible dust from the wide brim. "I'm not old. I'm well seasoned. Besides, everyone knows with age comes wisdom. Rachelle likes me just the way I am."

Despite his cavalier words, his voice wobbled.

"What does all that wisdom tell you? Does it say you should have regrets you waited so long?" Declan slipped another horehound cough drop in his mouth. The strong licorice flavor instantly filled his mouth. The acrid scent cleared his nostrils. His goal was to get through this wedding service without coughing. And without running into Bethel.

"A little, I reckon." Toby stared at his boots as if contemplating their perfect shiny blackness. "Life is short, Bruder. In some ways, I was a *fuhl* to wait so long. But then, Gott's timing is perfect. It took just the right moment to realize that Rachelle was the woman for me and me the man for her."

"You are a fuhl, for sure and for certain." Jason shoved the bedroom door open. "We'd better hightail it to the barn before Rachelle regains her senses and runs away as fast as she can."

That would never happen. Rachelle's love for Toby was written all over her face every time their paths crossed. Which only made Declan think of Bethel. The way she stared up at him, her dark eyes almost black against the moonlight a few nights ago. The sadness in her voice. The slump in her shoulders. Her words conveyed one message; everything about her body said another. Even a novice at courting could see that.

She had her reasons for keeping Declan at arm's length. He had his reasons for doing the same with her. Reason. Rational thought. Common sense. All head talk that ignored the heart's message. The heart would be heard over the head's infernal nagging.

"Don't cry, Bruder." Toby man-patted Declan's shoulder. "You'll have your wedding day too in the not-so-distant future."

I hope. I pray. "I'm not crying, dweeb."

"Is it the cancer that's worrying you?"

This was Toby's wedding day. His happy day of celebration. "Nothing's bothering me. What's bothering you?"

"Don't lie to your bruder. I know you too well. You're leaving tomorrow to go to Richmond for cancer surgery. You're not in the celebrating mood, I reckon." Toby pushed the door shut again. Jason would wonder why they weren't right behind him. "We can't know what the future holds, it's true—no one knows. That's why it's called faith. We have to step out in faith."

"I know."

"Do you?"

"Bart already gave me this talk."

"Dat would, too, if he had the words. Mamm's putting her head together with Layla and Rachelle for another matchmaking campaign. She's sure Bethel is the one for you." Toby crossed his arms and leaned against the wall like a man who had no place to be anytime soon. "I'm not trying to get into your private business, but if the worst comes to pass, don't you want to have lived your life to the fullest?"

"You need to get to the barn now."

"We still have a few minutes. Besides, the service is three hours long. Rachelle and I don't meet with the minister for another hour."

While the congregation sang hymns, Toby and Rachelle would meet with the minister at a picnic table for about forty minutes so Jed could admonish them and bless them before they started their married life. Only Toby would take time beforehand to give his little brother advice. He was used to running the business, which seemed to make him good at running people's lives.

At least he thought so.

"Mamm needs to get her facts straight." Declan eased onto the foot of the bed. His church boots felt tight today for no good reason. "She has no idea what's really going on. Bethel's worried about adding to my burden."

"That's narrisch. Bethel's a hard worker, a gut caregiver for her brieder and schweschdre, and she works hard at the nursery. She's faithful. Everyone can see that. What more could a person ask? She'd be a great help, not a hindrance."

"Have you ever heard of something called the founder effect?"

"Jah, of course."

Everyone but Declan, it seemed. He'd been too busy living the life he loved auctioneering to pay attention. "It doesn't worry you?"

"Scripture tells us to hold ourselves apart from the world. It seems there are consequences, however unintended, for not mixing more with those out in the world. It doesn't matter. Gott takes care of us in our imperfections."

With age comes wisdom. Toby had received a large dose of it. Still, it didn't seem right that children bore the brunt of those consequences. Jesus loved the little children. He said to let them come to Him. He said to be like them. "The consequences are inflicted on our boplin, our kinner. Why would Gott allow that?"

Frowning, Toby rubbed both hands across his clean-shaven face. Soon it would be covered by a beard. "I don't consider Sadie or Jonah consequences. They're gifts from Gott. I wouldn't change a thing about them."

"I know. I agree—"

"Bethel should lay her worries at the foot of the cross and get on with life."

"Easy to say. Hard to do." Still, Toby was right. Bethel had lessons to learn, just as Declan did. With those lessons would come wisdom. Maybe God's timing was still ticking its way toward the moment their hopes and dreams would align. Maybe worry was sucking joy from their lives needlessly. Declan stood and opened the door. "This is your day, Toby. Let's go get you hitched before Rachelle changes her mind, like Jason said."

"Like *that* would happen."

Toby sounded very sure of himself, but he straightened and strode past Declan through the door like his pants were on fire.

It took another three hours of prayer, song, and preaching to get to that moment when Declan's siblings Layla and Jason and his sister-in-law Caitlin followed Toby to the front of the barn where they stood at his side across from Rachelle and her witnesses: Corrine and Henry Plank, Rachelle's brother John Lapp, and Bethel King.

Bethel. She huddled close to the others, her head bent, her cheeks bright pink. She wore a dress the same deep royal blue as the other women. They'd likely sat around together in the evenings cutting out the dresses from patterns, then taking turns at the treadle machine, sewing the material into the dresses. The entire time they gabbed about what Rachelle's married life would be like. They would live in the roomy former English house Toby had purchased on ten acres of land only a half hour's drive from the Lapps' place. That way Rachelle could spend time with her mom, helping out with the children while Toby was away on the auction circuit. Her mom would be close to help Rachelle with her babies, once they came along. They would laugh about the wringer-wash machine Rachelle purchased at an auction Toby called the day he proposed to her.

They wondered whether the babies would take after Toby or Rachelle, or a bit of both.

They discussed the wedding guests—those who would attend, those who wouldn't be able, the wedding gifts, the menu for the reception, the party games and singing, and the pranks that might or might not be played.

They giggled over the whys and wherefores of the wedding night.

All the while, had Bethel wondered if her day would ever come? Had she thought of Declan at all?

"Do you promise that if he should be afflicted with bodily weakness, sickness, or some similar circumstance that you will care for him as is fitting for a Christian wife?"

Bart's deep bass dragged Declan back to this moment in front of row after row of wooden benches filled with family, friends, and guests from across the country. Bart delivered each word of this time-honored question in a slow, deep, solemn processional leading to profound commitment.

Rachelle's immediate answer rang out clear and high, without equivocation. "Jah."

She had no way of knowing what that vow might require of her. Yet she was willing to make it in front of her community, her bishop, and, most important, her God.

Declan had no choice. He glanced toward Bethel. She stared at him for a split second. Angst fought longing. Neither won. She broke away first.

The ache in Declan's throat had nothing to do with cancer. He swallowed hard. A tickle threatened to dislodge a cough. *Gott, help me.*

Only a few moments left. Toby and Rachelle completed their vows. Bart presented them as husband and wife. They all took their seats.

Done. As simple and as hard as that. Toby grinned so widely his dimples threatened to pop. All the brothers kept smacking him on the back until Grandpa leveled a fierce glance at them and they quieted down. Declan snuck a look at the women's section. Bethel had squeezed into her seat between her mother and Claire. Her mother gave her a quick one-armed hug.

What did that mean? Claire took Bethel's hand.

They were offering her comfort. Why?

More songs, more prayers. The service ended. An immediate excited buzz filled the lofty wood building. The boys ran to slide open the doors. A fresh gale of crisp air overcame the stuffiness of so many people congregated together for so long.

"Come on. Let's go. I'll escort Toby to the eck. Then Dat will want us in the back helping grill the meat." Jason grabbed Declan's arm. "We need to make sure the buwe are lined up to act as ushers—"

"Everyone knows what to do." Declan tugged free of his grasp. Bethel and the other witnesses had surrounded Rachelle. They would guide her to the spot of honor next to her new husband and then assume their other assigned duties. There would be no chance to talk. Was there anything to talk about? Did she feel even an inkling of what he'd felt? Like they were fools letting life pass them by? "I'm right behind you."

"No, you're not." Jason stepped into the aisle in front of Declan. "Not now. Not here."

"I'm leaving tomorrow." For a surgery that would change everything in his life.

"This is Toby's day. Don't spoil it."

Jason was right. Declan sucked in a breath and coughed. Pain seared his throat. Not today. Maybe not ever. He followed his brother from the barn. The flood of people swept them into the yard toward the house. No looking back.

No need. Bethel, Rachelle, and a cluster of other women hurried past him, laughing and chattering. Bethel never glanced his way.

She never looked back.

Maybe that was Declan's answer.

———————

Chapter 22

*N*othing smelled as good as fresh dirt warmed by the late April sun. Finally spring had decided to stick around. With another deep inhale, Declan sank his hoe into the earth. He loosened and broke up clods to make it easier for his mother to plant the tomatoes. He paused and wiped his face with his sleeve. The newly rototilled plot stretched the length of the huge garden his mom had started planting in March. The cabbage, turnips, carrots, peas, radishes, spinach, and onions flourished under her watchful eye. She seemed to know just which vegetables could withstand cold soil and late freezes, which needed longer growing seasons, and which needed to be planted as seeds or started in her small greenhouse and then transplanted. Most Plain women did.

Until now Declan had paid little attention to the how and why of their system. Gardening was fun, but he never had time for it. The auction season started about the same time as the spring planting. The Miller women took care of the gardening—and the store where they sold much of the produce—and the Miller men ran the auctioneering business. Until now.

For a brief flash a microphone replaced the hoe in Declan's hand. He stood on the platform, a sea of straw hats, bonnets, John

Deere caps, and bare heads in front of him. Energy crackled in the air. *"Who'll give me 300? 300, I got 300. Who'll give 350, 350, now 400 . . ."* Bid cards in the air. Good-natured competition. Laughter. The smell of hot dogs, hamburgers, and cotton candy floating in the air. His brothers bickering. His dad giving them the stare. Grandpa's chuckle.

Supper at a diner or drive-through fare. Bubble gum and songs. Card games deep into the night.

Life on the road with the Miller brothers.

All gone. Just gone.

For now, not forever. Maybe. Maybe not.

"Are you tired?"

Back in the garden, Declan stabbed at the dirt with his hoe. Tired. How could he be tired? He'd done nothing but sit around on his behind for more than a week. "I'm fine."

Mom peered up at him from the spot where she knelt tucking tender tomato plants started from seed in her greenhouse into the soil and covering their roots. "Maybe you should sit down for a bit."

"Nee," Declan growled. He didn't need to be coddled. "I said I'm fine."

"Don't growl at me, Suh."

"Es dutt mer."

He turned back to his work. Since his surgery, this was his work. The surgery had gone well, according to Dr. McMann. They'd been able to remove "most" of the cancerous tissue. How was that considered successful? Most was not all. Two days in the hospital and he was sent home to recuperate. The doctor gave him an A at his follow-up appointment two weeks later. Healing well. No signs of infection. All his lab work was good.

He'd also reiterated his earlier instructions. No auctioneering. Not never, just "not for the foreseeable future." No one could foresee the future. Eventually, Declan would start physical therapy to retune his voice, so to speak—no pun intended.

A seven-week period of radiation was intended to eradicate any remaining cancer cells. Five days a week. Seven weeks spent in Richmond. Dollar signs danced in Declan's head. Not only could he not earn money, but he represented a money drain for his family.

He dug deeper and turned over the dark, moist, rich soil. So this was where the saying "tough row to hoe" had come from. People kept saying cancer treatment was a tough row to hoe. Except preparing the soil and planting the vegetables wasn't difficult work. In fact, it was satisfying. In a different way from calling auctions. The Plain people had a long history of being farmers, of being in touch with the earth and working outdoors. No audience. No crowds. The only noise the blue jays and cardinals chattering in the ash, red maple, and black oak trees amid the rustle of their leaves.

Farming on the scale of his ancestors wasn't an option now. His family didn't have the necessary acreage or the equipment. Farming was far more expensive nowadays, and smaller farmers rarely made a profit—especially if they used what the English called old-fashioned equipment for sowing and reaping.

"You don't have to pretend it doesn't hurt." Mom rose and trod barefoot toward him. "Are you taking the pills the doctor prescribed?"

He shook his head. People kept talking to him as if they expected him to answer. Part of his voice box was missing, gone, cut out. With it had gone his plans for a long career as an auctioneer. Maybe even his plans for a long life.

No wallowing. He smiled and offered an exaggerated thumbs-up.

"What if I bring you a chocolate milkshake?"

Another smile but a thumbs-down. Milkshakes were preferable to the steady diet of pureed foods, scrambled eggs, mashed potatoes, gelatins, and puddings, but the painkillers dulled his appetite.

Disappointment flittered across Mom's face. She ducked her head and returned to her flat of tomato plants. She wanted so much to help.

Declan's heart did a painful *thump-thump* routine. He closed his eyes, craned his neck, and raised his face to the sun. *Gott, sei so gut, let me heal fast. My mamm is worried. She wants to help. Let her know I'll be okay, sei so gut. No matter what, I'll be okay.*

He tapped her shoulder. *Talk to me.* He mouthed the words, just short of a whisper. The memory of the moment he'd heard his voice at his follow-up appointment with his doctor surfaced. Raspy. Barely recognizable as human. Guttural. Words unrecognizable.

Physical therapy would help, the doctor promised. Gone were the days of shouting over the crowd, but one day soon Declan would tell his nieces and nephews jokes. He would sing "The Itsy Bitsy Spider" song, if not to Melinda, to his nieces and nephews.

One day he might even speak wedding vows.

The memory of Bethel's sad smile that night in her kitchen when she'd said they were simply friends took its place next to the sound of his decimated voice.

A person couldn't give up. He had to get his voice back. Find a job. Then he would show Bethel he had the strength, the perseverance, and the seriousness of character needed to share a life with her—no matter what challenges their mixed-up genes presented them.

It would take time and patience.

Patience. Of all the fruit of the Spirit, the hardest to manage.

Wiping her hands on her apron, Mom stared up at him. "Talk about what, Suh?"

He shrugged. *Anything.* He swept his arm in an arc across the endless neat rows of vegetables.

"Gardening? Whatever you say." She chuckled. Then her smile faded, replaced with acute discomfort. Her cheeks, already ruddy from the sun, turned a deeper red. "Es dutt mer, Suh."

He summoned a smile and shrugged. *No worries.* So many simple phrases had become potential land mines feared by his family. They were only words.

Mom picked up her trowel. She bent over the row and dug with unnecessary vigor. "It's not gardening, not really. It's farming. We plant more than most families because we sell more. Not just at the store, but at the produce auction house and restaurants in Lee's Gulch and other nearby towns."

All facts well known to Declan, but at least she was talking. He returned to his hoe. *How do you know when to plant?*

"I plant when my mudder planted, when her mudder planted. I always thought they just knew." Warming to her topic, she waved her trowel enthusiastically. "Then *Mammi* told me they planted according to the *Farmers' Almanac* on when the last freeze was expected in the spring and the first one in the fall. They had learned which vegetables have longer growing seasons and can withstand cooler soil temperatures. They knew which ones to start from seed in the nursery and which ones could be planted as seeds later in spring because they had shorter growing seasons."

An intricate calendar Mom kept in her head just as Grandma had and Great-Grandma. *Cabbages, turnips, carrots, onions, peas, radishes, spinach . . .*

"All planted toward the end of March." She pointed at the tomatoes. "These need a longer growing season but can't tolerate freezes, so we start them in the nursery. After they're well established, we introduce them gradually to the great outdoors. Finally, in late April we transplant them after the last freeze."

She was a wealth of knowledge and experience.

"I never knew you to be interested in gardening." Her smile fading to a grimace, Mom let the trowel sink to the ground. "I suppose you had no need. It's gut to see you making the best of your situation. Wanting to learn about the planting season while you adjust to working in the garden is a positive thing."

For now. Or maybe forever. Bart's less-than-gentle nudge toward finding a new vocation resounded in Declan's ears.

It feels gut to work outdoors.

"I agree." Mom was obviously in her element, happy, with a trowel in one hand and a plant in the other. She appeared younger than her fifty-plus years. "I enjoy baking and cooking. I don't mind cleaning house or sewing. But after the endless cold winter months with short days and long nights, I love being outdoors again. I can't wait to work on the flower garden."

Mom was known for her unique flower garden. The previous year she decided to forgo the usual neat, organized flower gardens found in all their Plain neighbors' yards for what she called native flowers.

Milkweed, butterfly weed, golden asters, and ragwort? Declan mouthed the question.

"Of course. It's nice that you remember their names, Suh. You've been paying attention, unlike your brieder and schweschdre. They think I'm a little crazy. Some flowers native to Virginia are going extinct. Native plants don't have to be watered as much, and they feed the hummingbird—"

I know.

All the Miller siblings had heard her sermon multiple times on the many reasons everyone should plant native flowers. That they tended to tune her out came as no surprise.

"Sorry. I personally think they're just as beautiful. The black-eyed Susans, sweet alyssum, and butterfly weed did really well last year. So did the golden aster and sundrops."

Declan nodded again. Not being able to actually talk tried his very soul. His jaw, tongue, and lips longed to leap into action. To tell a joke. To see her laugh. To argue with Toby. To sing with Sadie.

"Sadie is a great help with the garden. She loves getting her hands and her feet dirty." A curiously hesitant note crept into his mother's voice. "You could take a lesson from Sadie Maedel."

As if Declan's mere thought of his little sister caused an immediate segue in his mother's meandering mind. And what did she mean by that? No doubt she would tell him in great detail.

"Sadie gets up and goes about her business without feeling sorry for herself every single day. Don't tell me it's because she doesn't know she's different. She does. Other kids make sure she knows. People give her that pity look in the store. They carry on about 'the poor little thing' in front of her like she's deaf too."

Mom leaned back on her haunches. She stabbed at the air with the trowel. "That maedel lives up to her potential every day because she has tenacity and no fear of the future. She's fiercely independent. She makes her own way even when it's a hundred times harder for her than the next kind."

Anger blew through Declan. A second later it dissipated, spent like a sudden storm, over and done with. He knocked on his chest with his fist. *And me?*

"You have big trials, I'll give you that, but you're also a child of Gott baptized in His Son's name."

Flowers. Vegetables.

Mom snorted. "Of course, you'd rather change the subject. Gott can make gut come from all circumstances. Scripture says so."

So much for putting on a happy face. His mother saw right through him. *Have faith. Also realistic.*

Pursing her lips, she brushed her hands together as if scattering his mouthed words. "If you had faith, you'd let Bethel King walk through this trial with you. You'd be getting to know her better, finding out if you're meant to be together, instead of wasting time, alone and bitter."

They hadn't spoken a single word since that evening not long before Toby's wedding. She hadn't sent him a card after his surgery. Yes, it was his fault too. He'd been careful to avoid her at church. He hadn't taken another buggy ride to her house to try to change her mind. He didn't need to be told twice. On that his heart and his head agreed—for once. "She doesn't want it."

Even those few words hurt. Declan rubbed his throat, as if that would help. "Ach."

"No talking." Scowling, Mom tugged her scarf down on her forehead, leaving a smudge of dirt above her eye. "You're not getting any younger, Suh, but you're definitely getting old and sour before your time."

Declan clenched his jaw. He would not play the so-called cancer card. His mother knew. She'd suffered through the surgery with him. She'd sat with him in the hospital. She'd prayed with his dad, Bart, and the others. She knew.

She says just friends. I agree.

"Plain men and women aren't friends." Mom's scoffing tone matched her wrinkled nose. "And you don't agree. It's obvious from your expression every time you see her. Always has been. Bethel's smart, a hard worker, kind, faithful, and not hard on the eyes, I suppose. She won't be single forever. Mess around and some other lucky sap will snap her up."

Matchmaking at a time like this. That was Mom. *Isn't Elijah next?*

Still frowning fiercely, she chuckled. "He's getting his own swift kick in the seat of the pants, believe you me."

A horn honked. Brakes squeaked. The English school bus. One of the disadvantages of attending the English school—at least in Declan's mind. Sadie loved school—too bad it didn't let out for the summer as early as the Plain school.

"That'll be Sadie. Don't tell her all the nice things I said about her." His mother rose. She picked up the now-empty flat and trotted down the row to the wheelbarrow, where she had a bucket of seed potatoes already cut into chunks, each with at least one eye. "I don't want her getting a big head."

Sadie was the last Miller child in danger of being full of herself. The sound of her voice singing an English song about a farmer in the dell floated on the breeze. She'd learned so much English since starting at her new school. Speech therapy had helped with her pronunciation as well. A few seconds later she rounded the corner of the house and skipped across the yard. Matilda the Cat followed. "Mamm. Declan. There you are."

"Here we are. How was school?"

"Gut. I want to plant." She plopped onto the grass and tugged off her shoes. Her prayer covering was crooked, revealing more of her blonde hair than she should. Her brown-rimmed glasses needed a good cleaning. Matilda wound her skinny body around the girl's legs. "Matilda the Cat does too."

"You can drop the potatoes into the holes. Just remember, eyes up."

"So they can see to grow?"

"Something like that."

"Jonah says we see each other at plate sale on Saturday."

Bucket in one hand, shovel in the other, Mother halted. An expression that could only be described as guilty suffused her face, making her already rosy cheeks turn beet red. "I reckon."

Plate sale?

"I'm surprised you haven't heard. The district is having a barbecue plate fundraiser in front of the Hershbergers'. Martin is donating all the meat and the rolls for the pulled pork. The women are making sides and desserts. I'm making my spicy hickory barbecue sauce. Don from the English grocery store is donating condiments and paper goods. Everyone is pitching in to help families with medical bills this spring."

For my bills, you mean.

"It's not all about you." Mom packed plenty of acerbic bite into her response. "The Kings have bills for the buwe and now Claire too."

Right. Declan laid aside the hoe. He knelt and went to work making six-inch-deep holes about a foot apart.

"I'll do that." Mom squatted next to him. "You should work at the fundraiser. They could use help with grilling the meat."

Nudge, nudge. Mom wasn't concerned about volunteers for the fundraiser. She was all about throwing Declan and Bethel together. *We'll see.*

"See what? Dat and the buwe are in Intercourse at an auction this weekend. You have nothing to do."

She didn't mean to rub it in, but it still stung. The fairgrounds in Intercourse were perfect for big auctions. This one would require four simultaneous auctions. All the brothers would be on platforms—except Declan. Instead, he'd be at home, doing what? Planting flowers? Filling in for Josie at the family store?

"Layla and Corrine and Bethel and Josie and Sherri and me will be there." Sadie ticked off the names on her chubby fingers. "And Jonah and Robbie and Judah and Rachelle and everybody."

Except the menfolk, of whom Declan was one. Pouring more alcohol in the wound.

They were raising the money for his bills. The very least he could do was volunteer. It was better than sitting at home, moping around.

Bethel would be there. Good. The bills were piling up for her family too. The least he could do was to help them as well.

Besides, he was no coward.

Chapter 23

Whoever decided Declan should be in charge of grilling the meat for the fundraiser plates had a twisted sense of humor. He used tongs to deftly flip the chicken quarters while trying to ignore how his mouth watered. The sizzling chicken, along with homemade spicy pork sausage links, spread out on three racks of the oversize grill, smelled delicious. The aroma drifted on a soft breeze across the parking lot in front of Hershbergers' Grocery Store. With any luck every customer headed to the store this fine first Saturday in May would smell it and stop at the white canopy where the fundraiser was well underway.

Too bad Declan wouldn't be joining them for a tasty plate of homemade food. He was still limited to soft foods. Better not to say anything or Mom would try to puree it for him. She was an expert now. Sadie called it Declan's baby food. She wanted to eat her food pureed, too, in solidarity. Never mind that chewing made eating more satisfactory.

"More chicken, Declan, more chicken." Speaking of Sadie. She skipped, did her version of a cartwheel, legs wonky, and hopped the last few feet to the area where the men had set up the grills and the smokers. Once again her prayer covering perched precariously to one side. Her glasses slid down her nose. "Miriam says they need more chicken and more sausage. And more pulled pork."

Declan held up two fingers and pointed at the chicken and sausage. "Got two." He jerked his thumb toward Enos and Aaron King. "Pulled pork."

"Mamm says you should carry the meat."

"You can't carry it?" He patted his sister's head.

"She says it too heavy."

"*It's* too heavy," he whispered.

"Jah. That."

Sadie had been instructed by her teacher to practice her English over the summer. Declan was helping. He'd also been avoiding approaching the canopy—or at least one volunteer working in it. He wasn't a coward, but neither was he a glutton for punishment. "You handle it fine."

"Not *and* the pulled pork." Sadie pushed her glasses up her nose. Her eyes were the same blue as the sky. "Besides, Mamm said."

And what Mom said went. "Fine." He pointed at the chicken. "When it's done."

His technique would involve dumping it and running without getting caught in Mom's matchmaking shenanigans, which would involve overly long conversations about nothing.

I'm not a coward.

Jah, you are.

Declan deposited mounds of chicken and sausage into a huge pan lined with paper towels to soak up excess grease and covered it with foil. He turned down the gas grill and closed the lid. With Sadie close on his heels, he made a stop at the Kings' smoker—not to delay his approach to the canopy, really. Seriously, no. He swiped a glance at the canopy while waiting for Aaron to load Sadie down with a pan of pulled pork ready to be served on oversize sourdough buns. A line of English and Plain customers snaked its way across the parking lot toward a playscape the Hershbergers had erected for their smallest shoppers.

The women would be far too busy for conversation. *Sei so gut, Gott.*

It was ridiculous to avoid Bethel. They were friends. They understood each other better than most. Maybe that's why his heart insisted on going where his head knew he shouldn't. It wasn't enough to be friends. He'd never wanted to be simply friends—not the entire time they'd been fellow students in school. He'd waited too long to get his act together, and now it was too late. He had no occupation and a more uncertain life expectancy than most.

"How are you doing?" Enos's low voice interrupted Declan's silent argument with himself. His gaze flicked from Declan back to the smoker. "Heard you had the surgery."

"I did." Declan settled the pan on their picnic table long enough to adjust the foil. "Doing okay."

"That's gut." Enos picked up tongs and a long-handled fork. "You're done then?"

"Nee. Radiation next."

He shrugged. "Hope it goes well."

"Danki."

"Gern gschehme." Enos went back to pulling apart a hefty chunk of meat.

With the exception of the few words they'd exchanged in front of Dr. Matthews's clinic in February, that was the most conversation Declan had ever had with Bethel's oldest brother. To say the man wasn't much of a talker was an understatement. Nor did he seem to have much of a sense of humor. Serious apparently ran in the family.

Which was fine. Declan was in no position to attempt to humor him into a smile.

He picked up his pan and, together with Sadie, strode to the canopy. Entering it was like diving into a beehive. It buzzed with women all simultaneously working and talking. The line still snaked across the asphalt parking lot. Saturdays were the busiest days at the grocery store. For customers who chose the pulled pork, the women cut rolls, assembled sandwiches, added pickles, and wrapped in a steady assembly line beginning with the Styrofoam plate that then went to others who added scoops of potato salad and coleslaw. Chicken and sausage were a combo alternative. Customers also had their choice of three kinds of pie, chocolate or vanilla cupcakes, or huge chocolate chip cookies. Iced tea or lemonade rounded out the ten-dollar offering.

Quite a bargain. Everything had been made and donated down to the plates and napkins, which meant every penny went into the medical relief fund.

He set the pan on the closest table and helped Sadie with hers. In and out. Easy-peasy.

"Suh, there you are." His mother touched his arm, forcing him to turn back. Frowning, she shook her finger at him. "Don't run off. Pop into the store and get us more ice, more cups, and another container of tea. We're keeping the tea in Martin's refrigerated case by the bottled water. You know where the ice is."

"Jah, ma'am. Right away."

"Don't get cheeky with me." She clucked like a mama hen robbed of her eggs. "Bethel, go with him, sei so gut. You can help carry."

"No need—"

"Hurry, run." Mom flapped her apron in the air. "Can't you see the line? We don't want to keep these hungry folks waiting, do we?"

Without a word, Bethel wiped her hands on a dish towel, squeezed between the prep tables, and traipsed out the back of the canopy. Adopting an exaggerated meek pose, Declan followed. "Not delicate, is she?"

"She means well." Bethel adopted a brisk pace. She entered the store two steps ahead of Declan. "You get the tea. I'll take care of the ice and the cups."

"Jah, ma'am."

Finally, she met his gaze. "Like your mamm said, don't get cheeky."

"Or snippy."

"I'm not snippy. Just busy. I don't want to leave the other women in the lurch. We've been super busy since eleven o'clock. People are so kind—"

"Or so hungry."

"True, but they can go home and eat for less."

"People like food someone else prepares," he whispered.

"We could use some more napkins too. Martin said to help ourselves to whatever we need."

"Fine."

"Fine." She pivoted smartly and turned into the picnic aisle.

Was this how friends acted? "Bethel."

She halted, then turned.

"Do you treat Hattie like this?"

"Like what?"

"Like she has cooties?"

"I'm not acting like anything." She picked up a package of paper plates, studied them, then replaced them on the shelf. She straightened boxes of plastic forks and knives. She chewed her lower lip, then heaved a noisy breath. "We're busy. This isn't the time or place."

Declan held up three fingers. "Home three weeks."

"That's funny. I haven't seen you anywhere except on the church pew."

"Friends usually visit when a friend has surgery." All this talking made his throat hurt, but he couldn't stop himself. She had said she wanted to be friends. Why didn't she act like one? "They send a card."

"It's different with Plain men and women." Red blotches worked their way up her neck and across her cheeks. "You know that as well as I do."

"You were sure we could be friends."

"Do we have to do this right now, in the middle of a grocery store?" Her trembling voice dropped to a whisper. "I'm sorry, I can't do this now."

"Richmond tomorrow." Declan touched his neck. "Radiation on Monday for seven weeks. *When* do you want to talk?"

"Seven weeks?" She put her hand to her mouth for a second, then let it drop. "You're not coming home for almost two months?"

Declan moved into the aisle with her, letting an elderly English woman pushing a cart pass. "Radiation five days a week. The doc says weekends are for resting and recovering."

"You're not going alone, are you?" She drew two steps closer. Her dark eyes filled with a warm sympathy that was a balm to Declan's sore heart and soul. "Where will you stay?"

"Worried about me?"

"Don't tease, Declan, sei so gut."

"With Aenti Joy and her mann." Declan's hoarse voice grated on his own ears. "They have a farm near Richmond."

"Will it hurt . . . the radiation?" Her hand crept out. Her fingers touched his.

Declan let his gaze sweep the crowded store. College students in shorts buying bags of pita chips and hummus. Moms with strollers. Plain women discussing the cost of cleaning supplies. Intertwining his fingers with Bethel's in the middle of a grocery store filled with Saturday midday shoppers was out of the question. He did it anyway. Her skin was warm and soft. "Doc says no. Side effects, though."

Bethel didn't need to know the details. The skin on his neck might blister or peel. He would likely experience mouth sores, dry mouth, trouble swallowing, and, of all things, hoarseness. As if he didn't have enough of that.

"And when it's over you'll be cancer free, ready to come home and get back to work?"

"That's the plan."

They didn't call it "cancer free" anymore. The radiation was designed to ferret out and destroy any cancer cells remaining after the surgery. But no doctor could guarantee there wouldn't be a recurrence. Declan faced follow-up scans and exams for years to come. Again, Bethel didn't need to know that.

"What aren't you telling me?"

"I'll be fine."

Katherine King came around the corner. "There you are, Dochder. Elizabeth says to bring more napkins and plastic silverware too."

Declan dropped Bethel's hand. In tandem they edged apart. "Can I write to you? Friends write, don't they?"

"Coming, Mamm." Bethel turned so her mother couldn't see her face. "Jah, sei so gut," she whispered. "I'll write to you too. I'll be thinking about you."

"About your friend."

"You keep saying that like it's a bad thing." Warring emotions—annoyance, concern, sympathy—flitted across her face. "Just take care of yourself. Do what the doctors tell you to do."

"I will."

"Promise?"

"Promise."

Even with her mother bearing down on them, Declan couldn't break away from Bethel's gaze. It held far more promise than her words. "Seven weeks."

"See you in seven weeks."

The promise in her eyes would hold him in good stead, no matter how bad the side effects were. Declan might not have a job or a future, but he had a reason to come home.

Chapter 24

 ethel held out her arms. "You can just hand it to me, please."

"Expecting a big check, I guess." The mail carrier grinned as he loaded Bethel's arms with a stack of mail. "Can't be bills or you wouldn't be standing out here by your mailbox, waiting for me to drive up."

"Thank you. Hoping for a letter." Bethel pulled the stack against her chest to keep the envelopes from plummeting to the ground. Surely Declan would've written by now. She'd been standing out in the warm May sun, sweating, every day for the last week. "Something besides junk, that's for sure."

"Good luck with that. It seems like 90 percent of what I deliver these days is pure junk."

"You got that right. Poor trees." Bethel shifted the mail to one side so she could use her other hand to return his jaunty wave. She forced herself to wait until he drove away in his U.S. Postal Service Jeep to sort through the stack. A seed catalog, *The Budget* newspaper, several pieces of junk mail, a Clinic for Special Children newsletter, and a letter from Mom's Mothers of Children with Physical Disabilities round-robin group.

Bethel flipped through the stack a second time. Nope. No letter from Declan. Nothing with a Richmond postmark.

It had been two weeks since Declan left to start his radiation treatments. Maybe the side effects were worse than he expected. Maybe the fatigue made it hard for him to muster the energy to write. He'd done a good job of downplaying these side effects, but Bethel now knew better. She'd gone to the library in Lee's Gulch and researched it on the internet. Fatigue, mouth sores, peeling or blistered skin, dry mouth, trouble swallowing, change of taste, and worsening hoarseness.

Still, the physical side effects weren't as worrisome as the mental and emotional ones. Claire's LGMD diagnosis had reinforced this lesson for Bethel. Claire tried to hide her depression. Bethel knew her sister too well to deny the changes in her once happy-go-lucky personality.

Losing his voice surely affected Declan in the same way. If only Bethel could write him a letter to tell him about her thoughts, how Claire's trials were similar, and how Bethel wanted to walk through this season with him.

But she couldn't. He had to write her first so she would have his address.

She could ask Declan's mother for the address. Would that be too forward? Would it be a flame to gasoline in Elizabeth's tendency to go overboard with matchmaking? Would it be inappropriate for a single Plain woman to write letters to a single Plain man?

The questions went round and round in her brain.

"That must be some awfully interesting junk mail."

Startled, Bethel dropped a slick oversize postcard from a company promising to replace their gutters cheaper than any other company in the entire state of Virginia. She swiveled. Dad stood on the cement porch in front of his warehouse shop. A smattering of sawdust decorated his fluffy gray beard. He'd stuck safety glasses on top of his straw hat. Whether he'd remember where they were later was questionable.

"I get the feeling you're waiting for something. I don't think it's a magazine or a sewing pattern."

"Just . . . a letter. It would be nice to get some real mail, that's all." Not a lie. It would be nice. Better not to tell Dad from whom Bethel wanted that letter. "We get so much junk mail. It's a ridiculous waste of a good tree."

As a furniture maker, Dad had a good understanding of the cost of lumber and the ebbing supply of harvestable timber.

"I agree with you, Dochder." Dad stretched and took a few steps out into the sunshine. The second week of May and the air had turned warm. Summer intended to make itself felt finally. "Maybe you should join one of those round-robin thingies like your mom does. Or maybe you should spend your spare time with friends who are right in front of you."

Friends who were right in front of her? "I do. Hattie and I are going fishing with the kinner tomorrow. We might even take them for a dip in the creek."

Getting Judah and Robbie down to the creek's rocky shoreline was an ordeal, but they loved fishing as much as they loved hunting. Claire liked to fish, but hunting was her favorite. She'd always been good with a rifle—better than Bethel, whose soft heart had a hard time taking creatures' lives. She tolerated fishing more, even though it wasn't her favorite activity. Liam and Melinda liked to do whatever the older kids did. If it made the buwe and Claire happy and got them outside in the fresh air and sunshine, Bethel would jump in to match their enthusiasm.

"I meant something fun for you and friends your age." Dad wiped his face with a semi-clean blue bandanna. Sawdust fluttered in a tepid breeze. "It's none of my business, but time is passing.

You're spending all your time working at the nursery or taking care of the kinner. Both are gut and honorable activities, but you must not let either stand in the way of your future as a fraa and mudder of your own kinner."

He'd been talking to Mom. Bethel picked up the postcard. She wrapped her arms around the mail to keep anything else from escaping. Not to avoid the conversation. It was time to start supper. Really. "I love working at the nursery. My earnings are needed to help pay the bills." She eased a few steps down the gravel road toward the house. "Being here to take care of the kinner is a blessing for me. And for our whole family, I hope."

"I reckon you're right, but that don't mean you can neglect your future."

"I know. Believe me, I know."

"I'm not spying on you, don't get me wrong, but I know you don't leave the house in the evening." Dad fell into step next to Bethel instead of going back inside. "Makes me wonder if you've run off all the men of courting age."

"Run them off?" Bethel's voice rose. She scrambled to bring it back down. This was not a conversation she wanted to have with her father. And this wasn't a subject she would expect him to broach. What was going on here? "How would you know if I go out in the late evening?"

"I can't sleep."

He sounded matter-of-fact, but insomnia had to bother a man who worked as hard as he did.

"Is this a new thing?"

He didn't answer immediately. His boots crunched on the gravel. Ginger and three of her siblings woofed as they engaged in rough-and-tumble in the yard. An airplane's engines rumbled overhead.

"Nee."

Leave it to a man to think one syllable was an adequate answer. "Why can't you sleep?"

"If I knew the answer to that, I'd know how to fix it."

"Are you worried about Claire?"

"Worrying is a sin."

He could go on and on about Bethel's courting or lack thereof, but Dad couldn't share his feelings about the trials faced by the entire family, especially the children. "I still worry. I guess that makes me the only sinner in the house."

"Point taken." His stride slowed. He scooped up Ginger and gave the puppy a brisk scratching behind her ears. "It does no gut to fret, but the minute I lay down at night, the thoughts begin to pester me. No matter how tired I am, I can't fall asleep."

"I have the same problem."

"You shouldn't. They aren't your kinner."

"They're my brieder and schweschdre."

"We'll share their care until your mudder and I no longer can."

"Then those of us without the disease will take care of those with it."

"As it should be."

"So why worry?"

Dad blew out air noisily. "Because we have three now, but there's nothing to say there won't be more with Liam and Melinda. How will you and Enos take care of them and your own kinner?"

"We'll manage." Now Bethel was the one not opening up about her true feelings. This was her chance to bridge the divide with her dad. To reverse the order of daughter and father. To offer him comfort. "Not to be full of hochmut, but I think I do a gut job of taking care of the buwe. Enos is solid too. He doesn't say much, but he loves his brieder and schweschdre. He won't consider it a burden. Neither will I. Sleep well knowing that, Dat."

"You do a gut job. Maybe too gut a job. Know that your mamm and I want you to have a life of your own as well. Never forget that."

"I won't, but isn't it all our jobs to take care of our family? Even if it means making sacrifices?"

"Sacrifices, jah, but shared sacrifices. It's not just on you. The community will help. Remember that."

"I will. I promise."

Dad's hand came up and touched her sleeve for the briefest of moments. "You make my heart happy." His words were steeped in harnessed emotion. "Your mudder and I know we can count on you and Enos. We try very hard to see Gott's hand in our trials. We know He brings gut from all things. We fall short, though, when we question His plan."

"How can we not? It's hard to fathom why." Bethel clenched her jaw to keep the questions from spewing out. *Breathe in, breathe out. Breathe in, breathe out.* "Gott forgive me for my stupidity."

"It's not stupidity." Dad clomped up the steps to the porch in front of her. He gently dumped Ginger into one of the rocking chairs. The puppy squeaked in protest, jumped down, and trotted away. Chuckling, Dad held open the screen door so Bethel could pass through ahead of him. "It's human sin. Our brains aren't able to understand such a grand plan. We don't have to understand—we just have to hang on for the ride."

"My hands hurt from clutching the reins." Bethel laid the mail in a neat pile on Dad's desk. She turned to face him. "Yours must too. You've been doing this a lot longer."

"I talk to Bart when it really gets out of hand." Dad kept moving, headed down the hallway to the kitchen, and Bethel followed him.

"You could do the same. He would have a gut word to help you with your situation. You need your sleep too."

Her gaze pinned to Dad's back, Bethel halted. "What situation would that be?"

"I admitted my worry to you. Daeds don't do that. They don't like their kinner to know they're plagued by doubts. I thought you might do the same."

She'd walked right into that one. Bethel picked up speed until she passed her father and entered the kitchen first. "I'm pouring a glass of tea. Want some?"

"So it's like that."

"I'm fine."

"That's why you've been staking out the mailbox, hoping to see a letter from Declan Miller."

Not Dad too. Bethel needed to work on harnessing her expressions. "Declan is a friend. He's sick. I want to know he's okay. I remember when Mammi had radiation. It wasn't easy. I want to send him a card, but I can't until I have an address."

"It's not possible for grown Plain men and women to be friends." Dad's statement lacked oomph. His faint smile belied it as well. "I reckon your mamm has an address. She'd be thrilled to give it to you."

No doubt about that. "I'll ask her. Do you want tea?"

"I'll take it to go." Dad stuck his hand in the cookie jar and pulled out a handful of oatmeal-raisin cookies. "Put some ice in it. I need to get back to work. The Schultzes want their table and chairs this week. I told them we'd deliver them tomorrow."

Bethel poured the tea into a tall travel mug, added sugar and lemon juice, and carried it to her father. "What would you think if a single Plain woman wrote a letter to a single Plain man? Is there anything wrong with that?"

Dad took a long swig of his tea. He held up the travel mug and seemed to contemplate its contents. "Sweet and sour, just like life. If a man and a woman were courting, a person would expect them to exchange letters to stay in touch."

"What if one of them is sick and the other one just wants to express her—or his—concern for him . . . or her?"

Dad finished chewing a big bite of cookie. He cleared his throat. "Your mamm has Declan's address. She asked Elizabeth for it so she could send him a get-well card. Elizabeth told her they're starting a card shower, announcing it in *The Budget* and everything. They reckon he's feeling homesick up there in Richmond. He likely enjoys getting mail. I reckon everyone should send him one."

In other words, no one would think twice about it if Bethel joined the crowd. "Danki, Dat." She planted a quick peck on her father's cheek. "I'm glad Mamm's sending Declan a card."

"What was that for?" He pretended to rub his check clean with his sleeve. "Have you gone daft, maedel?"

"Just happy you're my daed, that's all."

"Humph."

Tea in one hand, cookies in the other, he stalked from the kitchen. He would never admit it, but her dad was pleased. His small grin and red face said so.

Bethel followed him as far as the living room. She veered toward the desk, took a seat, and opened the drawer where her mother kept her writing supplies for her round-robin letter group. Her familiar scrawl appeared on a sticky note attached to a box of assorted greeting cards. It had Declan's name on it and a Richmond address.

Her heart did a strange hippity-hop-hop. Bethel rummaged through the cards for just the right one—not too syrupy-sweet, not too impersonal. She settled on one with a colorful drawing of a sunrise over a cabin. A "hoping for quick healing / can't wait until you come home" message inside.

Two sheets of stationery—no, better make it three—and Mom's favorite bright blue pen completed Bethel's supplies. She slipped upstairs to her bedroom where she deposited them on the small desk situated in front of one of the floor-to-ceiling windows. She'd have to wait until after supper to write.

That would give her time to think about what to say. The address and stationery were only half the battle. Striking the right tone in the letter would require all the finesse of a woman needle-pointing an intricate tablecloth design.

Bethel was terrible at needlepoint.

Chapter 25

Multitasking. A fancy way of describing what all women, especially mothers, had always done—half a dozen tasks simultaneously. Bethel stuck Judah's straw hat on his head. She handed a wet washrag to Melinda, whose hands were filthy. While Melinda pretended to wipe them clean, Bethel pulled a stack of bologna and cheddar cheese sandwiches from the cooler parked on the ground a few yards from the creek and doled them out.

Robbie whooped when she handed him his, along with a bag of potato chips. His face was pinkish red, and they'd only been fishing for an hour. Mom would have her hide if the kids came home with a sunburn instead of fish for supper.

"After we eat, we should head back to the house." Bethel tugged the water jug closer so she could pour water into the plastic cups she'd lined up on a flat rock to her right. "I still have to finish the crib quilt I'm making for Caitlin and Jason's bopli."

Nothing like being a month late. Hattie rolled her eyes. "Like there's a big rush. Retta will be in school before you finish."

Bethel's quilt making was on par with her needlepoint. That was to say, average to poor.

"Nee, not yet." Melinda spoke through a mouthful of sandwich. "I want to swim with the fishes. Maybe I can catch one then."

"Me too. Me too." Liam rummaged in the cooler and came up with a green Granny Smith apple. "We just got here. We can't go yet."

"I told Mom I'd make hush puppies and sweet potato fries to go with the fish."

"We haven't caught enough fish to feed two cats, let alone the whole family." Judah's face darkened. "I haven't even caught one."

He was right. So far Robbie had snagged a channel catfish, a sunfish, and a small bass, while Claire had managed to hook two good-sized smallmouth bass. The rest of them were coming up fishless. "I just don't want you to get sunburned."

"Ha. You're the one with the red nose." Hattie rose. She tossed a chunk of bologna in the vicinity of a turtle sunning on a nearby rock. He lost no time—considering he was a turtle—in gobbling it up. "Besides, it's just hot enough for a swim. My sweaty feet are clamoring for a good soak."

Bethel had promised swimming. She hadn't thought that one through. The swimming logistics for the boys were even more challenging than getting them down the narrow, uneven path strewn with rocks, pine cones, and clumps of weeds. Claire's metal walker with neon-green tennis balls on the two front legs was worse. She'd run out of energy to lift and set, lift and set, long before they'd run out of path. She tripped over a rock, stubbed her toe, and nearly toppled over by the time they finally arrived at their favorite fishing spot.

Bethel didn't want Claire to think she couldn't still do the things she loved. Other reasons for not swimming could be had. "The water's probably still cold. The weather's just started to warm up. It's not really summer yet."

"No way. It's May." Claire dropped her half-eaten sandwich in the trash bag. She made a feeble attempt to brush away the flies after her peanut butter celery. "I'm so hot and sweaty. The water will feel gut."

"You didn't bring a change of clothes."

"I'm just going to wade. I won't get completely wet."

Bethel had heard that one before. "First we fish. Then we wade. Otherwise, we'll scare away the fish."

The creek's depth varied from shallow to neck deep with a rocky, uneven bottom. The current ran at a good clip, bringing with it flathead catfish, sunfish, crappie, and a variety of bass, both small- and largemouth.

Hattie telegraphed *Sorry about that* with her eyes. "Your schweschder is right. You've hardly eaten anything, Claire. Have some of my chicken salad sandwich. It's yummy."

"I'm not hungry." Claire had been listless for days. Bethel's hope that fishing would improve her mood hadn't been fulfilled. Her sister stood. Her skinny arms dangled at her sides. "But danki."

Her lack of appetite was catching. Bethel stuck her sandwich back in its wax-paper wrapping. She swallowed some water. "How about watermelon? It's cold."

"After we swim."

"Brownies?"

"After we swim." The kids, Hattie included, chorused together the last time. Then giggled.

Seriously. If they could wait on a chocolate dessert, there was no hope of convincing them to eat anything now. "Fine, fine. Your job is to each catch at least two more fish, nice big fish, not those little sunfish. Including you, Hattie. Once you've done that, we'll cool off in the water. *If* you keep your hats on and *if* you let me slather on some more sunscreen."

Everyone agreed to her demands, but not without some good-natured grumbling regarding the sunscreen. When they were suitably covered with white goopy stuff, they went back to baiting their hooks with minnows.

Which meant Bethel still had time to write her letter. She yawned widely at the thought. She'd been up well past ten o'clock the previous evening trying to write that letter. It was a disaster, a fiasco, a . . . any other word that came to mind. Two hours of word wrangling and most of the paper had ended up as crumpled balls in her trash can. The kids' steady chatter like distant music, Bethel picked a loblolly pine several yards from the shoreline for her writing spot. She used an old notebook like a clipboard and laid a slightly wrinkled piece of stationery on it.

Where had she left off? Two pages of gobbledygook meandering all over the place without saying anything of importance. He would think she was a goof. Maybe she should tell a joke. Bethel chewed on the end of her pencil. Did she know any jokes? She scratched her forehead. She swatted at a mosquito. Surely she knew one joke.

Nothing. "Hattie, tell me a joke."

Her fishing pole in one hand, Hattie swiveled. Surprise bloomed on her red, damp face. "Are you kidding? You poo-poo my jokes all the time."

"Just one. One good one."

Hattie scooted around so she faced Bethel. She wrinkled her forehead. "I'm thinking, I'm thinking. Hmm, okay, this is a gut one. What does a horse say when it falls?"

"I don't know."

"Help me. I've fallen and I can't giddy-up."

Melinda hopped around, howling with laughter. Liam joined her. Judah giggled. Robbie snorted. "Another one, another one!"

"Nee, one was enough—"

"What do cows like to read?"

Bethel pretended to sigh. "What do they like to read?"

"Cattle-logs."

"What?"

"You know, c-a-t-t-l-e-logs."

"That was bad." Judah's line jerked. "Wait, wait, I think I have a fish. Don't tell another one until I get him."

He did indeed have a fish. A nice smallmouth bass that likely weighed a couple of pounds.

"One more and then we're done." Hattie grinned. "I still have fish to catch."

"One more."

"Why can't your nose be twelve inches long?"

"I'm afraid to ask."

"Because then it would be a foot."

Judah, Robbie, and Claire groaned in unison. Melinda and Liam jumped up and down and hooted. Bethel simply shook her head. "Okay. That's gut. Catch your fish."

"Why do you need jokes?"

"Just you never mind."

"Jokes for the jokester. You want to impress Declan."

Not impress him, just not bore him to tears. "Fish."

Even if the jokes were terrible, they might make him smile. Bethel used all three. She wrote about the fishing trip, about the chicken coop falling over during a thunderstorm earlier in the week, and about the apple pie the puppies demolished before she had a chance to serve it to her family.

"Ach nee!" Claire's startled shriek split the air.

Her heart suddenly banging against her rib cage, Bethel jumped to her feet. Her sister's walker lay half in the creek. Choking and coughing, Claire floundered facedown in the water.

"Schweschder!" Melinda took a flying leap into the water before anyone could stop her.

"Nee, nee!"

Bethel reached the shore even before Hattie, although she was closer. The two of them leaped into the water. It was icy cold. Her dress's long skirt weighed Bethel down. She struggled to come up for air. Where was Claire? Melinda?

The current dragged her downriver. Bethel broke the surface. She gasped for air. There. She grabbed Melinda around the waist and hoisted her up. The little girl coughed and sputtered. "Claire, Claire!"

"I've got her." Hattie struggled to stand in water up to her chin. "Stand up, Claire. Come on, maedel, help me out."

Claire was younger but almost as tall as Hattie. "I can't get my balance." Claire went under and came up sputtering. "My legs won't hold me."

Her legs were weak but not useless. She was panicked. Melinda cried out and wiggled. Bethel tightened her grip. "She's fine, she's okay." Bethel struggled to move against the current toward Hattie and Claire. "Everyone's fine."

"I've got her." Hattie pulled Claire upright a second time and began dragging her toward the shore. "Let's get out of this cold water."

Claire sank into the water yet again. She came up sputtering. "I hate this. My legs are so weak."

"When you're using a wheelchair, come talk to us," Robbie yelled from the water's edge. He'd rolled his chair as close as he dared. Judah was right there with him, holding Liam in his lap. "It's not so bad. People wait on you hand and foot."

"Yeah, and Mamm brings you cookies hot out of the oven," Judah joined in. "Dat bought a new chess set for us. We're spoiled. You will be too. You already have your own room."

They weren't spoiled. They were trying to make Claire feel better. They were sweet brothers. Bethel slogged onto the bank with Melinda. She dumped the girl onto the closest towel. Then she turned to help Hattie with Claire. Her sister collapsed in a heap next to Melinda. "The buwe are right. I know it's hard. I can't imagine how hard, but you'll adjust." She squatted and tucked a big, fluffy beach towel over Claire. "Sit here in the sun and let it warm you up. What were you thinking? Jumping in the water on your own."

"I caught my two fish. I was hot." Claire pushed wet, tangled hair from her face. Her prayer *kapp* was missing. Her teeth chattered. Her lips were blue. "Besides, I didn't jump in. I stumbled and fell in."

Like that was better. Bethel spun her gaze across the creek. No prayer cap. "You should've said something. I would've helped you. Hattie would've helped you."

"I'm not a bopli. I've been in the creek tons of times, millions of times."

"Not since—"

"Not since my legs stopped working?"

Bethel wrapped a towel around Melinda, who put her arm around Claire as if making sure she didn't decide to jump into the water again. Bethel patted her hair and face dry. "Claire, you need a little help, that's all. We can all use help. So what if you got wet? Wasn't that the idea?"

"I fell."

"And we were here to help you up. That's what family does. We take care of each other."

"I hate this."

"Don't you think we hate it?" Judah spoke up. "I'd rather run the bases than watch from the sidelines. I'd rather climb trees and jump off into the water. But it doesn't do no gut to fuss about it."

"It won't change a thing. That's what Dat says. Being whiny doesn't help," Robbie chimed in. "It just makes you miserable."

"I know I shouldn't complain. I got more years of running around than you did." Claire swiped snot from her cheek with her wet sleeve. "I'm just a big bopli."

"Nee. We've had time to get used to it." Judah pulled his fishing line from the water and laid the rod aside. "We'll give you another week or two—maybe three—before we start nagging you about it."

"Danki." Claire's bedraggled expression bordered on a smile. Not quite, but almost. "I'll try not to make more work for you, Beth."

"Just promise you won't scare the dickens out of me." Bethel handed her a napkin. "Wipe your face." She turned to Melinda. "And you, maedel, what were you thinking?"

"I wanted to save my schweschder."

"That's a nice thought, but wait until you're tall enough and a gut swimmer before you go on any rescue missions in the future."

"How was the water?" Liam plopped down next to Claire. "I wanted to get in, but now I don't know."

"It was cold." Claire tugged the blanket tighter. "I think I'll stick to fishing."

Hattie picked up Claire's rod and handed it to her. "Your schweschder is right. The water's too cold for swimming. I reckon I can catch another fish before you do. Before you buwe do."

And just like that, the tension faded and the kids went back to good-natured competition. Bethel took off her waterlogged sneakers and socks. She wrung out her apron and skirt. The wind blew. The tree limbs dipped and bowed. The leaves danced. At this rate her clothes would dry quickly. The adrenaline buzz of fear and worry gradually fizzled. *Danki, Gott, that Claire isn't any worse for wear.*

Which was more than she could say for her letter. In her mad dash to rescue Claire, Bethel had scattered the stationery across the damp ground. Her shoe print decorated one sheet. Mud obscured her handwriting on another.

Barefoot, Bethel padded through the trees, scooping up the sheets. What could she say to Declan about her day now? That her sister took a header in the creek because Bethel had been busy writing a letter to him? That Claire's decline was breaking her heart? That Bethel's job had grown and her shoulders were bowed under the weight? How hard it was to care for a sibling with a debilitating disease? How much harder—or maybe easier—it would be if it were her own child?

Declan didn't need to hear her sob stories. He was walking through his own season of trials at this moment. What he needed was her support—everyone's support.

She could start with finishing her letter. Bethel chewed on her lower lip. Starting now. Pencil. Where was her pencil? Not with her pack of stationery. Not next to her travel mug of water. It couldn't have gone far. Bethel crawled around on her knees hunting for it.

"What are you doing?"

She craned her head to peer up. Her forehead wrinkled, hands on her hips, Hattie stared down at her. "You remind me of a crazed squirrel searching for acorns."

"I'm trying to find my pencil. I'm going to finish this letter if it kills me."

"A bit dramatic, aren't you? What's this behind your ear, my dear?" Harriet reached down and tugged something from Bethel's hair. She held out the pencil. "You're starting to scare me."

Bethel snatched the pencil from her friend's hand. "You and me both. Can this be our secret?"

"Are you going to tell your mamm and dat about Claire's adventure—I guess you'd call it a misadventure?"

"I reckon I have to. They need to know her disease is progressing. They'll want to take her back to the clinic."

Harriet tsked. "Somehow they have to encourage her to slow down and take care before something worse happens than a splash in the creek."

"We can't ever let our guard down—"

"I've got one, I've got one!" Judah whooped and hollered. "It's a big one."

At least someone was having a good time.

Chapter 26

A person could get a fat head with such a big stack of mail lying on the table next to his supper plate. As if it was a sign of popularity. Declan plopped into his chair and reached for it. The different-colored envelopes suggested cards. This had to be his mother's doing. She probably stuck an announcement in *The Budget* asking for a card shower like Declan was a poor kid laid up with a broken leg or a widower missing his newly passed wife. She shouldn't have done that. He didn't need folks feeling sorry for him. He was fine. The sore, blistered skin on his throat, the fatigue, and the mouth sores begged to differ. Radiation wasn't awful, but neither was it a picnic.

"You got yourself a pile of mail, don't 'cha?" His cousin Remy squeezed into a chair across from him. The twelve-year-old wrinkled his nose and sniffed. "I ain't never got that much mail. Aren't 'cha gonna open it?"

"If you're going to speak English, at least speak it right." Remy's older sister, Jennifer, who'd graduated from school in April at age fourteen and therefore felt herself to be all grown up, nudged her brother with her elbow. She set a bowl of mashed potatoes on the table next to an enormous platter of breaded pork chops. "It's none of your beeswax if Declan opens his mail. Maybe he wants to do it in private."

"I'm just saying you'd think he was dying or something—"

"You just shush your mouth, Remy Hershberger."

"It's okay. I'd rather he be honest than pussyfoot around the way most adults do." Declan managed a grin despite the way his own voice grated on his ears. "People are just trying to be nice."

His palliative care social worker called it "being supportive." The brochure she'd given him saved him from having to ask the embarrassing question: What did *palliative* mean? *Palliative care is specialized medical care that focuses on providing patients relief from pain and other symptoms of a serious illness, no matter the diagnosis or stage of disease. Palliative care teams aim to improve the quality of life for both patients and their families.*

Not to be confused with hospice care, which made a dying patient comfortable in the last days of his life. Declan didn't need hospice care. Not yet, anyway. *Danki, Gott.*

What palliative care really meant was another medical appointment in another building, more paperwork, more endless questions, more people asking him if he was okay, if he needed anything . . . until he wanted to run screaming from the building. If he could scream, which he couldn't. A little less support and a little more alone time spent outdoors digging in the dirt and planting vegetables would be much more helpful.

Neither of his cousins would understand any of this English stuff. Jennifer was still picking at her brother. "He's old enough to know how to keep his mouth shut instead of sticking his foot in it, boot and all."

"I'm sorry." Remy fiddled with the knife and fork next to his plate. "I didn't mean nothin' by it."

"Don't worry about it."

"You're not dying from the cancer, are you?"

"Nee." Not anytime soon, God willing. "Not planning on it, anyway."

"Is the cancer why you don't have a special friend?"

"How do you know he doesn't have a special friend?" Jennifer's exasperated sigh expressed exactly Declan's feelings on having this topic come up in conversation again. Even his kid cousin thought about these things. Was there anyone who didn't?

Jennifer lifted Remy's hat and let it flop back on his head, covering his pale blue eyes. "Again, it's not any of your beeswax."

She did have a way with words. Jennifer and Remy bickered all the time. It made Declan feel more at home. Besides, he didn't have a special friend. Not exactly. Still, the suggestion propelled him to sort through the cards. The return addresses were mostly from the outskirts of Lee's Gulch. But also from family in Bird-in-Hand, Strasburg, Intercourse, and Ephrata in Pennsylvania. Even other parts of the country. Plain folks were like that. Any of the ones northwest of Lee's Gulch could be from Bethel. The Kings' exact address was anyone's guess. The Plain families all lived down the road from each other. No need to know house numbers.

Remy grabbed a purple envelope. "This one is heavy. I bet it has money in it. Sometimes people send money when they know you're doctoring—"

"Give me that." Aunt Joy snatched the envelope from Remy with her free hand and handed it to Declan without missing a beat as she placed a basket of rolls on the table. "The bu has yet to learn proper respect for the possessions of others. Remy, go wash your hands. The backs too. They're filthy."

Remy was right, though. Declan's aunt Millie in Bird-in-Hand had included a bookmark, two ten-dollar bills, and a coupon for Oreo cookies in a card featuring a cardinal on a tree branch. *Treat yourself* was all she'd written inside.

"Millie has a big heart." Despite her words for Remy, Aunt Joy had the same gleam of curiosity in her hazel eyes. "Anything from your mamm?"

"Probably. I'll open them after supper."

"Gut idea." Aunt Joy couldn't quite hide her disappointment. Everyone loved to get mail, even if it was one step removed. "Food's getting cold."

No need to be stingy. After managing to eat potatoes, gravy, creamed corn, and a helping of homemade applesauce Aunt Joy had made just for him, Declan opened the cards and shared the contents with his extended family while the girls cleared the table and washed and dried the dishes. He read the tidbits aloud while his youngest cousin, Carly, counted the bills. By the time he got to the last one, which was from a rural route Lee's Gulch address, Carly was up to $172.

Some of his younger relatives had sent chewing gum, hard candies, playing cards, and crossword puzzle paperbacks.

"People are so generous . . ." A thick folded sheaf of paper fell from the last card featuring a sunrise over a rustic cabin. Declan paused. He unfolded the paper, pushing aside pages to see the signature. Bethel had signed her name in a compact, angular script. Declan stood. "I think I'll walk off this gut food before I turn in."

"Don't you want to take the money with you?" Carly held up the bills in one hand and a pile of change sent by youngsters in the other. "You don't want it to get lost."

"Would you mind putting it in my room for me? With the cards?"

"I'll make sure she does." That same curious glint in her eyes, Aunt Joy dried her hands on a dish towel. "You didn't eat enough to need a walk. I'll leave a snack out for you to eat later."

Again, generous. Declan tossed his thanks over his shoulder as he headed for the door. It took less than five minutes to get to the spot he had in mind. A stand of statuesque loblolly pines offered shade and a quiet space where no one but the flies and mosquitoes would find him. He picked one of the older trees—more than a hundred feet tall and its scaly bark a gray-red color—as a backrest. First he brushed away the rusty-brown pine cones. Sitting on their sharp spines would not be fun. He swished around the aromatic pine needles to make a comfortable cushion. He settled down, back against the trunk, and inhaled. *Stop procrastinating.*

Dear Declan,

I got your address from my mamm. I hope you don't mind me writing. We'd talked about it, but I never heard from you. It worried me. I know. We're not supposed to worry. I long to set a better example, but my humanness is showing, as usual.

Anyway, now that I'm writing, I don't know what to say. Isn't that silly? I can't imagine anything about my life is interesting enough to scribble it in a letter to a man who has so much on his mind. On the other hand, maybe it will take your mind off your troubles. If you have troubles. I'm not suggesting you do. I can't help but wonder why you haven't written. Which makes me imagine all sorts of bad things.

Not that you have any obligation to write me.

Seriously. This is the worst letter I've ever written. I'm tempted to tear it up and start over. (Which I've done several times already.) Only then, what would I say? Am I going around in circles? Well, it's best that you know how ridiculous I am now rather than later. If there is a later. Not that you won't be around, but that you'll see what a terrible letter-writer I am and decide to have nothing more to do with me.

Laughing, Declan dropped the letter in his lap. He laughed so hard his gut hurt. He had to wipe his eyes with his sleeve. In all likelihood Bethel wasn't trying to be funny, but she was funny. Cute. Sweet. And funny.

She'd discovered the reason Declan hadn't written first. He didn't know what to say. How could he write her about the way the radiation side effects kept him from sleeping at night or about his fears that he would never call an auction again? His nightmares that the mask he wore during the treatments was stuck on his face and wouldn't come off? His fear that he'd go through all this treatment only to have the cancer recur? The way his imagination went wild late at night painting pictures of what his life would be like after treatment?

Bethel had her own worries. Maybe she'd come up with a way to overcome them.

Slapping away a buzzing fly, Declan picked up the letter.

What does a horse say when it falls?

"I don't know."

Help me. I've fallen and I can't giddy-up.

Jokes. She'd resorted to jokes. Bad ones. The second one about *cattle-logs* was worse. No doubt provided by Hattie. They had the ginger-headed woman's fingerprints all over them. Still, Declan laughed. Sometimes jokes were so bad that a person couldn't help but laugh.

Bethel was trying so hard. He should've written to her too. He would. As soon as he finished reading her letter.

Today Hattie and I took the kinner fishing at the creek. We were quite the procession with two wheelchairs and a walker. I carried the water jug and Hattie carried the cooler of food. The buwe propped the fishing rods across their chairs' arms, and Liam and Melinda carried the bait: minnows. Everyone caught at least one fish and Robbie caught four. He was on a roll. We had enough for a fish fry for supper. I made hush puppies and sweet potato fries. Mom made her coleslaw and onion rings. We had quite the feast.

It truly sounded like a feast. Declan's mouth watered. When was the last time he ate real food? Food that had to be chewed. A steak. In a minute he'd be slobbering. *Stop torturing yourself.* He swatted a mosquito and went back to the letter.

I wish that was all that happened on our fishing expedition, but it wasn't. Claire tripped and fell into the water. Melinda decided to dive in and "rescue" her. I took my eyes off them for a few minutes to work on this letter. Then she's hollering and splashing and Melinda is in the water after her. I went after Melinda and Hattie grabbed Claire. Claire couldn't right herself. Her skirt and apron were wrapped around her legs. They're getting weaker faster than Robbie's and Judah's did. She's frustrated and sad. Which makes me frustrated and sad. And guilty. I feel like I let her down. I don't want to wrap her in a protective cocoon too soon, but neither do I want her to be hurt. I should've been watching her.

I can't watch them every single second of every single day. Can I? Is that how Mamm and Dat feel? Do they wonder and worry about how well we'll take care of their kinner when they're gone? They needn't worry. Enos and I will do everything we can for them. And, Gott willing, Liam and Melinda.

I know you understand what I'm saying. You pretend to be a silly clown, but I see a deep well of seriousness buried under your jokes. I think you want to be liked and you think being funny will make people like you. The fact that you want to be liked is sweet. ~~I do like you. I wish you were here.~~

She'd scratched out those last two sentences, but Declan could still read them. Why would she try to remove them? If only he could be there to ask her. Homesickness enveloped him. He missed Sadie and Matilda the Cat and his horse and buggy and the auctions that were going on without him. He missed Mom's flapjacks and blackberry syrup, her biscuits, butter, and sorghum, her lemon meringue pie.

Aunt Joy was a good cook, but Mom's food was familiar and homey. All he had to do was walk into the kitchen and smell her lasagna cooking and he immediately felt better.

One final paragraph in Bethel's letter:

I reckon you're anxious to return home. I'll pray for quick and complete healing. That you'll be able to get back to your first love: auctioneering. If that's Gott's will for you. And if it's not, that you'll make peace with it.

That was exactly how Bethel should pray, but it didn't make the sentiment any easier to swallow. No pun intended.

She signed the letter *Your friend, Bethel King.*

Like Declan wouldn't be sure which Bethel had written him. *Your friend.*

If she was just a friend, would he miss her this much? Would he think about her first thing when he woke up in the morning and last thing before he fell asleep at night? Would he wonder what she'd think of his surgeon or his oncologist or the way his voice sounded these days?

Would she be in his thoughts morning, noon, and night?

It didn't seem likely.

Chapter 27

*F*inally. Peace. Quiet. Solitude. Bethel turned the flame up
on the propane lamp in the living room. She had the place
to herself. Stories read and prayers said, Melinda and Liam went
to bed not long after supper. Bethel and Mom helped Judah and
Robbie with their bedtime rituals. They settled down after a bit.
Mom and Dad worked on a five-thousand-piece Noah's Ark puzzle
for another hour. An hour and six minutes, to be exact. Staring at
the clock didn't make time move any faster, it turned out. Neither
did reading the latest Kathleen Fuller novel—as much as Bethel
liked the author's stories.

She settled into the rocking chair next to the open windows. A
warm late May breeze did little to cool the room. It didn't matter.
Bethel turned the envelope over on the palm of her hand. The
handwriting was a surprisingly neat script. Somehow she'd imagined it would be sloppy and all over the place, written in a rush
like the man. She smoothed her fingers over the envelope. Finally,
after five weeks, Declan had written.

Enough with the anticipation. Bethel ripped open the envelope.
She slid out the paper. Two sheets, one-sided. Not bad. Not long,
but not bad.

Dear friend.

He would start with that. His little poke in her side.

I'm sorry—

An anguished shriek broke the silence. Big, heartrending sobs followed.

Claire.

Bethel shot from the chair. She jerked open the door to her sister's new bedroom. Claire sat upright in the double bed. Her eyes were wide. Tears rolled down her cheeks. She clutched a pillow in both arms. "Ach, Beth, it was awful, just awful."

"I'm here." Bethel whipped over to the bed. She tossed the letter on the side table and scooted onto the mattress so she could get close enough to put her arm around Claire. "What was awful? What happened?"

"Light the lamp, sei so gut. I don't like the dark. It's too dark."

Claire had never been afraid of the dark, not even as a toddler. Bethel did as her sister asked. Then she crawled back under the sheet. "What has you so upset?"

"I had a bad dream." Claire rubbed her eyes with her fists. "It was so real. I heard Melinda screaming. She was in the creek. I ran—I could still run fast and hard—to the water. She was drowning. She was drowning, and I couldn't save her."

"It was just a nightmare." Bethel rubbed her sister's back. "It wasn't real."

"I know, but it seemed so real. I jumped into the water and then my legs stopped working." Claire's voice broke. "It was just like the day we went fishing. My dress was so heavy. It got all twisted around my legs. I couldn't move them. My arms were heavy. Everything weighed a ton. She was drowning, and I couldn't do a thing to help her. Then I was drowning."

The words came faster, half garbled by the sobs. "I tried to breathe. The water filled my mouth and my nose. I sank and sank deeper and deeper. I could see Melinda floating, her eyes open and staring . . ." Claire buried her face in Bethel's shoulder.

Bethel hugged her sister close, rocking her gently. "Just a nightmare, just a bad dream. A very bad dream. You're awake now. You're warm and dry in your bed. Melinda's upstairs sleeping."

Deep, dreamless sleep, Gott, sei so gut.

A nightmare wasn't surprising after what Claire had been through. Bethel rocked and rocked. Gradually, Claire's sobs quieted. She relaxed against Bethel. Finally she raised her head. "I'm such a big bopli. I know it, but I can't seem to stop myself."

"You're not a bopli. You're going through something hard. The grief of it, the hurt, has to come out somewhere."

Bethel pulled away long enough to snatch a box of tissues from the nightstand. She handed it to Claire. Her sister tugged one from the box, sopped up tears, and blew her nose loudly.

"It's even worse when I dream I can run. I wake up and it breaks my heart all over again." Claire grabbed a clean tissue and mopped her face. "I can't be left alone with the kinner. If something bad happens, I won't be able to save them. I can't even get them out of the house, let alone drive a buggy."

"We'll take care of the kinner together. There're lots of us." Bethel smoothed Claire's hair from her face. "We have big families. None of us has to do it alone. We have each other."

"You don't want to spend your life taking care of me." Claire pulled away. She shredded the tissue with shaking hands. "You'll get married and have your own kinner. So will Enos. I'm praying every day this doesn't happen to Liam or Melinda. Let me be the last one to get it."

"I do want to spend my life taking care of you, Robbie, and Judah. I have room for all of you and my own kinner."

So why had she been so hesitant to forge a bond with a Plain man like Declan? He'd been brought up with the same beliefs. He loved his sister Sadie and would care for her if given the chance. He'd argue with his siblings over who would be her caregiver when his parents passed. Why did she underestimate him?

Because of the cancer. It came down to the cancer. *O ye of little faith.*

However God chose to heal Declan—here or in heaven—Declan should have a chance to love and be loved.

No doubt. But should it be with a woman with Bethel's genes?

Gott, I'm so confused. Help me in my confusion, in my doubt, in my uncertainty.

The prayer of a weak person, but the best she could do.

"I know. I just hate being a burden." Claire slid down on the bed so her head lay on her pillow. She pulled the sheet up around her skinny shoulders. Her voice had grown sleepy. "I can't imagine not being able to carry my bopli from his cradle to the kitchen. Or give him a bath."

"We can't see the future. Gott can do anything. He works miracles, doesn't He?" So easy to mouth platitudes. To walk in Claire's shoes would put Bethel's words to shame. "I'm so sorry you're going through this. I'll pray Gott chooses a mann for you. I'll pray He gives you your heart's desire. If He sees His way to give you a bopli, we'll all help you take care of him."

"His will be done." Her voice soft, drowsy, Claire closed her eyes. She turned on her side and tucked her hands under her pale cheeks. "But I sure would like that. A lot."

"So would I."

Bethel inched away until she could reach the letter on the side table. *And while you're at it, Gott, could You heal Declan, sei so gut? If it's Your will, sei so gut.*

Of course God knew the truth. He knew Bethel wanted what she wanted.

Didn't most people? What would Bart say to Bethel's insistence that God heal Declan? That there be no more LGMD in her family? What had Jed said in their baptism classes? Obedience and Gelassenheit. The two pillars of the Plain faith. The minister's gruff voice sounded in Bethel's ears. *"Yield fully to Gott's will. Forsake selfishness. Not my will, but Thine be done."*

Jed had said it wouldn't be easy, but yielding to God's will—even when it meant loss, grief, pain, and suffering—was the mark of a mature believer.

Which made Bethel a puny baby believer at best. Such pride. To be so sure she was all grown up in her faith when she took her baptismal vows.

I'm so sorry, Gott. Please forgive my hochmut.

His response would likely be, *You're forgiven, My child. Go and sin no more.* Because that was the kind of God He was. Gracious, merciful, just.

He would be so disappointed in Bethel. She swallowed tears. The ache in her throat grew fiercer. She wanted what she wanted. She could no more stop than the sun could decide not to rise in the morning.

Claire heaved a big sigh. Little baby snores followed.

I'm trying, Gott.

Did she get points for trying? Jed would likely say no.

How was Declan doing with this conundrum? Maybe his letter would shed light on this problem. Bethel smoothed open the stationery.

Dear friend,

I'm sorry it's taken me so long to write. You're about to see why. I'm awful at it. There's a reason I was no good at book learning in school. I'd rather pull pranks, play games, and tell jokes.

Just remember you started it. So what do you get when you cross a cow with a duck?

More a riddle than an out-and-out joke, but Bethel was willing to play along. "What do you get when you cross a cow with a duck?" she whispered.

Claire mumbled in her sleep.

"Nothing, Schweschder, sleep."

Milk and quackers.

Bethel stifled a giggle. So bad. So very bad. "Ha-ha."

You didn't like that one? How about this one? Why do roosters never get rich?

"I give up."

Because they work for chicken feed.

Even worse. Still, Bethel smiled. Silly jokes were fun. But they could also be used to fill space and avoid real conversations, real sharing of thoughts, feelings, and the heart. A person needed both. Would Declan see that and open up his heart to her? She read on.

I'm sorry you had such a scary time at the creek. It's strange how a simple outing, meant for family fun, can turn into a bad thing from one second to the other. But you and Hattie handled it together. You make a good team. I'm glad you have Hattie around to keep you from taking life too seriously. She's a good friend.

I can see your cheeks getting red, your forehead wrinkling, and your eyes spitting fire at me. I know life is serious. Believe me, I know. But how can we get through it if we don't learn to laugh in the moments between the painful whacks life brings when it wields its mighty ax, breaking our backs and our hearts?

He had a point, and he said it well. Declan wasn't as bad at this writing thing as he liked to pretend.

Speaking of which, things are going okay here. Five weeks down, two to go. It's not a hike in the pasture, but it's not terrible either. They made this crazy mask for me to wear on my face. My throat is sore and red. My skin is peeling. It'll be worth it if the radiation goes on a search-and-destroy mission, getting rid of every last cancer cell.

Staying with Aunt Joy is good. Her kids remind me of my siblings. All that bickering. I feel right at home. Except I have my own room. At night I sit by the window and stare at the moon and the stars. That's when I'm most homesick. Should a grown man admit to being homesick? That can be our little secret, okay? I don't want Mamm and Dat to worry. Mamm has a store to run. Dat is on the road with Toby and my brothers auctioneering. Life goes on. As it should.

I don't just miss home. I miss you. I miss talking to you. Am I allowed to say that to a friend? A man can miss a friend, can't he?

I miss holding your hand. I miss arguing with you, my serious friend.

I miss your dark eyes and somber expression. I miss the sound of your voice.

I don't care if you don't like it. The truth is the truth.

If nothing else, my words might cause you to write me back quick so you can argue with me. That's my secret plan. Ha.

Ten more treatments. Twelve more days until I come home. I'm jumping in a van and heading straight to Lee's Gulch the minute that last treatment is done. The oncologist wants me to stay a few more days for follow-ups with my team, but forget that. I'm coming home. I can always come back here if I want to. Which I'm sure I won't.

See you then.

Your friend,
Declan

Bethel folded the letter. She slipped it back in the envelope. No reading it again. Her bedtime had come and gone. She rose and turned off the lamp. On tiptoe, she slipped to the window. The half-moon cast a pale light that flickered in the treetops. The same moon, the same erratic twinkling of stars. Separated by miles upon miles of asphalt, they could share this moment. Declan was homesick. He missed her. He also thought he knew so much. He thought he knew Bethel so well.

She missed the feel of his hand on hers. She missed his dimpled smile. She missed his silliness. She missed bickering with him.

Bethel missed all of him.

Chapter 28

*H*ome. It smelled like home. Declan paused on the rug that lay inside the front door of his family's home. His nose filled with the spicy scent of sausage mingling with a mouth-watering aroma that had to be cake. Supper would feature some of Declan's favorite foods. A wave of uncertainty, an odd whiff of nervousness coupled with a strange longing, swept over him. After almost two months, the feeling that he was a different man than the one who'd last stood in this spot swelled inside him, making it hard to breathe. He swallowed against the nausea that continued to plague him. The living room might be a carbon copy of Aunt Joy's with the same green curtains, propane lamps, lumpy sofa, rocking chairs, and desk with neat stacks of magazines, bills, and round-robin letters, but now this one was foreign territory.

"I thought I heard the screen door shut." Clutching a dish towel in one hand, Mom trotted down the hallway from the kitchen. "You're here. You're here. Welcome home, stranger."

Stranger. Even his mother felt it.

"I'm here." He shifted from one foot to the other. He cleared his throat. It didn't help. "Mike dropped me off."

His gruff, rough-as-gravel voice could've belonged to a stranger.

Mom's expression didn't change. She kept right on coming. "It's so gut to see you." She wrapped her arms around Declan's waist in a hug so quick he didn't have time to respond. Frowning, she stepped back and eyed him up one side and down the other. "What has Joy been feeding you, Suh? You're skinny as a rail. Are those red patches on your neck from the radiation?"

Mom didn't usually talk this much. A case of nerves plagued her as well. Declan shook his head. "It's not Joy's fault—"

"Of course it's not. It's the cancer's fault. Let us thank Gott that you are healed. We'll fatten you up in no time." Mom grabbed Declan's arm and tugged him toward the living room. "You just sit yourself down and rest while me and the maed finish fixing your celebration supper. Venison sausage on rolls, onion rings, French fries, coleslaw, pickle roll-ups, chocolate cake, and homemade ice cream. Your dat and the buwe got home from the road yesterday. Everyone's here. Toby and Rachelle. Jason's bringing Caitlin and the kinner over. Layla and Micah. It's a welcome-home celebration. Your daadi and mammi Miller are in Bird-in-Hand or they would've come too."

Declan had no choice but to plop into the rocking chair by the empty fireplace. He had to wait until she ran down to squeeze a word in edgewise. "You didn't need to do anything special."

"We sure did. You're home. You're gut to go. No more cancer, praise Gott." She grabbed a pillow covered with a needlepoint of a flower garden from behind his back. "Just rest. Sadie is in the barn playing with a new litter of kittens. She usually helps with supper, but she was so excited about you coming home, she was like a jumping bean. I had to send her outside to check on the cat. She's so excited to see you. Everyone is."

After two months of sitting on his behind doing nothing, the last thing Declan needed was to rest. "Mamm—"

"Just hush. Rest. Supper will be ready in a jiff."

"I don't need . . ."

She was gone, leaving Declan alone with his thoughts in the living room where he'd sat at his grandfather's feet and listened to story after story about life on the road. Where he'd practiced calling so Grandpa could critique his style. Where he'd raced to show off his auctioneer certificate.

All gone—for now. The doctors and the physical therapist didn't know him. He'd get his voice back. No matter how long it took, he'd pick up that mic and call another auction.

In the meantime, he needed to find a job that allowed him to help with the medical bills.

In the meantime, he wanted to drive to Bethel's, sit on the porch swing, and listen to her stories about what had happened at the Kings' house while Declan was in Richmond. What did she think of his idea of working at the nursery? How did she think Atlee Schrock would react to the idea? Did Atlee even need another employee? What did Bethel think about working side by side with Declan?

The screen door squeaked open. In traipsed Dad, Toby—who carried Sadie piggyback style—Emmett, Elijah, and Micah. Jason must have been running behind with Caitlin and the kids.

"Woo-hoo, the cat dragged in a live one." Toby let out an exaggerated hoot. "Sadie, do you recognize this guy? What's he doing in our living room?"

Declan stood. "It's not your living room anymore."

Toby didn't wince at the mangled sound of Declan's voice. He clapped. "Right you are, Bruder. I sometimes forget I'm an old married man."

"Ha, emphasis on the old part," Elijah murmured. Their brother rarely raised his voice, preferring to fade into the background. He ducked his head and studied the pine floorboards. "Welcome back. It's a gut thing you showed up. Mamm and the girls are making enough food to feed the entire town of Lee's Gulch."

"Danki. So I gathered." Declan peeked at his father's face. He had much the same broad grin as Mom. Whatever came next, in this moment, they were happy. To their way of thinking, Declan was done with cancer treatment. They deserved that happiness and the celebration. "They didn't need to do that, but I'm happy to eat as much as I can."

Sadie wiggled from Toby's grasp. She grabbed Declan's arm and tugged. He obliged by squatting to her level. She placed her damp, chubby hands on his cheeks and fixed her owlish gaze behind her thick glasses on him. "Are you all better, Bruder? Toby say the doctor took away bad stuff in your throat. Mamm too. She make a big cake, chocolate—"

"Let the man get a word in edgewise, Sadie."

"It's okay, Dat." Declan hugged his sister and planted a kiss on her prayer cover. He'd missed her sweetness most of all. "You're talking really gut these days. I reckon you've been practicing with Rachelle since school's out."

"She says I do gut." Sadie returned the hug. "Even better than Jonah, but she says not to tell him that."

Declan laughed. "Jah, you don't want to hurt his feelings."

"Enough chitchat." Dad took off his straw hat and ran his hand through damp hair. "Go wash up. Supper will be ready. You know how your mamm hates for it to get cold."

She did indeed. Suddenly overcome by a powerful hunger, Declan let Sadie pull him to the kitchen ahead of the other men. There the gaggle of women had set places at the big table and a card table for some of the kids so everyone would have a seat at the celebration. At the center of the table Mom had placed a huge flat pan cake decorated with fluffy white frosting and letters in purple that read: HAPPY CANCER-FREE DAY, DECLAN!

The women descended on him. Hugs from Layla, Rachelle, Josie, and Sherri. The back door opened. Jason and Caitlin swept in with their kids. Bedlam ensued. More hugs, more exclamations over how the kids had grown.

Hugs were the best medicine doctors never prescribed.

Finally, Mom demanded everyone sit before the food got cold.

Declan's throat ached, but not from the treatments. His family was so happy to see him and so optimistic about his future. They weren't obsessing over where he'd work or who he'd love or who would love him enough to overlook an uncertain future. Their optimism was the best kind of medicine. The weight of his treatment slid from his shoulders and disappeared—at least for the time being.

"Have a seat, Suh." Dad pointed to the chair close to the end where he sat. "It's been forever since we talked."

Dad didn't do much talking, unless it was for something important. Declan heaved a breath and sat. Dad made small talk about the weather and Richmond while the women brought the food to the table. Sherri poured water in their glasses. Dad cleared his throat and bowed his head. The chatter ceased.

He raised his head and picked up the platter of venison sausages tucked in mammoth homemade sub rolls. "You first, Declan."

And the chatter, this time at the highest volume setting, resumed.

"Coleslaw?" Dad handed Declan the bowl. "Are you able to eat whatever you want now?"

"Pretty much. I'm careful, though. Sometimes it gets sore."

It being his throat.

"You're not sounding too bad."

Trying so hard to be optimistic. "Dat."

"In comparison to before the radiation," Dad hastened to respond. He handed Declan a glass casserole dish filled with sizzling-hot homemade onion rings. "It's getting better."

"A lot better than it could've been if they'd had to take the entire vocal cords. So that's a blessing. Plus I did a lot of physical therapy in Richmond." He would continue to do the exercises on his own as well as make an appointment with a local therapist the Richmond doctor had recommended. "But I still sound like a grizzly bear somebody woke from hibernation a month too soon."

He didn't have enough voice left to project it to a crowd, even with a mic, for hours at a time.

"Did they give you a timeline for how long until your voice gets back to normal?"

"Nee. Truth is, they don't know. They said it might never be the same, but they don't know me. I'll get it back. That's a promise."

Dad squirted mustard on his sandwich. He handed the condiment to Declan, who did the same. His gaze fixed on his loaded plate, Dad took a healthy bite of his sandwich and chewed methodically. So did Declan. The conversations flowed around them. A strange English shopper dressed in pj's and moccasin slippers at the family store. The blown tire on the trailer. The big estate auction in Roanoke. A first tooth, potty training, learning to read high German. All the patches of material sewn together in a quilt unique to this family. Declan's family.

"It doesn't matter." Dad dabbed at his mouth with a napkin. "You don't have to call the auctions. There's plenty of other work to go around. You can handle the paperwork or help move the inventory to the stage. You can bid spot. You can coordinate with the sellers."

The words weren't unexpected. Declan's dad couldn't really understand. Declan laid his sandwich on his plate. "Nee, I really can't."

Dad's head snapped up. His forehead furrowed, he stared at Declan, his expression full of concern. "What do you mean, can't? Do you still feel bad? If you need time to get your strength back, I understand that. A week or two at home resting and you'll be back to normal, I reckon."

I mean I can't go on the road and pretend like I'm happy doing everything except the one job I love.

His appetite gone, Declan laid his napkin over his plate. Maybe Mom wouldn't notice how little he'd eaten. "It's not that. The last thing I need is to sit around doing nothing, but I don't want to go on the road with you until I can call auctions again."

"Why not?" Dad's frown deepened as his voice rose slightly. Toby, who sat on Dad's right side, glanced up from his conversation with Micah. Declan shook his head at Toby's raised eyebrows. "It would be . . . like dumping a load of salt in a gaping wound to trail after the rest of you and not be able to call an auction. All the jobs are important, I know, but auctioneering is the only one for me."

"You're one of the Miller brothers. You're expected to help in the business however you can." Dad tossed his napkin on his plate. He pushed the plate away. "You need to know how to run all aspects of our business. One day I'll retire and you'll have to step up. I can teach you to take care of the trailers and the equipment, if you don't want to spot. But no job is better or worse than another. You know that."

So many words. Only on the topic of the family business would Dad bother with such a long response, so full of passion. He and

Grandpa thought like that. A family business meant every male member of the family. But the business would survive fine with Toby at its helm, with Dad as the hands-on worker of miracles with equipment, and Jason and Toby as the lead auctioneers. Dad could call when three auctioneers were needed for the bigger sales.

Elijah might differ from Dad regarding working in the family business, but he would never say so aloud. Emmett would be of age soon. There were plenty of Millers to keep the business healthy. More auctioneers than they knew what to do with.

Declan took a breath. He chose his words with care. "This isn't just about not being able to call. It's important for me to find an outside job where I could earn money to pay my doctor bills."

"We're doing fine with the bills."

No, they weren't. Dad wasn't lying. He believed they *could* pay the bills because they'd always found a way. Declan had seen firsthand the bills for the surgery, radiation, lab work, imaging and physical therapy, as well as the social worker and all the other medical people. According to the financial counselor, cancer was one of the most expensive diseases to treat in healthcare around the world. Declan was blessed that Dr. McMann's office had coordinated those appointments. In normal circumstances, uninsured patients had to pay for medical services when they were provided. Or they weren't provided. Amazingly, the Plain tradition of paying these bills in a timely manner was taken into consideration in this part of the country.

In the non-Plain parts of the country, he would've had to wait to receive care until they had the money. No amount of barbecue plate fundraisers would cover his bills. The staggering amount owed could deplete the district's medical fund. The elders would reach out to other districts for help.

Dad didn't know all this. He didn't need all this weight on his shoulders—no matter how sturdy they were.

"The money earned from Miller Family Auctioneering is used to support this family. So is the money earned from the store." Declan kept his tone soft, respectful, but firm. "We have several families in the district with medical needs. I can't let my bills jeopardize this family or the district."

"It won't—"

"Charlie."

Mom leaned between Declan and Dad with a water pitcher in her hand. She refilled their glasses.

"We're just talking about Declan coming back to work."

She leaned closer to Dad. "This is a celebration. Can we leave the business talk for later?"

Mom might be a fierce mama hen with other people, but she chose diplomacy when it came to her husband. Dad's expression turned contrite, like a boy in trouble for talking in class. "I reckon it can wait."

"Gut." She straightened. "I see that napkin over your food, Declan Miller. Eat more and talk less. That's my prescription for putting some meat on those bones. Now get busy."

She might be soft-spoken with Dad, but not with her children. Declan did as he was told. He managed to eat most of the sandwich and the coleslaw, but the fries and onion rings were soggy—his own fault, but Mom would have to be satisfied.

Sadie insisted on being the one to cut the cake and serve Declan his piece. It was twice the size of everyone else's and came with two scoops of vanilla ice cream topped with chocolate syrup and caramel sauce. That didn't keep Declan from slurping up every last bit of goodness. Stuffed to the gills, he pushed back his chair and patted his belly. "Where's the wheelbarrow? I need someone to haul me out of here."

"Me, me," Sadie crowed. She waved her spoon in the air, splattering drops of ice cream on Sherri and Josie. "You see new kitties. They cute. Like me."

Everyone laughed except Josie and Sherri, who were busy wiping ice cream from their faces.

"Nee, Sadie Maedel. You got out of helping with fixing supper." Mom stood and picked up her plate. "You will help clean up."

"A walk might be better for the digestion than a wheelbarrow." Toby put his hand on Declan's shoulder. "Why don't you and I walk down to the office? I can bring you up-to-date on the schedule—"

"I'm not coming on the road—"

"Declan needs to rest." Mom blistered Toby with her infamous "I'm the mom" glare. "Just a slow walk to the office and no work. He's to take it easy. Mudder's orders."

Toby's hand tightened on Declan's shoulder. "No work. Just talk. I think Rachelle has something she wants to tell you, Mamm."

With that he let go of Declan and headed for the back door. Declan stood and strode after him, the sound of the women's voices suddenly loud in his ears. Toby had lit a match and dropped it in a pile of hay. The entire female portion of the Miller clan would descend on poor Rachelle.

Declan only had to deal with Toby. Whatever he wanted, Declan was prepared to handle it.

Chapter 29

"What news?" Declan sidestepped Matilda the Cat, who strolled past them toward the house without acknowledging their presence. Only Sadie counted as far as Matilda was concerned. He quickened his step to keep up with Toby's longer stride toward the path that led to the auctioneering office. "Or were you just trying to get Mamm's mind off me? If that was the case, danki."

"Gern gschehme. Both." Toby slowed his pace. He pushed his hat back, giving Declan a better view of his smiling face. "Rachelle is in a family way."

As much as he tried to sound nonchalant, Toby's grin told the real story. The man who'd intended to be a bachelor for life was thrilled. That he'd told Declan at all said as much. Plain folks didn't make a big deal out of announcing babies.

Declan clapped his brother on the back. "Mamm will be happy. She dotes on her *kinnskinner*. She can't wait until they're old enough to need matchmaking."

Toby unlocked the door to the building that housed the family business. He held it open. "After you."

Inside, the air was stuffy, evidence that the men had been on the auction circuit for the last three weeks. Declan sank into a chair across from the oversize, institutional gray desk with its neat array of folders, a computer and keyboard, a phone, writing utensils, and an assortment of office supplies. Josie could be thanked for the organization, now that Layla was married and applying her administrative skills to Micah's hog farm. "So what did you want to talk about?"

"What makes you think I wanted to talk?" Toby took a seat behind the desk. He picked up a letter opener with a rooster head on the end and flipped it through his fingers. "I just wanted to get you away from Mamm's attempts to smother you."

"I saw the glare you gave me at the supper table." Declan met his brother's gaze head-on. "You could hear what Dat and me were talking about. You have concerns."

Toby stuck the opener in a ceramic pencil holder shaped like a saddle. "You really don't want to go on the road with us?"

"It would be hard, but that's not the only reason. I need to earn money for bills."

"Gott will provide."

"Bart already gave me this talk."

"I'm the oldest bruder. It's my place to repeat it."

"I know you mean well. You all do." Declan snagged a mint from a bowl next to the pencil holder. He took his time unwrapping it. "Try to imagine how you'd feel if you might never stand on the platform and call an auction again. Try to imagine watching others do it while you stand on the sidelines."

"Believe me, I have. I get this awful feeling in my gut." Toby grimaced and rubbed his belly. "I've never wanted to do anything else. If I could've, I would've so that I didn't have to spend so much time away from Rachelle."

"But Gott's plan is for you to keep doing what you love to do, while Rachelle stays home with your kinner." Declan sucked hard on the candy, letting the mint soothe his throat. "I know it's full of hochmut on my part to object. I know I should be willingly obedient. I'm trying. I really am—"

"I have no business judging you. I would never."

"You must have an idea of the bills I'm racking up with this disease." Declan rolled the wrapper into a tiny ball, round and round, in the palm of his hand. "If I go on the road with you, I'm more of a burden. I'm costing you—the business—money. If I stay here and get a job, I'll have an income we can put straight into knocking down those bills."

His expression thoughtful, Toby craned his head from side to side. He nudged the wastebasket in Declan's direction. Declan aimed and tossed the wrapper into it. "Two points."

"He shoots, he scores." Toby scrubbed at the short, ragged blond beard he'd acquired since his marriage. "You have a very gut point. Truthfully, I think Dat misses having you on the road with us. He's like Daadi. He wants all his buwe working together."

"I understand that, but it's not possible. Not right now, anyway. If my voice improves, then I can get back on board as an auctioneer. In the meantime, I need to get a paying job." Declan rearranged the pencils and pens in the holder on the desk. "I do wonder, though—"

"Don't wander too far."

"Hardy-har-har. I thought about going out on my own." Declan took the pencils from the holder and returned them one by one. "I even told Dat I was considering it. I wanted to be able to stretch out my arms and not smack a Miller brother."

"Dat mentioned it."

Declan caught his brother's gaze. "He didn't like the idea. He said nee. Adamantly. Now I have to do it. Like Gott saying, 'You wanted it, and now you've got it. Be careful what you wish for.' I never wanted to leave auctioneering."

"Just us, your family." Toby pulled the pencil holder from Declan's reach. He selected a pencil and flipped it through his fingers in a repeat performance of the letter opener. "I don't reckon I'm wise enough to discern Gott's will on anything, but I do know Scripture says He'll walk through trouble with us. He didn't give you cancer to teach you a lesson about family."

"I know you're right." Declan's throat throbbed. He needed to take his meds. "Bart said I should seek out other work I enjoy. Like a backup plan. But I can't give up on being an auctioneer—not yet. I plan to do the PT and work hard to get my voice back."

"What did you have in mind?"

"Schrocks'."

"You selling plants?" Toby made no effort to hide his surprise. Then a slow smile spread across his face. His dimples appeared. "Ah."

"Ah, what?"

He shrugged. "None of my business."

It certainly wasn't. "What's none of your business?"

"Bethel King works there, doesn't she?"

"That has nothing to do with it." Declan grabbed a flyer from the desk. He proceeded to fold it into a paper airplane. "I like plants. I like grubbing in the dirt. I like talking to people. It's something I can do that'll keep me from sitting around feeling sorry for myself."

"We can't have that. I reckon the pay isn't great."

"It's not like I have the skills to do anything else. I put all my eggs in the auctioneering basket."

"Nobody could've imagined this would happen."

"People never think bad things are going to happen to them. I don't know why that is."

"In this world, there will be trouble . . ."

Declan nodded. "Jah, exactly."

"Don't think I didn't notice you moving the conversation away from Bethel."

Persistence was Toby's middle name. Declan smoothed the folds in his plane. He aimed and fired it at his brother. It did a loop and landed on the desk far short of its intended target. Toby laughed. Hearing that sound after weeks away from home made it impossible to be sad. "I don't talk about courting. It's not done."

"So you're courting then."

"I don't know."

Louder guffaws. Toby's shoulders shook. He wiped tears from his eyes. "And I thought I was bad with women. If you don't know, who does?"

Declan shrugged. "Bethel?"

"Let's hope so."

"I planned to pay her a visit tonight," Declan admitted. "But Mamm—"

"Had other plans. You could still go later—"

"Declan, Toby!" Sadie raced into the office. "The buwe put up the volleyball net. Jason says to come quick before the maedel beat him and the buwe. Mamm says we can have seconds of ice cream."

She grabbed Declan's arm and tugged with all her strength. Declan took pity on her and stood. He picked her up and tossed her over his shoulder. She shrieked with laughter. Declan couldn't help but laugh too. The best medicine.

He smiled at Toby. "I don't know about volleyball, but seconds of ice cream can't wait."

"I guess your love life will have to wait."

"Declan has love life?" Sadie patted Declan's back. Her sneakered feet kicked aimlessly. "Nee, nee, nee. He no go. I say nee."

At this rate, Sadie needn't worry.

Chapter 30

The sign in front of Schrocks' Nursery and Landscaping announced a sale on two cubic feet of all pine bark and nugget mulches. Just the written words summoned the earthy scent of mulch Declan associated with shoring up trees, shrubs, and flowers in the family yard. A good dose of mulch helped them suck up and retain water, a handy remedy when rain wouldn't come. And it smelled good.

Raising his face to the brilliant mid-June sun, he strode across the uneven cement, gravel, and dirt parking lot, past raised pallets of four-packs of beet, cucumber, and bell pepper plants, all on sale for $1.79 each. Most folks had planted theirs weeks ago. Long wooden tables held a variety of large decorative clay, ceramic, and metal pots interspersed with caladiums, geraniums, cacti, and succulents on clearance. He hadn't entered the store yet, and he was already at home.

If only Atlee Schrock saw it that way. A job at the nursery might be just the medicine needed to pull Declan from the murky haze that kept him from seeing the path to a future that didn't include calling auctions anytime soon—maybe ever.

Heaving a deep, steadying breath, Declan pulled open one of the double glass doors. He stood aside to let an English woman pass carrying a twenty-five-pound bag of tomato and vegetable fertilizer over her shoulder. "Can I carry that for you?"

His scratchy sandpaper voice still surprised him.

"I got it." She smiled and nodded. "Take care of that cold. Chamomile tea with honey and lemon always does the trick for me."

Declan tipped his straw hat and let the door swing shut behind her. People assumed. It was easier to let them. They also felt free to dispense medical advice. He swallowed a retort that involved giving her unsolicited advice for everything from her sunburn to the big mole on her upper lip to the cold sore on the lower one.

He dodged an old man with a cart full of yellow, red, pink, and white antique rosebushes, then edged past a woman examining a pegboard on the front wall featuring pruning shears, trowels, and soil knives. The nursery was doing brisk business this Saturday morning. Finally he made it to the counter where Atlee stood behind a cash register, discussing topsoil with an English man. The patch on his short-sleeved cotton shirt identified him as a local landscaper.

"Hey, Declan, gut to see you. I didn't know you were back." Atlee handed the man a receipt and wished him a good day, then turned back. "Your mamm has been one of my best customers all year long—especially for all those native plants none of the other folks will try their hand at. Did she send you for more? I just got in a shipment of oxeye daisies, black-eyed Susans, and salvias. 'Course, she'll want to pick them out for herself, I reckon. So how are you?"

Hattie got her talkativeness from her dad. The best strategy was to wait for him to take a breath, then jump in. "I'm gut. Nee, she didn't. I wanted to talk to you—"

"Hattie, Declan's here. Come say hallo."

Declan's family and the Schrocks had been good friends over the years. Some probably had wondered if Declan and Hattie would be a good fit. But they'd never been more than classmates.

A watering can in one hand, Hattie glanced up from her vantage point among a display of rhododendron, hydrangea, chokeberry, and witch hazel shrubs. With a smudge of dirt on her forehead and mud caked on her forest-green SCHROCKS' NURSERY AND LANDSCAPING apron, she was pure Hattie. She splashed water on a white hydrangea bush, set the can down with a thunk, and trotted over to the counter. "You're here. You're here. Does Bethel know? Of course she doesn't. She's here. Did you know that? Of course you did. That's why you're here, right?"

"I just got back to town last night—"

"She's tidying up around the trees in the greenhouse." Head cocked toward the wide-open doorway that led from the metal building to the greenhouse, Hattie pranced in place like a grade schooler who needed to use the outhouse. "You must've stopped by to tell her you're back—"

His intentions involving Bethel were none of Hattie's business. "I came to talk to your dat—"

"Sure, sure, but if she walks in here and finds you talking to Dat, not having said hallo to her, she'll be hurt. You don't want to hurt her feelings—"

"Dochder, Dochder, how you do go on." Atlee's craggy face had turned a deep red. His desire to give Declan a nudge obviously didn't extend to out-and-out matchmaking of the kind Hattie was intent on doing. "You'd better restock the gardening implements— especially the rakes and hoes. We've had a run on them over the past few days."

Hattie rolled her eyes, but she slipped around the counter and headed for the door that bore a sign that read STOREROOM—EMPLOYEES ONLY. "It's your funeral, Declan."

"Hattie!" Atlee's brown eyes bulged behind thick rimless glasses. He tugged at his gray beard with one hand and slid back his straw hat with the other. "That girl has no more tact than a four-year-old. It's no wonder she's not married."

The red turned to a nice shade of purple. The poor man might have a seizure. Declan summoned a reassuring smile. "It's okay. I don't mind." Hattie's comment about funerals and the fact that Atlee had voiced concerns about his daughter's marriageability to a Plain single man had sent the poor man to the very edge. No sense in toppling him over the cliff. "I've known Hattie since we were both in diapers. She doesn't have a mean bone in her body. She's a gut friend."

To Bethel and to Declan. There was that *friend* word again. Atlee likely ascribed to the same sentiment as most Plain folks—men and women couldn't be friends. It was sinking sand. Besides, this particular woman needed a husband who enjoyed her odd sense of humor and flights of fancy. Declan couldn't help there. As much as he appreciated a kindred spirit, he'd already given his heart away.

"You're right about that." Atlee rubbed his forehead as if he had a headache coming on. "What did you want to talk to me about?"

"A job."

"Ah." The nursery owner's face was getting a workout. His eyebrows rose. His mouth dropped open. After a second he thought to close it. "So the rumors are true. Your voice is gone for gut? No more auctioneering?"

Rumors. As much as people claimed to hate gossip, they couldn't help themselves. The grapevine thrived in the sunshine and fertile soil of Lee's Gulch. "Time will tell." Bart would be proud of that answer delivered in a raspy, hard-to-understand voice. "In the meantime, I need to work. We have medical bills to pay."

Not the subtlest appeal, but the truth.

"Huh."

For once Atlee seemed at a loss for words. He turned back to the cash register where an English woman in fancy workout clothes proceeded to buy a cart full of flowering annuals. They chatted about the weather, local politics, and the price of eggs. By the time she pushed the cart toward the doors, Atlee's color had returned to normal.

"Why the nursery?"

"I like gardening. They say I should do something I like so I can be more content."

They being the bishop and the palliative care social worker who had said Declan had to embrace his "new normal." *You're a cancer survivor. Not everyone gets to say that. You're one of the lucky ones.*

Luck had nothing to do with it. God's will had been done. Where Declan went from here was unknown. He would get a job, work on strengthening his voice, and learn to accept his fate—whatever it was.

Be content. Gardening is good. Gardening is fine. Content. Declan forced his fisted hands to relax. Would ringing up flats of tomato plants, shrubs, and bird feeders give him the same satisfaction he received from drawing folks into bidding wars that resulted in good sales that benefited both sellers and buyers?

How could it? He had no childhood dream that involved plants or bird feeders. But maybe it could be a second best that served the purposes necessary for his family. Setting aside his pride and accepting God's will. His heart and his head continued to circle like two hounds claiming their territory.

Ignore the turmoil. Do the right thing. "So do you have the need for another worker?"

An absentminded expression on his humidity-dampened face, Atlee waved away a bumblebee. He straightened a stack of receipts. "This is the busiest time of year for us. I'd been considering it, but I just moved Bethel from part to full time. I don't know if I can afford to pay another full-time employee."

Since he seemed to be talking to himself, Declan held his peace. He would be the last person to try to convince a small business owner to take on another employee if he didn't really need one or couldn't afford one. Miller Family Auctioneering had a decent profit margin—according to Toby—but they only had income six months out of the year. The combination store helped make up the difference, if they kept expenses down for both businesses.

Atlee waited on another customer. Then another. Declan eased away from the counter. The seed packets on display next to the gardening implements needed straightening. Someone had removed packets and then replaced them in the wrong slots. Declan busied himself righting the situation.

"You're back?"

Her normally warm voice was soft, quiet, cool.

In his rush, Declan stuffed the packet of radish seeds into a slot for leaf lettuce. He turned. "Hallo, Bethel. I mean, jah, I am . . . back."

She didn't respond. She stood there staring at him, waiting, a hurt expression on her pretty face.

From the bright red spots spreading across his cheeks, Declan knew exactly what Bethel wanted. She stifled the urge to stick her hands on her hips. She wasn't a mother scolding a small child. Still, that didn't mean she couldn't let him stew for a minute. He'd said in his letter he was coming home Friday. That he would be over to see her on Friday. It wasn't his fault she'd sat on the porch swing all evening, waiting for him. Elizabeth probably had a party for him. That's what Bethel would have done if it was her loved one.

If it was her loved one.

So, fine, Bethel could deal with him not coming over on Friday night. This was Saturday, the day after Friday. Here he was in the store, the store where she worked. Surely he knew from Atlee and Hattie that she was in the store as well. They were in the same place at the same time for the first time in seven weeks, and he hadn't bothered to find her.

"I was going to find you as soon as I—"

His voice was rough, gravelly, breathy, nothing like the bass he employed calling auctions. It had to break his heart every time he opened his mouth. Bethel took a breath. She summoned a smile. "As soon as you finished rearranging the seed display?"

"Nee, jah, nee, I mean, I was just waiting to talk to Atlee."

That explained everything. Declan had lost at least ten pounds, and his skin was pale from lack of sun. Except where it was red on his neck, likely from the radiation. None of that made him any less a handsome man. Which was totally beside the point. "You had a sudden need of advice on plants?"

"Nee, no plants."

"Then what?"

"I came to ask him for a job."

That answer certainly came out of the back forty acres. Bethel forced her mouth to shut before a fly flew in. A job at the nursery. A job at the nursery could mean only one thing. He was no longer an auctioneer. No wonder sadness etched his face.

Bethel edged closer. Between an English couple bickering over whether to buy a mountain laurel or a dogwood for their front yard in one aisle and an elderly lady talking quietly to the houseplants in the other, this was a terrible place for this conversation. "Ach, I'm so sorry."

"It's not forever. It's just that I still have a lot of work to do on my voice." The muscles in his jaw worked. His gaze bounced from her to the bickering couple and back. "In the meantime, I like working with plants and I need a job to help pay medical bills."

Truth be told, Declan likely saw gardening as women's work. It wasn't the same as sowing milo, alfalfa, and corn, like farmers did. He was trying so hard to make the best of the situation. Bethel's throat tightened. "Gut. I do too. It's fun working here. What did Atlee say?"

"He said he wasn't sure he could afford it." Declan picked dead leaves from a hanging pothos plant. He deposited them in the dirt. He avoided her gaze. "He's thinking."

"This place is packed morning, noon, and night. The customers are running us ragged." What was Atlee thinking? To have an employee like Declan who had a wealth of knowledge about plants, gardening, farming, and the like would be invaluable. He had another important tool that he wouldn't necessarily write on an application. He was a people person. At least the pre-cancer Declan had been. Atlee had known Declan his whole life. He knew this. "The fact is, he's just tight with the money."

Atlee would call himself frugal.

"Let's go." Bethel forged past Declan, headed for the counter. "I need to talk to him."

Atlee had a line six deep in customers. Instead of interrupting, Bethel turned to Declan. "Have you ever worked a cash register?"

"Jah, at our store."

"Then get in there and show Atlee what you can do."

Declan shot Atlee an uncertain look. The store owner was concentrating on a cart filled with a dozen different flowering plants. All the customers behind this one had similar carts. "Are you sure?" he whispered. "You work here."

"The scanner does all the work. Atlee needs more hands." Bethel nudged Declan. "Go on. I'll see if any of them have questions. I hate for them to wait in line when they really just need information."

Sure enough, a Plain woman Bethel recognized from the south district wanted to know which insecticide was best for a mite infestation killing her tomato plants. Bethel chatted with her about mites, beetles, fungi, and other fun stuff while leading her to the best products for her need. By the time they returned, the line had dwindled to two customers. The one Declan was helping laughed at something he said. Declan's dimples were showing. Atlee appeared less stressed.

Her face damp with sweat, Hattie emerged from the storeroom. Her smile reappeared when she saw Declan at the cash register. She elbowed Bethel. "So you saw he's back. Happy, happy day, right?"

Bethel elbowed her in return. "You knew he was here, and you didn't come to tell me?"

"He said he would do it. He wanted to talk to Dat first. I have no idea why."

"He wants to work here."

"You don't sound happy about it."

"I would love to work side by side with him, but don't you see what it means?"

Hattie's smile disappeared. "Ach."

"Ach indeed. He says he's still working on his voice, but I'm sure there are no guarantees he'll get it back."

"He could still work with his family."

"Would you want to be stuck on the sidelines watching your brieder do the job you love?"

Hattie swiped at her face with her sleeve. A cobweb dangled from her prayer covering. "Nee, I reckon not."

"Besides, he's in the same boat I am."

"Needing to earn money to pay medical bills?"

"Jah."

"Then Dat better hire him." Hattie smoothed her wrinkled apron. "I'm on it."

"Just don't be too direct. Make it seem like his idea."

"He's my dat. I know what I'm doing." Hattie tapped her temple with her index finger. "Stand back and watch the master work."

She sauntered up to the counter like a woman without a care in the world. Her father was wiping dirt and water from the countertop with an old dish towel. Declan still had a customer. "Dat, you really need—"

"Hattie, there you are. You'll be happy to know I just hired Declan."

"You did?"

Declan, Hattie, and Bethel spoke in unison. Declan smiled. Hattie laughed. Bethel closed her eyes for a split second and praised God.

"I did. He knows how to use a cash register and the customers like him." Atlee's grin suggested he was mighty pleased with himself. "You can have next Saturday off like you wanted, Dochder. But don't make a habit of it. Saturdays are our busiest days."

He put a spray bottle of cleanser back under the counter, along with the dishrag. "Bethel, can you and Hattie handle the cash registers while I take Declan into the office to fill out the paperwork?"

"Happy to." Bethel peeked at Declan. He grinned. She returned the grin. "Welcome to the nursery family."

"Danki."

She picked up a leaf that had fallen from a customer's plant. "I guess we'll see a lot more of each other now."

Declan glanced at Atlee, who was headed for the office, then back at Bethel. "It appears that way."

"Jah, it does."

"Egad, you two." Hattie hacked like a cat trying to dislodge a hairball. "Can't you say what you have to say before my hair turns gray and my teeth fall out?"

"Hush," Bethel and Declan said in unison.

"Don't you have work to do in the greenhouse?" Bethel added. "I can handle the customers. If I need you I'll call you on the two-way radio."

Hattie rolled her eyes. "Dat's waiting for you, Declan."

"Then go." Declan made shooing motions. "Skedaddle."

"You didn't just skedaddle me—"

"Now." Bethel and Declan spoke as one. "Hurry."

As soon as she disappeared from sight, Bethel turned back to Declan. "Are you really done with treatment?"

"I go back every three months for a CT scan, but it's precautionary. The surgeon got all the visible cancer cells. The radiation finished off the job." Declan came around the counter and stopped within arm's reach. "I have to fill out that paperwork, but I'll come to your house tonight. Late. Mamm is intent on making up for lost time."

"Me too," Bethel whispered.

Declan squeezed her hand. "Tonight, then."

"Tonight."

Tonight couldn't come soon enough.

Chapter 31

$\mathcal{N}$ ow that they were in the same place at the same time, a strange awkwardness prevailed. Bethel clutched her hands in her lap. She studied the nearly full moon, so bright against a black sky that it hurt her eyes. *Say something. Say something. What?* Their conversation during the buggy ride from her house to the dirt road that meandered between her parents' farm and Declan's had been full of meaningless prattle: Declan's new job at the nursery, their families, the weather. *Gott help us, we're talking about the weather.*

"It's a fine night for a buggy ride." Declan pulled on the reins. The buggy slowed. He pulled into a clearing that led to the road—a trail really—that would take them to the creek. Instead he stopped. "It's still cool after the sun goes down, even in June."

"Seriously?"

"You don't think so?"

"Declan."

He shifted on the seat. It squeaked under his weight. His horse tossed his head and whinnied. Even he felt the strain. The reins bunched up in Declan's big hands. He had nice hands. Bethel tore her gaze away from them. She studied the leafy shadows that danced in the moonlight. Crickets sang in harmony. A frog croaked and fell silent. Mosquitoes buzzed by her ear. She batted them away. An owl hooted. All of nature could think of something to say, but not the two of them. *Come on, Declan.*

"I've waited two months to be . . . here." Declan's fingers went to his throat. He rubbed the reddened skin. His hand dropped. "With you. Why is this so hard?"

"I reckon it's because we imagine how something is going to be so much and so often, we get so we're afraid it won't live up to our expectations." Bethel shifted her gaze to her own hands. Her fingers were white. She loosened her grip. "A person wouldn't want to spoil it by saying the wrong thing."

Declan's hand crept toward her. His fingers covered hers. "There's nothing you could say that would spoil this. Me, I could crater it any minute by telling a silly joke or saying something stupid. It's my specialty."

"I'll start then." Her heart thrummed against her rib cage. The breeze failed to cool the sudden heat that rushed through her body. "Have you decided not to let your cancer stand in the way of courting?"

"The scan didn't show any cancer cells. The chances of it coming back are small." Shadows hid Declan's expression. "Have you decided not to let your family's genes stand in the way of courting?"

"I can't change my heredity. I see other couples having boplin and not worrying. I reckon I'll have to learn to do the same." It was either that or remain a single Plain woman who deprived herself of the most important things in life every Plain person wanted— marriage and children. "Have you decided being friends—if it's even possible—isn't enough for you?"

"Have you?"

"Jah." Bethel whispered the single syllable and let it ride on a sudden gust of wind that carried it away into the treetops and across the sky. "I have no choice. My heart refuses to let my head win the argument."

Declan chuckled softly. "Mine either."

"So what now—?"

Declan's lips covered Bethel's. The kiss was soft, deliberate, almost a question. Bethel turned so she could slide her arms around his neck. Question answered. Declan's embrace tightened. Uncertainty fell away in a rush of heat from a flame that burst from dry kindling at the first struck match. Soft turned fierce, deep, determined. *Don't ever let him stop. Don't ever let him stop.*

Declan leaned back. "I've wanted to do that since fourth grade."

Bethel drew a shaky breath. "You have not." Her voice sounded high, like someone else's. "Okay, maybe *you* have, but *I* wasn't thinking about it in grade school."

"Miss Prim and Proper." Looking mighty satisfied with himself, he grinned so wide that his dimples nearly popped. "I happen to know from eavesdropping on my schweschdre and their friends that girls do wonder what it's like to kiss a guy . . . and such."

"I didn't say I didn't wonder about it." Bethel managed a weak laugh. "I said I didn't think about kissing *you*."

The heat roasting her cheeks rose another hundred degrees.

The chuckle turned into outright laughter. "Fair enough." Declan drew closer. So close Bethel could see a tiny scar over his left eye she'd never noticed before. "As long as you think about it now."

The second kiss went on and on. Declan's hands ran down her arms, touched her hands, then clasped her face and held her there. She couldn't have moved if she wanted to. She definitely did not.

Everything about it was so perfect. *Danki, Gott, danki.*

Was it right to thank God for kisses?

Startled, Bethel opened her eyes.

Declan did the same. He let go. "What's the matter?"

"Nothing. Nothing, I, we should probably slow down a bit."

Declan touched her face and let his finger trail down her cheek and across her collarbone. Sparklers danced across her skin in the wake of his touch. He picked up her hand and kissed her fingers. This had to be what grasping a live wire felt like. "You're right." He slid farther away. "It's just that I've waited so long for this I sort of exploded. I'm sorry if I got carried away."

"You didn't. I promise you didn't." Bethel clasped her hands to keep them from reaching for him. Even distance couldn't dampen the fire. "I think you have so much pent-up emotion from everything going on in your life that it all came rushing out at once."

"There might be truth in that." Declan leaned back and stared at the sky. Then at Bethel. "But my feelings for you were driving that train."

His tone was matter-of-fact. No embarrassment. A simple statement of truth. "That's gut." A laugh burbled up in her. "I'm glad to hear it. It was nice."

Declan's eyebrows rose. "Nice?"

"Gut. Wunderbarr. There's no word in Deutsch or English or German to describe how it—how you make me feel."

"We should probably try courting before we do that again."

"That's a gut idea." So why did it take every ounce of self-restraint to keep from sliding across the bench and kissing him again? "What did you have in mind?"

"I think we should take a walk down to the creek." He dug around under the seat and came up with a flashlight. "Then if I get fresh with you, you can shove me in the water to cool me off."

"Or vice versa." Bethel laughed. Laughter never felt better. "You keep your distance. I'll keep mine."

Promises, promises. By the time they reached the creek, they were holding hands. Even the full moon didn't provide enough light to lead the way to the water. They had only one flashlight. Taking Declan's hand was the smart thing to do. That's all there was to it.

Was God laughing at her now? Or frowning? *He's leading the way, Gott. It's nice to have someone lead the way. I can rest in knowing I don't have to be the one in charge.*

God would understand. He saw. He knew. He knew what came next. Each breath of cooling night air, damp with humidity, fragrant with wet earth and leaves, came easier for the first time in forever.

"How's this?" Declan flashed the light at a patch of grass at the water's edge. "It might be a little damp. Sorry, I didn't think to bring a blanket to sit on."

"I don't mind." Nothing could burst her balloon at this moment. It carried her floating above drab day-to-day details like getting her dress dirty. She let go of Declan's hand and eased onto the grass. "A little mud never hurt anybody."

Declan joined her in one long, lean motion, much closer than she'd expected. His scent of soap and man wafted over her. Bethel leaned into it. Their shoulders touched. He heaved a sigh.

Bethel tried to make out his face in the darkness. "What was that for?"

"What was what?"

"The sigh."

"Truth?"

"Sei so gut."

"I've spent the last three months gritting my teeth and telling myself to just get through it. Get through it. Get to the other side. I begged Gott to make it go fast. Now I want time to stop. I want this time to last forever."

"Me too. Forever," Bethel whispered. There he was. The real Declan. The one she'd waited so many years to meet. The one who spoke his heart. She leaned closer. "Danki."

"Danki for what?"

"For telling me how you really feel. For letting me in. It makes me feel . . . special. I know we're not supposed to want to be special—"

"You are special to me." Declan put his arm around her and squeezed. "It's taken us forever to get here, but I'm thinking it was worth the wait."

Bethel leaned against his solid frame and closed her eyes. Somehow she had to capture this moment and hold it in her mind, wrap it up in tissue paper, and carefully store it away to be enjoyed again and again. The feel of his muscles straining under the soft, faded cotton shirt, the clean scent of store-bought soap, the roughness of tiny whiskers on his chin nuzzling her cheek, the sound of his raspy voice that had never sounded sweeter. All of it. "Let's just sit here then. Let's just be here in this moment."

Declan gently laid his head on hers. He held her close. A wispy cloud drifted over the moon, obscuring it for a few seconds, then moved on so that the moon's light was all the brighter.

"It's perfect," Bethel whispered. "Just perfect."

Chapter 32

*O*ne way or another, ordinary life had to be lived. Mountaintops gave way to valleys—or the plateaus in between. Declan lugged another forty-pound bag of fall lawn fertilizer from the shelf to the cart. He planned to replace them with winter fertilizer alongside a sales display of clay pots and terra-cotta pots with matching saucers in hopes that folks would plan ahead and buy them now. Despite the nippy October weather outside, the nursery still held dank, warm air. Sweat dampened his face and his shirt. His shoulders ached, but in a good, hardworking way.

Bethel stood behind the counter talking to a customer while she rang up his purchases. Just the sound of her voice was enough to send Declan hurtling back through time to that first buggy ride in June, to the feel of her arms around his neck, her soft skin against his, and her scent of lavender shampoo enveloping him. They'd taken many buggy rides since then, eaten many sack lunches together at the picnic bench out back of the nursery, and made sure their paths crossed at every church lunch, every work frolic, and every social event in the four months since. But they'd always limited themselves to a few sweet, chaste kisses before saying good-bye after a buggy ride.

What was it about Bethel that made it so hard for Declan to let go of her hand when she said good night? She had such sweet regret on her face that perfectly matched what he was feeling inside. He wanted to kiss it away. And keep kissing her.

His boot hit the corner of a pallet of fertilizer bags. He stumbled, caught himself, swayed, and hung onto the bag on his shoulder. A man wearing overalls and a John Deere cap grabbed Declan's arm to steady him. "Easy there, bud."

"Thanks." Declan dumped the bag on the cart. He took stock of his feet. No pain. Likely the boot's steel toes had kept him from breaking at least one.

No place for spinning wool, he silently scolded his wayward self. *That's how accidents happen. Keep your mind on your work.*

How could he when Bethel was right there with her warm brown eyes, her fair skin, and a smile that beckoned him to come closer?

"Declan, could you come up here for a minute?" Atlee's bellow carried over the hum of the fans, the murmur of customers, and the squeak of carts.

Declan let the last bag of fertilizer fall onto the cart. A reprieve. "Coming."

Dusting off his hands as he strode toward the counter, Declan kept his gaze from Bethel. They'd agreed to act like coworkers and nothing more while at the nursery. One, courting was private. Two, no one liked to be forced to observe couples acting couple-y in public—not something Plain folks did, of course.

Atlee laid a clipboard stuffed with invoices on the counter. Murmuring to himself, he swiveled and glanced at an old-fashioned paper calendar on the wall. He opened the storeroom door and bellowed again. "Hattie."

A few seconds later Hattie appeared. She had a dirt smudge on her nose and something that might be strawberry jam on her upper lip. "Jah, Dat?"

"Quick announcement." He paused. "As soon as Bethel helps out Duke."

Duke being the man in the overalls and John Deere hat. He purchased a huge bag of birdseed and a pile of mouse traps, nodded at Atlee, and went on his way.

"What is it, Dat?" Hattie wiped her face with the back of her hand, spreading more dirt across her left cheek. "I'm almost done with the inventory. I need a DQ hamburger, a slushy, and maybe even a Blizzard. I don't know if I'm more hungry or more thirsty. I have a powerful thirst—"

"Dochder." Atlee held up his hands like twin stop signs. "The sooner you stop talking, the sooner you can have your lunch."

Hattie dutifully closed her mouth, but no way Atlee missed the eye roll. He waited another full minute to resume speaking—testament to that fact. "Even you don't know about this, Hattie. I got a phone call from your daadi and mammi in Pinecraft this morning. My dat had a heart attack last night. Me and your mudder are headed down there on the next bus—which is at seven tonight."

"Is Daadi going to be all right?" Hatti rushed around the counter. She launched herself at Atlee, who caught her up in a hug. "Is he dying? I want to go too. Can I go too?"

Atlee peeled her away from his chest and gently backed her up. "Doctors say he'll be fine. They're doing some kind of surgery to clear up blockage this morning. He'll have to stop eating all the steak, fried potatoes, sausage, and bacon he likes and take more pills than he'll want, which will make him crankier than all get-out."

"Can I go too?"

"Nee, we need you here in Lee's Gulch. Your aenti Leeanne will help you and Hannah with the younger kinner. You can come here a few hours a day to return phone messages, fill the computer orders, and pay any bills that can't wait." Atlee pointed a callused index finger at Declan and then at Bethel. "You two, I need here at the nursery. Declan, you're in charge, especially of the cash registers and the deposits, but also the work schedule. You'll need to be here six days a week. Bethel, you'll handle displays, customer service, watering, and making sure shelves are restocked with the help of whoever else is on the schedule that day."

"Declan's in charge?" Hattie's voice squeaked with indignation. Bright red spots bloomed on her white cheeks. "I've been working here since I had to stand on a step stool to wipe the counter—"

"I can't leave a young girl—"

"I'm twenty-two years old—"

"Don't interrupt me, Dochder." Atlee's expression turned steely, his tone stern. No doubt Hattie walked a thin line. Atlee wasn't as strict as many of the Plain fathers in the district, but neither did he allow his children to disrespect him. "You don't act your age and you know it. Besides, I'll not leave a woman in charge of money deposits and locking up the store at night. I wish your brother Ben was here, but that's water under a Lancaster bridge. I need a man in charge."

"I understand that." Hattie managed a meek voice that didn't match the angry spark in her eyes. "But even Bethel has more experience in running the store day-to-day. She's been working here two years. Declan's worked here four months. Bethel knows everything about what we stock, how to prepare lawns for winter, when to plant winter gardens, and when to start the spring gardens—everything."

Declan swiped a glance at Bethel, who hadn't said a word. Her head turned side to side as if watching a ball bounce back and forth over a volleyball net as father and daughter talked. Only the way she chewed her lower lip gave a hint of her feelings. She wanted to say something but likely knew it was better to ignore the urge. She caught Declan's gaze. Her eyebrows went up. She gave a tiny shrug.

Did she think she should be in charge? Plain women often ran bakeries, gift stores, restaurants, and other girlier businesses—it was the only word that came to Declan in the moment—but not nurseries. Usually they stopped working altogether when they got married, unless it was a family business in which their children would one day work.

Would they be able to live on his salary if he still worked at the nursery after they were married? If—when—he returned to calling auctions in the spring, he might be able to work at the nursery during the offseason. His voice continued to improve with physical therapy, but it was still raspy. He didn't have the volume or stamina needed to call an auction—not yet, but soon. The therapist was very sure of it.

The possibilities ping-ponged around Declan's brain. He'd barely allowed himself to imagine a time when courting Bethel would turn into something permanent. Only late at night when he couldn't sleep did he allow his imagination to conjure up such a sweet picture. He hadn't broached the subject, not yet. It was too soon.

"You agree, Declan, don't you?"

Atlee's sharp tone suggested he'd spoken to Declan more than once. Heat burned through him. Agree about what? Declan adopted his serious face as if he'd been thinking about the situation. "The three of us together, sharing responsibilities, can manage the nursery and other employees as a team. We each bring our strengths to the table. Plus, it's not like you're moving to Siberia. Maybe you can call once a day so we can powwow about any questions or issues that come up."

"Gut point, gut idea, gut idea." Atlee nodded so hard his hat shifted. "You'll make a gut manager."

Bethel lowered her head. She plucked at a scrap of paper caught on the cash register's corner.

"Do you have thoughts on the plan, Bethel?" Declan kept his tone casual. She had worked here much longer than he had. She deserved to be consulted. "Are you okay to come in every day? The kinner are in school, except for Claire."

Claire, whose symptoms had progressed more quickly than they'd hoped, was able to do less and less at home to help their mother. Bethel often poured out her heart to Declan about the pain this caused her parents and the sadness that had enveloped Claire as her disease progressed.

All he could do was hold her hand and nod. Platitudes didn't help in the least. They were better left unsaid. He'd learned that with his own disease. People meant well, but they had no idea how their words made him want to run bellowing into the closest cornfield.

The boys and Claire would always be Bethel's first priority. Which was fine. Declan planned to stand in line to take his turn caring for Sadie when his parents could no longer do it. Together they would do what needed to be done. Without complaint.

Sei so gut, Gott, don't let these tribulations change Bethel's mind about courting.

A wisp of a prayer God must be tired of hearing repeatedly for the last four months.

Her expression thoughtful, Bethel cocked her head. She directed her gaze to Atlee, as if he'd asked the question. "Do you have any idea how long you'll be gone?"

"Nee, nee." Atlee picked up the clipboard and handed it to Hattie. "Pay these invoices. Make sure you write the check numbers in the register. It all depends on how Dat comes through the surgery and how long he's in the hospital. Then Mamm will need help taking care of him, but my brieder and schweschdre likely will help out too. I'd like to bring my eldre back to Lee's Gulch, but I doubt Dat will agree. They love Pinecraft. They've made gut friends there. They're settled."

He sucked in air. No doubt breathless after such a long speech.

"So it could be a month or two?"

Why did it matter?

"Jah, I reckon."

Bethel squeezed past Atlee and went to the calendar. She tapped on the first week of December. "Declan, you have a CT scan and an appointment with your doctor in Richmond December third, don't you?"

For just a few hours, when he worked at the nursery, it was possible for Declan to forget he was a "cancer survivor." Maybe Bethel wasn't able to forget, as much as she insisted it didn't worry her. "That's right."

Three months since his first scan. Already. Every three months, then every six months. If there were no recurrences, after five years, he could go to once a year. *Sei so gut, Gott.* Another prayer that was on repeat in Declan's brain. Anxiety did its best to crowd out faith. *Do not fear.* Scripture said so umpteen times. Nowhere did it explain how the flawed, weak human was supposed to manage that.

It only took uttering the word *scan* to hurl Declan back in time to lying on his back staring up at the painting of turtles on the ceiling during his three-month scan. He felt the warmth of the blanket the technician tucked around him, the prick of the needle for the contrast IV. He heard the low hum as the table transported him into the "doughnut," the rush of the contrast spreading through his arteries, producing that strange sensation that he might wet his pants. The disembodied voice that ordered him to hold his breath, then breathe.

In a few scant minutes it was over. The endless dragging of time began afterward—the wait for the results.

Everyone said, "God is good" when the scan came back clean. No worries. They went about their business. Except the cancer survivor who then began the countdown to the next scan.

It would be fine. No way he went through all that treatment only to start over again in six months.

No way.

"I could very well be back by then. And anyway, you'll only be gone two days." Frowning, Atlee tugged at his ragged gray beard. "Bethel, you and Harriet can handle forty-eight hours. If I'm not back, I'll ask Jerry to make the deposit and lock up for you."

Jerry owned the hardware store next door to the nursery. He was a good neighbor.

Bethel pulled a notebook from a shelf under the counter, followed by a pencil holder stuffed with pens and pencils. "I'll make a to-do list." She loved her to-do lists. "Declan, do you know how to find the work schedule on the computer?"

Declan forced a grin. "Does a bear hibernate? For sure and for certain."

Bethel's expression turned somber. "Are you all right? You're pale."

Probably from working indoors all summer instead of at fairgrounds on the auction circuit. "Never better." He scoured the recesses of his memory, searching for a joke he hadn't told before. Not one came to mind.

An auctioneer without a voice. A comedian without a joke. What would he lose next? Nothing, he would lose nothing. The scan would be clear and he'd get his voice up to snuff, go back to calling auctions, marry Bethel, and have a huge passel of children. Period. End of story. He stopped short of "happily ever after," but as close as the hair on his chinny-chin-chin—sparse as it was.

"Go, Atlee. We've got this. Right, Bethel? Right, Hattie?"

"Right!" The two women linked arms and offered Atlee matching smiles. "Go."

Uncertainty etched on his face, Atlee grabbed a leather satchel from under the counter and stalked to the door, all the while mumbling under his breath. At the door, he turned and opened his mouth.

"Go, Dat." Hattie shook her finger at him. "Tell Mamm I'll be there in a bit to help her pack. Tell her not to worry about supper. I'll take care of fixing it for the kinner."

"Will do." Atlee shoved his straw hat down more firmly. "If anything—"

"We've got this. Go."

He went.

Chapter 33

Leaving Declan in charge of the nursery was a good thing. In theory. Bethel strode down the nursery aisle filled with snow shovels, windshield ice scrapers, and sundry other items needed to cope with the winter weather expected to arrive any day. The late November weather was chillier than usual for north central Virginia, but no snow had fallen yet. They still had an overabundance of pumpkins, gourds, and squashes, along with Thanksgiving decorations, pruning shears, rakes, and other tools used to tame autumn lawns. Where had the sales display gone?

"Looks gut, doesn't it?"

Bethel swiveled at the sound of Declan's hoarse voice. He approached behind her, pushing a wheelbarrow filled with winter lawn fertilizer and mulch bags. "Early bird gets the worm, you know."

"What happened to the sales display of autumn stuff?" Bethel worked to keep irritation from her voice. "We really need to sell it. Our warehouse is full and we don't earn back what we spent on it if it doesn't sell."

"True, true, true." Declan parked the wheelbarrow. He grabbed a bag and tossed it on the bottom shelf. "I moved the fall stuff to the front, next to the register, and marked it down to half price. Once I get these bags moved, I'll get started on a display for lawn prep for winter and spring."

He talked so fast, he ran the words together. Add the hoarseness and he could be difficult to understand. He'd been like this—like a popcorn kernel in a hot skillet—since Atlee left. Unable to sit or stand still.

"There's no hurry. We have so much autumn merchandise—"

"I know, I know. I just like to stay ahead of the curve."

He had dark circles around his bloodshot eyes. His skin had a gray pallor. He was working too hard. If he wanted to stay busy in order not to think about his scan the first week of December, that was understandable. Bethel inhaled the nursery's familiar musky scent of mulch and dirt. Maybe it would calm her worries. "Are you sure you're all right? You look tired. You can take an afternoon off now and then. Hattie and I can handle it."

"I'm fine. We just had Thanksgiving Day and the Friday after off. Plus we're shorthanded with the part-timer who quit." Declan tossed another bag on the pile. He paused long enough to resettle his straw hat on his head. Then he was back at it. "And then there's the English high school kid who didn't show up for his shift on Friday."

It *had* been a long week. A lost order of snow shovels. An invoice paid twice. Atlee wouldn't be back for at least another three weeks. In the meantime, they would simply have to make the best of it. Apparently intent on doing just that, Declan walked away.

"Declan, wait, how was Thanksgiving with your family?" Bethel hurried to keep up with him. She reached for his arm, then thought better of it. Not in the store. "You haven't said a word about it."

"Gut. It was gut." He slowed. His shoulders straightened. "I ate way too much stuffing and rolls and pumpkin pie—not that a person can ever eat too much pie. It's always gut to be reminded of your blessings. To give thanks."

"I felt like I had so much to be thankful for." Bethel gave in to the urge. She slipped her hand into his and squeezed his fingers. "I'm so thankful for you."

Declan halted. He squeezed her hand and turned to face her. "Me too. Always."

"So why do you seem so troubled? Is it the scan?"

"I'm just—"

The sound of raised voices—one male and one female—trumpeted through the aisles. "That doesn't sound gut." Declan shook his head. "I'd better go see what's going on."

"Let me. You can finish—"

"I've got it."

That was Declan these days. Always on the run. Bethel went after him.

It sounded as if the couple were debating whether it was too late to plant a garden in the ground. Which obviously it was. They stood in the aisle in front of a display of chimineas and outdoor heaters meant for patios or decks. The middle-aged woman's face, including her double chin, was bright red. Chunks of her husband's silver hair stuck up all over his head as if he'd been yanking on it.

Bethel could relate. At least she hadn't voiced that thought aloud. Declan skirted their empty cart and approached. "Can I help you folks with anything?"

The two launched into the merits of their positions simultaneously and at full volume.

"Whoa, whoa." Declan had to raise his voice to be heard over their bickering. He winced. His hand went to his throat, then dropped. "If you'll let me, I'm sure I can help you."

With a surly grunt the man ran out of steam first. His wife wrinkled her nose but stopped talking soon after.

"The best thing to do right now is prepare your yard and your garden plot for the winter. You can till whatever vegetation you have in your garden so it's mixed in with the dirt. That will provide nutrients. Mulch all your existing plants, shrubs, and trees." Declan's voice grew raspier with each word. "They say we'll have a mild winter, but you never know. Mulch protects plant roots, and it absorbs rain to keep plants hydrated. You might also consider feeders and birdbaths for our feathered friends."

They also wanted to have blooming flowers in the spring. Bethel slipped closer. "It is too late to plant flowers from seed, it's true, but you can grow both vegetables and flowers from seed indoors and transplant the seedlings in the spring after the threat of freezing weather has ended." Bethel touched a basket of primroses and then another of autumn daffodils. "Indoor gardens and hydroponic gardens can give you cherry tomatoes, chili peppers, and herbs year-round. Plus tending to them is said to reduce stress."

Which this couple definitely could use.

"We also have firepits, if you're interested." Declan went on as if he hadn't heard Bethel. They did have a surplus of materials to build firepits and a nice selection of the ever-popular chimineas, but the couple wanted plants. "We have some beautiful Adirondack chairs that would be comfortable. The whole family can gather around on one of these until snow comes. Which might not even be until January, what with the mild winter they're forecasting."

The Adirondack chairs, made by Bethel's father, would be a great bonus sale. Declan could sell milk to dairy farmers. His dimples were on full display. The missus nodded and smiled in return. "That does sound great. We have just the spot."

"But—"

"Come on. Let's check it out."

The mister didn't have a chance.

"We'll buy stuff to plant the indoor garden later." The missus patted Bethel's arm. She cocked her head toward Declan. "Lead the way."

Bethel nodded and managed a smile. She didn't fault Declan for being a good salesperson. He was far better at it than she was. Still, his manic approach to the job couldn't be good for him. He wanted to believe he'd recovered from any lingering side effects from his treatment. His face said differently. He wouldn't slow down long enough to listen to her concerns.

Shaking her head, she headed to the front to find Hattie. Her friend was the grease that kept the wheels turning smoothly at the nursery—something that came as a bit of a surprise. Hattie sparkled in her dad's absence.

"What's with the 'I poured spoiled milk on my oatmeal this morning' look on your face?" Hattie sprayed a cleanser on a front window and wiped vigorously. The oatmeal *she'd* eaten for breakfast was prominently displayed on her wrinkled apron. "You've been cranky all day."

"Nothing."

"Sure doesn't seem like nothing."

"You missed a spot."

"Did not and don't change the subject." Hattie applied a liberal squirt to the spot she had indeed missed and followed with appropriate elbow grease. "Are you and Declan squabbling?"

"Nee, not exactly. Does he seem . . . a little crazy to you?"

"Like he's drinking four gallons of kaffi before he comes to work in the morning? Jah."

"He keeps redoing the endcaps. He's setting up displays of winter snow shovels. Any day now he'll have a spring display up. And then he stays after hours to count the day's receipts and go to the bank."

"Comes with the territory. Dat was right about leaving him in charge."

"I tried to tell him to take a few hours off to rest. Instead, he grabbed customers I could've handled and rushed them off to see chimineas."

"He didn't listen? Surprise, surprise. What do you think being married to him will be like?"

"Who said anything about marriage?"

With a half snort, half chuckle, Hattie turned and toasted Bethel with the cleanser bottle. "Seriously? You two are meant for each other. Your goo-goo eyes are so sickly sweet I think I'm coming down with diabetes."

"You don't come down with diabetes."

"You're so sweet on each other it's a wonder you both don't have it too."

"I really don't see you being all demure and not sharing your opinion with James when you're married." Or with anyone. The thought made Bethel chuckle. "You've never let anyone—except maybe your dat and mamm—tell you what to do."

"I just know how to make James think my ideas are his ideas, that's all." Hattie curtsied daintily, her tone airy. "Besides, I won't try to change him if he doesn't try to change me."

James didn't have a life-threatening disease. *Danki, Gott.*

Hattie pulled a step stool from behind the counter. She slid it back to the window and climbed onto the top step. Not the best place for a wiggle worm like her. "What's really bothering you?"

Bethel flopped onto a glider rocker next to the wind chimes she coveted every time someone opened the door and allowed the wind to jostle their merry tinkling bars. "I don't know. I feel so . . . up in the air. His CT scan is coming up fast, and I'm . . ."

"Scared?" Hattie hopped from the step stool and landed with a thud. "How do you think he feels?"

"I think that's what this is all about, but I don't really know. He won't talk about it. That's what's so frustrating. I thought we were in this together, but he makes a joke or starts talking about the spring auction schedule like he has no doubt he'll be headed out in March with his brothers and his dad."

"You don't think he will?"

"You've heard his voice."

"Okay, folks, I'll let Hattie ring you up, if you don't mind." Declan brushed past Bethel without making eye contact. That he'd heard her remarks was apparent in the way the warm blue of his eyes turned to ice and his dimples disappeared. And that he chose Hattie to ring up the merchandise. "Sir, do you want help carting your items to your vehicle? Where're you parked?"

Mister did indeed want Declan's help. While the men took care of the heavy lifting, the missus enthused over the firepit they planned to construct in their backyard, the tiki torches she'd picked out, the bird feeder and birdbath, and an order for four Adirondack chairs to be delivered at a later date. Bethel's dad would be pleased.

"What about the indoor garden?"

"Oh, we picked up seeds, little planting pots, and peat moss." The missus proceeded to add a fireplace lighter to her haul, still talking all the while. "Declan's right. We can do both. We'll be ready to start our outdoor garden in March."

Declan's right. That was good. "I'm glad he was able to help you find what you really wanted."

Finally, Declan and the mister returned. The missus handed the long receipt to her husband, who rolled it up and stuffed it in the pocket of his plaid flannel shirt. He clapped Declan on the back, thanked him for his help, and propelled his wife out the door, all the while ignoring her excited chatter.

The door closed. "Declan, I—"

"I'm going to take lunch."

"Okay, I can—"

He tugged his coat from the rack behind the counter. He shrugged it on with quick jerky movements. "I think I'll go home for an hour."

Usually they ate their packed lunches together.

"Declan, es dutt mer. Let's talk."

He stepped around her and stalked toward the door. "I'm all talked out."

Bethel grabbed her coat and followed with it still tucked under her arm. "We need to talk. Now."

"Talk about how you don't understand why I don't want to talk about scans?" He paused, hand on the door lever. "What do you need me for? You can just talk to Hattie about it."

"I shouldn't have talked to Hattie about it. I'm sorry. Let's talk now, about why you've been running around, bouncing off the walls, for the last few weeks." Working to keep her voice down, Bethel edged closer. "You're burning both ends of the candle. You have three projects going at once."

"I'm trying to do a gut job for Atlee. Isn't that what I should be doing?"

He didn't wait for her answer. He shoved through the double doors. Bethel followed him down the sidewalk past outdoor displays of fall clearance items. A biting cold wind blew through her. The temperature had dropped instead of rising since they opened the store. Heavy gray clouds obscured the sun. "Of course, but you've been like a Percheron trying to pull the plow by yourself. Let Hattie and me and the others help carry the load."

Declan angled toward the path that led to the far back parking lot where he'd left his buggy and horse. It was hard to tell if he was listening. Bethel broke into a trot to keep up. "Whenever I bring up the scan in December, you immediately start to talk about calling auctions in the spring."

"So you don't want me to go back to calling auctions?"

"You know that's not it. I want you to do whatever you want to do. Only . . ."

"Only what?"

"Do you think your voice has improved enough?"

"Dad and Toby say it has or that it will have by March." His stride quickened. His voice grew raspier, belying his words. "I do all the exercises. I'm careful to rest my voice. I do everything the therapist says to do. She says improvement in these cases is slow and steady. There's still plenty of time."

The men might be inclined to tell Declan what he wanted to hear in order to encourage him. The therapist was a professional. She would give him her best medical opinion, wouldn't she? "Gut, that's gut. So why are you running around popping up like a jack-in-the-box?"

He slammed to a stop. Bethel ran into him. Her nose banged into his shoulder blade. "Ouch." She rubbed it. "See what I mean?"

He whirled and took her arm. He bent down and kissed her nose, a short, hard kiss. "Es dutt mer." He tugged her coat from her. "Put this on before you freeze."

Bethel did a quick 360-degree review of their surroundings. Two cars and two buggies in the lot. One was Hattie's. The others were empty as well. She hugged Declan, then tugged him down for a longer, softer kiss. He didn't pull away. He wasn't that mad. When they finally came up for air, Bethel no longer felt cold. From the look on Declan's face, neither did he. She squeezed his hands and tried to read his somber stare. "Don't be sorry. Talk to me. Sei so gut."

With a groan, he tugged free. He held out the coat. Bethel allowed him to help her put it on. He pointed at the buggy. "Get in . . . sei so gut."

Bethel did as she was told. Declan slid in next to her, but not close like he normally did. Instead of picking up the reins, he stared at his hands as if he'd never seen them before.

"I shouldn't have talked to Harriet."

"She's your friend. That's what women do."

Men didn't? Bethel scooched closer. She put her hand over his. "Talk to me. Sei so gut."

His gaze lifted. His frown deepened. He cleared his throat. "I'm scared all the time." The words were barely a whisper. "I know I shouldn't say that. I shouldn't be that. It shows how shallow my faith is."

Bethel tightened her grip on his hand. "You're only human. You're allowed. Gott understands." He should. He surely had a reason for allowing this cancer for this man, who wanted nothing more than to be an auctioneer. His former occupation made him so happy. He was good at it. He worked hard. He helped support his family. What good would Gott bring from Declan's affliction?

Tell me that, Gott, sei so gut. Tell me.

As if God had to tell a mealymouthed sinner like Bethel anything. "It's only been three months since you had a clean scan, only six months since you finished radiation. You said yourself, your voice is improving. Your oncologist had positive things to say. The odds are in your favor. He said so."

Bethel had prayed, *Don't let the cancer return. Let Declan have his heart's desire*, until God had to be sick of hearing the same request over and over again. Especially when it didn't end with *Thy will be done*. Surely Declan's entire clan prayed the same prayer. And the elders. And other members of the district.

Surely Bethel wasn't the only one who had difficulty adding that last part. *Thy will be done*.

Why wouldn't it be His will? Declan was young, otherwise healthy, a good man, a faithful follower, a good brother, son, and friend. Why would God not spare him this cross?

Why, Gott? "Whatever happens, we'll cross that bridge when we get there."

"You're right. You're right." Declan straightened his shoulders and sat up tall. "It's the in-between time that's making me crazy. The waiting. So I throw myself into the work. I don't know any other way to do a job but go whole hog. It's my nature."

"You're gut at it."

"I'm pushy and I'm stepping on your toes and Hattie's and the other employees'."

"Nee, you're doing a gut job. We want to help. That's our job."

"I'm sorry. I'll try to do better. Are you sure you're okay courting a man on the road six months out of the year?"

"We've been over this." Bethel elbowed him gently. "Whatever you decide to do, I'm fine with it. If Rachelle can do it, so can I."

Courting. He said courting, not marrying. He always tiptoed around that subject. How long would he make her wait? What was he waiting for? How many scans before he would allow her to take a chance on him? The last question skittered across her tongue and teetered on its very tip.

"If we're going to kuss and make up, let's do it right."

Declan tugged his hands free of hers. He clasped her face and brought her close. The kiss dissolved hurt and anxiety. It washed away doubt and impatience and warmed her down to toes tucked in thick socks and leather winter boots. When he finally raised his head, Bethel was light-headed—from lack of oxygen and a love so deep and so wide she could drown in it. "That's a good start," she whispered.

"A start? Okay, how about I take you for pizza at Chelsey's?"

"As nice as that sounds, we don't have time. And we can't leave Hattie alone here with a part-timer who still doesn't know a petunia from a pansy."

"You're right. I'll get it to go. I'll be back quicker than a lightning strike."

"Just be careful."

"I need another *kuss* to keep me going until I get back."

Who was Bethel to deny him? When they were both out of breath, she broke away and hopped from the buggy. She returned his jaunty wave and watched him drive away.

If he returned—*when* he returned to auctioneering—she would do this often. Watch him drive away, only for weeks instead of minutes. That was okay. Anything that made him happy would make her happy too.

Sei so gut, Gott.

Chapter 34

*O*ne more sigh and I'm going to send you home early." Hattie's resigned expression belied her tart tone.

Promises, promises. Going home early on a cold December day wouldn't be the worst thing in the world. "Sorry." Bethel grabbed the broom leaning against the wall behind the counter. She swept the floor with listless one-two-three swipes at a few dried leaves and some customer's missing-in-action bobby pin, gave up, and leaned against the broom handle. This was ridiculous. Declan's scan had only been a day earlier. He would call when he called. Plain folks didn't make phone calls to chat. Or reassure. "I just thought we'd hear something by now."

Hattie propped her elbows on the counter and nestled her chin in her hands. "It's only been a day and a half. Even if the doctor did that stat thingy Declan was telling us about, he wouldn't have the results yet. You don't even know what time his follow-up appointment was."

"I know, I know." Bethel returned the broom to its original spot. The lull in customers didn't help. Some would show up for Christmas holly, pine boughs, poinsettias, and even a bit of mistletoe over their lunch hour. Hopefully. The nursery did less business this time of year. It was cheaper to go to discount stores for Christmas decorations. Being busy was better. Time passed more quickly. Since Declan climbed into the van and waved good-bye through the open passenger window, Bethel had been unable to think about anything but what he was going through in Richmond. If the suspense was eating at her, how much more was it devouring him? "I wish I could've gone with him."

"Wouldn't that have scandalized the elders?" Harriet stretched both arms over her head, yawned so widely her tonsils showed, and scratched her nose. "Stop messing around and marry the man. Then you can go with him wherever you please."

"He hasn't asked." Besides, as much as he tried to be obedient to God's will, Declan was still struggling with an uncertain future as an auctioneer. "He's so determined to return to calling auctions. I think—I don't know because he doesn't talk to me about it—he wants to be able to offer me a clear picture of what our married life will be like. Will he be an auctioneer and all that means as far as travel goes? Or will he work someplace like this nursery?"

He didn't seem to understand that it didn't matter what he did as long as they did it together.

"Men are so dense, aren't they?"

Hattie's philosophical tone tickled Bethel. As if she had so much experience with men. James Eash was her first and only beau. "I guess James hasn't asked you to marry him either."

"Nee. He just natters on about Sheetrock and paint colors and the cost of lumber these days." Hattie snorted. "I'm beginning to think I'll have to ask him."

Wouldn't that turn James's life upside down? Of course, he was used to Hattie's less-than-decorous ways. He must like them, in fact. "Do you love him?"

"If you're asking me if he makes me swoon, then nee." Hattie threw pretend air kisses. "But I miss him when I don't see him for more than two days. I like the way he smells, and when he holds my hand, I think I'd rather die and go to heaven than have him let go."

"Sounds like love to me." No matter what anyone thought about Hattie's slapdash appearance, her silly flights of fancy, or her childlike love of fun, she would make a good wife. She would be a good mother—the kind children deserved. Surely James saw that. "If he doesn't ask you soon, I think you should ask him what his problem is."

"I just might—"

The front doors swung open with such force the bell ding-ding-dinged repeatedly. One smacked against the wall, propelled by a ferocious cold wind. Bethel's mom rushed in. "There you are, Bethel."

She sounded out of breath and peeved as if Bethel had intentionally hidden from her. "Here I am, Mamm, working as usual. Why are you here?"

"Claire was feeding the chickens and she fell again."

"Ach! Where is she? Did she break anything? Did she have to go to the hospital?" Bethel started toward the storeroom. She'd retrieve her bag and get to her sister. "Hattie, can you—?"

"She's fine. She's fine." Mom tugged at a crocheted shawl wrapped around her shoulders. A lock of gray hair loosened by the wind hung in her eyes. Her cheeks were red and chapped. Her eyes were wet with tears. Mom never cried. Not in front of her children, that was for sure. "We just came from the clinic. She sprained her wrist and skinned her hands and forearms, but nothing's broken."

"That's gut. That's gut." Bethel kept her hand on the doorknob. "Why wasn't she using her walker?"

"She used it to get out to the chicken coop. But she likes to hold the bucket with one hand and spread the seed with the other. Like she always has. She wandered too far from the walker. When she tried to return to it, she fell."

Mom explained this as if it made all the sense in the world. It did. Anyone still coming to terms with a worsening disability would cling to familiar tasks for as long as possible. Sometimes too long. "Did you want me to come home? Or did you just stop by to let me know?"

"We called the clinic in Strasburg. We need to talk about the Achilles' heel tendon surgery." Mom's voice quavered. She heaved a breath. "It helped the buwe with their balance so they could keep walking for a little longer. It'll help Claire too. Maybe we'll be able to keep her out of a wheelchair for another year or more. Anyway, they had a cancellation. If we go now, we can see the doctors in the morning so they can assess the progression, as they call it, and then decide whether surgery will help."

"If they say no?"

"Then they'll help us with ordering the right wheelchair for her."

At least the house had already been retrofitted with all the necessary ramps. Three wheelchairs. Claire's tearful question of, *"Who will marry me like this?"* battered Bethel. The ache in her heart intensified until it hurt to breathe. "Go home and pack. I'll be right behind you."

"I have chili simmering on the stove. I was going to make cornbread, but I—"

"Don't worry about anything. I'll take care of it. The kinner won't starve." Bethel scraped up a faint chuckle for her mother's benefit. "How's Claire doing?"

"It's hard to know. She hasn't said a word. It's like she went away. Far, far away."

Tears choked Bethel. She swallowed against them. "It's hard for me to understand. I can only imagine how hard it must be for her."

"She'll adjust." Mom turned back to the door. The rest of her thought hung in the air, unspoken. *She has no choice.*

"I'll see you back at the house." She rushed away.

Bethel slipped into the storeroom. She closed the door and leaned against it, head down. *Breathe, just breathe.* Declan. Cancer. Scans. Their future. Claire. Falls. Surgery. An uncertain future. The boys. Worsening symptoms.

Her legs trembled. She slid onto the tile floor, back against the door, and wrapped her arms around her knees. *Gott, Gott, where are You?*

The silence hummed in her ears. The smell of peat moss, dust, old cardboard boxes, and fertilizer enveloped her. She leaned her head against the soft cotton of her dress. "Gott?" she whispered. "We need You now. Declan needs You. Claire needs You. Mamm and Dat need You. We all need You."

I'm here, Dochder.

Three words, clear as Mamm's supper bell ringing on a late, hot summer afternoon, hung in the air.

So do something. Nee, es dutt mer, Gott. I mean tell me . . . I mean, sei so gut.

Shame burned through Bethel. She didn't have to say anything aloud. God knew her every thought. He knew she wanted desperately to tell Him what to do instead of waiting patiently, humbly, obediently for His plan to unfold. Not because she was selfish, but because she wanted it for Declan, for Claire, for Robbie and Judah, for her parents, for everyone touched—not just touched, but ravaged—by two diseases that had no cure and wreaked havoc on lives.

Sobs threatened to break through the dam of resolve she'd so carefully constructed over the years. "Nee, I will not cry." She breathed in and out until the sobs retreated. "I will not, I will not, I will not cry."

Rest in Me, Dochder.

Rest in Me . . . There it was. His answer. All Bethel had to do was rest in Him. Rely on Him. Depend on Him.

If only it were that easy.

Rest in Me, Dochder.

So that was the point of all this? At least it had a point. God wanted them to rely on Him in all circumstances. *I understand that, Gott. I've learned my lesson. Can't You work Your miracles of healing now?*

Rest in Me.

Bethel closed her eyes. She willed every muscle in her body to relax. Rest in Him. *I'm trying, Gott, I'm trying.*

The door pushed against her spine. "Bethel, are you all right? What are you doing in there?" Hattie sounded worried. Hattie never worried.

Bethel straightened. She opened her eyes. "I'm fine. I'll be out—"

The phone jangled. She jumped. "I'll get that."

Bethel heaved herself to her feet and ran to the desk. She scooped up the receiver just as Hattie opened the door and stuck her head inside. "Schrocks' Nursery and Landscaping. How may I help you?"

"Bethel? It's me. Declan."

He sounded far, far away, his voice even raspier than usual. She tightened her grip on the receiver. *It's him*, she mouthed to Hattie. Her friend nodded and withdrew.

"I'm so glad to hear from you. Did the scan go okay? I was just thinking of you." She told him about Claire's fall and plan to go to Strasburg. The words spewed out. Gasping for air, she forced herself to stop babbling. "More about that later. How are you?"

No answer. The sound of breathing signaled Declan was still on the line. "Declan?"

"It's back, Bethel. Es dutt mer."

Seconds ticked by.

"Bethel?"

The words were gibberish. Like he'd spoken in a foreign language. "What did you say?"

"The cancer is back."

Rest in Me.

Chapter 35

_S_ ilence met Declan's declaration. _Please don't make me say it again._ Each word brought a new wave of pain. He rubbed his throat. His fingers were cold. Aunt Joy's phone shanty was drafty and full of chilly December air. His whole body had turned icy when Dr. McMann gave him that somber look and said those words: _"Declan, your cancer has recurred."_ "Bethel, are you there? Did you hear me?"

Maybe her body was encased in ice too. Maybe her lips were too frozen to move.

"How are you doing?"

How did he answer that? Tell Bethel the truth and add to her burden of worry? Lie and dishonor their bond as a couple building a relationship that one day would be sealed with marital vows? At least that had been his dream. His hope. _"Do you promise that if he should be afflicted with bodily weakness, sickness, or some similar circumstances that you will care for him as is fitting for a Christian wife?"_ "Cold . . . I'm cold."

Would she understand that?

"I wish I was there. I wish I could hug you. I wish I could warm you." She whispered so softly Declan could barely hear her. She did understand. She didn't offer platitudes or the inevitable "I'm sorry." "I'm having trouble believing it. That you'll have to go through it all again."

"Me too. That we'll all have to go through it again." The news didn't just affect Declan. It affected his entire family. His friends. Bethel. "I'm the one who's sorry. You have your hands full with Claire and the boys. You don't need more of this. If you don't want—"

"Don't you dare say it." Now Bethel sounded like herself, full of snap, crackle, pop. "We're in this together. This setback changes nothing. What happens now?"

Declan leaned against the shack's unadorned Sheetrock. His throat ached but not from cancer. His head and his heart kept it company. "The doc called it a local recurrence. That means it's in the same place. It hasn't spread. Some rogue cancer cell escaped the radiation and started growing." His voice grew steadily hoarser. "He wants to do another biopsy to confirm."

"Then it's not for sure." Hope colored her words. Hope must be the same color as sunlight, lemonade, and lemon meringue pie. "When is the biopsy?"

"He's sure. It's back. But they have to do a biopsy. That's the way the process works." Declan sucked in air and let it out slowly, so very slowly. Emotion wouldn't help. It would make it harder for Bethel. "Monday. He was able to finagle a spot in the surgeon's schedule for it. He's pushing to fast-track the results too."

"If the biopsy confirms it, then what?"

"Surgery."

"Surgery again?"

"This time he'll take out more of the larynx. The voice box."

Another long pause. "I see."

She did see. She sounded as if her mouth were full of cotton.

"How big the tumor is will determine how much of the voice box they'll have to remove."

Pain reverberated in those last two syllables. She was imagining what life would be like with a man who could no longer speak normally, who couldn't do the one job around which he'd built his life. The future was full of gloomy shadows that hid how he would adapt to the new him. If he couldn't imagine it, how could he expect Bethel to imagine it?

He had to draw back the curtain and let her see exactly what to expect. Only then could she make her choice with all the facts in front of her. Declan forced himself to continue. "Complete removal will mean they'll have to leave a hole, they call it a stoma, for breathing. I won't be able to talk or swallow or eat or smell the way I do now." Might as well rip away the bandage completely. "I'll learn new ways. If it's a partial removal, my voice will be affected but not completely gone. I'll have to do speech therapy again. I'll learn to use it as much as possible. Anyway, I'll be here for a while longer. Tell Hattie I'm sorry. When is Atlee due back? Do you know?"

"Whatever happens, we're in this together. You can't scare me away. I hope you understand that."

She thought that now, but how would she feel in a year or two or three? How heavy would his burden feel on her shoulders? It was too much to ask. Far too much. "Are you sure? I can't ask you to—"

"I'm as sure as Sadie is that pie is a breakfast food. It's not too much to ask. That's what people who care about each other do. They show up and they don't give up—no matter what happens. Wouldn't you do the same for me?"

He would. Without a sliver of doubt. "That sure?" He managed a half-hearted chuckle. "I need to talk to Atlee."

How did a man with a fractured voice work in retail? How would he talk to customers? How would he joke with them, give them advice, share his knowledge with them?

"He's back next week. You know he'll have a job for you, no matter how long it takes for you to get better and get your voice back. Atlee is more than your boss. He's your friend. He's like family."

A fierce sob threatened to break through the hedge he'd constructed to hold back his seething emotions. Declan fought it back. Bethel was right. Bart had offered good advice. Seeking a new job, a new occupation, a new joy had been the right move. Miller Family Auctioneering was a family business. He would never lose the love of his siblings or his parents. But the Schrocks could serve as his family too. Plain businesses were like that. "I still have to call Mamm and Dat."

"I wish there were words to tell you how much I hurt for you." Her voice broke. "The word *sorry* is so paltry. I know how much not being able to call auctions hurts. I wish I could take this hurt from you."

There it was, the writing on the wall scrawled in permanent black Magic Marker. Declan was done. His career as an auctioneer had ended. "Jah."

"It breaks my heart."

"At least we know. No more struggling to make it happen. I have to go."

"Wait, Declan."

He gritted his teeth against the onslaught of tears. Grown men did not cry. Plain believers took what life offered. They ran the race set before them. *Thy will be done.*

"Before you called, I was arguing with Gott, and I think . . . I know this sounds full of hochmut and ridiculous, but I think I heard His voice."

Declan straightened. A flutter of laughter burbled up in him. The ache eased. Arguing with God? That Bethel would share with him such a revelation spoke of how much she trusted him. Others would scold or school her in humility versus hubris. "You heard Gott's voice? What did He say?"

"'Rest in Me.' He said 'Rest in Me.'"

Rest in Me. A wave of exhaustion swept over Declan. The idea of rest sounded so good. He closed his eyes. The muscles in his shoulders and back unknotted. Plain believers didn't argue with God. They believed God had a plan for them. They accepted the plan—whatever it was. But Bethel so loved her family—so loved him—she took her concerns straight to the Father Himself. She had great courage—or great delusions. Only God would decide which. "Why were you arguing with Gott?"

"I had a weak moment." She cleared her throat. "For a minute, just for a minute, it was too much. I thought He asked too much. I was being selfish, like it was happening to me and not to Claire and Mamm and Dat and . . ."

Silence filled the line.

"And me."

"Jah, and you."

"I'm telling you, if it's too much, Bethel—"

"You'll never be too much. My life would be empty without you in it. It would be empty without my brieder and schweschdre. Family is everything. In gut times and in hard times."

What could he say to that? The cancer might kill him. Then her life would have that empty space where he'd been, where their love had been. Maybe he shouldn't do that to her.

"I know what you're thinking." Her voice regained its wholeness, its steely determination. "Don't you dare try to back out now."

She was too smart for her own good, too wise. If that were possible. She was exactly what he needed, and what's more, she knew it.

Declan opened his eyes and stared at the metal slats that formed the shack's roof overhead. Tiny rays of light slipped through. Just enough to stave off darkness. "I wish you could come here."

Had he said that aloud?

"Me too. I just told Hattie that."

"You can't."

"I know. But that doesn't mean we don't have a right to our feelings."

Memories of how Bethel's hand felt in his, the softness of her skin, her lips, her warmth flooded Declan. The need for her washed over him like homesickness. She was home. To have her with him every day for the rest of his days wouldn't be enough. "You have responsibilities there. Besides, people would be scandalized."

A small chuckle sounded over the line. That Bethel could laugh at a time like this was a good sign, wasn't it? "This will sound stupid, but I'm glad you wish I was there."

"It doesn't sound stupid, but why?"

"Because it means you want me with you in the hard times as well as the gut times."

"In all the times." Declan wrangled tears that burned his throat. "Gut, bad, and otherwise." The words came out in a croak.

"Me too," she whispered. "Me too."

Declan loosened his grip on the receiver. The desire to keep talking to Bethel, to keep hearing her voice, warred with the knowledge that he had to break the connection. He had to tell his family. Make plans. Keep putting one foot in front of the other. "I have to go."

"Declan, wait."

His grip tightened again. He waited.

"I love you, Declan."

His heartbeat spun out of control. He straightened. The doctors might be able to fix his throat. They might be able to excise cancer cells. But they couldn't offer a medicine as strong as love. The ache in his throat eased. The tears receded. "I—"

"You don't have to say it back. It's not the kind of thing you say for the first time on the phone. I just wanted you to know."

He wanted to say it. He wanted to say it forever. He'd loved her first. "Bethel—"

"I have to go." She hung up.

Declan laid the receiver in its cradle. Bethel loved him.

Rest in Me.

He leaned forward, eyes closed, and laid his head in his hands. God's request was so simple. Except for a man used to solving his own problems.

And getting his way.

God had given Declan the gift of a smart, wise, strong woman, a helpmate who would be strong when Declan couldn't be. What more could he ask for?

He'd wanted to know why God allowed the cancer. Why let it recur? Why not answer prayers for complete healing? Why, why, why? God had to get tired—irritated, really annoyed—with such insistent prayers. The apostle Paul only asked three times for the thorn to be removed from his side. Then he went about his business. Was there a limit to the number of times a person could ask for God's help with a single trial? Surely not. Was it a lack of faith to keep asking?

More questions than answers. Maybe it was time for another visit with Bart.

Rest in Me.

Rest in Me. Not in his bishop or doctors or family or auctioneering. Not even in Bethel.

A hard word. A hard lesson. Declan raised his head. He clasped his hands in prayer.

If Bethel could lay her worries at God's throne, so could Declan. Bethel loved him. God loved him more.

Rest in Me.

I get it, Gott, I finally get it.

Better late than never.

Chapter 36

*C*ranky. That summed up Bethel's general state of being. Tonight. Okay. For the last three weeks. Resting in God was hard work when the man she loved was enduring surgery and recovery in a hospital in another state. His parents, his brothers and sisters, the elders—they were allowed to visit him, but not her. She could join her mother in delivering casseroles to his parents' house and helping the women with household chores. Otherwise she simply had to parrot platitudes and go about her business.

Christmas had come and gone. She'd done her best to join the festivities with a thankful heart for the celebration of her Lord and Savior's birth. Everyone tried to cheer her up—which only drew attention to the reason for her angst. Still, she appreciated them so much. She had so much for which to be thankful. Instead, she was cranky.

Sorry, Gott, for being such an ingrate.

Bethel wiped the last pot dry with more elbow grease than necessary. She plopped it on the stack on the shelf next to the stove. She couldn't take it. Not one more minute of the stuffy kitchen air that held the mingled aromas of pizza-biscuit casserole and sawdust pie.

"That's it." With exaggerated care she folded the dish towel and hung it on the rack. "Go on, Mamm. You're tired. Dat's already gone to bed. You should too." She shooed her mother toward the kitchen door. "The kinner are down for the night. You're surely tuckered out."

Her parents had just returned from Strasburg, where Claire had undergone surgery on her Achilles' heel tendon. The surgery had been pushed back because of the holiday schedules. Getting Claire in at all before the end of the year had been a major feat. The doctors believed the surgery would help her stay mobile longer. In a month to six weeks, she would return to have the other tendon done.

"I think I will." Mom paused at the door. "He'll be fine, Dochder. You'll hear from him soon."

Her mother saw too much.

And she was overly optimistic. Rachelle Miller had shared the news after church on Sunday that the surgeon had removed only a portion of her brother-in-law's voice box—about half. He'd declared the surgery a success. But Declan would have to learn to talk again. It had been two and a half weeks since Bethel spoke to him—one last call in the phone shanty to confirm the surgery date. His parents had gone to Richmond to stay with him at his aunt Joy's. He'd been in the hospital four days, including two days in intensive care. Then another ten days at Joy's so Charlie and Elizabeth could take Declan to follow-up appointments.

According to Rachelle, he was coming home Monday. Yesterday. To finish healing so he could start chemotherapy as well as speech therapy.

He was home. He'd been home for twenty-four hours. It was all she could do to keep from hopping in a buggy and flying down the road to the Miller farm.

Bethel couldn't pretend to her mother that none of this mattered. "I hope so."

Her mother rubbed her already reddened eyes. Dark circles surrounded them. "When he does, make sure he knows you'll put him first."

"What do you mean, put him first?"

"Your dat told me about the conversation you had a while back. About your worries. He's right. You can't let them stand in the way of marriage and kinner. Or think you need to be the one to carry the burdens of this family."

"Claire and the boys will need me when you're . . ."

"It's okay to say it. When your dat and I are dead." Mom smiled despite her words. "We'll rest easy knowing family extends beyond blood in this community. We have no worries about the kinner being well cared for. It's hochmut to think you're the only one who can do it."

An echo of Dad's words. A lesson to be learned again and again? Why did she keep picking up a burden after laying it down? God likely wondered the same thing. *I'll do better, Gott, I promise.* "Do you ever regret marrying a man who has the gene mutation that causes this awful disease?"

Mom shook her head. Her smile deepened. "Your daed was the only one for me. Gott brought us together. He can bring good from all circumstances."

Her tone was soft, but it still stung. How many times would Bethel need to hear variations of those familiar verses before they sank in? "I'll sleep in Claire's room. That way if she has pain during the night, I can give her some more ibuprofen."

"What were we just talking about? I'm Claire's mamm. It's my job to see to her, not yours."

"I'm not taking over your job, Mamm." Bethel managed a smile. Her mom was right, but that didn't mean she couldn't take a turn caring for her sister. "Tonight you're tired and I'll be up for a while anyway. You'll sleep better in your own bed."

"Danki, Dochder." Mom retraced her steps. She held out her arms. Bethel stepped into her hug. Somehow Mom's once-rounded frame felt less substantial than just a few months earlier. As if time had worn her down. "She's doing better. She actually smiled at the nurses and waved good-bye when we left to come home."

"That's gut. Really gut." Small steps. Any steps were a godsend. "What do you think made the difference?"

Mom gave her one more squeeze and let go. She stepped back. "She took part in a small group session with some other teenagers who have LGMD and similar diseases. Some use wheelchairs. Some have walkers or canes. She had a chance to see how other kids are coping. We didn't get to go in with her, so I don't know what they talked about, but she came out smiling. I think she feels less alone."

"That's so gut. She needs to feel hopeful."

"We all do." Mom's smile held a mixture of her own hope and a deep weariness. "You get some sleep too, Dochder."

"I will. I just need to get a breath of fresh air first."

"The wind is icy cold. Wear your scarf and your gloves."

"I will. Promise." Bethel waited until her mother's footsteps receded through the living room to the stairs. A walk might wear her out enough to sleep, but first she would check on Claire. She opened the door a crack. The lamp glowed.

"Claire?" Bethel peeked in. Her sister was sitting up, propped against her pillows, a notebook on her lap. She'd tossed aside the faded patchwork quilt so her thin legs were exposed. A white patch of bandage covered the lower part of her right leg and foot. Bethel slipped closer. "Why are you still up? Are you okay?"

Claire tossed her waist-length brown hair over her shoulder. She stuck a pen behind her ear. She made it easy to imagine what Mom looked like as a teenager. "I'm fine."

"Are you sure? Is pain keeping you awake?" Bethel slipped closer. No lines marred the smooth skin around her sister's mouth and chocolate-brown eyes. "I can bring you some ibuprofen and some water. Or tea if you'd rather."

"I'm gut." She snagged the pen and tapped it on the notebook. "You could just leave some tablets on the table. If I need it during the night, I'll grab it. That way you don't have to worry about it."

"I'm going to sleep in here. That way I'll be right here if you need me."

"You don't have to do that. I'm a big maedel."

"I want to. I like having company." Bethel settled on the edge of the bed. "Besides, you don't snore too much."

Bethel's little joke didn't seem to register with Claire. Her expression pensive, she twisted a lock of hair around her finger.

"Mamm said you went to some kind of small group session at the clinic. Did you like it?"

Claire smiled, the first genuine smile in forever. "I did. I made some friends." She held up the notebook. "I'm writing letters to a few of the kids I met. We exchanged addresses."

"Ah. That's wunderbarr. I'm so happy you made friends."

"I have friends, gut friends here." Claire shrugged, her tone almost apologetic. "They'll always be my friends. It's just . . ."

"They can't understand what you're going through."

"Nee, they can't. But Maryanne and Adam can." Claire's cheeks turned pink. Her gaze dropped to the notebook.

What was going on here? "Maryanne and Adam. Are they related? Where're they from?"

"Adam's fifteen. Maryanne's my age. They're bruder and schweschder." Claire doodled on the paper. Bethel leaned closer to peek. Lots of fancy A's and C's. No M's. "They live between Lee's Gulch and Nathalie. Mamm said we might share a van with them sometime if our appointments coincide. They said they could come by and pick us up."

"That sounds like a gut idea."

"It is." Claire waved her pen with a flourish. "It would be great to see him—them—again." The enthusiasm drained away. "But the chances of our appointments being the same day or even the same week aren't very gut, are they?"

"You never know." Bethel stole one of Claire's pillows and used it to cushion her back while she leaned against the headboard. "Besides, nothing says we can't invite them here for a visit. Or we could meet them for lunch in Nathalie."

"Do you think Mamm and Dat would let us do that?"

To see that smile light up their daughter's face? Yes, indeed. "I think it's a possibility."

Claire grinned. For a second she returned to the innocent girl who started riding horses at four years old, shot the first buck of the deer season two years in a row, and regularly blocked the most spikes in volleyball.

"So is it Maryanne you want to see or Adam?"

The pink in her sister's cheeks turned a becoming red. "Mmm, well, Maryanne is nice and she likes to read the same books I do, but Adam . . . Adam is funny and smart and he says he likes the wheelchair better because he can get places faster than with a walker. He challenged me to a race when my leg is healed."

She looked awfully pleased at the thought.

"You like that idea."

"You know me—I like to win."

Exactly what the doctor ordered. Anticipation. Hope. Fun with a cute guy. That kind of medicine couldn't be bottled. "You'll have to heal quickly."

"That's the plan." She yawned and stretched. "That's what I'm telling him in my letter."

"Then I'd better let you get to it before you nod off." Bethel returned the pillow and fluffed the pile. "I'm going for a walk. I'll try to be quiet when I get back."

"Don't tell Mamm about Adam."

"Don't worry, I won't."

Mom already knew because she was Mom, but there was no need to tell Claire that. She was too young to court, but not too young to dream of the day when she would. And to dream about a boy named Adam.

Everybody needed hope.

It was lovely to see the seeds sprouting in Claire. Bart and the other elders often preached about how God put the right people in His children's lives at just the right time. Sometimes that person came in the form of a teenage boy using a wheelchair to win races.

Bethel slid from the bed. At the door she turned for a peek at her sister. A sparkle in her smile, Claire was already engrossed in her letter writing.

Danki, Gott.

Chapter 37

*H*anging on to hope could be hard. Sometimes life took a ridiculously sharp left turn. But then God smoothed out the road. Bethel buttoned her heaviest coat all the way to the top and tucked her thick woolen scarf around her neck. She pulled on her favorite mittens and let herself out the back door into the night to consider this thought. Claire still had many miles to travel on her pothole-filled road. People were simply expected to keep putting one foot in front of the other. Or in Claire's case, find joy in using a walker to race with a boy in a wheelchair.

God put that boy in Claire's life. Did He nudge Bethel into Declan's life to help him find his way on another pothole-filled road? Or was it the other way around? Declan could show Bethel a thing or two about navigating life's sharp left turns.

The only way to make any forward progress was to rely on God. Pure and simple. Bethel got it. *You can stop teaching me this lesson now, Gott.*

Apparently not.

The wind cut through her. She bent her head against it and walked faster. She wasn't an innocent fourteen-year-old girl dreaming about her first puppy love. Love required work. Sometimes love wasn't enough. Hopefully Claire wouldn't have to learn that lesson anytime soon.

Bethel angled past the corral, past the barn, past the chicken coop, past the phone shanty, past the furniture workshop, and out onto the gravel road that eventually led to the highway. She swallowed against the ache in her throat. It didn't help. The ache had no beginning or end, no identifiable place of origin, and worst of all, no cure.

Not true. Declan was the cure. Dusk peeked through the trees and blanketed the road. A critter skittered across it, stopped at the edge, and stared back at her. Its eyes glowed yellow. A possum.

"Go on, git."

It skedaddled.

A flash of white and then the shrill screech of a barn owl filled the heavy silence. Bethel peered into the darkness, searching for its heart-shaped face and beautiful speckled body. It was likely hunting prey. Voles, insects, lizards, and mice beware.

She should go back, but she wasn't tired. Not physically tired, anyway. The second she laid her head down, the images would start to spin. Declan flat on his back in a muddy field at the fairgrounds. Declan carrying chairs for her after church. Declan with his sore throat at the medical clinic. Declan sitting in the kitchen talking nonsense about stand-up and sit-down comedians.

Declan.

A kaleidoscope of memories. No matter how she arranged and rearranged them, the end result was a man who touched her heart. A man who'd gotten under her skin and into her head against all odds. He couldn't be taken seriously, yet she did take him seriously. He was dealing with a terrible disease. She had her own family's health concerns. Her head said it was a precarious match. Her heart said two together were stronger than one.

Gott, sei so gut, help me have faith in the future, no matter what it holds.

The words turned into a song. A psalm. Like the ones David wrote for his Lord sung to the tune of a nursery rhyme.

Thy will be done should've been the refrain. But it was too much. The words wouldn't come.

Rest in Me.

I'm trying, Gott. You know how I'm trying. She would keep trying, no matter how hard it became.

The *clip-clop* of a horse's hooves drowned out the thought. The buggy's headlights drew closer. Bethel moved to the side of the road.

The horse whinnied. The buggy slowed. The driver spoke to his horse. "Whoa, easy, boy, what's the matter?"

A voice so like Declan's—before it was ravaged by disease. Bethel stepped back onto the road. "Who is that?" It couldn't be Declan. He wouldn't be able to speak at all for weeks.

"Whoa, whoa!" The buggy halted. "Bethel? Is that you?"

She stepped into the headlights. "It's me."

"Hey, it's Emmett."

Declan's seventeen-year-old brother. "What is it? Is something wrong? Did something happen to Declan?"

"Nee, nee. He's here."

Bethel peered into the shadows. Declan, who was sitting next to Emmett, waved. Bethel put her hand to her chest. Her heart thrummed. *He's here. He's here.* "You should be at home resting."

"I tried to tell him that, but he insisted we come find you." Emmett sounded exceedingly chipper—like a teenage guy about to pull off a silly prank behind his parents' back. At seventeen, he probably saw this jaunt with Declan exactly like that. "I'm just the chauffeur. Declan's not allowed to drive a buggy. Or talk. Or eat solid foods. Or sleep lying down. Basically, his life stinks at the moment."

"So you decided to make it better by taking him on a buggy ride after dark on a frigid night?"

"Kind of like you walking on the road in the dark with the wind knocking you around."

She wasn't recovering from surgery to remove a life-threatening tumor. "I couldn't sit still anymore. I was thinking about . . ." She might as well say it. Emmett knew about Declan and Bethel or he wouldn't have agreed to bring his brother here. "About Declan. I needed to take a walk to clear my head. But I'm not the one who should be resting."

"There was no talking sense to him. He wouldn't take no for an answer."

Bethel stepped closer to the buggy. Declan's expression was obscured in the darkness behind its headlights. "How, if he's not talking?"

Declan held up a small whiteboard in one hand, a marker in the other. Then he proceeded to write something on the board. He held it up. Bethel scooted closer still. She took the board and moved it into the headlight's beams. WANTED TO SEE YOU. He'd crossed out WANTED and scrawled NEEDED above it.

"Here I am." Here they were. Now what? They couldn't have a real conversation with Emmett right there between them. "What did you have in mind?"

"Hop in." His face the spitting image of his older brother's, Emmett jerked a thumb toward the buggy's back bench. "I'll drop you both off at your house. I've got places to go and people to see, if you know what I mean."

His playful tone suggested he was making the most of his rumspringa. Bethel smiled to herself. She had a few of those memories herself. She did as he instructed. The ride back to her house allowed Emmett to give Declan a detailed accounting of what had happened at the Miller household while he was in Richmond—specifically all the things Elizabeth and Charlie didn't know about and thus couldn't tell Declan. The siblings' antics filled the ride.

At the hitching post, Emmett paused long enough to let them jump down. "I'll be back when I get back." He grinned. "So be ready. I'll slow down to five miles an hour and you can jump in."

Everybody was a comedian.

"Be safe. Don't get into trouble."

"I'll do my best." His grin belied the seriousness of his response. "By the way, I already have a mudder." He took off without waiting for a response.

Bethel couldn't help it. She laughed. "He's working on being a comedian just like his bruder."

Declan nodded. He winced. His fingers went to the bandage on his throat.

"Does it hurt much?"

He shook his head. Winced again. He was lying.

Bethel touched his shoulder. "Let's go inside. Can you have a cup of hot tea?"

He shook his head again, then wrote LUKEWARM and held it up.

"Got it."

Bethel led him inside. He sat at the table. She headed to the stove. Declan caught her hand and tugged. Bethel turned back.

He pulled a cloth from his pocket, wiped the board clean, and scribbled. WHAT DO YOU GET WHEN YOU PLANT KISSES?

A laugh burbled up in Bethel. Declan the jokester was back. That spoke volumes about his state of mind. She shrugged. "I don't know."

Tu-lips (you know, two-lips)

Bethel rolled her eyes and laughed. "You don't have to explain. I got it."

He grinned and wiped the board clean. So you were thinking about me?

"Always. Every day. Thinking and wondering and worrying."

Rest in Gott didn't help?

"It helped, but I'm only human. I had too much time to think."

About what?

"About whether you really want to court a woman who could add to your trials by bringing a stupid gene mutation with her." Bethel let her fingers trail across his fine five o'clock shadow. "Watching Claire's mobility deteriorate has been really hard."

Another swipe at the board. This time he bent over writing for a long time. When he held it out, the words crowded the board. I've been thinking about whether you want to court a man who will always have cancer.

His handwriting had grown more ragged as he wrote.

"We're a pair, aren't we?"

One vigorous swipe wiped the board clean. Jah.

"Whatever happens, I'll help Mamm take care of the kinner."

You will.

"No matter what happens, we'll take care of each other."

You were walking toward me, not knowing I was coming to you.

"Jah."

I was coming to you, not knowing you were coming to me.

"Jah."

In our weakness He is strong.

"Jah."

He can make good come from all circumstances.

More repetition. God must know how badly Bethel needed the reinforcement. "Jah. He's teaching us to cling to Him in our weakness."

I MISSED YOU.

"I missed you too."

YOU SAID YOU LOVED ME.

The word *love* got tossed around with careless abandon. A person loved chocolate. A woman loved a fancy dress. People loved books and songs. Love didn't begin to describe Bethel's feelings for Declan. How could she express such a big feeling? "I do."

I LOVE YOU TOO. LOVE YOU SO MUCH. Declan laid aside the whiteboard. He pulled Bethel onto his lap. His eyes were full of an emotion that couldn't be mistaken. He cupped her face and tugged her closer until their lips met.

Sometimes words weren't what was needed. Love vanquished fear, doubt, worry, and anxiety. Wounds shrank and disappeared in a flood of certainty. Whatever came, they would face it together.

Finally, yet too soon, he leaned back. Bethel kissed his forehead, his cheeks, and his nose. "I couldn't have said it better myself."

He smiled and ducked his head. Bethel smoothed his thick blond hair. She touched his chin until he raised his head. She traced the fine lines around his blue eyes and full lips. "I want to be right here with you, come what may. Through it all. You understand that, don't you?"

Declan reached past her and picked up the whiteboard. Bethel handed him the marker. He nudged her until she turned her back so he could lean the board against it and write.

Another nudge. She turned. He held up the board.

WILL YOU MARRY ME?

Joy did cartwheels around the kitchen. Fears fled, chased away by the assurance God would carry them through the days that followed—however many that might be.

Bethel took the board from Declan. She turned so he couldn't see what she was writing. She held it up.

Jah. Jah. Jah.

Declan tossed the board aside. What came next required no words.

Chapter 38

*J*oy came in the morning. Every morning. Bethel eyed Declan's hand. His fingers were spread across the bleacher seat between them. She surreptitiously eyed the potential competitors for the Singer treadle sewing machine, the next and last item of the day at the retirement auction at the Knowles County fairgrounds. Men wearing ball caps or straw hats and women in bonnets were busy fanning themselves with their bid cards under a brilliant July sun. Or drinking from tall cups of lemonade and iced tea purchased from nearby booths. A few focused on Toby, who paced the platform, his deep bass filled with amusement as he tried to pump up the bids for two large dog kennels. Plain folks around these parts didn't put dogs in kennels—not much anyway.

"Come on, folks, even if you don't have a dog, I know there's a wife out there who has thought a time or two about putting her husband in the doghouse."

Hearty laughter broke out and spread across the crowd. Even Sadie and Jonah giggled from their spots sitting cross-legged in the green grass, eating snow cones next to Robbie and Judah in their wheelchairs. Sadie swiveled and grinned at Declan. Her lips were raspberry red. "Beth put you in doghouse, Bruder?"

"Nee. Not as long as I'm gut." Declan doffed his hat at his little sister. "You could always stick Jonah in one with Runt if you ever need to teach them a lesson."

"He can't be gut for very long. He's too narrisch." Josie elbowed Sherri and laughed. Declan's sisters were sitting on the second row, sharing huge buckets of kettle popcorn with Claire and Nyla.

Bethel's sister leaned back against the bleacher behind her. She giggled and held up two fingers. "Bid on both kennels, Beth. You can use one and give Mamm the other one. She can use it for Dat."

"Woo-hoo, uh-oh," Robbie hooted.

Judah joined in. "Don't let Dat hear you say that."

"Very funny." Declan stuck out his tongue at them. He might be a married man, but his inner child still showed up regularly. "We'll get both of them, and you three can take turns."

"Ha. You'll have to catch me first." Claire grabbed her walker and tilted it toward her as if ready to take off. The tendon surgery had helped her gait considerably—and her morale. "I've gotten pretty gut at using this thing."

"She has. She keeps up with me, and I'm fast." Nyla wiped sticky fingers on a napkin, which stuck to her hand rather than doing its job. "She tied with Adam when they raced last week. He was so sure he'd win."

Claire held up one finger high overhead, signaling *I'm number one.* "I'd have beat him, but he cheated. He started before Maryanne said go."

Seeing Claire smile and hearing her laugh was the cherry on top of a beautiful day. She still had low days, but time spent with her friends with similar disabilities had given her the ability to focus on all the activities she could still do instead of those she couldn't.

Kelly Irvin

Regular meetups with Adam and Maryanne in Nathalie, coupled with the round-robin letters they shared, helped. Nor had she been abandoned by her old friends. She was learning to live in the moment, one day at a time.

Just as Bethel was. Like being there at the auction with these youngies she loved. It might just be a picture of what her future— hers and Declan's—looked like. She slid her hand across the worn, green commercial plastic until her index finger touched Declan's.

He curled his finger around hers.

She suppressed a smile and stared straight ahead. They were almost holding hands in public.

Declan scooted closer. As close as he dared in the middle of an auction crowd. "So what sound do porcupines make when they kiss?"

A fraction closer and they could kiss. Bethel cocked her head. "I don't know, but I'm betting you're about to tell me, Mr. Sit-Down Comedian."

"Ouch."

Of course. She half groaned, half laughed. "I should've known."

Declan's impish grin made him look like a teenager despite the thick beard that had grown in a darker blond than his hair. "So what's gotten into you, Fraa?"

Hearing him call her "Wife" still sent a thrill racing up Bethel's spine, even after five months. "Nothing. Why do you ask, Mann?"

"I told you I'm okay with coming to auctions. It doesn't matter anymore—not as much, anyway. I'm happy. I'm surprised I still have to prove it to you."

He had to work so hard to make himself understood with his breathy, slurred, hoarse voice. Yet he smiled. Bethel fought the urge to kiss him right there in broad daylight in front of a couple of hundred folks who knew them both. "You don't have to pretend for me, ever. I know it's bittersweet. It has to be."

His expression turned pensive. He shrugged. "I suppose it always will be bittersweet. I miss calling auctions. I miss being on the road with my brieder. All that's true, but despite all that, I'm truly happy."

Declan didn't have to tell Bethel he was happy. It showed. He had plenty of side effects from cancer treatment, along with the dreaded three-month scans and lab work, to remind him of the blessing of simply being alive. His happiness showed in the way he popped out of bed in the morning so he wouldn't be late to the nursery. Atlee had retired not long after Declan finished his chemotherapy. He promoted Declan to manager and gave him full rein. Hattie served as assistant manager and happily took over the bookkeeping and payroll.

Declan's happiness showed when he kissed Bethel good-bye with gusto before leaving for therapy for his stiff neck and mouth muscles and seemingly insurmountable speech difficulties.

Since their wedding in January, they'd worked side by side to make repairs on the small A-frame house he'd purchased on five acres just outside Lee's Gulch city limits. It was good to have their own place but still plenty close for Declan's drive to the nursery and so Bethel could easily go to her parents' farm each day to help her mom care for Claire and the boys.

"I guess it goes to show that there's more than one road to happiness." *Danki, Gott, for that.* Bethel curled another finger around Declan's. "We learn how to be happy in our circumstances, whatever they may be."

"Jah. It can be a hard lesson, but a gut one. I'm glad I learned it with you." Declan's grip on Bethel's fingers tightened. "It appears I've become like a city boy now, working inside all the time. It's so hot today. Ice cream sure would hit the spot about now. We could go to the food tent—"

"Not yet. Maybe later."

"Bethel—"

"I thought we'd bid on the sewing machine that's coming up next." Bethel worked to keep her face serious. He would be so surprised. "It's a really nice Singer with a beautiful inlaid pine stand. The description says it's a vintage 1940s model. I tried it out while you were talking to your brieder. It still works really well."

"Why? You've been using your mamm's. You're at her house every day anyway." Declan rubbed his throat, a habit he probably didn't even realize he had. "Does she suddenly have so much sewing she doesn't want to share it?"

"I think we should have our own." Bethel rested her hand on her still-flat belly. "Once a couple starts a family, they should have their own sewing machine, just like they have their own washing machine. I won't always be spending as much time at my parents' house come . . . winter."

"Starts a family . . ." Declan's jaw went slack. His mouth hung open. Bethel patted his cheek. "Close your mouth, Mann, before you swallow a fly."

"We're starting a family?" He spoke so loudly an English woman in the row in front of them turned to stare. She smiled. Bethel returned the smile. "He's delirious."

The woman chuckled and turned back.

"Hush. Let's not tell the whole world."

Declan scooted even closer, then leaned toward Bethel. "But you are saying you're . . . we're . . . we're having a bopli?"

"I am." Bethel could no longer contain her smile. "We are."

Eyes wide with wonder, Declan's gaze fell to Bethel's belly. "You don't look . . . When?"

"If I'm counting right, late winter, early spring, February." She squeezed his hand and let go. "I'll know more after I see the midwife. I asked her to come over next week."

"Next week!" Declan half rose from his seat. "She should come over now. Today."

Bethel grabbed his arm and tugged him back down. "There's no rush. We're barely getting started. Besides, I've got my eye on that sewing machine. It has a pretty cabinet. See the four drawers and the nice handles? I could put it in front of the living room windows so I can catch the breeze."

"I can't believe you're thinking about sewing at a time like this." Declan snatched up the bid card he'd laid aside when they first sat down. "But if it's a sewing machine you need, I'll get it. I'm kind of an expert on auctions."

That he could say those words with a smile was a gift from God.

"If we can get it at a decent price," Bethel cautioned. "There will be other auctions, other sales, if the bids get too high."

She'd done her research. Old treadle sewing machines could fetch anywhere from a hundred dollars to $900—it just depended on how well the machine had been maintained, the quality of the cabinet, and who else wanted it. She had no intention of paying $900 for one—even if they could afford it, which they couldn't.

Fortunately only two other bidders took an interest in the machine. They both bowed out at $150. A decent price for a tool that would be used more and more as their family grew.

Gott, sei so gut, let our family grow. Healthy, happy kinner with a healthy dat and a healthy mamm.

There were no guarantees. If only there were.

Declan helped Bethel down from the bleachers as if she'd suddenly become a fragile porcelain doll. Together they examined their purchase. Between gulps of water from an oversize travel mug, Toby congratulated them on a good buy. "I didn't realize you were in the market for a sewing machine. We've had others at the last couple of auctions. I could've snagged one for you."

Declan opened his mouth. Bethel nudged him with her elbow and jumped in. "I've been using my mudder's. It seemed like a good time to buy our own, and this one's really nice."

With a small smile, Toby cocked his head to one side. "Huh, really? Well, it's a beauty, all right. Should work well for a growing family."

A growing family. He'd guessed. From the look on Declan's face, he might burst with the news. But Plain couples didn't do that. Their joy would become apparent in time.

"It should fit in the back of your buggy." Toby clapped Declan on the shoulder. "I'll find Emmett. He can help you take your purchase to the parking lot."

Declan offered him a goofy grin in return. Bethel swallowed a giggle. "Danki."

Whistling noisily, Toby took off. By then the crowd had dispersed. The sun hung low to the west in a cloudless sky. The scent of fresh-cut grass mingled with the aroma of barbecued pork and roasted turkey legs. Everything about the day was perfect.

Declan smoothed his fingers over the machine's pine stand. "So, no regrets? No worries?" The goofy grin was gone, replaced with a somber expression. Had the excitement worn off and reality set in? "Are you ready for this?"

No sense in pretending she didn't know what he meant. "Nee, no regrets. Worries, jah, some, I admit." She captured his hand in hers. If someone saw them holding hands, so be it. They were a married couple, after all. "I've come to realize that no matter how hard I try, I'll always worry. I'll fight off the worries with the sword of faith, trusting in Gott. They'll keep coming at me, and I'll keep repeating, 'Rest in Gott, rest in Gott.'"

"Gut for you." His shoulders hunched, Declan shuffled his feet. "Which worries you more—cancer or LGMD?"

Bethel's free hand went to her belly. "Honestly?"

"Jah, honestly."

"The LGMD." The strength of Declan's grip on her hand calmed the tremor that ran through Bethel. "But now that there's a bopli—our bopli—on the way, I realize it won't matter. We will love this bopli. He will have the life Gott wants him to have. He will be so loved by you and by me and by your family and my family. Nothing can steal my joy—our joy—at that thought. Not today."

"Or any day." Declan drew closer. He glanced around, smiled, then kissed her cheek. Such a soft, tender feather of a kiss, it might not even have happened. "I want joy every day. If the cancer comes back, I'll do whatever I have to do to be here for that bopli and you for as long as Gott wants me here. We'll both do our part to take care of each other and our kinner—come what may."

"You promise?"

"I promise. You?"

Tears choked Bethel. Happy tears. She nodded. "I promise," she whispered.

Declan glanced around. He drew her closer and bent down. "A vow deserves to be sealed with a kiss."

Sometimes a kiss wasn't just a kiss. Bethel lost herself in the feel of Declan's hands on her cheeks, his lips on hers, in his scent of soap and man, and the roughness of his beard. No matter what happened, they had today and joy in each day that came after—however many that might be.

Rest in Me.

Discussion Questions

1. Declan uses humor to distinguish himself from his many siblings. Bethel feels as if he isn't serious enough for her to court because of the difficult health issues her family faces. Do you find humor to be an important trait in your significant other as well as friends and family? Is laughter good medicine? Can there be too much of a good thing?

2. Declan loves being an auctioneer. It's the only job he's ever wanted to do. Then his cancer makes it impossible for him to do it. Have you ever been in a situation where something you loved doing was no longer possible, for any reason? How did you react? What advice would you have for Declan?

3. Bethel sees herself as a caregiver for her siblings with LGMD. She's committed to helping her parents. All Amish women dream of getting married and having children. She's afraid she'll have children with the disease as well, and the thought is overwhelming. What advice would you have for her as she navigates this difficult situation?

4. The Amish rely heavily on the knowledge that everything that happens to them is part of God's plan for them. Romans 8:28 says that "for those who love God all things

work together for good, for those who are called according to His purpose." What does that mean to you? How does it affect the way you approach your life, especially the trials?

5. Bethel is afraid she will have children with LGMD. With her family history, the chances are good. If you were in her shoes, how would you proceed? How does the mainstream world differ in its attitude toward having children with disabilities? Especially knowing in advance and considering "options"?

6. Declan can't understand why he had to get a cancer that took away his voice, his most important tool as an auctioneer. Do you believe God allows such situations in order to teach believers to rely on Him? Why or why not?

7. Amish families consider all babies gifts from God. They refer to children with disabilities as "special children." Knowing the impact words can have on people mentally and emotionally, how do you feel about this designation? People with disabilities in the mainstream world often work toward not being seen as special, but rather simply differently abled. For those of you who have disabilities or loved ones with disabilities, how do you navigate the semantics of disability?

8. Bethel has three siblings with LGMD, possibly more as Liam and Melinda grow older. What advice would you give Bethel for dealing with her guilt for being the one the disease passed by?

9. What would you tell Bethel regarding her fears of having her own children with the disease? How does her response reflect on her faith in God's plan for her? How do you respond when your faith is tested?

10. Have you ever been in a situation or a season of life in which you knew you should "rest in God"? Did you find it difficult? How did you find a way to rely on God fully (if you did)?

Acknowledgments

Writing these stories about living with disabilities—both the characters who have the disabilities and those who love them—is a labor of love. As a person who came to disability late in life, I know the challenges personally. Those feelings pour out into these stories. I've found so much kindness, compassion, and support from so many people—family, friends, and strangers—as I navigate my struggle with limited mobility and a chronic, life-threatening disease. These experiences give me hope for humanity and allow me to continue to write stories filled with the ultimate hope.

This book was a team effort, as usual. My thanks to the dynamic duo of Becky Monds and Julee Schwarzburg for making this a better story. I thank you on behalf of readers who would have to wade through a lot more unnecessary words if it weren't for you. I also appreciate deeply the work of the HarperCollins Christian Publishing marketing, publicity, and sales team. Y'all rock!

My agent Julie Gwinn and the Seymour Literary Agency team also deserve mention for years of support and encouragement.

I can never thank my husband, Tim, enough for supporting my writing career from the very beginning. His dedication to caregiving in the past eight years has been monumental, and I couldn't keep going without him.

A special shout-out to my readers who continue to read my books and support my writing career. You're the best!

Thanks be to God who in all things works for the good of those who love Him, who have been called according to His purpose.

Enjoy more stories by Kelly Irvin in the Amish Blessings series

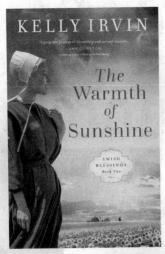

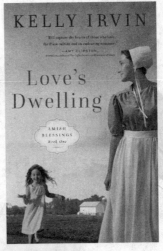

Available in print, e-book, and audio

From the Publisher

GREAT BOOKS

ARE EVEN BETTER WHEN THEY'RE SHARED!

Help other readers find this one:

- Post a review at your favorite online bookseller

- Post a picture on a social media account and share why you enjoyed it

- Send a note to a friend who would also love it—or better yet, give them a copy

Thanks for reading!

About the Author

Photo by Tim Irvin

*K*elly Irvin is a bestselling, award-winning author of more than thirty novels and stories. A retired public relations professional, Kelly lives with her husband, Tim, in San Antonio. They have two children, four grandchildren, and two ornery cats.

Visit her online at KellyIrvin.com
Instagram: @kelly_irvin
Facebook: @Kelly.Irvin.Author
X: @Kelly_S_Irvin